MW00463507

THE
SHADES

VACHEL THEVENOT

© 2022 Vachel Thevenot

All rights reserved. No part of this publication may be reproduced, distributed, or transmitted in any form or by any means, including photocopying, recording, or other electronic or mechanical methods, without the prior written permission of the publisher, except in the case of brief quotations embodied in critical reviews and certain other non-commercial uses permitted by copyright law.

Print ISBN: 978-1-66787-023-6
eBook ISBN: 978-1-66787-024-3

TABLE OF CONTENTS

WINTER

PREFACE

For the sake of clarity, unless stated otherwise, a "year" as described in this story corresponds to one standard Zystinian year, a length of time only marginally longer than one of our own Earth years. The same applies for hours, days, weeks, and months for simplicity's sake. This story, like the last, takes place within the confines of Zysti galaxy, only this time in a different corner, and this story, too, was translated from the language of Modern Zystinian into English for your convenience.

Here is the second story transmitted from the depths of another world: the translated rendition of The Shades.

TRAPPED IN DARKNESS,

MY WORLD IS BLACK.

THIS PLACE OF PUNISHMENT

CREATED BY ME.

WHY DID I HAVE TO BE THE ONE TRAPPED IN IT?

SPRING

CHAPTER ONE:
FACELESS

Partly cloudy. 9mph winds blowing northeast. Fifty-nine degrees fahrenheit. With wind chill, fifty-five point two. No rain is expected.

First day on the job.

Lam put on her apron, the store's logo and name printed on it in big, colorful letters. She pushed the kitchen door open.

She could see the inside of the store from behind the long granite counter. Dozens of empty chairs stood lit by the soft blue light of a cold morning. It was quiet and peaceful outside, and just as much inside. But it was time to get to business. Lam turned on the lights, put up the "open" sign, and waited.

A half-hour of silence later, the sound of a bell rang through the store. Lam straightened out of her slump and leaned over the counter to see her first customer.

It was a small boy, wearing only ragged clothes far too big for him, his skin a dark gray. But it was something else about him that startled Lam.

The boy had no face.

Despite this, he took his time looking around the store, at least as much as he could without eyes, and then finally he walked up to the counter.

"Is this place new?" the boy asked.

Lam didn't know what to say at first. All she could do was wonder how in the world this boy could talk, or see, or do anything at all. He had no foreign accent, but appeared to be from somewhere she'd never heard of before. And his voice was strange. It was obviously male and young, but Lam couldn't tell if she was actually hearing his voice or if it was just being projected into her head. Strange appearances were nothing unusual, not in a place like Nur—it was populated by people from all around the galaxy—but she had never in her life seen a person without a face. *Was it some strange type of Val?* Lam wondered.

"Yes, this is our first day in business here. We've been trying to expand our stores to other planets, and Manim was one of the first."

The boy was paying attention to the menu hanging above her.

"Where are you from?" Lam asked as politely as possible, awkwardly trying not to stare at where his face should be.

"I dunno."

This puzzled her.

"How old are you?"

"I think I'm nine. Maybe ten."

"Ten..." Lam quietly said to herself, almost disbelieving. "Zystinian years, right? Not this planet's years? Aren't the years here on Manim like... ten Zystinian years long?"

"Yup. Ten years."

"Then you probably only remember seeing winter and spring before, right?"

"I only really remember up to a few years ago."

"Really? That's strange. What's your name?"

"I don't have a name."

Looking at his disheveled attire, Lam wondered if the boy was an orphan. But with no orphanages in their small town, he was likely lacking any parental support. She felt a pang of pity for the boy.

"Is there anything you want?" she offered.

"No, thanks. I'll eat at Grano's. I didn't recognise this store, so I wanted to check it out."

He turned back momentarily towards the store window. A few other small stores and buildings lined a nearby block. Lam could see clearly one among them, "Grano's," in big comical letters above a red-painted store.

"Oh. Well, you can take something to go if you'd like. For free."

"Really?"

"Sure."

"Can I have a Bletim wrap?"

Lam turned away from the boy and prepared a Bletim wrap. The boy stood on the tips of his toes to watch her make the meal. After finishing, she reached over the glass on top of the granite counter and handed him the food, wrapped in aluminum foil. He took it and held it in his hands for a bit, looking at it intently.

"It looks yummy."

"That's good. You stay safe out there, okay?"

"Yeah."

And with that, he left the store with another ding.

The faceless boy was also nameless. He didn't have much at all, for that matter. Not even many memories. But he did have some, and one in particular was bothering him, distracting him from the wrap he was enjoying.

It was a vivid dream he had had the previous night: he was surrounded by inky blackness, flying in no direction in particular. Then, he saw tiny pinpoints of light, little stars shooting by at high speed. For a moment, he felt free, but then the view around him became obscured with dark-colored metal. He looked back in front of him, and the scene had changed; he was now falling down at high speed. He braced for impact, but instead of a jolt of pain, he found himself in a new location entirely. He was floating in a flesh-coated chamber now, completely immobile. All of a sudden, a thin, metallic rod protruded from one of the fleshy walls, slowly growing closer to him. But right before it was about to touch him, he woke up.

As strange as it was, and though it disturbed him, he knew he had other things to pay attention to. And since he had no idea of what the dream meant anyway, or if it meant anything at all, he found himself snapping back into the moment.

This was one of many unusual things about the boy, though he wasn't aware of how unusual some of these things were. He saw the world through different eyes, or in his case, none at all, gathering sight, smell, sound, and taste from an unusual organ attached directly to his brain. This organ was attuned to a specific wavelength of visible-infrared light that could penetrate the skin and tissue in the front of his head, thus letting him see. In lieu of a nose, a permeable membrane where his face should be let in oxygen and the right molecules to register smell, and his body registered the vibrations bouncing off of his head, transferring all of this information to this master organ in his brain. Unbeknownst to the boy, his anatomy proved to be a highly efficient way to achieve the goals of a face, but without a face at all.

Everything he needed was all there, but it was hidden under the barely permeable, slightly translucent surface where his face should have been.

At Grano's now, the boy pushed open the glass door and walked up to the plump man at the counter. The man noticed him quickly, and a big smile came across his face. The boy smiled too, or at least made a mental attempt. The plump man could tell the boy was happy to see him.

"Hey there, little buddy!" the plump man said.

"Hi Mr. Grano!" the boy cheerfully responded.

"You here for breakfast again?"

4

"Mm-hm."

"Alrighty then. Coming right up."

The boy sat down excitedly at one of the many tables, taking extra care to get himself comfortable in the leather seat. He grabbed his fork and knife and eagerly watched Mr. Grano prepare his meal from behind the counter. And when Mr. Grano had taken it out of the oven, he presented the steaming dish to the boy with pride.

"Grand Soman just for you," Mr. Grano said, sliding the platter onto the table.

It was a triangle-shaped bread with a scrumptious green sauce coating all but the crust, ground up meat sprinkled generously on top. It appeared far too big for such a small boy, but he ate it ravenously, to Mr. Grano's delight. Grand Soman was the boy's favorite.

With no mouth, or any face at all, the boy didn't eat the way other people did. Instead, the part of his face where his mouth should be became malleable, and he simply absorbed the food into his face.

Mr. Grano sat on the other side from the boy as he ate, patiently waiting for him to finish. When he did, the boy slumped down into his chair, relaxed as ever.

"How was your weekend?" Mr. Grano asked.

"I liked it."

"Good. Was the Soman good, too?"

"Yeah."

"How's the search for your parents going?" Mr. Grano asked, trying his hardest to be polite.

"Not well. I can't find them."

"Hm. Sorry to hear that. Did you see that they opened a new place a few blocks from here?"

"Uh-huh. I went there."

"Did they tell you where they came from?"

"No."

"They're from our galaxy's capital, Zephyr. I expect that if they have the money to expand all the way to Manim, they'll provide some good competition. Don't let them put me out of business, alright?" Mr. Grano joked.

"I won't. Don't worry, Mr. Grano."

The boy grabbed a handful of chips from a basket on the table and laid them out in front of him, eating them one by one.

"By the way Mr. Grano, why is our planet called Manim, anyway?"

"Good question. You see, Manim is the only planet for quite a ways out that has life on it. When the colonists who originally came to Manim saw our planet, the only planet for lightyears with life and plants and air, they saw it as an oasis."

The boy cocked his head, confused. Mr. Grano elaborated.

"An oasis is... think of it as a safe place. A small safe place in a universe of unsafe places. The colonists saw our planet as an oasis and named it Manim, which was their word for 'oasis' in their original Bedinian language. And, funny enough, Nur is the only town on Manim. An oasis on an oasis."

The boy was amazed. "Wow..."

"And while I'm sure you already know this, every year here on Manim is equivalent to 10 standard Zystinian years. Soon, you'll turn one here on Manim! Isn't that amazing?"

"I'll turn one?!"

"I know, right? Our galaxy is so cool. We're lucky to be in it, even though it can be strange at times."

The boy tilted his head and put it in his hands like he was deep in thought.

"Mr. Grano," he started, "is there anything strange about you?"

"Me? Well, everyone's strange in their own way. Everyone on Nur is from a different part of the galaxy. Some people have Vals, some don't, everyone has different skin color and hair color, and sometimes people are even different shapes and sizes. My species is different from yours. My species has better vision than many others, but no one from my species ever has a Val. We're even allergic to different things. We can actually eat most poisonous things, but my species is allergic to citric acid and thorium. Weird, right? My biology makes me intoxicated by those things, like I'm drunk. But you don't have to worry about being drunk for quite some time!" Mr. Grano chuckled, prompting the boy to laugh along with him.

Eventually, the faceless boy got up from his seat and walked to the door.

"I'm going on a walk. See you, Mr. Grano!"

"See ya, lil guy!"

And the boy walked outside again, passing between the small stores and shops of Nur before stopping in his tracks and pulling a small, crumpled sheet of paper out of his pocket. He studied the paper for a moment—it was a map he'd made of his neighborhood and the surrounding area, crudely drawn but effective. There were countless eraser marks and faded pencil scratches on the paper from dozens of corrections and alterations he'd made.

Beyond the sketches of the houses, stores, and streets that the boy was so familiar with was blank, untouched paper. He had only explored his immediate area of the town and had set aside room on the page for when he ventured further out, but he had yet to step outside the confines of his neighborhood and a couple small shops. The creek behind the abandoned house he slept in was too wide and the car-flooded streets were too intimidating. He didn't know what the colored lights and beeping machines meant or did, and he was too afraid to find out.

The boy followed his map to its edge where he stood on a sidewalk in front of a wide street. Fast-moving cars flew by on either end, and the boy felt his fear grow and grow before he decided to step back from the curb and onto the sidewalk's safe and familiar embrace. With a slight sense of disappointment, he started his walk back towards Grano's diner. He couldn't miss the morning news.

When the bell on the door indicated the boy's return, the morning news was already playing. Other patrons had come during his absence, occupying other red-painted seats in the diner. He picked the seat closest to the TV on the wall and sat down, listening intently to the overly cheerful news reporters.

"...really a great day to get outside, wouldn't you say?"

"Oh yes, absolutely wonderful. Especially if you love the cold! And in other news, a new business has come to Nur. Today is their opening day. Be sure to give Anak-Lespin *a visit if you can. I've heard their food is delicious."*

"They really are great, Rande. Did you know Anak-Lespin *originated all the way from Zephyr, our galaxy's capital?"*

"Really?"

"They sure did."

The boy spent much of his time watching TV. He admired the news reporters, how much they knew about their town and how much fun they seemed to have talking about it. The boy knew he wanted to be a news reporter one day.

"Now we'll hand the floor over to Artak with the weather. Take it away, Artak!"

The screen cut to a well-dressed man with a smile on his face.

"As you said, we can expect beautiful weather in Nur for the next few days, with highs in the mid-seventies and lows in the fifties. The sun should be out all week. That's all for me, now back to you!"

"Thank you, Artak. We're almost through our long spring season and migration rates to our little colony town of Nur are expected to be at an all-time high."

The camera switched to an aerial view of Nur, a view of the bustling town below as the reporter talked.

"The number of seasonal migrants to Nur has finally begun to increase again, some families enticed by the comfortable life Nur has to offer, some drawn here hoping to capitalize on Manim's unique supply of corvyte, and many scientists wishing to study the famous weather phenomenon here, The Shades."

The TV switched to a shot of the back of someone's car with a large bumper sticker. The sticker had a cartoonish drawing of a cloud on it, with the text below saying "I SURVIVED THE SHADES." It then switched to a video of Nur's town entrance, the text "Home of The Shades" emblemed beneath. Another shot showed the town's mayor among a large parade, waving happily to the crowd around him.

"If this news broadcast makes its way to a newcomer to Nur, then welcome to our town—proud home of The Shades, and only town on the strangest planet in the galaxy. Thank you so much for tuning in, and, of course, we'll see you tomorrow."

While the outro jingle played, a strange feeling crept into the boy. There had to be *so much* out there. The news reporters the boy so cheerfully watched were somewhere out in his own town, yet unknown to him. And the boy made another revelation: what else out there did he not know? He'd glimpsed new lights and sounds and people out beyond his map, just out of sight, just out of reach. How much was he missing by staying in his own territory? How many things just as cool or as wonderful as the news people were waiting for him? He knew he couldn't just keep watching the world safely from behind a TV screen.

With a rush of determination, the boy steeled himself and stood up. Making sure the meager pocket change he'd gathered and his map still remained in his coat pockets, he pushed open the front door to Grano's and stepped outside.

After a long walk he reached the edge of his map once more, looking down at the blank areas on the paper. Now, he'd finally see what was out there. The boy fixed himself on the street ahead of him, cars whizzing by at high speeds. He kept close watch on the number of cars on the street at any given time, and once the number finally shrunk, he stepped onto the street and made a mad dash across the road.

Immediately, the boy realized he was in over his head. Even with how fast he was running, the street felt impossibly long and the colored vehicles rushing by overwhelmed him. It felt like the entire street was erupting with honks and beeps, some cars narrowly missing him as he ran.

Nearing the end of the wide street, he noticed a car hurtling his way. It was too late to step back or leap forward—he was already in the middle of its lane. The car approached with a long, drawn-out beep, and for a moment the boy thought he'd met his end.

But then, he felt a rush of power flow through his body. His exposed skin emitted blackish steam into the cold spring air, and just before the car hit, the boy leapt into the air with astonishing speed. He soared over the car as it flew by under him, until he finally landed on the sidewalk on the other side with a painful thud. Hardly believing what he had done, the boy pushed himself to standing. *He'd made it.*

A moment later, a bus slowed and came to a stop in front of the boy. He watched the doors on the bus for a moment before they opened, revealing a friendly-looking driver who waved at him happily. The boy waved back. With no other idea of what to do, he stepped aboard.

He'd never seen a bus from the inside before; he knew people went in and out of it and what it looked like from the outside, but he never knew just how many people it held. An old man was on a phone call near the front, and a group of kids just a bit younger than the boy were crammed into a row in front of their mother, all staring and loudly commenting on a video game they were playing. It seemed everyone from every walk of life was there. The cloth-lain seats looked worn, and the boy picked an empty seat by the window to sit and watch the world outside.

The bus began to move again with a whine. He watched the cars and street begin to pass by for a moment, listening to the sounds of the bus and the people inside. The little kids playing their video game were shouting and groaning whenever someone won or lost a level, and the boy could hear clearly what they were saying.

"Go, go! Defeat the boss!"

"I'm trying!"

Then, a new voice sounded out behind him.

"Did you jump over that car?"

The boy turned around to see a bright-faced boy his age with spiky blonde hair standing in the middle aisle, gawking at him. Upon seeing his lack of a face, the blonde-haired boy jumped back.

"Whoa! What are you?!"

"Um…"

"Sorry. You surprised me—I've never seen someone without a face before."

"Well, neither have I."

"You can see?! Ah- sorry again. I'm Grif. What's your name?"

Grif sat down next to the boy, hand extended. The boy shook it tentatively, but wasn't sure how to answer the question.

"I don't have a name."

"Really? Well, surely you have something, right? What do people call you? I never really thought about not having a name. I already remember mine. I don't know *where* I remember it from, though…"

The faceless boy tuned out Grif's lengthy rant as he pondered the question. *What was his name, anyway?* The little kids on the other end of the bus suddenly yelled with joy and excitement.

"The laser! Fire the laser! Finish it!"

The mother sitting behind the loud children began to scold them, prompting apologies and whines.

"Um…" the faceless boy started, the gears turning in his head. He had an idea.

"Azer."

"Huh? Azer? That's your name? How do you spell that?"

The boy didn't know—he'd only just made it up. "Uh… A-Z-E-R?"

"Azer. I kinda like that. Well, alright, Azer, I meant to ask you, did you actually jump over that car earlier?"

"Yeah, I guess so," Azer replied. Having a name of his own filled him with confidence. "It's something I've always been able to do."

"You know most people can't do that, right?" stressed Grif. "That's unusual."

"How else are you supposed to cross the street?"

"There's a crosswalk. The cars stop for you," Grif answered matter-of-factly.

"Oh." Azer turned back around towards the window. Cars, people, and buildings were zooming by at a pace he'd never seen before.

"Man," Azer commented. "This bus goes fast! This thing could beat me in a race!"

Grif looked at Azer with awe. "You sure are a strange one. But to be fair, I'm not the most normal either. Check this out–"

Grif pulled up his shirt to reveal a huge scar where his heart should be. And Azer noticed that the usual thump-thump of a heart was nowhere to be seen.

"I don't have a heart. I think it was removed when I was little, but the crazy thing is: I don't remember it happening at all. And I can produce electricity from my hands."

Grif put his shirt back down and pointed a finger into the air. Little sparks of electricity shot out of it. Azer was in awe.

"Cool! I have a little scar too, on my side right here–" Azer pulled up the right side of his t-shirt to reveal a long scar on the side of his abdomen, right above his hip.

"Where'd you get it from?" Grif asked.

"No idea. But it seems like there are a lot of things about both of us that neither of us know, right?"

There was a brief pause and Azer took another look outside. He was already seeing more of the world than he ever imagined existed.

"You don't have any parents either, do you?" Grif inquired.

"Nope."

"We're not the only ones. Apparently, a bunch of people died when colonizing this town. There are a bunch of orphans I've seen."

There was another brief pause, Azer too focused on studying the outside world to pay full attention to Grif.

"So why'd you get on the bus, anyway?" Grif asked again.

"I wanted to explore."

"Same. School in the Battle Academy starts soon, and I wanted to get one last chance to look around the town before I went there," Grif said.

"The Battle Academy?" asked Azer.

The bus slowed to a stop with a creak.

"It's the school around here. Don't worry about it. I'll explain it later."

The passengers began to promptly exit through the folding doors, carrying their bags and briefcases. Azer and Grif followed the river of people out the bus and into the world.

They were deposited onto a sidewalk in front of a glamorous fashion store, with big, bright lights lining the windowsills and the clothes within sparkly and new. As the bus wheeled away down the road, it revealed another row of bustling streets, filled to the brim with family-run businesses and thrift shops. Every type of person was walking the sidewalks, hailing from planets and countries neither of them had ever heard of. Every skin color, every shade of hair, thousands of little quirks and details that set each person apart, walking and working and shopping on the streets of Nur, in the heart of the town.

The two boys began walking down the street, taking in the sights, sounds, and smells of Nur. It was a peaceful environment, the bluish sky shining down upon them. Just like the news broadcast he had seen that morning, Azer could spot a nearly infinite number of interesting things—statues, shops, art installations, and the scaffolds of emerging buildings. And, more interestingly, he saw many mentions of something called "The Shades." Bumper stickers, posters, and slogans all mentioned "The Shades." Passing by a gift shop, Azer saw a vast number of Shades-themed souvenirs, many depicting thick clouds or a lightning strike. Seeing all of this, Azer couldn't help but wonder.

Then, a voice from afar caught Azer's attention. Unlike the friendly, lighthearted clamor of the town, this voice was harsh, meaningful, and frightening. As they continued their walk, the source of the voice came into view.

A woman, dark-haired and tall, was speaking from atop a decrepit wooden crate. She was in her early twenties, well-dressed, sporting a red-tinted, sweeping black cloak with a strange symbol on the cloak's center. Her dark, narrowed eyes made contact with passersby as she spoke, and her skin appeared edged and hardened. Beside her was an unkempt, burly man with long hair, wearing the same cloak as the woman. He was silent and held up a red-lettered sign with the text:

FEAR THE SHADES. RETRIBUTION AWAITS.

The woman shouted, "You all live like your lives will never end. But your lives will end in three years! The Shades is coming, and if you do not join us, not one of you will survive God's power! Rapture awaits us all, and the only thing you can do is repent. Pray to God's will and you will live; you will ascend with us! Meet the lord in the blanketing clouds above, or die blasphemed!"

Azer was unable to look away, despite not understanding half of what they were talking about. The boys passed in front of the doomsayers, and the woman's haunting eyes landed on Azer and Grif. She pointed at them.

"God will not spare children! Listen to me while you have the chance: you must join our cause or die. Remember my name: I am Kovaki. Kovaki of Nova Noctis."

The two stood silent for a moment.

"Doomsayers," Grif scowled. "Just ignore them."

But Azer was intrigued. "Hey, Grif?"

"Yeah?"

"What the heck is The Shades?"

CHAPTER TWO:
DIVINITY

Sunny. 3mph winds blowing east. Eighty-four degrees fahrenheit. High humidity expected.

Eight years before Kovaki's speech in the town center, Kovaki stared out of the window in her classroom, lost in thought. Summer air warmed the window's glass and kids played in the courtyard outside. Beside her was her friend Haise, staring blankly at nothing in particular. Neither were paying any attention to the teacher.

Haise straightened herself in her seat, turned slowly, and leaned towards Kovaki. Haise quivered as she moved, as though she was old and decrepit, but she, like Kovaki, was only thirteen. An intricate pendant dangled from Haise's neck, swaying with her movements.

"There are... only fifty days left," Haise told Kovaki in her frail, high voice.

Kovaki turned to Haise, eyebrows raised.

"Seriously?" Kovaki whispered. "That was fast."

"I want to spend... more time with... you... since I will be going then," Haise whispered.

Kovaki looked at her friend intently. Haise had been brought up deeply religious by her parents, and even after their passing, she had maintained their spiritual fervor. Ever since Kovaki and Haise had met, Haise had made it clear that she wouldn't be around for long.

"My bones... are weak. My family and I are... not used to this... gravity," Haise had told her when they met. "My parents are gone... they couldn't survive... but I will be ascending... in a few years. I'll meet God."

Those words buzzed around for what had to be the thousandth time in Kovaki's head.

"Alright. Meet me after school, 'kay?"

"So, Haise, tell me," Kovaki started. Her friend was sitting with her on a bench, hot to the touch at the summer's peak. "And I don't mean to be rude when I ask this, trust me. But what *do* you think is gonna happen when The Shades comes? Are you really sure you want to be left behind?"

Haise turned to Kovaki, sweat dripping down her face from a mix of heat and everlasting exhaustion.

"Have I ever... told you where my family... is from?" Haise breathed.

"Not really."

"Somewhere... on a moon in a distant solar system... is a society... of people with the collective mission of finding... our galaxy's true God."

Kovaki bunched up her forehead. "What do you mean?"

"The different civilizations of Zysti galaxy... all had their own religions... before they discovered each other—the Great Discovery... and founded our galactic society. Many religions fell apart during the Great Discovery... and left everyone wondering... who really made the universe. Which religion was correct."

Kovaki pondered this for a moment. She hadn't considered how religions would have been affected by the Great Discovery over a hundred years ago. She hadn't even considered what pre-Discovery religions would have been like. To believe that people thought a God or Gods made just one intelligent species on only a single planet was hard to wrap her head around.

"Go on," Kovaki urged.

"These people... from all over the galaxy... formed a group called Noctis... on a moon somewhere. They dedicated their lives... to find where the true God was. This pendant..." Haise held up the pendant hanging from her neck and displayed it to Kovaki, "... is the symbol of Noctis. My family is from the moon... where they reside. My parents... heard about The Shades... and thought they found Noctis' true God. Remember that science lesson?"

"Which one?"

"The one on... gravity."

"Oh, yeah."

"My parents and I... grew up on the low-gravity moon... where Noctis is. The gravity here... was too high... and they died before they could see... The Shades."

The sudden mention of Haise's late parents left Kovaki speechless and uncomfortable. After a short moment of silence, she replied:

"I'm sorry about that."

"To answer your question... I know that The Shades... is when the true God pays a visit. I'm sure of... that. I want to stay behind for my parents and... a better path... forward for me. My disease makes my... bones deteriorate... and I want to see God before then. Before I die. Ascending will let me... escape death."

"You've said The Shades is when God pays a visit, but what do you think is gonna actually *happen* then? Like, what does it look like? How will I know that you've ascended when I come back to Manim after The Shades?"

Haise looked to the sky above, dotted with wispy clouds.

"During The Shades... Manim is covered in clouds. Every... inch of sky... gets covered in storm clouds. It lasts a day and then dissipates."

"I know. But everyone on the ground during The Shades vanishes; everyone knows that. What happens to them? Aren't you afraid of that happening to you?"

"Why would... I be? What happens to them is... a *miracle*. The souls who colonized this planet... who stayed behind during the first Shades... they ascended. The same will happen to me. I will meet God... and he will help me move to a... higher plane of... existence."

Haise looked Kovaki square in the eyes.

"To answer your question... I do not know what... will happen. But I imagine... it will be beautiful. If you want... you can join me... down here. Ascend with me."

Kovaki studied Haise's face for a moment. She bit her lip, deep in thought.

"Sorry Haise. My mom would miss me ... a lot. Also I... I haven't ever been the most religious. Not sure if God would be happy about that."

Haise smiled at her.

"That's... okay. We all meet God eventually... one way or another."

Today was the day. Kovaki stepped outside her home on the streets of Nur and looked at the sky. The weather was flawless. Not a cloud in sight. The temperature was mild and welcoming, and the sunshine felt warm on her hardened skin. But her heart was pumping. After today, she would never see her best friend again, and the anticipation of the event that would occur today only made her nerves worse.

Kovaki walked to Haise's house, mulling over what she'd say to her friend. Part of her hoped that The Shades was just some big hoax, a blend of legends that culminated in widespread hysteria. She hoped that every-thing she'd heard about The Shades wasn't true, that her friend was just wasting her time, but she wasn't sure what to believe. With how gorgeous the weather was, Kovaki was having serious doubts that a planet-wide storm would happen at all.

Kovaki knocked on Haise's door, and a few moments later, it opened, Haise occupying the doorway. The inside of her house was dim, lit only by ritual candles and cracks between blinds on the windows. The house was surprisingly big, considering that Haise was an orphan; apparently, her parents had left her a considerable sum of money upon their passing. Haise was wearing her Noctis pendant, heavy and intricately made of polished wood, coated with sigils on every square inch. The center of the pendant had a larger symbol, engraved in what looked like real gold, a strange series of lines surrounded by a thick golden circle. Haise looked overjoyed.

"Hi, Haise. I just wanted to say 'bye.' Thank you for... for being such a good friend."

"Thank you for being... a good friend, Kovaki."

Haise pulled Kovaki into a big hug, which Kovaki returned. She tried to fight the tears threatening to well up in her eyes. The tug of second chances told Kovaki to take her back, to make her come, to do anything to see Haise one more time, but deep down she knew it was already too late. Haise had made up her mind long ago.

After a long embrace, Haise pulled away. Her fate was sealed.

Kovaki racked her brain for something final to say. "Hey, uh... Good luck on seeing God. If that's how that works."

"Thank you."

Kovaki looked at her friend once more, and then waved goodbye, turning away to go back to her house.

The Battle Academy, Kovaki's school, was the pickup point for all students. Every citizen of Nur was to be evacuated in spaceships provided by the Zystinian government, and all students of the Battle Academy were to sign in at school before boarding the evacuation ships. After helping her mother board up the windows and doors of their house, they walked to the Battle Academy to await pickup.

Upon arriving in her classroom, Kovaki noticed it was filled with many unusual things. There was a disproportionate amount of adults– the parents of everyone in her class present to ensure their child's safe boarding of the Zysti-provided evacuation ships. Even Kovaki's own mom was by her side. The second thing she noticed out of place, other than the fact that all of the desks and chairs were pushed to one side of the room, was that the other wall was occupied by several complex-looking machines, with many of her classmates clustered around them. Each machine had a digital console with the Zysti galaxy insignia engraved above it and a flat, clear panel at the machine's base, and the rest of it was encased in dark plastic. Fingerprint scanners.

Having them present was justified—the Zystinian government had to take responsibility for the safety of their people. Everyone in the town had to scan their fingerprints on these machines, and anyone who didn't was reported as missing. Kovaki already knew how to fool it.

Kovaki and her mom walked over to a machine, and Kovaki followed the instructions on the screen. She pressed her thumb on the cool glass until the screen indicated she had been successfully accounted for. She gave a thumbs up to her mom, who smiled, and then hung around the machine for a moment, waiting for any attention to fall away from her. Once her mother and her classmates seemed occupied with something else, Kovaki swiftly pulled out five index cards from her pocket, each with one of Haise's fingerprints on it. She shuffled around through the papers until she found the largest one—the thumbprint. Kovaki shoved the rest into her pocket and pressed Haise's thumbprint on the glass. Beads of stress-induced sweat formed on her nose, as the processing was taking longer than usual. Then, after five heart-stopping seconds, the "approved" symbol appeared on the screen, and Kovaki finally let out a breath.

Her insides panged at the deed she'd done, but an uneasy sense of relief washed over her. Maybe, if The Shades wasn't all it was cracked up to be, Haise would still be around when she returned.

A long period of nervous waiting then fell over the classroom, everyone discussing The Shades, their parents' experiences with it, and every range of theories as to what its true nature really is. Alone, without her friend, Kovaki's nerves set in, anxious at what was to happen on her planet in just a few hours.

Almost making her jump, Kovaki's mom interrupted her thoughts.

"Where's that Haise girl?" she asked. "I haven't seen her yet."

"Oh, she's just running late," Kovaki said, fighting to keep the competing guilt and panic out of her voice. Her mom seemed to buy it, as she nodded and turned away. Kovaki, contemplating what she had done, kept looking outside the window for a sign of the storm, but the clear sky continued to shine down on them harmlessly.

Her teacher barked orders at the class, telling them to make their way out of the school. A long walk later and Kovaki found herself standing with her schoolmates in front of a huge silvery-gray ship with a ramp lying on the grass in front of their school. Zystinian officials ushered people inside, and as Kovaki's place in line got closer, she could see dozens and dozens of other similar ships nearby. The whole town was evacuating. Except for Haise.

Kovaki marveled at the ship as it flew out of the atmosphere and into orbit. The vessel, along with the dozens of others leaving Nur, was to dock with a much larger flagship already in orbit around Manim, housing all the inhabitants of the planet for a day while the storm below ran its course. But, so far, Kovaki couldn't see any storm. Her confidence was steadily growing, though cautiously, that The Shades was a hoax.

But then she saw it. Kovaki wasn't sure how she had missed it at first, but two foreboding walls of solid cloud were slowly, steadily emerging from both poles of the planet. Over minutes and then hours of space travel, Kovaki watched in horror as the light gray walls grew and grew until they swallowed the entire planet whole, meeting at the equator.

Manim was now a ball of thick gray cloud from pole to pole. She was so engrossed, Kovaki hardly noticed when their evac ship docked with the Zystinian flagship.

The Shades had arrived.

Stepping back onto Nur's soil once more felt wrong, almost. Somehow, in some way, everything had been left *exactly the same*. Kovaki's first instinct was to rush to Haise's house, but she wasn't sure she was ready to see what was there. Or wasn't there.

Every house in every neighborhood had the entrances boarded, nailed, or screwed shut. Except for Haise's. She had left her doors unlocked, welcoming whatever mysterious force the storm unleashed. Kovaki put her hand on the doorknob and pushed the front door open, heart pounding.

It was almost completely dark. The ritual candles had been extinguished, but aside from that, nothing seemed out of the ordinary. Except Haise's unsteady voice was nowhere to be heard.

Kovaki stepped inside, and the light pouring in through the front door illuminated something lying on the living room floor. It was a journal, emblemed with the same symbol Haise had been wearing on her Noctis pendant. Hand shaking, breathing ragged, Kovaki picked it up.

Opening the journal revealed Haise's diary, thoughts and ideas captured over many years. Kovaki flipped through each page, familiar with some of what she read, until she reached a blank page—blank except for a date and a few words beneath. The date was that of The Shades, and the words, unmistakably in Haise's handwriting, read:

> I see it. I see the image of God in front of me. It's getting closer.
> Kovaki, I was right. It is beautiful.

Kovaki read these words again and again before putting the journal down. She was dazed. Her previously terrified face transformed into a wide grin.

"Haise," she said, "you did it. You really did it."

"You met God."

Kovaki could only distantly hear the urgent voices of news reporters coming from her television.

"...Nur authorities have reported the absence of a thirteen year old orphaned girl named Haise Menss. Some suspect..."

A ringing in Kovaki's ears was growing louder and louder, slowly consuming all of her senses. It wasn't even grief—in fact, she hadn't stopped smiling for several minutes now. Realizations were consuming her mind in a euphoric symphony, everything in her life making sense in a way nothing had ever before.

There was a God. It was residing on the very planet she lived on. Her best friend Haise wasn't gone—she had ascended. Kovaki was filled with first a rush of joy and pride at her friend's triumph, immediately followed by a deep, burning jealousy. Haise was right. She had escaped the binds of mortal life and death and ascended into a higher plane of existence—and she had done it all without Kovaki. To think that she had been so close to ascending with Haise; it seemed inconceivably unfair. Kovaki had missed her ticket.

But who's fault was it? Her own. It was her own fault for not believing her only real friend and her religious journey. But it wasn't just Kovaki who hadn't believed—it was everyone. Nobody in her town had joined her, not even from Noctis. Kovaki had to correct this. She had to make up for the opportunity she had lost.

Now, she knew God had to be real. What else could explain such a phenomenon as The Shades? It was a routine rapture belonging only to the true believers.

Suddenly, Kovaki got up from her chair and started walking to the door. Her mom cried after her, panicked and confused.

So Kovaki would make them all believe.

After a short walk, Kovaki arrived at Haise's house to find police cars surrounding it. It had taken them days to figure out that Haise was gone. They'd pay for ignoring her—but that would come later. She snuck in through the unlocked back entrance, stepping into Haise's dark home with determination. She quickly located her living room where the Noctis pendant lay, grabbed it, and put it around her neck.

The mission of Noctis was to find Zysti's one true God, and Haise had found it. Now, the pendant Kovaki wore held a new meaning—making sure everyone else believed. She would form a new Noctis: *The Nova Noctis.*

"You all have come here for a divine reason. It is not a coincidence that, from every corner of the galaxy, you have ended up on this planet, in this room, all together as one community. You may think you are here to start a family or a business or to become another of Nur's many corvyte miners and live a prosperous life, but it is Manim's holy power that has brought you here. You are here because you… believe."

Kovaki's last word echoed throughout the dimly lit, white-walled room, resonating in the hearts and souls of her followers. She wore a long dark cloak held together by the Noctis sigil. Almost six years of work had gotten her here, preaching in front of dozens of dedicated devotees of Nova Noctis. But, finally, she had begun to make the people of Nur, if only a fraction of them, believers. Each of Nova Noctis' weekly meetings made her soul shine with joy and passion, and every additional filled seat reinforced her devotion and her foothold in Nur's society.

Out of the corner of her eye, she noticed a well-dressed man standing in the doorway to the room, fading sunlight around him pouring inside. His hair was sleek and well-combed, and he wore the signature black-green uniform of a representative of the Zysti Multiplanetary Government. Kovaki ignored him, continuing to wrap up the day's meeting.

"Sooner than you think, the day of salvation will come. We will all ascend together then. And when that day comes, and the fingers of God pluck you from the constraints of mortal life, only the true believers will be granted ascension." She threw a quick, almost indiscernible look at the Zystinian government representative patiently waiting at the doorway. "So tell your friends, your family, your children, and help pave the path for us all. Thank you."

The members of Nova Noctis rose from their seats and Kovaki stepped off of her podium to personally greet them. She shook the hands of some of her followers, embracing the ones with tears in their eyes, and once the last devotee left the room, she turned with a sweep of her cloak to the government representative.

"How may I help you?" Kovaki said, putting on a convincing smile. Before replying, the unsmiling representative briefly looked her up and down.

"Miss Kovaki Etonie, I have orders from the Zystinian government for you to shut down the religious organization by the name of Nova Noctis."

Kovaki recoiled at the words, her smile wiped away. A seed of panic formed in her mind.

"Nova Noctis is a legitimate religious organization," Kovaki responded, keeping any emotion or sign of weakness out of her voice.

The representative gave a brief, exhausted sigh.

"The foundation of your religion is collective suicide. Your organization is legitimate, yes, but The Shades is a dangerous phenomenon we don't fully understand yet. You are telling people to stay behind instead of evacuating the planet, and if that were to happen, it would lead to mass casualties. While we are not sure exactly what happens during The Shades, we know it kills people. Any religion, even a legitimate one, requiring people to die for its cause is forbidden."

Kovaki paused for a moment, staring at the representative while fighting the urge to bite her lip. If the Zystinian government was going to get in her way, that was going to be a problem. Possible outcomes and solutions whizzed by in her mind.

Before she could respond, the representative continued:

"You have three weeks to dissolve your religious group, and if it is not dissolved by then, an intervention will be necessary. Good day."

With that, the man walked away, leaving Kovaki to her turbulent thoughts.

Kovaki turned around, taking in the entirety of the Nova Noctis building. She then clenched a fist, her unusually hardened skin tensing up, and punched a small hole in the concrete with rage.

"But the freedom we are seeking is exactly what they want to halt. The nonbelievers want to keep us under their thumbs, keep us acting like good little citizens, but we can't let them control us. We will not!"

Since Kovaki had first proposed the idea of an anti-Zysti revolution to the rest of Nova Noctis, some members had left. But, while her numbers were fewer, the fervor and passion of her and her followers had grown exponentially.

"Many of us are already under their control. Thirty percent of all employed citizens of Nur work in the mines of Manim, mining corvyte for the Zystinian government. Some of us in this very room work there. You may think it brings our colony wealth like it did long ago, but now, they're just using it as a distraction from the truth! A truth only we are awake to—WE ARE SLAVES!"

The room filled with raucous yelling and fast-paced chants. She waited for it to die down, feeling a rush of intoxicating power through her veins.

"In just one week the nonbelievers will come to us, wanting to destroy all that Nova Noctis has built up and stop us from our ascension. We won't let them! We'll fight back! Be patient, but be ready, for their day of reckoning will come."

Right on cue, an immaculate Zystinian government ship, immense in size, landed in front of Kovaki. Before the shutdown sequence could even finish and the ship's high-pitched whir could fade away, the same green-suited representative as before stepped out of the ship, surrounded by four armed guards. The representative strode officiously towards Kovaki, whose cloak was flapping around in the wind. Behind her was the entirety of Nova Noctis, faces apprehensive. The representative's face was as emotionless as before.

"It's been three weeks," he said. "Are you going to shut down your organization?"

Kovaki let the words linger, giving him a long stare before answering quietly.

"Never."

The representative lifted his hand, raised two fingers, and pointed them at her. At once, the armed guards behind him split off and approached her.

"Arrest this woman," he ordered.

But as the words were coming out of his mouth, Kovaki reached over to his raised hand and broke his extended fingers. As the guards surrounded her, the representative let out a cry of pain and her Nova Noctis followers let out a collective yell, charging towards the guards.

Kovaki fought off the swings of the guards' electric batons, evading their well-trained attacks while sending punches and kicks to their unarmored faces. She was one of the lucky few of Zysti galaxy to possess a supernatural power—a Val—that made her skin into an impossibly hard, exoskeleton-like material she called "pure carbon." Her Val made Kovaki an unusually effective fighter, rendering their baton strikes and shoves from their riot shields useless, while also giving her an offensive advantage.

Quickly, the swarm of enraged Nova Noctis members overwhelmed the guards, shifting the focus of the confrontation from Kovaki to the angry mob. Screams, yells, and grunts overwhelmed the senses, and at first, it was hard to tell who was winning. As Kovaki emerged from the chaos, she saw the four guards pitifully trying to tackle dozens of her followers. But with their nonlethal riot gear, and with such small numbers, they didn't stand a chance. Emboldened, Kovaki led the way towards the ship where the injured representative was retreating, her followers in her wake.

Suddenly, great shadows and a deafening whir halted Kovaki's approach. The sun was obstructed by three more large government ships. As they landed, countless armed guards began to pour out. A small, indiscernible object soared out of one of the clusters of guards and landed in the middle of the angry crowd. Kovaki noticed an oddly-colored smoke billowing out of it only moments too late.

The effects of the tear gas were swift and painful. Kovaki's breath became labored and each inhale burned, blurring her vision with copious tears. She could feel herself coughing but couldn't hear her own coughs over the cacophony. The first image she could make out was a masked riot guard taking down and arresting a Nova Noctis member. She watched helplessly as her followers, one by one, were put in cuffs and dragged away.

One guard pushed Kovaki to the ground while another, in a swift, practiced motion, restrained her arms and began to cuff her. Was it going to end like this? Was she going to spend the rest of her days in a Zystinian prison, forever unable to ascend?

Rage and determination burned in her eyes. Not like this. One way or another, she would meet God. And she would do *anything* to achieve that.

Kovaki focused on the guard pinning her down and aimed a kick at his helmet. The helmet went flying off, and the guard was dazed. Kovaki lifted her chin and pulled back her head. With all the force she could muster, she headbutted the guard with a sickening *crack*.

Kovaki felt blood drip down her cheek. It wasn't her own. She was unharmed, thanks to her Val. But as she saw the guard fall limply to the ground, she knew he had been killed instantly.

For a moment, she watched the body. There was no remorse. It had been so easy to do the motions required to kill him. A life ended at her hands.

It felt good to punish the nonbelievers.

Looking around her, Kovaki noticed that some of her other followers had resorted to killing in order to escape. One of her earliest and most dedicated followers, Gorr, had strangled a guard. Kovaki ran over to him amidst the chaos.

"Find anyone you can! We're getting out of here before more of them arrive!"

Gorr nodded and urged along another fleeing Nova Noctis member, and Kovaki led them sprinting away.

Kovaki and the meager survivors of their confrontation with the Zystinian authorities huddled together within an abandoned house, lying against peeled-paint walls and a decrepit wooden floor. The stabbing cold of Manim's spring was particularly harsh that night. With the authorities still searching for them, they were left homeless and ostracized. The one thing they still had was each other and their undying faith.

Kovaki remembered her now long-past days preaching to the people of Nur, the days where she was looked at with reverence instead of fear and worry. What happened to that? She had only wanted to teach them to ascend instead of cower in fear from The Shades. Did the people of Nur expect to just run from salvation every time it came, for the rest of their days? But Kovaki's efforts to help Nur had only led to her ruin.

The fire of rage was now a steady burn alongside her passion. Her faultless devotion to The Shades was now tainted with the hatred of those who had wronged her, and she would take her revenge for it. Over time, she would rebuild her power and her followers, using any means necessary to do so. Kovaki had an idea—a way to force everyone to believe. She'd make the nonbelievers pay for her lowest moments.

And they would pay with their lives.

CHAPTER THREE:
A NEW GENERATION

Sunny. 2mph winds blowing northeast. Sixty-five degrees fahrenheit. No rain expected.

Azer stood in front of a titanic building resembling a small city, with different smaller buildings centered around the main entrance. The main portion of the building had a strange quality to its architecture—it was unlike houses and buildings in Azer's neighborhood, which had very traditional and simple designs. Instead, it was blocky in shape, with many outer rooms of the building appearing to jut out into the air. A large stone arch stood above him, the words "BATTLE ACADEMY" ingrained in the stone in dark black lettering.

"Are you sure this is the right place?" Azer asked Grif, also gawking at the massive structure. "It's huge!"

"What, the right place for learning things? Yeah, duh. It's a school. That's the whole point of a school."

"I've never seen a school before," Azer remarked.

"It sounds like you haven't seen much at all," Grif added. "Have you really only lived in that small western area of town?"

"For as long as I can remember."

"You really are an odd one. C'mon, let's head inside. You want to learn about The Shades? This is the place to do it, but we have to apply if we want to study here."

Azer followed Grif down the long path to the Battle Academy's main building, taking in more and more of the campus as he walked. People of all ages, shapes, and sizes walked up and down the path, adding to or leaving the large group of people crowded around the main entrance. Azer saw all of it as an exciting prelude to his education. He wondered if he would know as much as Mr. Grano one day.

"You seem to know a fair bit about the Battle Academy," Azer asked Grif. "Why aren't you already attending?"

"I applied too late. Apparently you have to apply before one of their 'semesters'. I've known about it for a while, but by the time I tried to apply, the semester had already started."

"What do you do there? Do you learn battle?"

"You learn all kinds of things, lots more than you can learn from just wandering around the town. When we apply, they'll explain it to us, but, yeah, you do learn how to battle. It looks pretty awesome."

By now the two had made their way into the cluster of people, and Grif's expression started to become confused.

"That's funny. We're supposed to find an adult to help us apply by now. I-"

Grif's sentence was cut short when he suddenly crashed into something tall.

"Oof!"

Azer looked up at what Grif had crashed into—it was a very tall man.

"Oh, I'm sorry! Here," the man said.

The tall man reached down to offer a hand and helped pull Grif to standing. Grif was dazed, at first unable to process what he was looking at. In the center of each of the man's palms were two metal-clad holes that went all the way through his hands. Azer could see the face of a kid his age through one of the holes.

"Sorry again. Are you alright?" the man asked Grif. Once Grif gathered himself and looked the man up and down, also noticing the strange holes in the man's hands, Grif nodded silently.

"Are you here to apply?" the man asked.

"Yep," Azer said, still in awe at how much the man dwarfed him. Azer and Grif only reached his waist height, and his head was adorned with well-combed silver hair. But the man didn't look old—to the contrary, he had a young face, with wide silver eyes and sharpened features. His silver hair was metallic in color and quality, fine and reflective and styled like a curving river.

"Then you've come to the right place. My name is Dr. Delvin Rawins, I'm a scientist and a scholar. I teach environmental science here at the Battle Academy."

Delvin shook both of their comparatively tiny hands. The metal in Delvin's hand was cool to the touch. "And you two are?"

"I'm Grif."

"I'm Azer."

Delvin gave a short nod and then looked past the two.

"Where are your parents?" Delvin tried searching the crowd for anyone resembling the two.

"We, uh, don't have any," Grif answered. "Both of us. We're not brothers, or, at least I don't think we are, but we're both orphans."

This seemed to intrigue Delvin, and he made a curious expression.

"May I ask where you two are from, then?" Delvin inquired.

"We don't know that, either," said Grif. "Or, wait, do you?" he asked Azer.

"Me? No, not at all. We're here because we want to find out."

"Well I'm sorry to hear all of that," Delvin said quietly. "But enough of my questions. You two want to apply, yes? I may have to pull a few strings to get that arranged, given you have no parents, but it would be a crime for me to deny two curious young gentlemen an education. Especially since you came to apply on your own volition. Learning is why life matters, after all."

Delvin then began busily typing away on the computer stationed at his standing desk, giving the two boys an uncomfortable moment of silence.

"What's 'volition' mean?" Azer whispered to Grif.

"No idea."

The silence persisted, filled with the chatter of other applicants and the swift keystrokes of Delvin. Azer felt a persistent awe in Delvin's presence, and not just due to his extraordinary height. Spending much of his time at Grano's Diner, most of Azer's unending questions he asked Mr. Grano. But the ones he really burned to know— where he came from, why the sunset changed the color of the sky, why everyone had a face but him—were never answered. Delvin, unlike Mr. Grano, was a teacher. Maybe he knew the answers to Azer's questions.

Azer's curiosity overcame his desire not to interrupt Delvin, and he blurted out:

"Mr. Rawins, what is The Shades?"

Delvin's bright silver eyes darted from the computer screen to Azer.

"We don't understand what it really is, but I've done some research into finding out. All we know is that, once every ten years, Manim is covered in clouds and everyone evacuates. After the storm blows over, everyone returns. Like nothing ever happened."

"Like nothing ever happened? Won't the storm destroy houses and stuff?" Azer asked.

"One would think so, but the surface before and after The Shades has been almost the exact same before and after every storm."

"What happens on the ground when the storm comes?"

"We don't know," Delvin replied earnestly. "But we do know that it's dangerous to be left behind when it happens." Delvin's face grew grim. "We can't confirm the cause, but eight years ago, a child at the Battle Academy van-"

Delvin stopped himself mid-sentence, gazing at the two young boys apprehensively.

"What?" Azer and Grif urged simultaneously.

"Never mind. I mustn't spread rumors," Delvin dismissed. He then got back to Azer and Grif's applications like nothing had happened. But the damage had been done—Azer and Grif were looking at each other slack-jawed, the fire of curiosity set aflame.

"Alright," Delvin said after a moment, "you two are officially enrolled in the Battle Academy. If you didn't know already, at the Academy you will get a full, Zysti-approved education, including learning, as the name implies, the art of battle. The Battle Academy also caters to children with Vals, teaching them to control and harness their powers to the greatest extent, including using them for good in the world. Because I teach a higher-level class, I will most likely not be your teacher anytime soon, but if you have any questions, please come to me in the building or find the Battle Academy's principal, Itell D. Ortum, or Dr. D for short. He's in the main office."

Delvin then pressed a button on his computer and printed several sheets of paper. He snatched them from the printer, bound them with a stapler, and held it out.

"These papers will tell you everything else you need to know about the Battle Academy, including when and where to go on the first day of school."

"Thank you," Grif said, taking the papers. The two began to walk away when Delvin shouted, "Wait!"

"If you want to get a headstart on the battle portion of school, I'm offering an extracurricular class for select students at the Battle Academy.

I call it the Combat Class. I hold lessons every other weekday after school as well as morning lessons on the weekends."

Delvin held out a small slip of paper, information printed in small text along with a photo of the class building.

"If you'd care to join, I'm teaching these classes at a low price."

Grif took the slip and studied it carefully. He looked at Azer.

"I'm not sure we'll be able to join, sorry," Grif told Delvin, who nodded understandingly. "We don't have much money. And I think we're going to be busy researching The Shades some more, so I don't know if we'll have time."

"Alright. But the offer is always open. If you ever struggle in the Academy's battle courses, we'll be open and ready for you. Just hang on to that slip; it tells you everything you need to know."

"Thanks."

"I hope to see you in school soon. Best of luck."

Azer and Grif walked away and, once out of Delvin's earshot, Grif jumped in front of Azer.

"You heard what I heard, right? The kid vanishing?"

"Yeah, I did! What was that?"

"There's something going on. Both with Delvin and The Shades. We gotta find out more."

"I know. Let's see if we can ask someone when we go to school next week."

Early in the morning, Azer ventured out into the cool spring air to attend his first day in the Battle Academy. But his mind was on other things besides school; he burned and burned with questions about The Shades, the missing child, and most of all, himself. Azer felt that, somehow, his unknown origin and missing face might have something to do with The Shades. But he had no idea how.

Yet.

The school day began with the principal giving a welcoming speech to the students, talking mostly about things that Azer unconsciously tuned out. One thing did pique Azer's interest, however: the principal, Dr. D, had an unusual appearance. He wore casual clothing and looked hauntingly pale, and his eyes were a ghostly white, like those of a corpse.

The first thing Azer noticed in school was the relentless attention that his missing face attracted. Every step in the hallway or moment sitting down in a classroom he'd find yet another kid staring at where his face should be, marveling or recoiling at the sight. Azer had hoped there would be other kids with something different about them, and he was right. Nur was filled with species from all corners of the galaxy. Kids had countless physical features he'd never seen before, but yet, Azer's missing face trumped all of that and then some. Nothing there was quite as unusual as the lack of a face. The attention was beginning to take a toll, and he was having regrets about showing up at school at all.

After his second class ended, Azer headed for the door as fast as he could to avoid the stares of the other children, hoping to get to lunch without much attention. He walked quickly through the hallway, but before he could enter the cafeteria, he was stopped by another group of children talking in the center of the hall. As soon as they noticed Azer's missing face, they began to surround him with a flurry of questions and exclamations. He tried to push to the left and then to the right, tried to escape around the back of the group, but it was no use—they had sur-rounded him in every direction. He couldn't get out without pushing them out of the way.

"Leave him alone, please."

A slow, clear, deep voice rang out from somewhere behind Azer. As if by some unknown power, the kids harassing Azer all went silent at once and scattered, leaving Azer by himself. He turned around to see the source of the voice.

It was the Battle Academy's principal, Dr. D. He was even taller up close, dwarfing Azer. Fear and intimidation kept Azer locked in place.

"I couldn't help but notice that you're getting a great deal of attention from the other students today, and now I see why. Don't worry. I'm sure you're tired of people talking about your face. Or lack thereof."

"Uh- yeah. I am," Azer answered.

Dr. D's white eyes moved down towards the book in Azer's hands, piled among his other worksheets and folders.

"Are you researching The Shades?" Dr. D asked gently.

Azer became acutely aware of the book he was holding, a bookmark sticking out of the section on The Shades. He pulled the book tighter to his chest.

"Yeah, I am. How did you know?"

"I can tell you're the curious type, like me, and I know that section of the book you've bookmarked well." After a pause, he asked, "Where are you from?"

"I don't know where I'm from. I have no idea why I don't have a face. But I wanna find out. My friend and I got this book because we want to know more." He paused. "I think The Shades might have something to do with it."

Dr. D looked at Azer meaningfully for a moment. Azer broke the silence.

"Do you know anything about The Shades? Other than what's in this book?" Azer asked.

"Not much," Dr. D sighed. "No one still alive has been on the ground when it happens."

"Is it really true that a kid vanished eight years ago, during the last Shades?"

Dr. D tensed up and his lips went thin. He looked at Azer again, gears turning in his head, before he sighed and rubbed the bridge of his nose.

"Well… yes. A student here, a poor girl named Haise vanished eight years ago. It's stuff a kid like you shouldn't have to worry about, but her disappearance was tragic to say the least. Why do you ask?"

"What happened to her? Did she disappear during The Shades?"

"Her disappearance happened to line up with The Shades, but we don't know what really occurred."

Azer could tell he was beginning to push his luck with the subject, and felt a small pang of guilt for asking about such a horrible thing. But the fire of his curiosity burned brightly at the prospect of a lead, and he couldn't help but feel a bit of reluctant excitement. Azer remained silent as Dr. D's face looked at him scrutinizingly, until his expression softened.

"You know, I admire your curiosity. What's your name?"

"Azer."

"I'll see you again soon, Azer. Don't let anyone harass you about your face from here on out."

Dr. D turned around and walked down the hall. Without another word, Azer walked into the cafeteria with a newfound confidence.

He quickly found Grif at a sparsely-populated table, grinning and waving an arm in the air at Azer. Azer sat down next to his friend, taking in the bustling cafeteria around him.

"This place just keeps getting more amazing," commented Grif. "You didn't get troubled too much for your… you know, not-face, right?"

"It's not a big deal anymore. I saw the principal, Dr. D, in the halls before I got here."

Grif eyes went wide.

"Seriously?! What was he like? Is he as boring as he was during the assembly?"

"He seemed… nice."

"That's good. Were you able to ask anyone about The Shades?"

"Yeah, I asked Dr. D. He said a girl named Haise disappeared here eight years ago. That's all I found out."

"So there *was* a missing kid!"

"But I think it's a sensitive subject. We probably won't be able to find out much more by asking the teachers."

"Fair. Why don't we ask some other students, then?"

A moment later, a pair of faces showed up behind Grif. It was two boys. One was a smaller boy with leaves and vines poking out from under his collar and sleeves, and the other a much taller boy who looked like he belonged in a higher grade. The taller boy had deep, dark purple skin and pastel blue eyes that almost seemed to glow.

"I... uh... can we sit here?" the smaller boy asked timidly, pointing to the seat next to Grif.

"Sure," Grif replied.

"Uh... I'm Milo, by the way. Thank you. Most of the other tables were taken up..." Milo's voice was quiet and soft. "This is Torbe. He's my neighbor and my friend. I hope it's okay if he sits here too."

"Hey," Torbe said, waving a hand towards Azer and Grif, who gestured back.

"Have you guys heard about the girl who went missing eight years ago?" Azer asked the newcomers readily. Torbe's face became confused, and Milo's instantly went pale.

"M- missing? Here?!" Milo exclaimed.

"When I said ask other students, I didn't mean for you to ask like that," Grif told Azer. "You're freaking that guy out."

"It's probably nothing, Milo," Torbe reassured. Torbe's voice matched his appearance, seeming several years older than the rest of them. "Just a rumor, I'm sure."

Azer found himself apologetic for scaring Milo, but felt undeterred in front of two new potential friends. Neither Milo nor Torbe looked at Azer with disgust or fear. *Maybe school wasn't so bad after all.*

As the first week at the Battle Academy came and went, Azer found himself swamped in schoolwork, a disappointing amount of it relevant to his past or The Shades. The Battle Academy, which he expected to answer all of his biggest questions, seemed to offer little in the way of life's greatest mysteries. What he did learn, however, was that he was years behind on his education; a fact indicated by the piles of papers he was assigned daily covering things he should have known years ago. His memory of Nur hardly reached that far.

Regardless, he was finally learning. And even with hours of work to do after school, Azer still found the time to search for the answers to his own past.

On the first day of the second school week was a grade-wide field trip to Nur's famous corvyte mines—the industry that brought great wealth to Manim in the first place. While he knew next to nothing about corvyte, Azer was eager to learn more.

He found Grif among the crowd of students boarding the school bus and walked by his side into the vehicle. School buses, Azer had quickly realized in his first week of school, were nothing like town buses. School buses stunk of old leather, were filled with rowdy kids instead of peaceful townspeople, and always seemed to be poorly ventilated no matter how many windows he opened.

Since Azer and Grif were in different classes, the only time they could talk with each other was on the bus. After discussing school for a moment, Azer asked:

"Grif, what're the corvyte mines?"

"No clue. I've only ever heard of it in passing."

"I heard that corvyte is why Nur was founded in the first place, but I don't know what it is."

"I don't either, dude. You ask me all this stuff like I know everything, but I don't think I've been on Nur that long."

"What do you mean?" asked Azer.

The bus started moving with a shudder, and Grif gave him a serious look.

"I mean I don't remember that far back. Only about five years or so. I have no idea how I ended up here on Nur or what I was doing before then. All I remember is my name."

Azer didn't frown, but he thought about frowning.

"I'm the same way, except I only remember two or three years back, not five. My earliest memory is walking into Grano's Diner, totally confused. I remember I was soaking wet."

Grif looked like he'd been slapped. "How is that possible? That's almost the same first memory I have."

"You came to Grano's Diner?"

"No, I remember being in the scrapyard instead. But I was soaking wet, just like you."

Azer took a second to process this, letting his mind wander. He and Grif had a lot in common, but almost identical memory loss and almost identical first memories? It couldn't be a coincidence.

"What is Grano's Diner, anyway?" Grif asked, trying to steer the conversation from something less enigmatic.

"Oh. I basically live at Grano's Diner. Mr. Grano's not my dad, but I've learned everything I know from him and the people who eat there. He took care of me when I first showed up. Mr. Grano said that since I don't know my birthday, I should use the date when he found me instead."

"Huh. You spend all day there?"

"Pretty much. He usually lets me eat for free. I used to either spend the day there or try to map out the area, and I sleep in an abandoned house not far from there." Azer turned to look out the window of the bus. "Though, I think I'll have a hard time mapping Nur out now..."

"Man, I should have stayed at a diner. Since I spend most of my time in the scrapyard from my first memory, I just built a little shelter for myself there. The workers don't bother me, and sometimes they give me free stuff, like food or money. I should have come up with a birthday the way you did…"

"You still can! I'm sure Mr. Grano can give you one."

"Really?!"

Gradually, the surrounding buildings of Nur became more sparse, replaced by brightly-colored foliage and increasingly tall trees. Azer could feel the bus rolling over subtle, stretched-out hills, warmly lit by the sun peeking through between teal-colored leaves. Eventually, with two small bumps, the bus passed onto a bridge, rolling over the river that indicated they were officially leaving Nur.

From what Azer had seen in school and in posters around Nur, the cities on Zysti galaxy's major planets largely looked the same. Which, logically, made sense—the humanoid beings which comprised 97% of Zysti's intelligent life gravitated towards making environments fit for humans; large expanses of land designed to stack as many people in one place as possible, filled with towering buildings.

But the planets on which these cities were built obeyed no rules. Every planet containing life of some form was impossibly different from the next, with plants and animals and terrain in so many colors that not all of them appeared in the visible spectrum. Manim was an outlier even on this front—its natural beauty alone brought settlers from across the galaxy. Swaths of cool-colored, lush scenery dotted with explosions of vibrant pinks and reds, the entire visual structure of the planet seemed deliberate and alive.

Once the forest began to clear, the Octane fields came into full view, appearing as vast waves of blue-tinted grass, interrupted only by an exceedingly distant mountain range that the eye could barely register. Now only two signs of civilization rested on the horizon: the town of Nur behind them, with its modest sized buildings peeking out from behind the forest, and the corvyte mines ahead, a massive industrial wasteland tainting Manim's natural beauty with walls of scaffolding and smoke-billowing towers. While he knew the corvyte mines had brought Nur its wealth, he felt disheartened and, as a member of the town, almost personally responsible for the hideous brown-grey patch of land spreading across the plains from the heart of the mine.

The bus stopped at what looked to be the main center for the corvyte mining operations. The exterior was hopelessly dull, comprising maybe two or three shades of grey—a theme that held true throughout the rest of the mine. The buses unloaded their cargo, placing the kids at the mouth of the huge building. Chaperones, some tired-looking and some genuinely excited to be there, ushered everyone inside.

The inside of the facility was filled with hisses and loud clanks, the cool, moist air smelling of oil, ozone, and a weaker, organic scent Azer didn't recognize. A stout worker wearing a yellowish-green hard hat and an infectious smile stood before the congregating group of curious children. Once the last group of students arrived and chaperones split the kids into several distinct groups, the worker spoke.

"Hey everyone! Welcome to Manim's corvyte mines. A few of my coworkers and I will be taking you on a tour through the mines, teaching you all about what corvyte is and how we produce it. This group–" he pointed at Grif's group, which Azer quickly snuck himself into—"come with me. And don't forget to take your own hard hat on the way out!"

After putting on a hard hat and following the worker deeper into the large facility, Azer found himself fixated on the worker's kind face. He wondered if he would have had a wide smile like that had he been born with a face of his own.

"Corvyte," the worker started, walking the group in front of a text-filled infographic, "is a highly valuable mineral unique to Manim. It starts out looking like this," he pointed towards an image of a rugged, unrefined piece of rock with a light grey mass inside, "and once we've refined it, it looks like this," he pointed at an image of an offwhite, putty-like blob on a table.

"Corvyte is so valuable because of its astounding medicinal proper-ties. While we consider it a mineral, it's actually made of a bizarre organic compound and is almost soft to the touch. We don't know exactly what it's made of yet, and scientists all over the galaxy are researching it. What makes corvyte special is its ability to mimic, transform into, and even repair any and every organ across any species. Corvyte can mimic your skin to heal a cut, or even transform into a fully functional heart to be used in a heart transplant."

The worker led them a few paces towards a station with a fist-sized blob of off-white material on a plastic tray. He grabbed a pair of thin plastic gloves from a nearby dispenser, grabbed a knife-like tool, and with apparent effort, began dividing the blob into several small pieces.

"Now, after you put on a pair of gloves, I'll give you each a piece of corvyte to play with."

Everyone rushed to the glove dispenser and frantically pulled out a pair of gloves, the worker patiently passing out balls of corvyte to the kids. When Azer received his, he found that it was surprisingly light. The corvyte was barely warmer than room temperature to the touch, warm enough to feel like it wasn't a rock or metal but not warm enough to provide the illusion it was alive. Azer tried playing with it like putty, but he found that molding the ball into different shapes was astonishingly difficult. It was stubborn, requiring substantial effort to mold, but by applying enough strength, it would take any shape. Azer's corvyte had an organic, unpleasantly sour smell.

Eventually, the worker instructed the students to place their corvyte back onto the table, each ball absorbing the next until it was one whole blob again. Azer took one final look at the strange material before they were led out the door to the facility and to their next destination.

"Next we'll be walking around the actual corvyte mines where the process starts. Come with me."

He pushed open a door and led the group outside onto an elevated catwalk between two large facilities. The catwalk looked out upon the swaths of stripped land where corvyte mining took place. Instead of great tunnels that led to ore, the corvyte mines were composed of mostly flat land where the first few meters of topsoil had been dug away, exposing the rock underneath. Dozens of miners moved about the mines like insects, crowded around the parts where corvyte was abundant. Extensive conveyor belts ran through and around the mine, funneling the ore to another facility.

"This entire area is the corvyte mine. Our miners look for veins of corvyte—usually taking the shape of long lines underground. Corvyte isn't found far underground—only twenty feet below at the shallowest—so our mines are wider than they are deep. Right now and during the fall are peak mining seasons, since the weather gets too cold to mine efficiently in the winter. So if you're interested in mining here when you're older, make sure to catch us in the spring or fall!"

Azer raised his hand, drawing the eye of the worker.

"Why can't you mine in the summer?" he asked.

"Great question! The reason we don't do much mining in the summer is because three days before The Shades, the purity of our corvyte decreases. It's one of the ways we know when it's about to happen, aside from occurring near the end of the summer. We're not sure why or how, but it does."

Azer turned to find Grif staring bewilderedly at him. Another familiar hand rose from the group. It was Milo.

"Won't this mining hurt the environment?" he asked timidly.

The worker scrunched his face in an apprehensive look. He looked like he was finding a way to avoid the true answer.

"Our mine is environmentally friendly. Manim is a big place—we're only taking a very small amount, relatively speaking. Don't worry."

The worker scanned the crowd for any further hands.

"Well, if there are no other questions, we'll head to our final stop—the corvyte refinery," said the worker.

The group was led into another building where, after climbing a surprisingly long spiral staircase and walking along a series of catwalks above the ground floor of the refinery, they finally came to a stop.

"Since corvyte is unique to Manim and it's so revolutionary to Zysti's medical industry, almost all of our refined corvyte is exported off-planet to the Zystinian government. And the government expects only the finest quality of corvyte. Which is why, after mining it, we put the corvyte through a rigorous refining process, which you can see below." He gestured downwards to the immensely complex series of machines and conveyor belts. "Follow me and I'll show you how it all works."

The students followed the worker as he took them to the entry point of the refinery, where an endless stream of unrefined corvyte was flowing onto a fast-moving conveyor. The worker stopped and began to speak when Grif said to Azer in a low voice:

"This corvyte stuff is linked to The Shades."

"I know," Azer replied. "It's really weird. How?"

"I don't know, but we've gotta look around and find out."

Azer wished he had a face to express how taken aback he was by this.

"What, like split off from the group?!" Azer hissed in a whisper.

"Yeah! There's no way this guy is going to tell us any more about corvyte aside from how they make the stuff pure. And besides, I'm getting bored already."

"I think they really don't have any other answers! Besides, why don't we just get back to the Battle Academy and ask our teachers? Or better yet, that Dr. D guy! He seemed to know a lot!"

Grif mulled this over for a moment.

"You're right. Good point. Let's do that instead."

The group was led down the conveyor belt and past a large, rumbling machine that looked like it was eating up the unrefined corvyte. As the worker explained what it was, Azer tuned out his words and watched the machine and its hypnotic, pre-programmed movements, resting his hands on the metal railing that barred him from touching it.

All of a sudden, a loud *thunk* surprised Azer and made him jump. A boy had leaned against the railing next to him. The boy had fiery blonde hair and spikes behind his ears, a self-assured look on his face. He looked faintly familiar to Azer. Upon seeing the newcomer, Grif frowned.

"Hi there. I'm Copycat, I'm in your class. Well, Copycat's not my real name, but I like Copycat better. How you doing?"

"My name's Azer. Nice to meet you."

Copycat looked him over, spending extra time examining the spot where Azer's face should be. Grif nudged Azer and urged for him to lean close.

"Azer, I think-" Grif whispered.

"You know, we should be friends," Copycat interjected. "Since we go to the same school, you must live nearby, and I live nearby too. I could show you my house, it's really really big. Our family is rich."

"Are you from another planet?" Azer asked. The idea of making a new friend was appealing to him.

"Yeah, we are. We moved here a long time ago."

"Say, Copycat... Copycat, right?" Azer clarified.

"Yep."

"Have you heard anything about a missing kid in the Battle Academy eight years ago?"

"Hell if I know," Copycat replied, disinterested.

Azer and Grif looked at Copycat with apprehension and awe.

"What? Yeah, I can curse. I'm almost eleven."

Azer returned to watching the conveyor belt go by, carrying masses of now half-refined corvyte. It was satisfying to watch the way it passed through each machine looking a little bit nicer, the color looking a little bit whiter.

Then, without warning, Azer's legs were swept out from under him. He hit the factory floor painfully, crashing his hand on the railing. The loud clattering sound caught the attention of the rest of their group, along with their tour guide, looking at him with worry.

There was a brief moment of embarrassment and panic as Azer processed what had happened, acutely aware of his peers staring at him. Copycat grabbed Azer's hand and pulled him up to standing.

"Hey, he's getting away… the guy that knocked your legs out from under you!" Grif yelled, pointing at a figure Azer didn't recognize receding into another tour group deeper into the factory.

"Some people are real jerks," Copycat said.

Once the attention had moved away from Azer and their group had resumed travel around the facility, Grif leaned in to Azer, making sure to keep Copycat out of earshot.

"I don't trust that Copycat guy."

"Why not?"

"I think he overheard our 'exploring the factory' scheme. He just rubbed me the wrong way."

All of a sudden, a "beep" resounded around the factory and a voice began speaking from intercoms in the ceiling. Constant echoing made the voice almost indistinct.

"Attention all staff. Nova Noctis activity has been reported in town. The local bank has been robbed and several people are injured. Put all security on high alert."

By the reaction of the factory worker, Azer understood that they had just heard information not meant for the students. Kids in the group began speaking to each other fearfully, the worker attempting to calm them down, but Azer had a different reaction. The name in the announcement rang a bell for Azer, and by the look on Grif's face, it did for him, too.

"Isn't that-" Azer started.

"Yeah, that doomsayer lady from before. They robbed a *bank?*"

Azer pulled out the slip Delvin had given him two weeks ago, buried deep in one of his pockets. In big letters, the slip read "Combat Class."

Azer and Grif looked at the slip, then each other. They knew what they had to do.

CHAPTER FOUR:
COMBAT CLASS

Cloudy. 10mph winds blowing northeast. Seventy-one degrees fahrenheit. No rain is expected.

The combat class building matched its appearance on print—short, only the essentials, and with an unassuming exterior. The windows were shaded, but warmly-colored light poured out from beneath the front door. The building was sandwiched between other buildings in a mostly unassuming strip mall not far from the school. After taking in their surroundings for a moment, Azer and Grif opened the door and stepped inside.

Azer was shocked by the depth of the building—from the outside, only its width and height were visible, which were modest at best, but the combat class facility extended a long way in, leaving ample room for the numerous students scattered around. And the students weren't just kids Azer and Grif's age—some of them appeared to be twice as old. While the inside was welcoming, warmly-lit, and filled with lighthearted chatter, the oppressive stench of stale sweat was ever present.

Grif placed crumpled money on the counter beside the door and then approached Delvin, who was standing on the mats beside a group of other students—two dozen or so, it looked at first glance. Seperate groups of students with their own instructors were deeper into the combat class room, each group standing on different colored sparring mats. As Azer looked at the other groups of students deeper in the building, he noticed that the students seemed to get older as they got further from the building's entrance, going from kids roughly Azer's age, to scary-looking teenagers, to students who looked college-age. In the group closest to the front Azer recognized Milo, Torbe, and Copycat, along with some other kids he saw in his school on his first week. Upon seeing Azer and Grif, Delvin motioned for them to join the rest of the group.

"And this should be just about everyone. Welcome to the beginner level combat class. If this is your first class, don't worry, students of all combat skill levels will be accommodated. You'll learn the basics of all types of fighting and refine any skills you already have. Now, I don't like to be the kind of person who spends too long on introductions; I believe it is due time to get started with the lesson."

Delvin pulled a small device out of his pocket and flicked something on its side.

"Please step off the mats for a moment."

Everyone obliged, slowly walking away from the mats. A loud rumble and a clank came from the floor. A circular portion of the mat, ten feet in diameter, twisted in its place slightly and then slowly lifted into the air, mechanical clanks vibrating the floor for the entirety of the platform's ascent. Ladder-like divots, aged and worn, donned the sides of the cylindrical rising platform. By the time the cylinder stopped moving with a clunk, its top had risen to well over Azer's height. Beside him, Grif gulped.

"Your first lesson is to spar with a randomly selected partner. The best way to learn is through practice, and today that is what you shall do. Do not worry, you will be fighting students of your age group. The results of each fight will tell me where each of you are in terms of fighting skill and how to proceed for further lessons. Excuse me a moment while I grab cushions. The practice fights will begin very soon."

Delvin walked into a large closet and returned with large cushions, placing them around the base of the cylinder, prompting the whole group of students to whisper amongst themselves.

"We're gonna be fighting *on* that thing?" Grif whispered.

"I guess so."

"This guy is the real deal. I thought our first few lessons were just going to be introductions or icebreakers or something. I had no idea we were already fighting each other!"

Delvin called the name of two students who Azer didn't recognize and led them, both looking unsure, to the top of the platform. They glanced at each other apprehensively.

"There is never one true perfect method to fighting—depending on who you are and what your Vals are, any fighting style might be right for you. Fight the way that feels right to you in these matches, and we will work on perfecting your techniques in future lessons. But I must stress, if you have Vals, you must use them to fight in some way. There is no such thing as learning without risk."

"Now, the goal is to push your opponent off the platform and onto the cushions below, and you may not injure your opponent to do so! Ready?" He paused. "Three, two, one, fight!"

As the two began to fight, the rest of the class watching in awe, Azer noticed that Grif had a mortified look on his face.

"Uhh oh," Grif said.

"Yeah, I know. I don't even think I have a Val. How am I supposed to do this?" Azer seconded. "Not to mention, this scar on my side hurts every time I twist and turn..."

"No, not that. Well, all that too, but I think I can help you out—I just meant that I have a terrible time controlling my electricity Val," said Grif.

"Really? It didn't seem like that when you showed me the first time."

"That's 'cause I only made a tiny bit of electricity. If I make too much electricity and try to control it, it just goes boom."

Azer cocked his head to the side.

"No, literally 'boom!' I always short-circuit and the electricity just explodes in my hands. My control over my Val comes and goes, and truthfully I've never had to really use it much before. Much less on another person…"

"Seems like we're both in the same boat," Azer said, watching the students on the platform show an eye-opening display of their flashy Vals. "You can do it. I doubt those guys started out being really good with their Vals."

"Yeah, you're right. I'll give it a shot."

Azer let his focus drift for a moment as he watched the two students fighting on the platform.

"I think I have a different problem, though, I don't think I have a Val at all…" he said.

One of the students—the one who seemed to be losing—suddenly curled back his fingers and jammed his palm into his opponent's nose. Immediately, Delvin's raised voice broke out over the scuffles of battle, accompanied by a pained yelp from the other student. The hurt student grabbed his nose and stumbled backwards.

"Stop the match! Geraas, that is a forbidden move!" Delvin shouted, immediately grabbing the attention of every student in the group. "You could kill him if you did that any harder or hit his nose at the right angle."

Geraas, the offending boy, looked at Delvin with terror, and then at his injured opponent. His opponent's eyes were watery from the strike to his nose.

"I'm so sorry! I thought that was just a stunning move, I saw it in a movie-"

"Be careful not to injure your opponent!" Delvin interjected impatiently. "Now, if your opponent is up for it, resume the match."

Geraas apologized to his opponent, who nodded understandingly, and they resumed.

"About you not having a Val and all," Grif started, turning back away from Delvin and facing Azer again, "I think you're already using your Val, but just unconsciously. Before we met on the bus, I saw you jump over a car. And I think I saw some kind of strange mist coming off of you then, too. If I could guess, your Val is like some kind of super-boost to your body."

Azer recalled the many times in his life he had performed extraordinary physical feats. At the time, he had just assumed it was a normal thing anyone could do. But Grif had a point; when Azer jumped over the car on his first trip across a busy street, he had felt a strange energy fill him, a burning sensation in his veins like liquid vitality was flowing through his body. Was that his Val all along?

There was a loud "oof" from the platform, and Azer turned his head just in time to catch one of the students falling off the cylinder and onto the cushions below. The other students cheered, and the winning student atop the platform jumped in celebration.

"Well done," said Delvin, helping the fallen student to his feet and the winner off the platform. "Now, will Copycat and Milo come to the base of the platform?"

Milo and Copycat split off from the group and made their ways to either end of the cylinder. They climbed to the top, and by the time they saw each other across the platform, Milo looked noticeably more intimidated than Copycat did.

"Three, two, one, fight!"

Immediately, Copycat walked towards his opponent, and as he walked, perfect duplicates of himself seamlessly emerged from his back and walked alongside the original. And in a sick moment of realization, Azer recognized the back of Copycat as the same person he saw walking away from him after his legs had been swept out from under him the previous day. Rage boiled inside Azer.

Grif appeared to have come to the same conclusion. "Hey, isn't that...? That looks exactly like the one who–"

"Yeah, the guy who kicked out my legs yesterday," Azer finished, anger tainting his voice.

"He must have cloned himself—one of him talked to you during the tour, pretending to be your friend, while the other knocked you over! I knew there was something up with him!"

"He wasn't my friend at all," Azer growled.

Copycat and his clones lunged mercilessly at Milo, who flinched. Out of Milo's sleeve came a twisting root that grew into a flimsy shield, which Milo used to guard himself. It blocked the punch of the first clone, but the other Copycats promptly destroyed the shield and sent Milo flying off the platform. Victorious, Copycat put an arm in the air and turned around to face the group, which was cheering loudly. Copycat looked at Azer with a smirk.

"You'll be able to get back at him soon enough, I'm sure of it," Grif reassured.

Azer hoped that was true.

"Next," Delvin announced, helping Milo up, "are Saa and Grif. Come to the top of the platform and fight on my go."

Azer gave his friend a silent nod as he left, which Grif returned. The girl Grif was about to fight climbed up the ladder onto the platform, and Azer recognized her as one of his classmates. Her face was multicolored, the color of her skin split down the middle—the right half of her face was a pastel pink, and the left was a bluish-green, the hair on either side of her head matching the split colors. Grif shook out his arms and legs and they shook hands.

"Three, two, one, fight!"

Grif came in for a punch, a harsh electrical crackle filled the air, and alarm filled his and his opponent's face as she ducked. In an explosion of electricity, with Grif's fist at the epicenter, Grif and Saa were launched backwards, skidding almost to the edge. Frightened murmurs filled the crowd of students. Delvin looked shaken.

"I'm sorry!" Grif said to his opponent and to Delvin, still panicked.

Now it was Saa's turn to attack. She moved her hands together and pointed them towards him, prompting Grif to leap out of the way. Neither of them knew what her Val was yet, or even if she had one. It seemed as if Grif didn't want to take his chances. Seeing an opening, he went in for another attack, attempting to push her off, but his shirt suddenly burst into flame.

Grif yelped and scrambled to put it out, but still didn't look half as mortified as his opponent.

"Easy! No injuring your opponent, either of you!" Delvin yelled.

Flustered and surprised by her unexpected combustion and Delvin's warning, Saa let down her guard. Grif took this opportunity to rear back his leg for a kick, and the familiar crackling filled the air once more.

BOOM! Just in time, Saa leaped out of the way and a blast of powerful electricity arced between Grif and the platform. Shrieks and screams erupted from the crowd again and Delvin stepped forward.

"I'll stop the match if neither of you can control your Vals! The goal is to push your opponent off the platform, not to injure!"

"I'm so sorry!" Grif said to Saa after recovering and realizing his mistake. She didn't respond, a look of pure fear plastered on her double-sided face.

Grif didn't resume the fight immediately, trying to gain his composure, and eventually he saw Azer among the crowd. Azer gave the same nod as before, and then Grif looked back at his opponent, a renewed determination in his face.

Saa was now trying to ignite the ground under Grif to make him lose his balance. Grif danced around the attacks with growing ease, until he weaved under her punch and straightened himself in front of her. He extended an arm away from her, another behind him, and a massive crackle and boom shook the air again. Azer expected the worst at first, but then realized it wasn't an attack at all—it was a distraction. Upon hearing the explosion, Saa flinched and instinctively let down her guard. Grif swept Saa's legs out from under her and continued his attack.

He stomped both of his feet to the ground and another crack split the stuffy air. Small craters had been carved under his feet from the explosions, and Saa, surprised, couldn't duck in time. She was shoved further off the edge of the platform, then slipped, fell, and now was hanging on by her forearms.

Grif backed up to the other end of the platform and ran towards his opponent at full speed, electricity tracing his body. Azer noticed something new—the electricity didn't have the uncontrolled crackle this time. Unconsciously or not, Grif had his electricity in balance, not using too much or too little.

Mid-sprint, he tripped over the craters he had made in the platform just moments earlier. The determined look on his face was wiped away and turned into wide-eyed surprise as he soared over his dangling opponent and into the cushions beneath.

A moment of shocked silence, and then—

A mass of loud, slightly confused cheering. Saa, realizing her victory, accidentally slipped down onto the cushions as well. The two fighters hauled themselves off of the cushions and shook hands. Grif made his way over to Azer, a proud grin on his face.

"I was so close! I totally forgot about the craters!"

"I know! Did you see what you did at the end there, though?"

Grif's smile lessened and he cocked his head to the side.

"You had total control of your electricity. You probably didn't even realize it."

And then Grif's expression became excited again. "Really? Awesome! I totally did it!"

As the next few battles passed, Azer felt an increasing foreboding as his turn grew closer. He had a scar on his side that hurt when he twisted, but that was the least of his worries now—what if he couldn't match his opponent's abilities? Even if he could fight well, would it even matter if he couldn't use his Val? He'd only ever used it unconsciously before, like a heartbeat. How was he supposed to harness it enough to be effective in battle?

"Next is Azer and Torbe!" announced Delvin.

Azer's anxiousness spiked as he began to walk up to the platform, and he could feel acutely the gaze of the other students watching him. As he climbed up the ladder, Azer could see his opponent on the other side. Torbe's face was intimidating, but without malice.

"You ready for a good battle?" Torbe said, smiling.

"Y- yeah. Let's do it." And they shook hands.

Azer got into his best battle stance and, without hesitation, tried to focus on the feeling that he experienced before when he unconsciously used his ability. He tried to remember the desperation of watching the car hurtling his way, and the ease at which he had jumped over it...

But nothing helped. He wasn't fighting a car. And while Torbe looked like he was going to put up a fight, Azer wasn't at risk of dying. So, for now, Azer would have to rely on his non-Val fighting skills. *It has to come back to me at some point*, he thought.

"Three, two, one, fight!"

Torbe came at him with a kick, his long legs giving him incredible reach. Azer ducked, but saw around him that a strange, large bubble was forming, translucent and floating in midair, distorting the air and half as wide as he was tall. *Was this Torbe's ability?* Azer dove underneath Torbe, using his opponent's height to his advantage, and the bubble fully materialized just as Azer rolled out of the way. It was between him and the crowd of students now, and through it, the view of their faces and figures were distorted and warped. Torbe turned around to face Azer, clenched his fists, and the bubble vanished as he lunged.

Although Torbe was very large, and equally as strong, Azer's relative size made dodging a lot easier. However, if he were to fail to dodge, he was sure that the attacks would be damaging.

After weaving around Torbe's kick, Azer backed up and readied his counterattack, a fake kick and then a punch. But only moments later, another bubble was appearing in the air in front of him. Azer's momentum carried him forward, and-

Azer's top half entered the bubble, and he felt an incredibly strange sensation—as if his torso was pulling uncomfortably on his waist, tugging as if he was about to snap in half.

He reached an arm outside of the bubble and immediately regretted it. His fingers, once leaving, tugged painfully behind him as if someone was tightly gripping the portion of his fingers that were outside the bubble and holding him back. His arm dragged behind, twisting his shoulder painfully. He worked to correct himself, trying desperately to pull his arm back in, nearly falling over due to his legs lagging behind in time.

That was it: *time.*

But as he made this realization, Azer saw the long leg of Torbe flying in slow motion towards Azer's exposed chin. And before he could stop it—

A jolt of pain seized Azer as Torbe's leg hit the bubble and sped up, impacting Azer's chin with astonishing force. He was knocked out of the bubble and fell down in a heap, rubbing his throbbing chin. Everything seemed to move normally again. Torbe leapt into the air towards the bubble and pulled his legs into his chest. Torbe entered the bubble, which rapidly sped up his movement, and he landed in front of Azer far faster than expected.

"Do those bubbles speed up time when you're in them?" Azer asked.

Torbe grinned proudly as Azer had figured it out.

"And they can slow down time, too."

Torbe reached out a hand. Azer took it and Torbe helped him up.

"Ready to continue our fight?"

"Yeah," Azer responded, a new confidence filling him.

"Show me your Val," Torbe said, returning to his battle stance. "I want to fight you at full strength."

For Azer, it wasn't just about winning anymore—he'd fail completely if he didn't figure out how to use his Val.

He tried yet again to focus on the sensation he had felt before when he jumped over the car, but in the heat of battle, he couldn't recreate it. And the pressure of avoiding Torbe's time bubbles didn't help, either.

Torbe, on the other hand, was perfectly adept with his Val; possibly even more so than any other student Azer had seen. He'd summon a time bubble in the air around Azer to throw him off or force him to dodge, and then Torbe would enter it in just the right moment to make his attacks frustratingly unpredictable.

After dodging a particularly fast punch, Azer took a moment to rest on the edge of the platform opposite his opponent. Torbe's size and superior battle prowess were exhausting him, and while Azer was able to dodge most of Torbe's attacks, he couldn't land any of his own.

The damage had already been done. Azer's moment of hesitation caused him to find his head in another slowing bubble, with the sounds and sights outside the bubble sped up to an unnatural pace. Torbe, in a quick motion, jumped into the air and kicked Azer square where his face should be. Azer flew out of the bubble again, his skin tugging painfully as it left the bubble's borders, and barely caught himself on the precipice of the platform. Torbe clenched his fists again and charged after Azer, and the bubble disappeared.

But just as Azer regained his balance and was steady on the platform once more, he felt the distinct feeling of entering a bubble, again with time slowing. But before Azer could even get a chance to try and escape, a distorted leg crossed through the bubble and struck Azer in the side where his scar was.

The pain struck him faster than the kick did, and seemed to double by the millisecond. His vision and surroundings changed abruptly, and he saw and felt himself in the dark fleshy chamber he had dreamt about. He was utterly alone, floating aimlessly and unable to move—his surroundings, Torbe, the platform, all had disappeared into nothing. He tried to call out for help but couldn't talk. He was completely helpless.

But he wasn't completely distant from reality. He still felt the jabbing pain in his side, and looked towards it to see a horrible sight—the thin, metallic rod that had ended his dream before was stabbed into his side, exactly where the kick had hit.

Despite the fact that his mind was now desperately racing, he was still completely immobile. He couldn't wriggle away from the rod, which extended all the way from the edge of the chamber into his skin.

And then, in a brief flash of searing pain and a burning sensation in every vein of his body, something began to spread rapidly inside his nerves and arteries, coming from the point where he was stabbed. Something was flowing into his body and circulating around, as if replacing his own blood, and then...

The burning suddenly stopped. The rod left his side, retracting back through the wall of the chamber, and an immense, almost godly strength filled him. The force in his veins no longer felt foreign or unwelcome—the burning had transformed into an energizing warmth.

The chamber shook slightly with the rumbling of a deep and distinct voice. It said, slow and booming:

"S..."

"R."

Azer felt himself snap back to reality, his feet grounded beneath him, the kick just having impacted his body. The pain in his side was gone, and Torbe's leg was still hanging in the air.

But something had stayed. He still felt that warm, liquidy substance inside his body. The energy that flowed through him made Azer feel intensely awake. It was as though he'd been asleep his whole life up until this moment. His heart was pumping furiously, circulating energy through every extremity.

After his mind had stopped racing and his stance evened, Azer realized...

He was *fast*. And it wasn't because he was in a time bubble, either.

His movements came with a flowing ease he had never felt before. It was like his limbs were being controlled not by his muscles, but by his mind alone. His legs stepped with impossibly little resistance, and the strength he was feeling came with no fatigue.

Azer ducked to leave the bubble and avoid Torbe's next attack. He had gone from standing to crouched so quickly, he hardly recognized even performing the action.

As Azer gazed at his own hands and arms, he noticed a dark mist rising off of him, like his skin was alight with a translucent black flame.

Torbe had noticed Azer now, crouched below his attack, the dark fire emanating from his body. It seemed as though Azer's awareness had sped up, too; he could watch Torbe's expression change to shocked amazement.

Azer sprung up from his position, hitting Torbe in the chest and tackling him. Torbe was sent flying from the impact. Azer was about as shocked as Torbe was from the strength of the attack. Torbe cleared most of the platform before landing near its edge, looking worriedly at the cushions below. Azer knew he'd have to restrain himself from using his full power, or he could accidentally injure his opponent.

The time bubble disappeared as Torbe got back up, fists clenched tightly. And Azer made another revelation—Torbe's time bubbles had a trigger: *his hands.* Opening his hands let him create a bubble, and clenching his fists destroyed them.

Azer's opponent came at him again for an attack, both hands open now. And, right on cue, a time bubble materialized behind him. After it fully appeared, Azer swiped his hand through it—*a slowing bubble.* Just what he was looking for.

Torbe locked hands with Azer, trying to push him into the bubble. Torbe's larger size made Azer's feet skid on the platform as he resisted. He let Torbe push him closer and closer, approaching the edge of the platform, the bubble's strange time-bending effects beginning to warp around the back of his head. And then, using his now monstrous strength, Azer swung around, gripping Torbe tightly and pushing him into the bubble instead. Torbe's expression grew panicked as his head slowly entered the bubble. Azer mustered all of his newfound power to push Torbe further and further, the time bubble slowing his movements more and more.

Azer felt Torbe's hands tighten, trying desperately to escape Azer's grip to close his fists and destroy the bubble. But Azer only resisted more, prying Torbe's fingers apart.

And then, with a great heave, Azer pushed Torbe off the edge of the platform. Torbe fully entered his own bubble and fell slowly onto the cushions below with a thud.

The crowd erupted into a deafening cheer, and Azer felt his heart rate slow as his Val began to fade and the strength left his body. He leapt off the tall platform and onto the mats, reaching a hand towards Torbe to help him up.

Upon seeing this, Torbe grinned widely. Without the extra strength, Azer could now properly feel the weight of his opponent and the tiredness of his own muscles. He walked off the platform next to Torbe, and joined his cheering classmates, pride filling his spirt like the strength had filled his body.

"What was that?!" Grif exclaimed, looking more proud than even Azer felt.

"S.R." Azer answered. "That's what I think my Val is called."

"Where'd it come from?"

He paused, thinking, and then answered:

"That'll have to wait until after class."

Azer sat in a comfortable chair at Grano's, watching the sunset-dyed clouds outside. He was gripping his stomach with paralyzing hunger, unsure why he felt so hungry in the first place.

"Ugh..." Azer groaned.

"You know, you're probably so hungry from that Val of yours," Grif pointed.

"What do you mean?"

"It looks like your S.R. boosts your physical functions to the max. You're probably using a huuuge amount of energy."

"Yeah... I guess I'll have to be careful."

"And by the way, from all the things we've found out, I think we need to stop The Shades."

"What? How?" Azer was incredulous.

Grif leaned forward in his comfortable chair, glancing briefly at the other customers in Grano's as if he was afraid of them listening in.

"Think about it. We know that something really horrible happens down here during The Shades, like that girl who disappeared eight years ago. Every single time The Shades happens, everyone has to be evacuated but some people get left behind and disappear. We've gotta do something about it."

"But how?"

"I dunno, but it has to be possible!"

"I think The Shades is just a type of weather we don't know anything about. You can't stop the weather, Grif."

Grif gave him a look, and then looked down at the menu.

"Hey, they have a breakfast menu. Huh...? Pancakes? What the heck are pancakes?"

Just then, the plump and jovial figure of Mr. Grano came into view, holding a steaming dish in his hands. Upon seeing Grif, Mr. Grano's face became immediately pleased and surprised.

"Ah! This must be the Grif I've been hearing about?"

"That's me," Grif smiled.

"Well I've got you two a hot and steaming plate of Grand Soman, freshly baked. But be careful, Grif, Azer can really put it down! Get some before he eats it all!"

Mr. Grano placed the dish on the table. Azer's stomach growled yet louder.

"I see why you wanted to bring us here," Grif said, hardly able to divert his attention from the food.

"Yup."

Grif took an indulgent bite of Grand Soman and found himself even more pleased than he had expected. After he got down the first slice of Soman, he asked Azer:

"So, if you don't think we should stop The Shades, then what should we do?"

"I think we should start smaller. We need to find out more about The Shades first, especially that missing girl Haise."

"Mm! How about we break into the Battle Academy?" Grif mused.

"What?!"

"You heard me. We should break in and see if they know more than they're letting on. And I definitely think they know more than they're letting on. That Dr. D guy you met has got to know something."

"But he already told me everything he knows!" exclaimed Azer.

"You sure? You said it yourself, that Haise girl is a sensitive topic."

"But we just got into the Battle Academy! You already want to start breaking into it?"

"Relax, I'm not saying we should break in now. We need at least a few more weeks or so before we break in. We'e gotta make a plan and everything, and we're gonna need some time to get more familiar with the school anyway. And it's not like breaking in is gonna hurt anyone, not if we do it right."

Azer wrestled with himself, trying to find a way to talk sense into Grif. But Grif had a point—breaking in might get them the information they wanted. Azer finally relented.

"Fine, but I'm only helping if we do it right. I don't want to hurt anyone."

"Awesome. And, hey, I had a cool idea."

Azer ate another slice of Soman. "Yeah?"

"You said you sleep in an abandoned house, right? Why don't I move in with you? We could have our own house, all to ourselves, with all of our favorite stuff in it!"

Even without a face, Azer felt like he had just cracked the biggest smile in the world.

CHAPTER FIVE:
GRUDGES

Partly cloudy. 19mph winds blowing southeast. Seventy-eight degrees fahrenheit. With wind chill, Seventy-two. Rain expected in the afternoon.

Azer and Grif waited patiently among the other early combat class students on the worn mats. For the past two months, the two boys had been routinely early to their classes and usually found ample time to discuss their plans and findings about The Shades—today's class was no different. Grif looked both ways at the other nearby students and then leaned close to Azer.

"How's the map?" Grif asked in a whisper.

"Huh?" Azer replied loudly, confused.

Grif put a finger to his lips and raised his eyebrows, panicked.

"Quiet down, man! The map of the school! The plan! How's it going?"

It came back to Azer in a rush. He condemned his own stupidity at not getting it earlier.

"Yeah, it's going fine. I finished it today. It was hard to map all the way around the outside of the school without getting noticed or getting suspicious looks, but I did it. I'm pretty sure Copycat saw me at some point, though. I wasn't able to map out the security patrols of the school, but I think there's a blind spot that's easy enough to get to."

"Awesome. I knew you could do it."

Azer put a finger to his not-face to indicate to Grif to be quiet. He nodded subtly over to Copycat, who was standing by the entrance, looking at them. Copycat had a large bruise on his face.

Noticing this, Delvin asked about it. "What happened?"

"Someone went too hard on me last class," Copycat replied simply. His mood seemed foul.

Delvin said nothing and instead pointed Copycat towards the group of students. He obliged and sat with the rest of them, taking care to shoot a vicious glare towards Azer and Grif, which Grif returned fully.

Combat class that day proved to be uneventful, both Azer and Grif getting a fair amount of practice fighting and Delvin helping them improve their stances. But one thing bugged Azer in a way that he couldn't shake, and it was something he'd been noticing ever since his first day of school a few weeks ago.

Every single person he came across on a day-to-day basis seemed so distinct. Everyone he saw had their own look, their own personality—the way they acted and interacted was unique to them. It was like everyone knew exactly who they were and how to approach the world, but Azer felt none of that. He noticed, amazed but infinitely jealous, that everyone's face looked different.

Azer wasn't particularly unhappy—to the contrary, he was enjoying his life since stepping beyond the borders of his home—but his lack of identity bothered him like an unscratchable itch. Grif had his own hobbies, his own way of speaking, quirks and details that would be easily missed—but Azer felt like he had nothing. He knew little about himself or where he came from. It was as if his own person had nothing to build off of. If the past is what defines you, and Azer had no past—what defined him?

All Azer had was the scant knowledge of the things he enjoyed—he loved to make maps, he loved to explore, and he loved spending time with his growing group of friends, Grif especially. Azer knew that if he built off of what he had, then maybe, just maybe he could find out where he came from. And the prospects of infiltrating the school soon filled him with excitement, a potential clue to his hidden past.

Azer said goodbye to Delvin and walked out of the doors alongside Grif, back to their now-shared house, discussing the events of today's class and the happenings of their lives in school. It was windy as they walked, some gusts threatening their balance.

"And, by the way, I think we need to infiltrate the school today," Grif said.

"Wait, what? Already?"

"Yeah, I mean, why not? You said it yourself, the map is ready, and I think I know how we're gonna get in. I was thinking about getting into the teacher's office through the window."

"Yeah, but this still feels a bit early! Shouldn't we like… prepare or something?"

"We *have* prepared! C'mon, man, it's not gonna be so bad! We're not stealing anything, we're not hurting anyone, we're just entering, looking, and leaving. No harm is gonna be done! Lighten up a little!"

Azer tried desperately to think of a counterargument, but found nothing. And the prospect of discovering more about The Shades and himself was too tempting.

"Fine. When do we leave?"

"I was think-"

Suddenly, a quiet *click* came from behind them, followed by quickly receding footsteps. Grif stopped talking and the two stopped in their tracks. They turned around to see the shrinking figure of Copycat, sprinting away from them in the direction of the Battle Academy. In his hand was a small recording device.

Grif sprinted after Copycat, Azer just behind. Desperation and seething anger surged through Azer. If Copycat had just recorded their plot, Azer and Grif could be kicked out of school. Terrible situations played in Azer's mind. But he wouldn't let that happen.

Just as Copycat turned a street corner, Azer activated his S.R. He let the burning energy fill his body and began to run at astonishing speed, sneakers pushing off the asphalt and catching up to Copycat quickly.

Azer tackled Copycat, knocking him to the ground, the recorder falling to the road with a clatter. Azer grabbed Copycat's collar and was about to demand an explanation, when, suddenly, Copycat dissolved before his eyes into dark grey dust. But only when the dust had settled did Azer realize he'd been fooled.

A clone.

Azer saw another Copycat a ways ahead, running along the sidewalk. He reactivated his S.R. and tore down the street in pursuit of Copycat once more, only for him to disintegrate into dust again upon contact. Azer's frustration was growing and panic was beginning to set in. How would he be able to take down all the clones, much less find the original?

Think. Copycat had to be taking the nearest path to the authorities in order to share the recording. Delvin had already left a while ago, and it seemed as if Copycat wasn't going home, either. That meant Copycat had to be going to the Battle Academy. And the original Copycat wouldn't be stupid enough to go straight to the Battle Academy; he had to be taking a roundabout path, maybe through the—

Azer saw Copycat disappear into the trees behind a building.

The scrapyard.

Azer sprinted towards the scrapyard, but came to a halt at the edge of the trees. He had no idea where he was going—if he got lost, he'd have no way of catching up to Copycat. But he knew someone who would…

"Hey," Grif said, stopping just behind him. "Why'd you stop?! We've gotta-"

"Tell me how to find the scrapyard," Azer said. "I'm gonna use my S.R. to catch up with him, so I'll be running ahead of you. You need to tell me how to get there and where he could be hiding."

"Oh, yeah. I know that place like the back of my hand. It's off to the left, just cut through the tall bushes and you can get there before Copycat does. He'll probably be hiding behind a scrap pile, so search those. Got it?"

Azer nodded.

"Alright, go, go, go! I'll be behind you!"

Azer sprinted towards the scrapyard, trying to ignore the fatigue that was beginning to set in from the use of his S.R. He pushed through the trees and tall-growing weeds, weaving slightly left, before he barreled through an overgrown bush. The environment opened up. The ground wasn't choked with plant life anymore—instead, extensive piles of scrap took their place, reaching great heights. Manned and unmanned construction machines, old and rusted, roamed the desolate, scrap-filled dirt. He had entered the city scrapyard. And Copycat had disappeared.

As a heavily-rusted bulldozer scooped up a massive pile of scrap, clanking and whirring by, Azer hid behind a pile of his own. Wherever Copycat was, Azer would find him.

Edging behind sharp metal scraps, he looked around the pile. There were fifteen to twenty other piles of scrap, some of plastic, some towering loads of cloth, some metal like the one he was behind. And in the center of the scrapyard was the largest pile of all, consisting of every type of trash and scrap imaginable. It towered disproportionally, higher than the machines should logically be able to reach. With its astonishing size, there had to have been trash there dating back to the very beginning of the colonization of their planet, eighty years ago. A strange feeling inside Azer told him—Copycat was there. Azer was drawn to the faraway center pile as if he had already been there before.

A moment later, a loud clatter from the nearest pile drew Azer's attention. A hubcap appeared to have duplicated itself dozens of times, displacing the other trash around it, clanking noisily. Azer left his refuge.

He sprinted towards the sound, out of view of a passing worker, and raised his fists. But, aside from the mysteriously duplicated hubcaps, there was no evidence of Copycat. *But if Copycat didn't do that,* Azer thought, *what did?*

Another clatter, different pile. Once the coast was clear, he leapt over an old television and sprinted towards the noise, fists raised again and S.R. pumping, only to find two identical, broken, rusted wheelbarrows fallen off the large pile and onto the ground. *How was Copycat doing this? Was he doing this? Surely Copycat's abilities were only limited to copying himself, right?*

Azer bent over closer. The wheelbarrows had identical rust patterns. They were both cracked a few inches into the handle, and the wheels were both bent a bit to the left. There was no doubt—the wheelbarrows had been cloned. Azer reached out a hand...

In an instant, another wheelbarrow erupted from the one he was about to touch, a perfect clone appearing out of it, splitting like a cell. It forced the first wheelbarrow out of the way violently, and the new clone rocketed towards Azer with equal force, crushing his outstretched hand and knocking him backwards.

Azer's hand throbbed, and he was bleeding from his forehead. The hit had filled him with dizzying pain and nausea, but he managed to push himself up slowly. *So he could copy anything.* He caught a fleeting glimpse of Copycat's figure hiding behind a massive stack of old tires.

As fast as his dazed body would allow, Azer sprinted towards Copycat, swaying dangerously, half from the concussion, half from the increasingly strong, whipping wind. Copycat ran, swerving past mounds of junk, touching everything he could with outstretched fingers.

As Azer reached the stack of tires, one of them suddenly burst into dozens of copies of itself, knocking the others back violently, threatening to knock Azer over again. He chased Copycat past a tattered bed frame which erupted into countless clones. Azer ducked and swerved past the falling and flying copies, splinters shooting through the air, some embedding into the bare skin on Azer's head. Not a single shooting jolt of pain slowed him down.

Azer leapt, dodged, and ducked through the multiplying mayhem, barely avoiding a hundred old steering wheels, a thousand shards of breaking glass, and a steel beam that had copied itself enough to where it was a pile of its own. After what felt like an eternity of running, and countless clones avoided, Azer finally cornered Copycat, recorder clutched tightly, equally exhausted, in front of the largest pile of all. And, somehow, through the pain and exhaustion, Azer felt that eerily familiar feeling again, looking at the pile. For a moment, he tried to put it aside.

"What is your *problem?!*" Azer yelled. "Why are you doing this?! What did we ever do to you?!"

"Don't tell me you don't know already," Copycat sneered without hesitation, his face hateful and his eyes flashing. "Don't tell me you don't know they're trying to recruit you."

Azer's rage subsided, replaced by confusion. "What?"

"I've known about it for *years*, Azer. Their stupid secret organization. I've wanted to join as long as I can remember, to be special, to be part of it, but instead of letting me in, I get *this!*"

Copycat pointed to the bruise on his face, tears in the corners of his eyes.

"Meanwhile, as soon as they come across you and Grif, some nobodies from nowhere, they're dying to let you in! Just because you're *special!* Because you're different! The last piece of the puzzle! Well, I'm never going to let you join them! Not if I can help it!"

"What are you talking about?! Who are 'they?'" Azer yelled.

"Team Virga," Copycat said with resentment. He held up the recording device threateningly. "But you won't have to worry about them once my clone delivers a copy of this recording to the school and you both get expelled!"

A massive BANG and Grif appeared behind Azer, electric charge surging through his body. Grif pushed Azer aside and lunged towards Copycat. Grif cocked back an electrified punch, but Copycat was already touching a rusted filing cabinet beside him.

"Grif, wait! He can-"

It exploded into dozens of copies, the heavy metal filing cabinets flying, propelled every which way by the sheer force of the duplication. It forced Copycat, Azer, and Grif apart, bruising and battering them. After the chaos had subsided, Azer found himself pinned to the ground by one of the cabinets and saw Grif rushing to his aid.

"Don't worry about me! Get Copycat!"

But Copycat was already escaping. Seeing Grif, Copycat picked up a stone and quickly cloned himself twice, the stone as well. From what Azer could see, it was a discolored, edged stone, and he could faintly make out some kind of strange symbols on it. The three Copycats all simultaneously hurled stones at Azer and Grif.

Azer, pinned down, was near helpless. It would take time to use his S.R. again. But Grif hadn't lost his determined glare.

A crackling sound filled the air as Grif electrified himself, and he stomped a foot to the ground. An electric explosion from his foot launched a metal trash can lid into the air, and he extended his hands out towards it as it fell back towards him. His hands sparked and arced, and a final, larger-than-ever explosion launched the trash can lid towards the quickly approaching stones. They impacted in midair with a loud, reverberating CLANG, and the stones were forced backwards, hitting the real Copycat on the head. He collapsed, the clones of him and the objects he touched disappearing into a thin dust, and the original recording device fell out of his hands unceremoniously.

"If we're lucky, that should have taken care of the clone at the Battle Academy as well," Grif said.

Azer felt the weight that was pinning him down lift off of him all at once. He pushed himself up effortlessly, and the two made their way over to Copycat and stood for a moment.

"Should we leave him here?" Azer asked.

"Probably not. But I honestly think he might deserve it."

Then, heavy footsteps behind them.

"Hey... what in the hell?" a gruff voice said. It was a scrapyard worker, staring between Azer and Grif.

"WHAT THE HELL ARE YOU KIDS DOIN' HERE, EH? GET OUTTA HERE!"

"Guess we have no choice! Run!" Grif said, wide-eyed, stomping hard on the recording device before he sprinted away.

Although Azer had thought he'd done enough running that morning, he and Grif found themselves sprinting again to the Battle Academy in hopes of breaking in. Running down and across streets, they saw a familiar face.

"Hey! Azer, Grif! Over here!"

"Milo?"

Milo and Torbe were walking down the sidewalk toward Azer and Grif, waving happily towards them. Azer and Grif slowed down, much to the gratefulness of Azer's aching legs, and stopped by the other two boys.

"What are you guys running for?" Milo asked.

"Nuh- nothing," Grif panted. "Don't worry about it."

Milo's eyes widened. "Wait, what happened to you guys? You guys are hurt! Come with us back to my house. My mom can help you!"

Azer touched a hand to his injured head, wincing. "It's a long story. And, sorry, Milo, we have to go to the Battle Academy. We don't have time."

"Why are you guys going to school? It's a weekend!"

"Just- don't worry about it, Milo, we're fine," Grif said. "If we find time, we'll head to your house."

"Alright, well, me and Torbe are taking a shortcut back to my place. Hopefully we'll see you there!"

And the two left, leaving Azer and Grif behind.

"Grif, hurry! We still don't know if Copycat's clone told someone yet!"

"I'm trying! I've never picked a lock before!"

The two were stationed outside of the darkened teacher's office, Grif fussing with the lock on the window.

"Someone's gonna see us!" Azer hissed.

"No they're not! It's the weekend! You heard Milo, we're probably gonna be the only people here!"

Grif returned to his work, concentrating hard, until with a tiny click, the lock on the window popped open.

"Alright, go, go!"

Azer climbed in, careful not to bump his injured head, and stepped into the clean, dark teacher's office.

"I'm having second thoughts, Grif!"

"Chill out! We're not breaking the rules if we don't get caught! Now stop complaining and search!"

"For what?"

"Anything! Everything! Find anything you can on that missing girl, or us, or The Shades that they might be hiding. Just look!"

But it was easier said than done—the number of cabinets, and the files in them, was immense. Every teacher, every student had their own file.

Azer dug in a desk, but only found a graded test. He searched through one of the many cabinets, but only managed to find the files of older students. The process repeated with countless student files as the minutes stretched into hours. He was growing frustrated, but then took another look at the files of the older students. Maybe...

Azer searched through the files, hoping to see Haise's name. Eventually, he found it, and pulled it out. A large red strip of paper hung off of the edge of the file, and the text next to her picture read:

Name: Haise Menss.

Gender: Female.

Appearance: Teal, pale skin. Yellowish eyes and long, thin hair.

Species: Yuuta.

Val(s): Elasticity manipulation of objects.

Date of Birth: Cievu 40, 3264 ZST

Notes:
Orphan. Suffers from a skeletal decay condition due to poor adaptation to high gravity.

There was nothing else of interest in the folder. Still curious, Azer continued to dig in the other old files. Did the red strip of paper indicate that something had happened to her? Azer searched for another red strip of paper, hoping for more clues.

And he found more—another file had a red piece of paper poking out from the surrounding white documents. Azer pulled it out to see something surprisingly familiar.

The picture showed a young girl who seemed familiar to Azer—he couldn't forget that face. It was the doomsayer who Azer and Grif saw after they first met: Kovaki.

Name: Kovaki E. Etonie.
Gender: Female.
Appearance: Marine blue skin. Reddish-purple eyes and medium length bluish hair.
Species: Silankieli.
Val(s): Skin is an incredibly hard exoskeleton-like material.
Date of Birth: Dyrrachis 2, 3264 ZST

Notes:
Occasional temper issue with teachers and other pupils. Past acts of violence. Belongings confiscated.

Azer closed the drawers and went back to looking around the room, searching for the belongings of Kovaki's that reportedly had been confiscated. He found a hidden dusty drawer inside an old metal cabinet, protected by an old rusty lock. Was this it? Pumping S.R. through his body, he snapped the lock in two and pulled it open to see an assortment of belongings—gloves, laptops, weapons, and more. Digging around, Azer saw a familiar symbol that caught his attention: the same symbol that the doomsayers had sewn into their cloaks, but engraved in gold on a dusty, leather-bound notebook. Hands shaking slightly, Azer pulled it out.

He opened the notebook to its front page. Light and small handwriting indicated that it was owned by Haise Menss. Azer turned the pages further, skimming the passages and ramblings of this long-gone girl. Then he reached the last page, and the words written there gave him goosebumps.

I see it. I see the image of God in front of me. It's getting closer.
Kovaki, I was right. It is beautiful.

"Grif, I found something," Azer said grimly. "And it looks like The Shades is a lot more mysterious than we thought."

"What do you mean?" Grif asked, still digging around in file cabinets. "What did you find?"

"A notebook from Haise. It looks like she knew the doomsayer person we saw a while ago, Kovaki."

Grif made his way over to Azer and looked over his shoulder at the final page. When Grif finished reading, his eyes went wide and eyebrows raised far.

"What does this even mean?" Azer asked.

"It probably means exactly what you said. The Shades is something a lot more sinister than we realized. Obviously when it happens... *something* arrives." Grif shivered. "But let's keep looking around for stuff. I think that Copycat's message obviously didn't get through or we'd already be found. Let's see if they have any information on us."

But before Azer could even start looking for his own file, the school loudspeaker suddenly gave a harsh beep and a voice spoke:

"Emergency alert to all staff: two missing children have been reported, by the names of Milo Arbona and Torbe Sorlen."

TWO HOURS EARLIER

Milo looked at Azer and Grif with confusion. "Why are you guys going to school? It's a weekend!"

"Just- don't worry about it, Milo, we're fine," Grif replied. He and Azer seemed to be in a rush. "If we find time, we'll head to your house."

"Alright, well, me and Torbe are taking a shortcut back to my place. Hopefully we'll see you there!"

With a quick nod from Grif, he and Azer ran off, turning a corner and passing out of sight.

"What was up with them?" Milo asked nobody in particular. "They looked all beat up."

"It's probably nothing," Torbe said, looking back at where Azer and Grif disappeared. "I'm sure they're fine. They know what they're doing."

Torbe led Milo down an unfamiliar street, taking them closer to an older side of town. The air was cool and moist, high humidity making Milo's shirt stick to his chest. The monochrome clouds overhead colored the town a bleak gray. He examined a worn-down advertisement pasted on a nearby bus stop to distract himself from the fact that he was getting further and further away from the roads he knew how to navigate.

"You sure this is a good idea?" Milo asked Torbe timidly, turning to his much taller friend. "My parents told me not to go to this area of town."

"I'm really late for some music lessons," Torbe said "Would you mind if we went this way instead? It's a lot faster, trust me. I've been down here loads of times."

Milo and Torbe stood at the mouth of a dark, long, and narrow alleyway, the odor of trash and rusted dumpsters in the air.

"Okay…"

They walked, Milo periodically stopping his pace at any noise. Milo kept close to Torbe, who was much taller than he was, and it gave him a sense of security.

"Torbe... it feels like someone's watching."

But as he turned around, he was horrified to realize Torbe wasn't there.

Torbe was pinned to a wall, wide-eyed. A disembodied hand covered his mouth, muting him.

"No, the other boy!" a voice said.

A thin-fingered, calloused hand grasped Milo's hair, pulling him back, and then an arm wrapped around his neck and squeezed him tight to a raggedy-clothed body. A terribly skinny, crooked-toothed man held him down, a strong stench of booze and a whiff of blood entering Milo's nostrils. He tried to yell for help, but his energy was being rapidly drained. He felt as if his eyelids would fall if it wasn't for the sheer adrenaline and panic pumping through him.

A grinding, sliding noise caught Milo's attention and he saw another hand opening up a window. Two figures stepped through the window and into the alley where Milo, Torbe, and the thin man stood. Another person then swooped from a rooftop, landing skillfully by the others.

The new figures were two women and a man, all dressed in sweeping velvety cloaks with hoods and a strange symbol-encrusted disc holding the cloaks together. The first woman was shorter than the rest with short, wiry hair, bloodshot eyes jutting out. The man, Milo noticed, was long-haired and missing a hand—and his remaining hand looked a lot like the one pinning Torbe to the graffitied wall. The second woman was taller, fuller, with dark, narrowed eyes that gleamed and edged, hardened skin. Milo could tell immediately that she was the leader.

Beneath their well-kept cloaks were stained, raggedy clothes. They stunk of alcohol and sweat, and had stitches and scars covering their bodies. They were the type of people his parents had warned him about—criminals. And judging by the almost ceremonial look of their clothing, criminals with a cause: *Nova Noctis.*

"Now," the leader said, looking towards Milo. "Fico, knock this one out and take him away. Gorr, kill the other kid. We don't need him."

Torbe let out a muffled scream. The tall woman looked amusedly at Torbe, the disembodied hand still covering his mouth.

"You got something to say about that?" the leader challenged Torbe. "Gorr, let him speak, I want to hear what this kid's gotta say."

The hand uncovered Torbe's mouth and hung in the air for a moment.

"NO!"

"'No' what, kid?" the leader taunted. "Afraid of death, already?"

"DON'T TAKE HIM AWAY! I WON'T LET YOU!" Torbe screamed.

The tears hanging in Milo's terrified eyes now flowed freely. The four cultists laughed.

"Torbe, you can't!" Milo sobbed.

"Think you're tough, huh?" the leader said, smiling now. "Think you can fight us?"

"I can and I will! Milo, this is exactly the stuff we've been training for in the Academy! This is what we need to do! Don't let them take you!"

"He can and he will!" Fico, the skinny man holding Milo chuckled hoarsely. "He can and he will! Didja hear him? There's a time and a place for heroism, *Torbe,* and this isn't it! Your friend here is gonna make us a lot of money! He's got some seriously rich parents who are gonna pay a pretty penny once we ransom him off! If there's anything left of him, that is…"

"Hey! Fico!" the leader barked. Fico's attention snapped to her. "We take him alive, alright? We can't get ransom money if he's already dead!"

"To be fair, Kovaki," the wiry-haired woman started, her voice loud and thin. "We could probably find a way to make him look alive enough to get paid."

"QUIET!" Kovaki yelled. "We take him alive! Gorr, hurry up and kill the other kid!"

"I don't know, his little speech has got me inspired," Gorr said in his deep, gravelly voice. "Let's give him a fighting chance. Just me and him. I wanna see this kid fight."

"Me too," said the hoarse voice of Fico. "Lemme at him."

"Fine!" Kovaki said, growing angry. She stormed over to Milo, grabbed him by the hair, and pulled him away from Fico.

"And you," she growled to Milo through gritted teeth, "get to watch."

The disembodied hand, waiting to apprehend Torbe again, flew back towards Gorr. It reattached itself to a red stump on Gorr's arm, and Gorr held his reattached hand up in the air, flexing and curling his fingers threateningly.

Torbe lunged towards his two towering opponents and swung wildly at Gorr. It missed and he hit the alley wall. He felt a shameful frustration as the gang laughed.

"Torbe!" Milo shouted, grabbing Torbe's attention. "Fico can sap your energ-"

But before he could finish, Kovaki's hand muffled Milo.

"Don't even worry about it!" Fico boasted after dodging a kick from Torbe. "It doesn't matter if the kid knows my Val. How's that gonna help him?"

Torbe dodged and attacked both of the men, but nothing landed. Fico was wrong—Milo had helped him. Torbe now prioritized dodging Fico's attacks first, narrowly avoiding the strikes from the limb-separating powers of Gorr. After leaping out of the way of Fico's grab and ducking under a kick from a disembodied leg, Torbe found himself cornered in front of Gorr. There was a sick, yellow-toothed smile on his face.

"Ever been hit, kid?"

Gorr slammed his fist into Torbe's side, sending him flying down the narrow alleyway. Brutal pain shot through his body, and he gasped for air as the wind was knocked out of him. The laughter of the kidnappers and the scared cries of Milo were quieter for a moment.

Torbe's mind suddenly felt clearer. The fear was gone, and all that resided inside him now was his wits and battle instinct. A memory, somehow stirred by the impact, came back to him. It was a memory of fighting Azer and saying to him:

"Show me your Val," Torbe had said, *"I want to fight you at full strength."*

Back then, Torbe had felt like Azer was holding back on him. He had thought, *Where is his Val? If he was using it, whatever it is, I would be losing.*

And in this sudden, clear state of mind, Torbe realized that he, right now, was holding back. The kidnappers still didn't know what his Val was—they didn't even know he had one.

So he would use it to win.

His time bubbles were nearly invisible—and in a dark alleyway like this, and on a cloudy day, the kidnappers would have no idea his bubbles were even there. He flexed his hands and a speeding bubble appeared near the ground, just large enough for Torbe to fit in while curled up. He watched as Gorr's disembodied arms approached him. Just before Gorr struck, Torbe leapt past the arms and into the bubble.

Entering the bubble and feeling the now-familiar sensation of time warping around his body, everything else began to slow. He changed direction and dove again towards Gorr.

Torbe watched the two sparring students at combat class intently, studying every movement and nuance of battle. The way the fight ebbed and flowed like an agitated liquid fascinated him. All of a sudden, one of the students curled back his fingers and slammed his palm into his opponent's nose.

"Stop the match! Geraas, that is a forbidden move!" Delvin shouted in Torbe's memory.

Torbe left the time bubble with a unnatural pulling on his skin and bowled into Gorr's legs. With no arms to cushion him, Gorr fell clumsily to the concrete with a thud, hitting his head on the asphalt.

Torbe curled his fists to destroy the speeding bubble and then flexed them again, concentrating all of his energy on creating the slowest time bubble he could. He could see it materializing in front of the shocked figure of Fico.

"You could kill him if you did that any harder or hit his nose at the right angle."

Torbe dove once more in front of the bubble, focusing all of his strength onto his legs, squatting down and preparing for a jump. Now in front of Fico, he looked the decrepit criminal dead in the eyes.

"Ever been hit?" he said before jumping as fast as he could into the bubble.

From the outside, it was as if someone pressed a pause button on Torbe. He floated and very slowly rose into the air.

"What the hell?" Fico exclaimed. "The hell happened to this kid?"

Milo, still staring at the scene wide-eyed, knew. He knew how fast Torbe was really rising in the bubble.

"Just hit him already!" Kovaki said, having abandoned Milo to help the injured Gorr. "Kill him!"

Fico formed his thin, calloused hand into a fist and swung it at Torbe. But before it could hit Torbe, it suddenly halted in midair, traveling at the same snail-like speed Torbe was. Surprised, Fico tried to pull his hand back, but it was stuck in midair as if the atmosphere itself had become solid.

Fico lunged with his other fist, but the same happened. The moment his fist entered the invisible bubble, it stopped, all momentum lost. At that moment, Fico's cocky and confident expression snapped into panic. He was desperately trying to free himself from these invisible binds of time, but it was futile. Torbe rose higher and higher inside of the time bubble, and Fico was trapped where he was. Before any of the other kidnappers could come to his aid, Torbe reached the top of the bubble, fist extended, and punched Fico's nose from below with blinding speed.

A spurt of blood, and Fico collapsed against the wall. He was completely limp, dead, panic forever etched into his eyes.

A deafening scream, who knows who screamed it. There were shouts and yells and people shouting Fico's name. Before Torbe could say another word to Milo, Kovaki's leg kicked Torbe square in the temple with an audible *crack*.

Torbe, specks of blood flying through the air after him, hit the alley wall, blood trailing behind him as he collapsed to the ground.

"TORBE!"

CHAPTER SIX:
HIDDEN EVILS

Drizzle. 22mph winds blowing northeast. Seventy-five degrees fahrenheit. Rain expected to intensify.

Drops of moisture and rain accumulated in Azer's hair as he ran, yet again, down the streets of his town. They fell onto his bare face and dripped down into his collar, making his clothes uncomfortably wet from a mixture of rain and sweat. Grif ran alongside him, in a similar state of discomfort.

The only thing that could top the shock he felt from discovering the information on Haise was the sudden disappearance of his good friend Milo. And so, Azer ran as fast as his diminished stamina could take him to the last place he saw Milo, praying he could make it in time.

Before Milo could make it to Torbe, he was halted by Kovaki's looming, furious figure.

"You're not going *anywhere.*"

She aimed a kick, but Milo was ready. He put up a forearm, and numerous vines and roots sprouted out in the shape of a shield. Her steel-like leg impacted the shield, cracking and breaking through his guard, throwing him far across the alleyway. Milo skidded across the wet asphalt, tiny specks of rain falling on his face. He stared up into the air.

"If you know what's good for you, you won't run!" she taunted. "Don't make it any worse for yourself! After what your friend did, I don't think we'll be as nice to you!"

As Milo pushed himself up, he felt a moment of strength. His paralyzing fear was evaporating by the moment.

"I'm not running! And I'm not going with you either! I'll fight you! I'm not afraid anymore!"

"Kid, don't you understand what's happening? With the money I'll earn from your ransom, I'll be one step closer to bombing the next round of evacuation ships from The Shades. You think you have willpower? You think you have a grudge against me? You don't have shit compared to what I have against nonbelievers like you. But when you're all left to die, to face The Shades alone, then you'll believe."

Torbe had been right. Milo cursed himself for not realizing it earlier. These kinds of people were exactly the ones Milo ought to be fighting. The hidden evils of his town who had to be vanquished. Cowardice and fear didn't matter—complacency was letting evil run free. And they would run free for no longer.

"Ether, get the kid. He's a Valin too. If he wants to play, he can play," Kovaki said, stepping back to let Ether pass.

"Roger," the wiry-haired woman said. Her wild demeanor became more focused, as if she was hunting Milo like prey.

"And don't forget to leave him alive, if only a little!"

The first thought Milo had as Ether dashed towards him was wondering what her Val was. As she wildly swung out her arm, Milo saw her shooting something small at him through the air, too fast for him to make out. Milo dodged and weaved, but he knew that his target wasn't really

Ether—it was Kovaki, who was standing back, watching the fight carefully. She was their leader.

Ether forced Milo further down the alleyway with her still unseen attacks, farther and farther from Kovaki, preventing him from getting close enough to attack or counter. And although Milo wanted to focus on the attacks as much as possible, he couldn't help but think that there was more to her ability.

Milo saw an opening and kicked Ether hard in the face. She staggered back, but quickly recovered and grabbed his airborne leg. There was a sinister smile on her bruised face.

"You've fallen for it, boy..."

She forced him backwards violently, holding his leg tightly, and then finally let him go with a great shove and a yell. He fell backwards, unable to right himself, and saw a horrible sight where he was about to land.

Ether's weapons were paper-thin, fist-length, white needles—and all along, she had been collecting them in one place. The javelin-like needles were floating above the ground like a menacing bed of nails. Nearing the ground, panic shooting through his body, Milo reached a fingertip to a bare spot of asphalt between the floating needles and, just before the mass of needles pierced his body, his fingertip made contact.

A great tree erupted out of the ground, cracking through the moist asphalt and rising incredibly fast. It grew and grew at high speed, like watching a timelapse. It pushed Milo off the ground, throwing him into the air moments before he would have landed. He soared over Ether, who was enraged and surprised, her popped-out eyes even more bulging than usual, and began to fall towards Kovaki. Without hesitation, he reached out his arm, which wrapped itself in a thick mass of vines and wood.

Falling and yelling, droplets of rain dancing in tandem, Milo swung his encased arm towards her for a final attack.

The wood smashed to splinters as it hit Kovaki's unfazed face. The roots and wooden pieces fell to the ground with clunks and thuds.

Milo stood in front of her, mortified, the fist he used to attack bleeding and crushed.

"You might have guessed by now," Kovaki said with a dangerous calm in her voice. "My Val is a powerful, hard exoskeleton over my entire body. My skin is made of 'pure carbon.' And I will also tell you that, since I realized my Val sixteen years ago, I haven't bled once."

She grabbed Milo by the neck and pulled him into the air, choking him.

"You've got a lot of cheek for a damn kid."

A sharp pain in his back told Milo that Ether's needles were piercing him. She was approaching Milo slowly as Kovaki continued to choke him.

"I'll give you credit; I didn't think I'd be losing a member of my faithful group today. You and your friend have caused me some real grief. But it's done now."

Milo gathered his strength for a kick towards Kovaki's torso, but it was held back by someone new. Gorr, pushing himself off the ground, was missing an arm—an arm that was gripping Milo's leg tightly. Gorr was bleeding freely from the head.

"Don't count me out yet!" he growled.

"A useful property of my pure carbon Val," Kovaki spoke again, removing an obsidian-like finger from his neck and placing it on his cheek, "is I can cover more than just myself in pure carbon. I can convert anything—living matter, for example—into a hard, immovable substance, bit by bit."

And, from the spot where her finger touched, Milo felt a painful sensation—as if his skin ripped and then healed itself, except impossibly hard. This spot now had no feeling—he could no longer feel the edged finger of Kovaki pressing against his cheek. And this feeling spread, a painful cracking and snapping that slowly crossed his face and neck, becoming hard and unfeeling. At last, he screamed.

"HELP ME!"

Milo could hardly see from the rain and tears clouding his eyes. Something… someone's foot? Something had impacted Kovaki's head and kicked it violently into the alley wall. Milo fell to the ground, the hardening sensation gone, and looked up to see Azer and the grim face of Grif looking at him. *He was saved.*

"What happened to Torbe?" Grif asked. Milo's tears fell faster.

"He…" Milo started, looking over at Kovaki, whose head was embedded into the cracked concrete wall. "She…"

But then, Kovaki's arms rose up, gripped the wall, and pulled her head out of the smashed concrete. She glared at the three boys with rage. Milo then realized that Gorr and Ether were looming, imminent.

"GET AWAY!" Milo screamed.

They leapt out of the way to dodge a mass of floating limbs, needles, and hardened punches. Gathering themselves, they saw Kovaki striding towards them, fury etched into the crinkled lines of her hardened face.

"I've told you!" she said. "Not one drop of my blood has been spilt! I've survived car crashes. I've fallen off of buildings. And not once has my pure carbon skin cracked! You cannot defeat me!"

Azer and Grif looked at each other with curiosity, rain dripping down their faces.

"Not once?" Grif whispered to Azer.

"Seems like it. That was a hard kick, too," Azer replied.

"Your call," Grif said, looking back at Kovaki and her fellow kidnappers as they approached.

"Let's do it."

"Milo," Grif said, looking at Milo seriously. "Stay back."

The moment Milo stepped back, Azer and Grif sprinted towards the three attackers, focusing on Kovaki. They dodged and weaved around Gorr and

Ether's attacks with grace as if they'd fought the kidnappers dozens of times before. They ducked and slid under every kick, punch, and attack. Grif slid under the legs of Ether and Azer, throwing aside Gorr's floating limb.

And, finally, after knocking away Ether and Gorr, Grif positioned himself behind Kovaki. He let out a blast of electricity, knocking her towards Azer. And, at the same time, Azer was sprinting towards Kovaki, fist raised and poised to strike.

Through the rain, a black mist rose out from Azer's skin. It flared from his whole body, leaving a short, dark trail behind him as he ran, and something strange began to happen. Subconsciously, Azer was focusing his will onto the arm he was ready to punch with. This subconscious moved the black mist, that fiery energy in his body, into his shoulder and arm. Invisible floodgates opened within his body, letting the energy flow and surge into his biceps.

Whether he knew it or not, Azer's arm contained all of the S.R. in his body.

Kovaki, still flying towards Azer from Grif's blast, hit Azer's fist, which was traveling at sonic speed into Kovaki's chest. The punch released a boom and made a cracking noise as it landed. Kovaki and Azer both staggered back.

Kovaki was slumped over, eyes wide, clutching her chest. She let out gasps of pain and surprise.

Azer, shocked at his own power, stood in tired stillness for a moment as the S.R. wore off, the power trickling away like water. He looked at his fist. There was blood on his knuckles, and it wasn't his own. He collapsed from sheer exhaustion, causing a tiny splash in a rainwater puddle.

Kovaki's chest dripped blood, pooling on the ground beneath. A great crack in her ultrahard skin stretched all the way from her chest to her neck, up to a portion of her face. She let out an agonized scream that pierced the humid air.

Milo and Grif rushed over to Azer, helping him up and praising him. But Azer couldn't hear anything over Kovaki's drawn-out shrieks.

For a moment, it felt like the fight was over. But that hope vanished a second later when an enraged Gorr grabbed the heads of Azer and Grif and smashed them together. Pain shot through Azer's injured skull. Gorr, with Azer too tired to fight back, repeatedly hit his absent face into the alley wall, cursing.

"YOU!"

But before Gorr could utter another word, he shook violently as Grif unloaded amperes of electricity into his body.

"Azer, get up! Please! We have to finish this!" Grif pleaded.

The words hardly reached Azer's mind. He was in too much pain and far too shaken to react. The surge of S.R. he had produced had all but shut down his body.

But he mustered his willpower. His broken and drained body got up slowly, one fist on the ground at a time.

A flurry of needles shot through the air towards the two, but were blocked by a large vine that had sprouted out of the ground, shielding the blows before disintegrating.

"You're not hurting another one of my friends!" Milo roared towards Ether.

She let out a frustrated growl, threw her arm to the side, and a massive metallic needle materialized in the air and fell into her hand—a long, thin javelin. Milo, in turn, sprouted a wooden plant from the ground, also javelin-shaped, and plucked it from its roots. He faced her with determination.

"Kovaki, I'm not leaving him alive anymore!" she yelled. "This kid dies!"

But Kovaki could not make a noise in response. She was still slumped over in agonized shock. Her eyes were unfocused and red, staring aimlessly. Ether attacked Milo wildly with the giant needle.

"Azer, listen to me," Grif said, cautiously watching the cultists, talking fast. "I know you're hurt. I know you're tired. But I need you to get up one more time. I need you to do what you did to Kovaki, one more time. She's almost down. She's in shock. You've completely destroyed her pride. One more strike, I beg you. Please, Azer. Get up."

Azer groaned and pulled himself to standing. Everything hurt, everything was so heavy—his battered head, his stinging arm, his clothes, the rain falling on his body. It was all so... heavy.

He gathered his voice.

"I'll do it."

A heavy splash sounded behind them.

"What... are you doing...?"

It was Kovaki. Her eyes were darker and redder than ever. She towered over them, her stance lopsided, blood no longer flowing from the crack in her exoskeleton. There was no longer any hint of a calm or collected demeanor—she was hellbent on killing Azer and Grif, whatever the cost. Her bloodlust was palpable.

She raised a flat hand and swung it down at them with frightening force. The two ducked and dove, but Azer was nicked by her strike, his shoulder now cut and bleeding. Her hand hit the wall behind them, smashing it and creating an explosion of dust and rubble.

The wall, from the spot Kovaki hit, cracked and morphed as it turned into hyper-hard pure carbon. The change in density and hardness caused more cracks in the wall, until pieces began to fall out. Concrete dust spewed out into the air as the pieces cracked and crumbled.

"What kind of power is that?!" Grif exclaimed. "Is she turning that wall into pure carbon, too?!"

And then, without hesitation, she prepared another attack. She lifted a leg and stomped the ground near Azer and Grif, who barely rolled out of the way. The ground cracked and snapped as it morphed into dense pure carbon, spewing yet more dust into the rainy air.

"Azer, hurry! She's gonna kill us!"

"I'm trying!"

He was, but the energy wasn't coming. There was no longer any hint of his Val.

Kovaki went for another attack—a kick, this time—and it forced both Azer and Grif to roll away, sprawling on the ground. Azer got up again, but Grif wasn't as quick. Kovaki stomped on his fingers, causing Grif to yell out in pain.

When Kovaki lifted her foot, Grif's fingers were still on the ground, now made of Kovaki's pure carbon. The ground underneath was fusing the two together. Grif couldn't move his own hand.

"I- can't- get- up!" he yelled with panic.

Kovaki looked up toward the sky. In her state of cold fury and blood-lust, she smiled. She smiled as she let the rain hit her face.

"Isn't the rain beautiful?" she asked nobody in particular. Azer was still in shock, but he began to feel energy return to him. Kovaki was silent for a moment as Grif struggled to get up.

"Haise told me that The Shades is a storm. I wonder what kind of rain falls then? Rain falls fast, you know," she said, extending an arm over Grif. "And I can turn *anything* into pure carbon."

Her hand extended over Grif, as if blocking the rain from hitting him. Nothing seemed to be happening at first, but, suddenly, Grif let out a yelp of pain.

A small wound appeared on Grif as he tried to desperately remove his hand, fused to the ground. Then another wound appeared, then another. They kept appearing at random intervals, each one making him grunt with pain. Azer tried to help, but nothing worked; Grif was being attacked by something Azer couldn't see.

Azer looked at Kovaki's hand, dripping with rainwater. He noticed that the rain she touched was turning hard and dense, made of the same enigmatic pure carbon she manipulated. And it fell at the same speed, retaining its momentum. Incredibly hard and dense, it created powerful bullets of rain that struck Grif's body, puncturing his skin.

"STOP!" Azer cried, grabbing Kovaki and doing everything he could to move her arm. But his efforts were fruitless. She continued to rain havoc down on his best friend.

"STOP HURTING HIM!" Azer cried again. He tried shielding Grif, but the hard and dense raindrops were even enough to pierce Azer's abnormally tough skin. Grif spoke, his voice raspy and pained:

"Don't... focus on me. Get Kovaki. Finish her."

Azer left the carbon rain and turned towards Kovaki, who was still staring down at Grif. He felt the welcome sensation of S.R. fill his body, and then, with enough concentration, focused the hot energy onto his arm. His muscles were screaming with fatigue, but he continued. And, with one final swing, he threw his arm into Kovaki's torso.

Another crack, another boom, another sensation of infinite exhaustion. He heard Kovaki backing away. He willed his body to look up at her, to make sure she was dead, to make sure she was gone... but she was, in fact, still alive. Azer fell to his knees.

A gurgling and pained laugh emerged from Kovaki, filling the narrow alleyway.

"I... I knew... you would go for another attack..." She went into a coughing fit, and then spit out a mouthful of blood. "So I turned the concrete dust around me... into a shield of pure carbon..."

The floating concrete dust around Azer had a different quality to it—edged and hard, it had slowed Azer's punch enough to be survivable.

Kovaki's laugh grew into a cackle as Azer fell to the ground.

"You lose!" she boasted, approaching him slowly. "My faith is unbeatable! I-"

Whether it had been there the whole time or if it had magically appeared, Azer noticed a dark, black figure behind Kovaki. Tall and cloaked, the figure stood still, and Azer could just barely make out a pair of ghastly white eyes underneath the cloak.

The figure reached a hand out towards Kovaki, and in a blast of darkness, she was thrown across the alleyway. It must have been Azer's imagination, he thought.

Portals, perfect ovals in midair, as dark as nothingness, spontaneously appeared, from which rotted hands emerged, grabbing Ether, who was frozen with shock. She was pulled into the portal and disappeared with a surprised shriek. Gorr, getting up, stared at the figure with terror and awe, and ran away frantically.

It was principal Dr. D from the Battle Academy.

"LEAVE!" Dr. D boomed, his voice magnified. "OR YOU DIE!"

Before Azer could even consider whether the command was for him, Kovaki scrambled out of the alleyway and was gone in an instant. Dr. D kneeled down towards Azer and carefully removed the hood of his cloak, showing the full face of Itell D. Ortum. He looked down between Azer, Grif, and Milo sadly, his white eyes mournful.

"I'm sorry," he said quietly, yet Azer could understand him clearly. "I'm sorry it took me this long."

Azer and Grif stepped out of the hospital doors accompanied by Dr. D, greeting the wet and cool night. The hospital windows were the only source of light, save for a few street lamps illuminating the asphalt.

"I suspect you want answers sooner than later. Will you both grab my arms? I want to take you somewhere," Dr. D asked kindly.

They each grabbed one of Dr. D's arms, who closed his eyes. In a swift, loud whoosh and a puff of black smoke, they were gone, having disappeared from the outside of the hospital.

Azer felt like he had painlessly disintegrated into gas. He traveled in a dizzying whoosh of darkness and color, until he landed on hard ground again, fully back to normal, just outside the Battle Academy.

"Don't be alarmed, it's only my Val. I can transport myself into and out of any shadow within a certain radius."

Dr. D promptly brushed both of his hands together and then peered down at the two boys before gesturing for them to follow and enter the school.

"Now, I'm sure you are both brimming with questions, all of which I'm happy to answer. Let me first say, I regret that our first proper meeting had to happen the way it did."

"Is Torbe going to be okay?" Azer croaked.

Dr. D looked down.

"Torbe... did not make it. I'm sorry. Know that it's not your fault. What happened to Torbe was an act of evil in the world, evil that you bravely conquered."

They turned a corner in the hallway and traveled down a passage Azer had never seen before.

"It is unprofessional for me as a teacher to show any kind of favoritism to anyone. But I put that aside out of a mix of sympathy and self-reflection, seeing my own past in you two. Your curiosity towards the mysteries of this strange world we live in is inspiring."

"What past? What happened to you?" Azer asked.

"Like you, I found myself alone, stranded on a world I didn't understand. I explored and traveled my world to find my past, but found nothing. So I came here. I found my passion in teaching, and founded the Battle Academy."

"Wait, you founded the Battle Academy?!" Grif exclaimed. "But that was-"

"Eighty years ago, yes," Dr. D finished.

"But does that mean that you're-"

"Eighty years old? I am. Now we're getting closer to the mystery, aren't we?"

Azer and Grif stared at each other, bewildered.

"You two find your pasts a mystery. All three of us do not know precisely who we are or where we came from. I woke up eighty years ago at the same age I find myself today."

Dr. D opened an inconspicuous door and urged the two boys inside. It was a janitor's closet, with cleaning materials and a vacuum lying on one wall, the other wall bare and painted. Dr. D ran his long, pale fingers over a spot on the ceiling, and then watched as the bare wall became more and more transparent. A long, downwards-sloping corridor was visible behind it, and Dr. D walked through the now clear wall and down the corridor. Azer and Grif followed, taking second glances at the vanished wall.

"Dr. D, I have another question," Grif said. Dr. D's white eyes turned towards him. "Why did you show yourselves to us today? Aside from saving us and everything, I mean. Couldn't you have just blown up the kidnappers and ran away?"

"I showed myself to you because I felt that you are ready to join our cause. I wanted you to find me, and you did."

"What do you mean? We didn't."

"But you did. You found Haise's journal in the teachers room-"

Azer and Grif tensed up.

"No, you're not going to get in trouble for that. I practically led you there."

"You said *our* cause? Who are you talking about?" Azer asked.

"Ah, I'm glad you asked! When I told you I knew nothing of our pasts, that was not completely true. A group of very trusted individuals and I have formed a group dedicated to discovering that exact thing. Not just our pasts, see, but a theory that I believe may explain our pasts, along with many, many other mysteries of this world, and possibly worlds beyond. In fact, my fellow coworkers should be upon us now."

Dr. D pushed open another door to reveal an extensive laboratory, full of equipment and a massive store of maps, books, and files. Three other people were in the room, the closest one both Azer and Grif immediately recognized.

"Mrs. Korca?!" Grif exclaimed.

Mrs. Korca, Grif's wild-haired and big-eyed science teacher, turned away from a document she was sifting through at the sound of Grif's voice. Her face broke into a smile.

"Grif!"

"What are you doing here?! I didn't know you worked with Dr. D!"

Before answering his question, Mrs. Korca turned to Dr. D.

"I take it they're joining us, then?"

"Yes. They've been through a terrible ordeal, and I should get them back to the hospital soon." Seeing the shocked look on her face, he said, "I'll fill you in later."

The sound of their voices had grabbed the attention of the other two people, and they gathered closer around Dr. D. The first was Delvin, their combat class teacher, and another older man with blondish-white hair and a sullen face.

"Azer, Grif, I would like for you to meet Pascal," he gestured towards Mrs. Korca who waved excitedly, "who has a pressure control Val, hence her codename. You two already know her."

"Next I would like you to meet Zeph, with his wind Val." He gestured towards Delvin. "Who I believe you're familiar with as well. His real name is Delvin Rawins, an environmental science teacher at the Battle Academy."

"Finally, I would like you to meet Twice, a historian with the power of dual minds." Dr. D gestured towards the sullen-faced man, and Azer felt an odd sense of familiarity. "His real name is Okta Sastrugi, father of one of your classmates, Ecat Sastrugi."

And then it clicked—that face looked awfully similar to one Azer was all too familiar with, one that he despised greatly. It was the face of Copycat, who only that morning had attacked Azer and Grif. Okta must have known what had happened to Copycat earlier that day.

"And, finally, myself," Dr. D finished. "I am Shadow, otherwise known as Itell D. Ortum, or Dr. D. My Val involves the control and manipulation of Death. Together, we're called Team Virga."

"Team Virga is a cause dedicated to unraveling the many mysteries of Manim. For a long time, we've worked together on a grand theory. This theory, which also concerns my past and your pasts, is a long one, a theory that cannot be covered in a night. In truth, you two have already been uncovering pieces of it on your own. It is unfinished, but the significance I believe this theory has on our world is unheard of to the common citizen. But I will tell you this: this theory involves a few very interesting things: A virus, our planet, and the phenomenon that we all know as The Shades."

SUMMER

CHAPTER SEVEN:
THE GHOST AND THE GHOUL

Cloudy. 4mph winds blowing south. Eighty-three degrees fahrenheit. Sunny weather is expected over the week.

"You guys excited?" asked Milo.

Grif was desperately trying to beat Milo in a fighting game on Milo's TV, Azer watching intently.

"What for?" Azer asked, turning towards Milo. Grif, focused, paid no attention.

Milo turned away from the game, surprised.

"Well, a lot of stuff, right? It's Grif's 13th birthday tomorrow, for starters. And doesn't that mean one of you is old enough to be part of Team Virga? Is that what it's called?"

"Shh!" Grif hissed.

"Oh, sorry. I forgot we can't talk about that in the open," Milo apologized.

"No! Shaddup! I'm focusing on beating you!"

Azer felt stupid for forgetting. It had been so long since Team Virga had been properly brought up, he had completely forgotten that he and Grif would be officially recruited when one of them turned 13.

Azer could attribute some of the forgetting to the traumatic events that had occurred on that day, three standard years ago. Since the attempted kidnapping of Milo and the attempted murder of all of them, it was no wonder Azer's mind would try and forget such a thing.

School, for one, was a nightmare for months following the incident. Students and classmates talked about Azer, Grif, Milo and Torbe constantly, and the attention grew tiring. Copycat's hatred grew even deeper towards Azer and Grif, now directed at Milo as well. His arrogance increased yet more, and glares from their rival became the norm. Torbe's family moved off the planet only a week after the attack, a heartbreaking occasion that Milo had found difficult to accept.

But, like all things, the commotion died down, and even some positives came out of it. Mr. Grano had employed Azer and Grif in part-time jobs at Grano's Diner. Milo had grown less afraid. While the expectation following the attack was that Milo would shy away from it, he talked about the incident freely. His face, which had been partially converted into pure carbon from Kovaki's Val, still sported the warped scars of her attack. His sense of justice had been reinforced, and he enjoyed being the top of their grade in combat class, along with Azer and Grif. Their friendship had strengthened even more after the battle, and Azer and Grif enjoyed frequent visits to his massive house, full of gadgets, games and technologies the two could never dream to afford.

"Also," Milo said, now completely unfocused on the video game and intent on Azer, his fingers still moving rapidly over the controller as Milo's character slammed Grif's into the ground. Azer broke out of his trance of thought.

"The Shades is happening soon. Just a few months away, always around this time near the end of Manim's summer. It's gonna be our first time seeing it."

"I'm not too sure how I feel about that. I wouldn't exactly say I'm excited," Azer pointed, watching the TV again as Grif's character took another beating from Milo's. Grif let out a growl of frustration.

"That's fair," Milo replied. They both knew Kovaki's motivations had been deeply shaped by The Shades. And Azer still felt a creeping dread at the idea of the storm, as if a great evil was approaching.

Finally, Milo's fighting character grabbed Grif's and threw him to the ground a final time, prompting the word "FINISH" to cover the screen in big letters. Grif threw his controller to the ground, enraged, while Milo calmly smiled.

"Want a rematch?" Milo asked.

Grif glared sidelong at Milo, picked up the controller and sat back down on the comfy couch with a frown.

"Yeah... fine. Say your prayers."

The two boys celebrated Grif's birthday the moment they arrived home from school. Grif received an engineering book that Azer had saved up for, a remote control car from Milo, and, to the boys' surprise:

"Is that... cake?"

On their front door was an excellently-crafted cake, with icing that read: *Happy Birthday Grif!* along with a note written in slanted handwriting.

Meet at the school as soon as you get the chance. You know the spot.
Dr. D

"Isn't it a bit weird for our principal to be taking care of us like this?" Grif said, but he was grinning ear to ear.

"It's your birthday."

"We finally get to be part of Team Virga! Do you think we'll get our questions answered?"

"We'd better!"

Azer and Grif moved into the cramped, dusty janitor's closet they had visited so long ago and shut the door behind them. It was dark and cold inside, lit only by a single fluorescent light overhead.

"Hey, let me get on your shoulders. Dr. D did something involving touching the ceiling. We need to try that too," Grif suggested.

Azer obliged and Grif climbed on his shoulders, eventually able to touch the concrete surface around the fluorescent light, running his fingers along different edges of the ceiling.

"This *is* what we're supposed to do, right?" Azer asked, unsure.

"Pretty sure. Ah-"

Grif suddenly gasped and poked a spot on the ceiling. Silently and unnoticed, the uncluttered wall of the closet slowly became translucent, leaking light in from the secret tunnel.

"Guess that did it."

They made their way down the tunnel, turning left and right, sinking deeper as they walked. Finally, they heard muffled talking and found the door they had entered three years earlier, pushing it open.

The members of Team Virga were gathered around a table, documents and papers strewn about. When they heard the creak of the door, they quickly came over to greet Azer and Grif. Copycat's dad, Okta, stayed behind, looking at them expressionlessly.

"Welcome! We're so glad to have you here!" Dr. D said, striding up to them in his black cloak, hood down. Delvin, only steps behind, bent down to congratulate the two boys. He reached out a hand towards Azer and Grif in turn, vigorously shaking Azer's hand with both of his own.

"I cannot express how much joy it brings me to see you two here with us," he said, an excitement visible in his silver eyes. "I hope you can help us with our search."

Mrs. Korca, only moments later, opted to give each of the boys a great and choking hug.

"I'm so proud as your teacher to see you coming this far," she said, her magnified eyes tearing up a bit as she looked at them.

Dr. D swept Azer and Grif away from the tearful Mrs. Korca and over to a large table. The tabletop reached all the way up to the chins of Azer and Grif, who were only still half the height of the other team members.

"First thing's first, happy birthday Grif! It is our pleasure for you two to join us. We would have recruited you on our first meeting, but after you found us, we decided that anything much younger than 13 was too young. I warn you now, working with us will not be easy, and oftentimes it won't be fun or pleasant, either. Curiosity and discovery alone drive us. Do you still want to be part of the group?"

Azer and Grif turned to each other as if considering, but both knew the answer already. They nodded.

"Good. To start us off, I will review the theory that our discoveries revolve around, and this theory stems off of a collection of—the word is hard to find—*dreams* I have had. Distant, long-lost memories from another time and another life. Again, I warn you—this isn't for the faint of heart. May I continue?"

The boys nodded again.

"I have had these dreams since I can first remember, but I have not made sense of them up until quite recently when I founded Team Virga. I dreamt of a man, a sick man, very sick indeed, tall with the brightest blue eyes imaginable. This man was a scientist, not unlike us."

"The science he pursued was trying to find a cure to a deadly virus—a pursuit he and his colleagues had been working on for a long time. It was of impossible lethality and deadliness, and countless lives had already been taken. The fate of the world rested in the hands of this man and his team."

"But I have already said before that this man was sick. He was sick with the very virus he seeked to destroy, and his days were now numbered. The man feared death. He feared meeting the fate he had seen in others thousands of times before. He had watched patients' eyes go blank and their minds go dim, and above all else he feared having the same happen to himself."

"By some miracle, he and his team of scientists had created a cure. A single, miniscule vial that could stop the virus in its tracks. It only had to be produced in mass."

"And when the man internalized his fate, a desperate and powerful fear of death overtook him. Moments before his demise and just the day before the vial was to be widely produced, the man broke the glass casing holding the cure. As death was overtaking him, he gripped the vial tightly and consumed the whole thing."

An unreadable expression came across Dr. D's face. He stopped talking.

"And?" Grif urged, his mouth dry and his eyes wide and terrified. "What happened?"

After a moment of silence, Dr. D spoke again.

"The dream ends there. Everything else I will tell you after that is speculation into the dream's meaning."

"There is no way to put it lightly—I believe it's not a dream at all. That man existed, and his selfish attempt to save his life did, in fact, result in the death of the rest of his kind," he paused. "And that man was me."

The shock Azer and Grif felt was palpable in the room. It was apparent that the other members of Team Virga had heard this story before, but it did not stop their faces from going pale.

"So... you survived?" Azer asked.

"I didn't. That man died the instant he took the vial, curing him of the virus as the virus killed him. The theory is that something inside the cure, some chemical or substance that is unknown to me, gave me life the second that I died. A bizarre fluke of science and nature took my body as it passed over the threshold of life and death and suspended me in the middle. I was alive when I died, I passed away while I lived. A grim state of superposition combined my passing soul and my living, breathing self, turning me into a new being, a new person. During that moment, my eyes turned white, like those of a corpse. My living death gave me a second chance, a rebirth of sorts. And when I could think again, I had the power of Death itself at my fingertips. I still do today."

"Any memories that hadn't closely preceded my death are entirely forgotten, save for a few random memories I might recall every so often. Aside from that, I may as well be a different person. But, even then, I still have a feeling of certainty regarding the weight of this virus, and, this may surprise you," he paused. "I feel a kind of deja vu when I'm around the two of you. I think, somehow, you are instrumental in this search. Something in my past life is telling me."

"Wait," Azer said, hardly able to wrap his head around the information being thrown at him. "I thought you said the virus killed your kind? Wouldn't it have died out after that? Isn't the virus gone now?"

"That's where the theory really starts," Dr. D answered. "I think, somehow, my planet wasn't the only planet to be attacked by this virus. We believe the virus is interplanetary, hopping from planet to planet. Evidence that Team Virga has been gathering over the years gives merit to the idea that other planets have fallen victim to the same infection that killed me."

"How many?" asked Grif.

"We don't know. Part of Team Virga's purpose is to find out."

"But what does this have to do with The Shades? Didn't you say a long time ago that this theory had to do with The Shades?"

"I did, but any evidence I once had to connect The Shades with this virus is currently unknown to me. Part of why we're trying to discover all of this is to unravel that mystery, as well. All I know is, somehow, they're related. We just have yet to find out how."

Azer backed up and sat down on a large seat, his hands on his head. Grif just stood there, mouthing silently, bewilderment on his face. The knowledge was overwhelming. They could now see why Dr. D had decided to wait so long to tell them.

"Are you two alright? I know that was a lot at once," he said, walking over to them.

"You can say that again," Grif said, shaking his head and rubbing his face. "Is there really that little evidence about this theory? So much of it seems to be make-believe!"

"Ah, but that's the nature of a theory. In reality, I could be completely wrong about everything. But that's why we're here, isn't it? Our purpose isn't to prove me right; it's to discover what *is* true and build off of that. Whether I'm right or wrong, we're here to get questions answered. And so, that brings me to the first mission I have for you."

The two boys looked up.

"Your first mission is to discover your pasts. I've told you all that we know thus far, and I firmly believe the histories you two and your species have will help us piece things together. I don't think it's a coincidence you both ended up on this planet without any information about yourselves or where you came from. Use any resources and means you have to find out. I'd help if I could, but your pasts belong to you, not me. Find them."

A moment of tense silence between everyone, and then Dr. D looked at his watch.

"But before that, I do believe it's your birthday today, Grif. The day is young and so are you, so spend the rest of your birthday having fun. Today's meeting is done, so you're free to go."

Reluctantly at first, Azer and Grif got up to leave the room. After tapping the solid-seeming wall they entered through, it grew more transparent until they walked straight through, turning opaque behind them.

A knock at the door. Azer and Grif happily rushed to it and swung it wide open, revealing the grinning face of Milo, who was holding a sack of pillows and sleeping bags that was larger than any of them. Grif closed the door behind him as Milo's mom drove away, and he plopped his numerous belongings on Azer and Grif's couch.

"Is anyone else coming?" Milo asked.

"Yep," Grif answered, getting a glass of water. "Saa's coming too."

"Cool. I brought my games and controllers. You want to try a round of Battle Heroes?"

Grif sighed and frowned. "Fine. You owe me if I win!"

Milo laughed and sat down, plugging his controller into Azer and Grif's TV.

"If."

Azer, Grif, Milo, and Saa all lay comfortably on or dangling off their sleeping bags, pillows, couches, and cushions on Azer and Grif's living room floor. The TV, in view of all of them, was quietly playing cartoons with spirited characters and bright colors, and Azer and Milo watched in silence.

The windows were dark, as the sun had fallen away over half an hour ago. Saa stared out of the nearest window, at nothing in particular, and asked:

"You guys like scary stories?"

Everyone turned her way. A pause.

"Well? Do you?" she repeated.

"I've never been the biggest fan..." Milo said quietly.

"Are you kidding? Of course!" Grif said.

"I guess..." Azer said.

"People who like scary stories want to hear them, and people who don't like scary stories need to hear them. So I'll tell you guys one," Saa said, sitting up straight and clearing her throat.

"Have you ever heard of the Manim deadzone?"

A chorus of "yeah" and "uh-huh" in response. She spoke again, her heterochromic eyes darkening.

"It's about Manim being the only planet in this corner of the galaxy with life, right?" Grif asked.

"Yeah. My brother told me a story about the deadzone planets, it's a true story. So, a bunch of rogue scientists, just having gotten kicked out of their jobs, decided to explore one of the forbidden deadzone planets. Just for fun. They had nothing to lose."

Milo unconsciously scooted closer to Azer.

"They ignored all of Zysti's rules about not going to the deadzone planets and decided to land on one called Nimon, a few lightyears from here. They had a group in orbit to take care of the ship and a group on the ground, and after a few days they would swap roles and the other team would get to explore. So they sent the first group down, letting them explore and stuff, and every few days they would swap out, right?"

"The first group explored Nimon for a while, mapping out the area, but nothing seemed out of the ordinary. Until, one day, the surface group contacted the orbiting group and told them there was a strange red light glowing from cracks in the ground."

"A few days passed without a word from the surface group, so everyone in orbit tried contacting them. Nothing. Getting worried, the orbiting team decided to go down and investigate..."

Saa paused for dramatic effect, and then looked at the boys again with a malicious grin.

"None of them were ever heard from again. Disappeared... as if they were never there. Only their ship's log was left behind. Legend has it that a monster was roaming the planet, waiting for unsuspecting travelers to show up."

Azer and Milo were shaking and hugging each other, Milo's eyes wide. Grif, on the other hand, sat separate from them, unfazed and unamused.

"Nice story. Who made it up?" Grif said.

"No, it's true!" Saa said dramatically. "My brother knows this kind of stuff! It's really a true story!"

"Then why haven't I heard it before? Or, why did your brother hear it and not you? Or, why didn't we hear about this in history class? Or science class? It's so obviously a made-up story, anyone with a brain can tell."

Saa looked disbelieving and frowned, while Milo and Azer let each other go.

"You mean it's not real?" Azer said, relieved.

"Obviously not. It's a good story, though. I'll give your brother some credit," Grif replied, lying back down.

"I don't know... It sounded pretty real to me," Saa said, still uncertain. "Maybe I just didn't tell it right."

Grif was adamant. "There just simply can't be a creature like that. How would the Zystinian government not catch it? There's no life at all on the deadzone planets."

"Hey, nobody knows everything. The creature easily could have been hiding. Even those Team Virga guys might not have heard of it."

Now Grif looked somewhat uncertain, frowning doubtedly. He stayed silent.

"Can I tell a scary story?"

Everyone looked towards the source of the voice. It was Milo, looking disconcerted.

"Of course. I thought you didn't like scary stories?" Saa said.

"Well... no, I don't... I just heard this one from Copycat a long time ago when he was trying to scare me. Thought I'd share it."

"Please," Grif urged.

"Well... I think it goes something like this... so, you know how there's a shrine just outside of town? Like, that really old one people talk about sometimes? Well, the story goes that there's an evil spirit that haunts the shrine and never lets people near it at night. It's called Nur's Ghoul. Apparently, anyone who goes near it gets t- taken by the ghoul, and nobody sees them again. Copycat told me he'd feed me to Nur's ghoul if he found out I told anyone that I caught him stealing Torbe's lunch money."

But by the time Milo finished, the rest of the group was already looking at him, scared and amazed.

"Wow... that was really good," Azer complimented.

"Yeah, that was amazing," Grif agreed.

Saa didn't say anything, but was instead staring off into space wistfully.

"That shrine's not far from my house," she said quietly.

Milo looked at her, afraid.

"You're not suggesting-"

"We NEED to go there!" she erupted all of a sudden, startling the others. "We've TOTALLY got to check it out!"

"But I thought you said horror stories were real?" Azer said over Grif's cheers of agreement.

"Not *all* of them! And besides, even if Nur's Ghoul is real, I've totally got to check it out! Actually, I think I've heard of it before! C'mon, let's go!"

"All in favor of sneaking out to see Nur's Ghoul!" Grif said, raising his hand up high. An instant later and Saa's was up, too. They looked expectantly at Azer and Milo. A moment of silence.

"Really? You don't want to?" Saa asked, disappointed.

"Doesn't matter! It's my birthday, so my vote counts for two! Let's go!" Grif exclaimed, promptly standing up and ushering everyone out of the door. Milo gave one last pleading look to Azer, who shrugged.

Trekking between trees and under street lamps, joking, laughing, and shouting, the four walked together. They went through Azer and Grif's neighborhood, over a bridge and a dirt path, between brambles, thorns, and branches. They walked to the outskirts of town, their feet aching and the joking replaced with an anxious sense of wonder. After an hour or more of walking, they reached a cleaner path that transitioned into a path of brownish-gray brickwork. It wound and twisted, eventually opening into a larger area, the same brickwork covering the ground all around.

There was the shrine, unexpectedly tall, a massive wall of aged gray stone. It was full of designs and symbols, draped with long strings of beads, flowers, and other signs of worship and respect. Despite much of it having crumbled away, and its appearance old and ruined, it still held a symmetric beauty, as if it was once part of a larger whole.

"It's so pretty," Saa commented, awed.

"No kidding," Grif agreed.

"What's the shrine for?" Azer asked, turning to Saa. "Aren't they usually for religious ceremonies?"

"I heard it was built not long after Nur was colonized as a form of respect to not just one god or religion, but all of the religions of everyone from every planet who lived in Nur. It's really something."

"That's amazing," Milo agreed.

Azer, however, felt differently from the rest. He wasn't feeling awe like the others. Instead, he felt an unplaceable nostalgia, a strange and otherworldly feeling of familiarity for somewhere he's obviously never been—and, after hearing what Saa said, a feeling of doubt.

"Are you sure it's only that old?" Azer pointed, walking up to the shrine and running his fingers over the symbols on the wall. Upon making contact with the wall, he was struck with a bizarre, electric feeling of... something. The familiar feeling had spiked for a fraction of a second and left his heart racing. "It looks a lot older than that."

Azer removed his fingers from the wall and looked at them. They were caked with black dust.

Saa said, "No, I'm pretty sure that's when it was built. It probably looks so old because it hasn't been cleaned for years. But you're right, it is strange... even though it was built by us, nobody knows what the symbols mean."

This made Azer laugh a bit.

"What are you talking about? They're perfectly readable. It's not *that* dirty and old."

There was silence from the others for a moment, and then Azer turned around. They were all smiling at him as if he just said a funny joke.

"What's up? I wasn't being sarcastic."

Their faces slowly transitioned from amusement to doubtful confusion and concern. They were all staring at him.

"But you said you could read them. Is that not what you said?" Saa asked, no longer smiling.

"Because I can." He came to a moment of realization. "Wait, can't you guys read it?"

"No," Saa answered emphatically. "Nobody can. Nobody's ever been able to."

"You're joking! You can't read this?! Here-" he pointed up to the start of a line of symbols- *"'We inscribe this first relic to preserve the knowledge of the Hivanian people and the properties of the world they currently inhabit.'* Can you guys not read that?! It says those exact words! Clearly!"

But they just continued to stare at him, shocked.

"'This historical relic enshrines the known qualities of and is to remain here as a guide in the case of a powerful force called the Magna virus, which the Hivanian people believe is imminent...'"

But then, Azer trailed off, thinking. An incredible realization had hit him. The Magna virus? This virus... there was a deadly virus being described on this shrine. No—it wasn't a shrine at all. It was something different. The symbols described it as a *relic*... but was it really that? Was this wall actually a part of a bigger, complete record of this species and this virus? Would this truly be the answer to their search? Azer turned towards the others, but they were no longer looking at him. Instead, they were staring fixed and mortified at a spot behind him, faces turning pale white.

Raspy breathing came from behind Azer.

A terribly ragged, pale… something… was standing behind Azer, far taller than he. The creature's skin was stretched tight over his bones and appeared almost translucent with sickening whiteness.

A growl came from the ghoul's throat.

"Don't move!" the creature rasped.

Azer stood petrified from fear. It wasn't that he wanted to obey—he was simply paralyzed with terror. Milo's lip quivered, and then-

"GHOUL!"

They all screamed as they ran for their lives, the petrifying spell that had lingered over Azer broken in an instant as he sprinted away. The ghoul yelled as he chased after them.

While stomping over the brickwork surface and crashing into tree branches, Azer could hear the ghoul behind him, shouting words he could barely make out.

"COME BACK HERE!" he said, his deep and gravelly voice damaged. "I'M GOING… YOU!"

The stone-laden ground was now thinning out into the dirt path again, peppered with the shoe prints of the four as they sprinted away.

"THE RELIC!" the ghoul cried, his voice faint now.

Azer slowed, eventually coming to a stop and turning back towards the voice. He no longer heard the ghoul chasing them; the only foot-steps were Grif, Saa, and Milo slowing down as well and approaching him, panting.

"Why… did you stop…?" Grif wheezed.

"I think we already lost him," Saa said.

"No," Azer said finally. "I heard him say something about the relic."

"And that wasn't a ghoul at all!" Saa exclaimed. "That was just a super skinny old man!"

"He certainly looked like a ghoul," Milo said, shivering.

"Wait! Guys!" Azer yelled. "Did nobody else hear what he said?"

"I could hardly make it out. I thought he was just threatening to eat us," Saa answered.

"He mentioned the relic!" Azer yelled again. "That isn't a shrine at all, it's an incredibly old monument! Way older than the earliest colonists! And the relic mentioned the virus Dr. D has been looking for!"

A moment of silence. Grif spoke up.

"Are you sure?"

"Yes! Someone's trying to cover it up by telling everyone it's a shrine! I could read it clearly! Maybe we should go back..."

"No!" everyone else yelled in unison.

"Okay, fine! But, please at least let's come back here tomorrow. I'm sure... I'm sure there's something there."

Azer and Grif went to the shrine first thing next morning. They traversed through neighborhoods, crossing busy streets and eventually passing into a far more wooded and lush path. While expecting to hear rustling leaves on their way, they were instead greeted by faint beeping and the whir of engines, which grew louder and louder until colored tape blocked their paths. A sign read:

CAUTION: CONSTRUCTION IN PROGRESS

Large bulldozers and excavators were tearing at the ground where the shrine had stood, while workers donning reflective vests pointed, shouted, and commanded. Azer and Grif stood, stark still, at the sight. Neither of them spoke a word over the noise. A worker approached them, exhausted and sweaty. He wiped his eyebrow and then spoke:

"What're you kids doing here?"

"Where's the shrine?" Azer asked, ignoring his question.

"We tore it down. The mayor wants to build a parking lot; it's been scheduled for a while now."

Another moment of silence. Azer returned to the spectacle.

"Excuse me..." Grif spoke up, looking haunted. "What happened... was there a man here? By the... shrine?"

The worker didn't speak, but instead pointed to the far side of the clearing, behind an idle piece of construction equipment. It was an ambulance, lights flashing.

"Heart failure, he's already dead," the worker said. "Must have spooked the poor man."

CHAPTER EIGHT:
RUMORS

Mostly sunny. 5mph winds blowing east. Eighty-nine degrees fahrenheit. Clear weather expected all week.

"**D**amnit!"

Dr. D slammed his fists on the table in the center of Team Virga's headquarters. Anger burned in his albino eyes.

"Language," Mrs. Korca warned from a chair, also looking grim. "There's more than just adults here."

"So Nur's shrine being built by the first colonists 80 years ago was a coverup," Delvin said. "How many other of these fictions has he created?"

"I should have expected something like that from him!" Dr. D seethed. "This wasn't an accident or a coincidence! Orbo's got a whole town to build a godda… a stupid parking lot!"

He paced around, unaware of Mrs. Korca's scolding glare. But only moments later she returned to pondering with the rest of Team Virga, Azer and Grif standing nearby, looking tense. Delvin was sitting in a chair by the main table, leg propped up, scratching his chin thoughtfully.

"There's nothing we could have done about it," he said. "Nobody is— I mean, *was* able to read the shrine— there's no way we could have known it had to do with the virus. And, besides, don't we now know that it was, or *is* real?"

Dr. D stopped mid-pace.

"Yes, I suppose we do. And it seems like we can infer that this race of, what were they called again?"

"Hivanians," answered Azer and Grif simultaneously.

"Yes, these Hivanians—they must have been wiped out by the virus. If that's the case, then that can only mean that the Magna virus has been here before."

Azer gulped.

A moment of silence followed. Dr. D stopped pacing. Everyone was lost in thought, in one way or another.

"What are the chances," Delvin started, breaking the silence, "that there is more than one of these relics? Azer, what you read said 'this first relic,' is that correct?"

"Yes, why?"

"Then that could very well mean that there are others. Itell, have you heard of anything Mayor Lindwoter could be hiding? Anything like the relic Azer and Grif saw?"

"I have my suspicions," Dr. D answered without hesitation, following the same train of thought. "I've heard things about the public library on the edge of town, rumors of some kind of secret chamber underneath. Though, up until now, I'd only thought it was just a myth."

"I think we've learned that rumors may not be as fake as we usually make them out to be," Grif mused, shuddering at the thought of the ghoul that chased them the night before. Azer nodded in agreement.

"I can plan a field trip," Dr. D spoke again, "to the public library. It could double as a secret Team Virga mission, digging into the idea of the secret chamber. Though," Dr. D said, looking serious and turning to Azer and Grif, "don't forget that I'm still your principal. Don't let Team Virga get in the way of your learning."

He paused, white eyes fixed on something no one could see, then spoke again without taking his eyes off this point in space.

"If the Magna virus is real, and still out here... then we'll need as much information on it as possible."

"But... it *can't* still be here, right?" Azer said worriedly. "Wouldn't the virus—the Magna—not be able to spread after the Hivanians died? And it seems like that relic we visited was really old, right? Surely it's not still here?"

Dr. D looked seriously at him, his frustration subsided.

"We can only hope not," he said grimly.

Dr. D stood in the middle of the Team Virga laboratory, a large map of the library laid out on the main table.

"It'll be a career discovery exercise," Dr. D started. "I've been meaning to do one for a while now. That's our disguise. A perfectly normal lesson. Once we get to the library, I'll instruct all of the chaperones to have their students pick out a book related to a career they're interested in, for, we'll say, half an hour. And at this point, Azer and Grif, you really will need to follow the lesson. Don't forget, you're students, too. Once everyone's picked out their books, the students will find a reading spot and read whatever they picked out for the rest of the field trip. At that point you all will split from your other non-Team Virga group members and begin looking for any kind of secret object or entrance, any sign of the next relic. Remain in the groups I assigned you while you search, and if you find anything, contact the rest of Team Virga."

"Whose group will you be in?" Grif asked.

"I'm not coming," Dr. D replied simply.

"What? Why?" Azer asked.

"Remember, Mayor Lindwoter doesn't trust me. If he finds me snooping around where another relic might be, who knows what he might do. He could go and destroy all of the others for all we know."

"Why hasn't he already destroyed all of them?" Grif interjected.

"That, I don't know. He's a mystery, too."

"In other news, some exciting events are coming up. We hope you are enjoying the ever-warming weather, because in only three months the great Perihelion festival is starting, hosted by Mayor Lindwoter himself."

A picture of Nur's mayor, plump and jovial, appeared on the television screen inside of Grano's. Azer scowled while Grif simply frowned silently.

"But before that," the newswoman said, the screen changing to an image of the cloud-filled sky, *"the mysterious weather event called The Shades is coming up. The Zystinian government recommends planning and preparing for the annual evacuation that is now less than a month from today. Remember: blockade your doors and windows, board them up if you can, bring all pets and treasured belongings with you during evacuation, and never, ever, be on the ground when it happens."*

The TV turned off. Mr. Grano was holding the remote, looking apprehensive.

"You boys don't need to worry about stuff like that, as long as you're following the evacuation instructions—and trust me, that won't be hard. They're going to be posted everywhere as The Shades gets closer. You'll be fine."

Without the TV on, the only sounds in the diner were mingled conversations from nearby patrons, the hum of the air conditioning, and the whir of an oscillating fan, alternating between blowing on Grif's face and Azer's missing one.

"Hot, eh?" Mr. Grano asked, trying to rectify his previously serious tone.

"Very," Grif replied weakly, staring absentmindedly out the window at the sunlight-covered ground.

"Mr. Grano," Azer started, turning away from the fan's cool breeze, "What's the Perihelion festival?"

"Ah. Yes, it's a festival held by our mayor every summer, once every Manim year, or ten galactic standard years. It's a big deal, since it's so long between each new Manim year. The Perihelion festival celebrates Manim's colonization eighty or so years ago. One of the few good things my brother does for this town," he added scornfully.

"Your brother? Who's your brother?"

"My older brother's the mayor of Nur. Senior to me by a whole thirteen years, but he doesn't act his age at all. We very rarely ever see him in town, even though he claims to be our mayor."

"Your brother's the *mayor?!*" Azer and Grif exclaimed in unison.

"Yes, but I hardly recognize him as the mayor; not many people here really do. That Dr. D down by the Battle Academy does loads more; he might as well be. I don't really see Orbo as a brother to me either, since he's so much older. He moved out when I was five and was elected mayor only two years later."

The school bus made a loud whine as it grinded to a halt in front of the Derecho Public Library. The Battle Academy chaperones ushered the kids out of the bus, some groaning as they were exposed to the sweltering heat. Azer and his class stepped onto the hot pavement and now had a full view of the large, well-kept entrance of the building. Two security cameras, one on each side of the covered entrance, stared down on the entering class, mechanical lenses subtly dilating.

Azer could hardly hide it; he was riddled with anxiety. It would be easy to pay attention during an educational field trip, and it would even have been manageable to follow the orders of a Team Virga mission, but to do both at once, while staying covert? The task seemed impossible.

Delvin stood by the entrance, motioning the stragglers inside, not giving a second glance to Azer or Grif, despite being part of the same mission. His intense, calm demeanor only filled Azer with pangs of worry. And as they entered through the glossy wooden doors, Grif shot him a look of wide-eyed fear that echoed Azer's thoughts perfectly. At least he wasn't alone.

The moment they entered the library, they were hit by a blast of air-conditioning, perhaps a bit too cold for the average person's liking, but just right for a group of overheating students. The inside was dead silent, broken only by the light hum of the air conditioners and muted footsteps. A papery, leathery smell filled the air.

The first thing Azer noticed was that there were more security cameras.

A *lot* of them.

In just about every corner, behind every bookshelf, stationed like insects along the ceiling, were the same type of security camera, each one positioned directly onto the crowd. And with every new camera he noticed, the odds of being able to complete the mission seemed to drop further and further.

Whether subconsciously or not, Azer searched for his fellow Team Virga members. This included Delvin, Mrs. Korca, and Okta, all having been scattered through the incoming crowd of students. He noticed them throwing glances at the ceiling and the security cameras that littered it. Even with faces, they looked a lot calmer than Azer did.

While the chaperones divided the crowd into their designated groups, Azer waved goodbye to Grif and joined his own. His chaperone was Delvin, and his only other group member was an older student he didn't recognize from Delvin's homeroom class. The three of them walked up to the bookshelves silently, and the other student picked up a book, reading it idly.

Azer scanned the shelves for something that caught his attention. Delvin had taken them to the nonfiction section, and he already had his nose buried in *Modern Chemical Innovations Vol. 2.* As he ran a pointer finger over the book spines, Azer stopped on a small, worn book titled *Sights to See in Zysti galaxy.* He pulled it off the shelf and flipped through it.

The first page was part of a two-page spread of a map of Zysti galaxy. Countless dots of varying size littered the page, each one with the planet's name written by it in small, uppercase text. The map was split into quarters by a thick-lined cross, each quadrant numbered.

His first instinct was to find his own planet, Manim. He scanned each quadrant, carefully reading each name until he found it in the lower corner of quadrant 3, far from the center of the galaxy but on the same horizontal plane as Zysti's capital planet, Zephyr. Underneath the planet's name was even smaller text that said:

PG. 173

He flipped to the page without hesitation. It had a large image of Manim taking up most of the top-left corner with a brief description:

> Manim is part of the Relar star system and is one of many planets colonized around the time of the Great Star Push, though it was not made part of the Zystinian Planet Union until several decades after its initial discovery. Since then, Manim has become a rapidly growing hub of interstellar travel and remains an attractive destination to tourists, settlers, and business owners alike.
>
> It features a temperate and livable climate, with lush forests, tall mountains and wide, open plains. Even today, its environment thrives with the presence of its inhabitants, and most of its gorgeous nature remains untouched. It is famous for its annual, planet-wide superstorm that inhabitants call "The Shades."

Curiosity now gripping him, Azer flipped to the section on the Relar star system, where he saw another, more zoomed-in map of the Zysti galaxy. It showed only one or two dozen stars, and each star and planet was labeled clearly. He noted how the named planets looked few and far between in relation to the massive scale of the map he was viewing— *perhaps a result of the Manim deadzone?* He looked at the planets that interested him, flipping to their respective pages and skimming their descriptions. He read about an icy planet inhabited only by its adapted native species, a tropical planet with innumerable islands in lieu of continents, and a volcanic wasteland whose only inhabitants were researchers developing new thermal energy technology.

A thought occurred to Azer as he read, and he quickly flipped to the front of the book. At the bottom of the front page, there was the publication date:

PUBLISHED 3270 ZST

He then flipped forward and found a specific line in the beginning of the book:

While there are just under a hundred different registered civilizations in the Zysti galaxy, tens of thousands of different planets have been discovered, some with life, and many more are being discovered every year!

If this book was published 20 years ago, Azer thought, *then what planets have been discovered since then?* Maybe there was new insight into the deadzone planets.

He located the nearest computer and booted it up, trying to ignore the webcam pointing directly at him. He did a search for an updated map of the Relar star system and wasn't surprised to see a few more planets than before.

Below the first link was a link to a news article from 11 years ago, published by a news station he had never heard of and with an enlarged picture of a half-buried, misshapen skull.

For an instant, something stirred inside him, but it was immediately forgotten.

The article read:

Remains of Unregistered Civilization Discovered on New Planet, Cause of Extinction Unknown

By Ingarus Hukt, 3279 ZST

A team of researchers recently discovered a planet within the Relar star system, dubbed R8-70, featuring indisputable evidence to have once been inhabited by an unregistered species. Innumerable humanoid skeletons are littered among what appears to be the remains of an intelligent species, with worn, destroyed husks of shelters, houses and towns.

Studies are still being conducted, but many experts agree that this planet is part of the mysterious Manim deadzone, an area in and around the Relar star system with a low 10 lifear (lifear: planets with life within fifty light-years), far below Zysti's average 150 lifear. As most life in Zysti is microbial or unintelligent, the remains of an intelligent species on R8-70 proves to be a rare and important finding, especially in the Manim deadzone.

While the cause of the mass extinction remains unknown, scientists have deduced it was not by war or natural disaster. Attempts have been made to identify the species, but in a surprising turn of events, it was discovered that the corpses had no form of DNA present. Numerous theories have circulated as to the reason for their abrupt demise, including a sudden gamma ray burst, an unprecedented solar flare, or, in a more unlikely scenario, an extinction-level weapon deployed by an unknown species.

Dr. Regus Maxim, a Galactic Exobiologist from the Tuxxis Academy of Planetary Sciences, comments on these possibilities:

"The tricky part is the absence of DNA found within the remains," he said in an interview. "A powerful enough solar flare could have caused the destruction we see in R8-70, not to mention bleach the DNA out of the bodies, but it's unlikely an intelligent society could be wiped out all at once by such an event. A gamma ray burst poses problems too: a burst of extinction-level proportions would have been easily foreseen by the Zystinian Department of Cosmic Threats, and any planets in its path would have been warned and therefore discovered. Not to mention, a GRB would have destroyed the planet's atmosphere, which is still intact. Though it is worth noting that the atmosphere is made mostly of methane, which could easily prove to be fatal to a species not adapted to survive it. Though, even then, the DNA problem remains, and atmospheres don't change chemical composition by the day."

When questioned about the potential of an alien attack, Maxim responded saying "such claims are baseless and are designed to start ghost stories among the masses. If we believe rumors like that, then surely it is our society that will fall next."

Azer finished reading, and before he could gather his thoughts, a voice came from across the library aisle. It was Delvin.

"It's been half an hour," he said, "enough book selection, it's time for *reading*."

For a moment, Azer sat in confused silence. Then, feeling stupid, he realized what Delvin was talking about, quickly standing up from his chair and walking to Delvin's side.

Delvin looked briskly from side to side, eyeing the security cameras to ensure no one was looking. He then pulled Azer close and moved behind a bookshelf.

For a moment, it looked as if nothing was happening. Then, Azer noticed a faint, airy hissing sound, barely audible. Delvin still looked as if he was checking the vicinity, but Azer could tell he was up to something.

"What's-"

"Shh," Delvin interrupted. "Stay silent."

It didn't take long for Azer to discover the hissing's source. The holes in the palms of Delvin's hands were circulating air at intense speeds, fast enough for ghostly strands of water vapor to form by the holes' openings.

The hissing then began to change in pitch, and in a slow, seamless transition, the harsh hissing became a low, soft whoosh all around Azer's body.

"While small, there's a blind spot between the cameras here. I had to find somewhere to hide us," Delvin whispered, barely a step above just moving his lips soundlessly.

"Hide us?" Azer echoed, trying to match Delvin's level of quiet. "How are we hidd-"

Then, in a shocking moment of awareness, Azer realized he could no longer see his own body. As he turned to Delvin, Azer realized he couldn't see him, either.

"Don't panic," Delvin said, reading his thoughts. "This is my doing. Look closely, you should be able to see me at least a little bit. But nobody else can."

Azer could, in fact, see miniscule slivers of himself and Delvin behind strands of invisibility. The quiet whooshing continued around them.

"Are we invisible? How are you doing this?"

Delvin now straightened himself again and looked both ways down the library aisle. "I'm circulating the water vapor in the air around us to refract light," he explained. "It flows through the holes in my hands at hypersonic speeds." He then left the aisle, urging Azer to follow. "My Val is wind," he elaborated. "With the holes in my hands, I can control air with atomic precision."

"Now, follow," he whispered again. "And stay close. If you leave my range, your invisibility will fade."

Slowly, Delvin walked deeper into the gargantuan, labyrinthine library, Azer trying his hardest to follow Delvin's translucent image. They strode past a long shelf of books, pressing themselves against the wall as a student passed. Delvin turned a corner, walked down a long hallway, turned another corner, and then came to a closed door. On it was a sign that read:

EMPLOYEES ONLY

Carefully, Delvin put his hand on the doorknob and pulled the door open, so slowly it was hard to tell it was opening at all. Once open, his ghostly figure urged Azer inside.

Behind the door was another large room, rectangular in shape, with expansive lines of books along tall shelves. But instead of being organized and user-friendly like the rest of the library, the books were worn and full of labels. Wooden tables were pushed up against the walls of the room, covered with mangled books, glue, and obscure tools. An office was stationed at the back of the room, with blinds down over the windows but warm light peeking through. This room revealed the machinations behind the scenes of the library—repair, stocking, and, according to a sign on one shelf, books that were forbidden to read.

"Is this it?" Azer whispered over the silence.

"I'm doubtful," Delvin replied. "The relic wouldn't be so large, and look so modern. Nor would it be this easy to get to."

Azer scanned the vicinity for any sign of the relic while following Delvin's side. They weaved through the rows of bookshelves and checked under tables, all to no avail. Azer's hope was beginning to dwindle and his mind was drifting.

"Delvin, why did you join Team Virga?" Azer inquired.

Delvin seemed ready for the question. "I was curious about the world, just like you are. A scientist. I came here from off-planet, one of the many scientists who came to Manim to study The Shades. I noticed that Manim's mysteries didn't end at The Shades, either—there are a thousand little enigmas about this planet. And while they may not be connected—each could have its own natural explanation, of course—if those mysteries were connected by some unseen force, I'd want to discover it. I'm not religious, but I think that force would be my idea of God. Itell saw that and took me in."

Delvin carefully slid a cabinet away from a wall before inspecting it and finding nothing.

"You know what's funny?" Delvin said. "I want to dedicate my entire life to science and discovery. That's all that matters to me. But if I ended up left behind during The Shades, I don't think I'd be afraid. Just seeing the force behind all of these mysteries would be worth dying for. Don't you think so?"

Azer didn't know if he knew the answer to the question.

"Can we check the office?" Azer suggested, fleeing the topic.

Delvin obliged and made his way towards the office, Azer in tow. He put a hand on the doorknob and pulled.

"It's locked," Delvin whispered, and then put his palm over the key-hole. A quiet, high-pitched whistle sang from the hole in his hand, and with a tiny click, he turned the doorknob and pulled the door open.

"Just a pin tumbler," Delvin pointed. "I can use the air inside the lock to manipulate the pins into the right orientation."

Towers of papers and documents, all lit by a circular light overhead, met the invisible intruders as the door creaked open. There was a large, ornate wood desk pressed against the far wall, littered with every type of office equipment. The office, compared to the previous room, was much smaller, just large enough to comfortably accommodate a single person, cramped by the countless documents stacked everywhere. Despite this, two seats stood at the main desk.

Flush with the ground, Azer noticed the edge of a small groove underneath a leg of the desk, covered by a worn old carpet that sat underneath the desk's chair. He leaned down and ran a finger over the groove, picking up a layer of dust.

He lifted a portion of the carpet to see that the groove continued along the floor, forming a square nearly a meter in length and width along the hard floor. Along one of its corners was another, smaller square. Ten different numbers adorned the smaller square, each labeling a thumb-nail-sized button.

"Delvin," he whispered as quietly as he could while staying audible, "is this it?"

Delvin, too, leaned down and ran his fingers along the edges of what was apparently a hatch. Moments later, Azer could hear a whoosh, and the dust covering the hatch flew in every direction.

"It won't open," Delvin stated. "It's airtight."

Wordlessly, Azer understood Delvin wanted him to try and open it manually. As tightly as he could, Azer gripped the edges of the groove and attempted to lift, S.R. flowing freely through his muscles.

For a few seconds, no results. And then, a heart-stopping, audible *crack* rang out deep in the floor.

"Stop!" Delvin hissed. "You're going to destroy the library before this lifts!"

Azer released his grip from the edges of the hatch. Delvin was right—the hatch was built deeply and immovably into the foundation of the library, and any strength he could muster wouldn't be enough to get it open.

"It's passcode locked," Delvin declared. "Electronic. I won't be of use here."

"Can we try random passwords?" Azer suggested, acutely aware of how stupid he sounded.

"If it's a four-digit code, then we have a one in ten thousand chance of getting it right."

"Can... does anyone else in Team Virga have a Val that could help?"

"I'm afraid not. Destroying it would be difficult, even for someone like Itell, and Okta's dual minds are for strategizing, not hacking. We have no choice but to find the passcode. For now, let's contact the rest. We-"

Then, suddenly, a creak rang out from the entrance to the maintenance room. Azer immediately straightened, tuned to the noise. Delvin, wide-eyed, motioned for Azer to follow him out.

Standing in the entrance to the maintenance room was a middle-aged woman dressed in an impeccably neat outfit, her narrow, sharp eyes magnified in intensity by her rectangular gold glasses. It was the seldom-seen head librarian of the building. She was scanning the room vigilantly, only pausing momentarily for her eyes to unfocus and soften in seemingly random intervals. Delvin and Azer stood just outside the office, trying to move away from the scene without making a sound.

Without warning, she began to stride confidently toward the aisle of books. Delvin's almost completely transparent figure quickened his pace, urging Azer along, trying to lead them around the aisle.

Then, as quickly as she had started, the librarian stopped in her tracks and stood. A pause, then she whipped around and sprinted back the way she came. Delvin, surprised at this strange movement, could only watch, Azer not far behind.

The librarian then turned down Azer and Delvin's aisle and continued sprinting directly towards them.

Adrenaline pumped through the two as they fled at equal speed.

"Can she see us?!" Azer asked.

"It's impossible!" his voice whispered in response. "I've refracted the light only to let you see me, and barely so!"

The librarian continued her pursuit, speeding down the aisles at a pace beyond her stature. Delvin dove behind a gap in the bookshelves, Azer nearly missing the cue before taking refuge by Delvin's side. The librarian suddenly slowed in pace, before stopping once more.

"I know you're here," she croaked, her voice deep and eerily soft, as though talking to a small child. Her soft tone poorly concealed a note of malice. Delvin flinched next to Azer, but continued to stay completely silent. Azer then heard a muted sound coming from all around him.

"This is Delvin. I'm muting the air around us. It takes a huge amount of my Val's power, but by no means can we be found out. The mission can't be failed. I'm talking to you by vibrating the air around you to create sound waves. Stay still and continue to remain silent."

It was a voice without tone or characteristics, like a spoken whisper. The voice sounded vaguely like Delvin's, but the words were embedded within a breeze-like whoosh. Azer heeded his command, baffled and amazed at the versatility of Delvin's wind powers.

"I'm sure you're well aware this is a restricted area, the office espe-cially," the librarian said, striding along Azer and Delvin's aisle. "Only two people are allowed in there, just Mayor Orbo and I." She then added, with a sneer, "Could you be the nosy no-gooders he warned me about?"

She continued to walk down the aisle, approaching their location. Azer tensed up. She walked right by their position, Azer unconsciously releasing the tension in his body before she stopped again.

"Found you."

In a lightning-fast movement, she whipped back around and thrust a hand towards Delvin's chest. Her hand penetrated Delvin's swirling cloak of wind, breaking it apart as the bizarre formation of breeze and water vapor split apart around her hand, revealing in full Delvin's mortified expression. Her open palm on Delvin's chest now, she clenched his collar and yanked him out of his refuge.

"This isn't the kind of place for teachers to be snooping around," she said acidly, pulling him along the aisle towards the entrance. "I wonder how you found out about this place... Regardless, you're going to be held for questioning. Mayor Orbo would love to talk to you."

Azer was bursting with things to say and scream as Delvin was taken away, but held himself back. Miraculously, for some unknown reason, Azer was spared, and he wasn't going to waste that chance. As long as he was unknown, his knowledge of the hidden door in the office was safe. The air still swirling around Azer's body told him Delvin hadn't given up on him yet, the air's quality full of Delvin's resolve. As soon as the door closed, he dove out of cover with the little, fading invisibility he had left.

Azer joined Grif's side at the entrance inside a disorganized group of students buzzing with words and rumors. He tried his hardest to hide his exhaustion and stress, having narrowly avoided being caught several times. Grif looked at him with worry and apprehension.

"What's happening?" Azer tried.

But Grif didn't need to answer. He pointed over the sea of students' heads at a group of adults. It was the head librarian accompanied by several police officers, Delvin's expressionless face visible behind one of them, in cuffs and looking dire. Azer felt a pang of worry and guilt. The librarian stepped up towards the students and cleared her throat.

"We have apprehended a suspicious figure inside the library. He will be going to the police station for questioning. The police suspect this man was not alone in his suspicious activity. Did any one of you happen to see this man with anyone else today in the library?"

The room was ghastly silent, the cool, musty air ripe with tension and fear. Sensing this, the librarian spoke again.

"You will not be arrested, just questioned. Now, again, does anyone here have any information about this man's activities today?"

Azer's heart was pounding against his shirt. How could it have gone so wrong? It felt like the mission had succeeded, but it hadn't. They had lost an important member of Team Virga. Azer didn't dare give away any sign he was affiliated. He could feel Delvin's will inside him, and it said to *not let the mission fail.*

Silently, frustratedly, the librarian returned to her spot next to the police, talking to them inaudibly before they walked out of the door, Delvin in tow.

The bus ride home was ripe with commotion among the students, and the news of a Battle Academy teacher being arrested for suspicious activity had spread like wildfire. Everyone talked about their theories and ideas as to what had happened. And all of them were so far from the truth.

Sitting quietly with Grif, he didn't know whether to be upset and who to be upset at, and if he should or shouldn't feel guilty, or regretful, or hopeful. His mind burned with questions about what had happened inside the library—what was really behind the trapdoor? How had the head librarian seen through Delvin's invisibility? And, incredibly, how had Azer made it out of there scot-free?

"It's worth noting," Grif started, "that we found the relic. Did you hear what she was talking about? You and Delvin found something that wasn't supposed to be seen. Don't beat yourself up about it."

"But-"

"Survivor's guilt. That's what you're feeling. We found what we needed to find, save for that password. And don't worry about Delvin. We'll figure something out. In the meantime, we should be more worried about The Shades."

CHAPTER NINE:
THE SHADES

HAZARDOUS WEATHER EVACUATION NOTICE: BOARD GOVERNMENT-PROVIDED EVACUATION SHIPS IN A QUICK BUT ORDERLY FASHION.

The TV that Azer often spent his time watching blared this message over and over—with bold red text on black, the Zystinian government's insignia was faintly visible in the background.

"Already?" Grif said, coming into the room. "I didn't think they were evacuating us until the afternoon!"

"I don't think they can risk it," Azer replied. "Imagine being that person piloting one of the spaceships and you realize someone's been left behind."

"Yeesh." Grif screwed up his face. "Though I wouldn't want to be one of the people left behind, either."

"I thought that hasn't happened since Haise?"

"Eh. Still."

Azer made his way out of the house, not exactly knowing why; did he want to see his surroundings one last time before he evacuated? Did he still feel troubled by the events at the library a few days ago? Was it because the sky was still so clear, the weather still so nice? He didn't feel like an unsurvivable meteorological event was approaching, in fact, just the opposite—today felt more welcoming and beautiful than ever. It felt as if nature itself was winking at Azer happily.

He sat on the front steps, letting the sun warm his unnaturally gray, dark skin, before Grif opened the door.

"Enjoying it while it lasts, I assume?" Grif asked, reading Azer's thoughts.

"Yup. Hard to believe what's about to come. Are they sure that The Shades is happening today? I don't see a single cloud."

Grif frowned. "Me either. Maybe they're just evacuating early?"

"You'd think we'd at least see some difference in the sky though, right?"

"Let's just get to the school—it's not worth worrying about."

They'd been instructed—more times than they could count—to attend school normally and on time today; the Battle Academy would take charge in making sure everyone there was evacuated properly. That's where the evacuation ships would be. Azer and Grif got to the bus, full of anticipation and anxiousness.

When they arrived at their homeroom class, it was buzzing with excitement. Their classmates and their classmates' parents had gathered, filling the room. One wall of the room was occupied by fingerprint-scanning machines adorned with the Zystinian insignia. Azer and Grif checked themselves in by scanning their thumbs. Azer found himself wondering if Haise had checked herself in before disappearing ten years ago during the last Shades.

Waiting in the classroom disheartened Azer. Every student had at least one parent or guardian present with them, ensuring their safety and ready and excited to spend the next day with them on an orbiting spaceship. Neither he nor Grif had parents, making Azer feel even more distant from his classmates. But he didn't need a parent to make sure he got on, anyway—he could take care of himself. Azer and Grif talked with one another as a voice on the PA called classes to be evacuated by grade, counting down. When their year was called, the mass of people began to flow out of the classroom, Azer and Grif with them.

"Wait for me, Kovaki."

The raspy voice inside the classroom made Azer and Grif stop in their tracks. They turned back around, leaving the flow of evacuees, only to see nobody inside.

Except for a symbol-encrusted journal lying in the middle of the classroom.

Azer rushed over to Haise's journal, picking it up and flipping through the pages in disbelief. He hadn't seen the thing in over three years. Grif appeared next to him, in a state of wordless shock.

"How did this get here?" Grif asked as if Azer knew. "I thought it was locked in the-"

"The teacher's office. I know. We haven't seen this since we broke into the school. Why the hell is it here now?!"

Azer flipped through the pages again, reconfirming he was holding the real thing. It was still worn and old, made of blackish leather and with the gold-encrusted Nova Noctis symbol on its front. It was undoubtedly real.

Or it was, until it began to dissolve into a thin gray dust between his fingers.

The door to the classroom closed, and a tiny *click* told them someone had just locked it.

The two started pounding on the door, shouting for help, but the figures of their classmates had already receded down the hall.

"HEY!" Grif bellowed. "LET US OUT!"

"What do we do?!" Azer asked, panicked.

"Wait- I'm sure someone's gonna find us. HEY! HEY!" he resumed yelling, his mouth by the ground, trying to reach his voice through the spot between the door and the floor.

They waited for a moment, looking frantically down each side of the hall for someone to come rescue them, when-

"Boo."

Azer and Grif jumped at the voice behind them. Azer could have sworn he'd launched himself several feet in the air with the shock.

They both heard a familiar, cackling laugh from behind them. It was Copycat, almost in tears from amusement.

"You- eh- you two were so funny... Oh man..."

"Copycat, I SWEAR!" Grif roared over Copycat's laughter. "Don't do that! This isn't even close to the time or place!"

After his laugh ebbed away slightly, Copycat spoke again.

"You guys- you guys actually thought you were gonna get left behind!"

"Let us out already or we will be!" Grif yelled.

"Okay, okay. Yeah, I'll let us out." He pulled a key from his pocket and put it in the door. It creaked open.

"Where'd you get that?" Azer asked. "The key?"

"Stole it," Copycat said nonchalantly. "Couldn't pass up an opportunity to scare you like this. I'd have done it with a clone, but I had to see it in person. Totally worth it."

"I swear," Azer mumbled, "you're such a lying, stealing little prick..."

"Hey, you want me to lock you back in? I just let you out. It's done, okay?"

They walked the halls of the Battle Academy towards the exits, Azer's ebbing adrenaline being replaced by shame and anger.

"How did you like my journal trick? I knew it would freak you guys out," Copycat boasted.

"How did you know about Haise?" Azer asked. "That was supposed to be-"

"A secret? Yeah. You two aren't that sneaky. You already broke open the lock three years ago. I read the notebook and see why you guys were so eager to find it. That's some spooky shit."

"Aren't you supposed to be with your dad? Students were supposed to be evacuated with their parents so they wouldn't get left behind."

Copycat didn't reply, instead giving Azer a contemptuous look before staring straight ahead.

"Which evacuation ship is ours?" Grif asked.

"We had number 26, but I just made us miss that. I'm not trying to kill us, don't worry. We'll just hop on number 27 instead, let them know we got on the wrong ship. It'll be fine."

They reached the end of the hall and stepped outside. The weather still looked flawless. However, Azer noticed, there were no other people around. Grif seemed to notice, too, as he gazed around with a frown.

"The evacuation ships should be that way-" Copycat pointed past the school, an area a ways away that was blocked by tall trees.

Azer's worry was growing. He trusted Copycat to guide them back, but something was off. He was longing to hear the sound of another voice, but no such sound was anywhere.

They turned the corner, passing a small brick building, and moved past the towering trees, only to find an empty, very large field surrounded by more trees. The grass, in many rectangular, house-sized shapes, was flattened down, and scorch marks were visible in large clumps of blackened foliage.

"I- it's fine," Copycat reassured, but his own voice was tainted with worry now. "I know that's not all of them, I'm sure of it. There's some more evacuation ships by the parking lot—"

The three boys looked up. Dark, silvery-gray spaceships littered the sky, putting black spots on the white clouds. They were receding into the atmosphere, away from view.

Grif let out a roar, grabbing Copycat by the collar and slamming him against a wall of the small brick building.

"YOU *IDIOT!*" he half-yelled, half-screamed.

"I'M SORRY!" Copycat cried, utter terror struck across his face. "I DIDN'T THINK-"

"YOU DIDN'T THINK WHAT? HUH? WAS KILLING US YOUR GRAND PLAN? YOUR NEW SICK PRANK?!"

Copycat didn't say anything; he seemed to be lost for words. Tears filled his eyes.

"THE SHADES IS COMING!" Grif screamed in Copycat's face. "AND YOU'VE JUST STUCK US HERE!"

Azer's heart dropped straight through his body. His stomach was now filled to the brim with nauseating fear. Distilled dread pumped through his heart, now beating madly. This had to be a dream. *This is a dream*, he told himself, his head spinning violently.

But the sun on his skin—the heavy breathing of Grif nearby—the tear-filled gasps of Copycat—they all felt too real. The clouds in the sky, the evacuation ships passing through and over them now, felt too real. The empty field felt too real.

They were going to die.

The dread filling every atom in Azer's body began to weaken his legs. He felt like he was going to pass out, fall over, scream in terror. But he couldn't—he was just stuck there, paralyzed with fear.

The three boys stood there for a moment, processing what had happened. Their breathing slowed. Grif was the first to speak.

"We need to hide. We need to do something. We need to get away," he ordered, his voice shaking.

And then it felt like Azer had never run faster. The three sprinted away to the neighborhoods, where the windows were boarded and the walls were reinforced. The beautiful, flawless sky felt taunting now, the absence of looming storm clouds somehow more terrifying than seeing them. He looked desperately into the sky for the source of the storm, just so he'd know from where it'd come. Every small breeze put him yet more on edge and doubled his panic. Every cell of his being was anticipating the storm.

By the time they reached the neighborhood, Azer noticed something off about the air. It was eerily darker, and a tension was palpable in the atmosphere, as if something invisible covering the whole planet was about to snap in two. It gave Azer a deep-seated feeling of unignorable anxiety.

Azer, Grif, and Copycat reached a neighbor's house, its windows and doors covered with thick metal plates. They stepped up to the porch and, without hesitation, Grif said:

"Break it open."

Azer gripped the steel handle and focused his spinning mind. His S.R. made his skin begin to burn. With an enormous tug, he ripped the steel door off of its bolts and bust down the wooden door behind. They stepped in the house and gathered themselves, sitting down in heaps.

"Okay," Grif said, pacing, his eyes full of fear and his face dripping with sweat. "Nobody's ever survived The Shades. Nobody's ever had their bodies found." His voice was breaking now. "But we're not gonna go out like that. I'm not going out like that. If we're gonna die, we're gonna go out fighting."

"Azer," Grif said, turning his face to Azer's missing one. "That girl Haise was the last one stuck down here during The Shades, right?"

"Yeah…"

"We're not going quietly with whatever Haise saw or was seeking out. And I know for sure that nobody who's been stuck down here has been half as determined as we are to stay alive. We're gonna survive, or we're gonna die trying."

The boys listened to Grif, and determination began to slowly replace the panic. Grif was right. There was no point in cowering in fear.

"I- I'll go outside." Azer said. "We should go outside for now before the storm starts. I want to at least see what's coming. I want to face it."

Steely determination began to appear in Copycat's eyes as well. They silently followed Azer outside and looked up at the sky.

The air was still tense, but, feeling the breeze on his skin, Azer noticed something else different about it. A moist coldness was in the air, prickling and poking at his exposed hands and neck. The sun no longer felt warm and comforting—its distorted light only served to make him feel colder somehow.

And, as if reading his thoughts, a powerful breeze of cool air blew over them. The wind was unfittingly cold, as if it had been delivered from somewhere far away, an icy essence in the breeze.

Above the nearby houses and trees, inside the darkening, distorted blue sky, thick clouds began to poke out. Azer walked further up the hill to get a better look.

It was as if there was an impossibly tall, black-gray barrier, stretching to the top of the atmosphere and wide enough to swallow the entire town a hundred times over. The dark clouds, an eerie green tinting their edges, were forming a wall that layered on top of itself, over and over, approaching them slowly. The clouds had a dense weight to them, as if whatever got in the way of their expanding path of sluggish destruction would get annihilated.

Azer realized immediately that what he had thought before was wrong—this was far worse than the unsettling silence and suspiciously good weather. He much preferred the quiet to the dark, rumbling hum of the wall of clouds above. Distant thunder echoed across the entire town like a voice.

"Let's go inside," Copycat said, his voice sounding like all the moisture in his mouth had evaporated.

On the way in, the breeze began to grow, cold wisps of watery air rushing by at an increasing speed. The sun was shining as bright as before, but the sunlight on his skin was chilling.

They slammed what was left of the wooden door behind them, and the three immediately split up. Grif was finding flashlights and emergency equipment, Copycat was attempting to fix the door, and Azer found an unboarded window through which to watch the storm.

Although the tempest was horrifying to watch, it was mesmerizing in a hypnotic way. The way the rolling clouds toppled over each other, the way the sunlight progressively diminished. Azer watched for a while, chin on the windowsill, while the clattering of Copycat and Grif filled the room behind him.

And soon, the soft patter of rain on the window joined the sounds of clatter. Thick, clear drops of water left splattering circular mist on the glass where they hit. Darkness was spreading outside, sunlight slowly blocked by dense clouds.

After less than a minute, everything went dark. It was as if someone had flipped a switch and turned day to night. The lights in the house were the only thing warding off the impending darkness now.

The rain intensified, the drops hitting the window at increasingly higher speeds. Copycat and Grif were more attentive now, taking occasional glances out of the rain-splattered window where Azer sat.

"With all that wind," Grif started, his voice low and serious, "we should be careful. Azer, let us know if anything happens."

And Grif was right—the wind was intensifying, great sheets of rain falling and being pushed around, forming fabric-like patterns on the street as they fell. The water pouring out of the sky bounced and dissipated as it hit the neighboring roofs and pounded harder on the window. This went on for a while, the wind speeds growing higher and higher, until, at last, a bright yellow-white light filled the sky for an instant.

"Lightning," Azer said out loud, half announcing and half surprised. Copycat and Grif looked up from what they were doing, flashlights and emergency supplies in hand, and stared out the window warily.

Only a few seconds later, a great shaking of thunder rattled the outside of the house, and the window's glass wobbled. The dread in Azer's heart seemed to double.

The storm, with lighting now dotting the pour of rain, continued to intensify, seemingly exponentially. The wind roared and slammed yet bigger drops of water against the window, a constant thumping in the room.

Trees, lining the front of yards and standing behind the houses, swayed uncontrollably. They leaned and leaned, far further than Azer thought possible. It was peaceful in an eerie way, watching the chaos outside while safe and dry inside.

Though the window was fogging and the hazy rain was turning everything cloudy and blue, Azer saw something approaching. Something, a dark blue-gray mass on the horizon, was growing larger and coming closer down the street. Though it was moving incredibly fast, it almost looked like a person.

But as it got closer, Azer realized it wasn't a person at all. It was a colossal tree branch, tumbling and flying down the street, riding the torrent like a sail. And it was headed straight for Azer's window.

"GET OUT!" Azer bellowed as loud as his body would allow. "RUN! GET OOOOUT!"

Copycat and Grif sprinted out of the door, frantic and as shocked by Azer's yelling as if they'd been struck by the lightning.

"GET OU-"

With a deafening crash, the massive branch ripped open the wall in an explosion of destruction, shooting all the way through the house and embedding itself halfway through the other side. Whipping wind and rain tore open the newly-made wounds in the walls, and the storm blasted through freely. Drywall and furniture lay in shambles all over the tattered house.

The three boys were outside on the front steps now, fully in the elements. The storm was no longer something to be watched in the distance—The Shades was here. The wind was deafeningly loud, and the rain was hitting them so fast that the drops were painful to the skin. They had to lean almost all of their weight against the wind.

"We've got to get to shelter!" Grif roared over the wind. "Stick together!"

They sprinted as fast as they could through the rain-filled streets and put their arms up to block the incoming debris, stumbling, the gusts threatening to push them over. Azer was filled with adrenaline, and the chaos felt as hyper-real as if he were using his S.R.

They approached another house, but nearby power lines were whipping around violently and sending sparks through the air. They struggled to the house next door, but a neighboring chimney had smashed into it, leaving a gaping hole in its side.

The three stayed as close as possible to one another and searched desperately for a sheltered house through the blinding wind and rain. After finding yet another ruined house, Grif stopped in his tracks.

"I HAVE AN IDEA!" he shouted over the deafening maelstrom, facing Azer and Copycat. "WE NEED TO GO TO OUR HOUSE!"

"WHY?!" Copycat yelled just as a bolt of lightning struck a ways away, illuminating everything with false daylight before decaying.

"WE'RE- MORE- FAMILIAR- WITH- IT!" Grif enunciated as best as possible, while a powerful gust of wind made the three wobble and readjust their stances. "IT MIGHT BE SAFE!"

"WHAT?! NO! LET'S ... WE HAVE TO GO TO THE SCHOOL INSTEAD!" Copycat roared angrily.

"ARE YOU CRAZY?! IT'LL BE DEMOLISHED!"

"COME WITH ME!" Copycat bellowed over the storm, now trudging off and beckoning for them to come. "IT'S GONNA BE SAFE!"

"IT WON'T! YOU'VE SEEN! YOU'VE SEEN HOW MUCH DAMAGE IS BEING DONE!"

"THEN WHY WILL YOUR HOUSE BE BETTER?!"

Grif was growing increasingly frustrated.

"BECAUSE WE KNOW THE AREA!"

"COPYCAT!" Azer yelled, joining in over the noise. "TRUST US! IT'LL BE SAFER!"

Copycat glared at the both of them with apparent distrust, water dripping down his soaked face. Then, without shouting, he said:

"Why do your ideas count more than mine? Why in the world are you just always right?!"

Grif's face contorted into disbelief. "You- what? Copycat, this isn't the time! Just come with us! It's safer where we're going!"

"WHAT ABOUT MY IDEA THEN, HUH?!" Copycat was back to shouting, rage mixed in with his panic. "WHY ARE YOU ALWAYS RIGHT BUT NOT ME?! WHAT MAKES YOU SO SPECIAL?!"

"THIS ISN'T ABOUT BEING SPECIAL!" Grif bellowed, louder than ever. "THIS IS LIFE OR DEATH!"

Copycat's wet face went white. He looked at Azer and Grif with fury and muttered something under his breath.

"You're just like… hate you."

Then he sprinted off.

"COPYCAT! COME BACK!" Grif shouted. "COPYCAT!"

"COPYCAT!" Azer yelled, joining Grif in the frantic shouts. After he had disappeared into the roaring wind and rain, they stopped.

"Dammit!" Grif said, stomping a foot in the ground. But before he could say another word, another piece of wood shrapnel was hurling their way.

Lightning wounded the sky with a snap and the two ran as fast as they could back home through the pandemonium. Every strike of sun-hot electricity illuminated the rain-filled air, filling it with fleeting light. Rain drops were now indistinguishable from the flying shrapnel; both were hitting the boys at such speed that they stung terribly, rippling their skin on impact.

The clouds, shooting by, spun rapidly and formed bizarre formations. Some swirled into tornado-like shapes before inverting themselves and forming a depression in the storm. Some clouds seemed to be turning sideways, and others spun and stirred as if someone above was dipping their hands in. It was unlike anything that seemed real or possible, like a fever dream taken form.

By the time Azer and Grif had made it into their neighborhood, the storm had fully evolved into this new, bizarre form. Wind roared in every possible direction, up, down, north, south, and the lightning arced and glowed in shapes they'd never seen before. They tore down the familiar streets, Azer trying as hard as he could not to look up at the sky.

Then a thought entered his mind. Azer remembered Kovaki's face, the pages of Haise's notebook. *Was God in the sky?*

The urge and curiosity couldn't be withheld any longer, and Azer gazed up. The sky was spinning, giving the sickening sensation that the whole world was rotating and falling away.

Azer tripped, dazed by the storm, and splashed into the flooding street. Hot pain swam in his mind. His knee had been terribly injured. He turned behind him to see blood seeping into the flood water—a fracture. Grif, unaware of Azer's injury, continued to run.

"GRIF!" Azer shouted as loud as he could, pain welling up in his body.

Grif, faintly hearing Azer's cry, stopped in his tracks, slipping slightly in the ever-pouring rain that filled the streets. Fear igniting his eyes, he began running back towards Azer.

But as he did, something strange began to happen. Blue light sparked out of the ends of whipping, mangled power lines and the remaining metal gutters of nearby houses. Azer could only watch, too distracted by the sight to notice that his soaked hair began to try and stand on end, and too focused on his pain to feel and hear the crackling of electricity all around him.

Grif, however, knew these were telltale signs of an imminent lightning strike right over them. He sprinted faster towards his fallen friend, and as the impossibly bright glow of lightning began to pierce the clouds overhead, Grif stopped, braced his stance, and threw his arm into the air. The lightning struck.

In an instant, blinding white light filled the town, nature's primordial force of electricity exploding the atmosphere apart. Millions of volts coursed into his hand, down his wrist, into his arm—the 50,000 degree heat of the coin-sized charge instantly vaporizing the beads of sweat and rain on Grif's skin into steam in explosions that tore apart his sleeve. It ran through his body, passing through his internal organs, before finally entering his left leg and traveling out of his soaked sneaker, breaking the sole apart as the charge grounded.

The air shook and rumbled across the town, the strike having expanded and contracted the atmosphere at supersonic speed. The flash left as quickly as it came, and Grif's body was left in the same position as before he was hit, now smoking. His sleeve began to catch fire, but the relentless rain halted its spread.

His body used to withstanding and producing electricity, Grif was spared from the worse effects of the lightning strike, his muscles and brain unharmed. But the burns against his skin screamed with pain, and the deafening boom left him dizzy. His consciousness slipped for a moment. About to fall, Grif slammed his injured foot into the rain-filled streets, stabilizing himself. He approached Azer and leaned down, his burnt hand outstretched.

Wordlessly, Azer took it. Both teetered on their feet, Grif's head still spinning and his burns still scorched, Azer's broken leg begging not to be upright. But within the endless maelstrom, the chaos of nature's finest weapon, they could do nothing but proceed further, into safety—to their home, should it still stand.

Azer and Grif, hardly able, trudged their way through floodwater, wires, and shrapnel, further and further into their neighborhood, until their house was in sight.

The turbulently swirling clouds crowned their home, now glowing with endless shades of colors. Behind the veil of thick, dark water vapor shone green light, a flash of red, and a low, droning blue. It was impossible to take in all of the sights at once. It was faint before, but now, finally, The Shades was beginning to show its true colors.

Nearly every house around Azer and Grif's was in tatters, the only pieces still standing being brick walls or the skeletal remains of plumbing. They walked up the rain-sodden steps of their home and stepped inside with relief, only to notice a horrible sight—the wall across their front door was torn open, rainy wind rushing by at high speed, ripped drywall hanging on by threads. Whether by exhaustion or a sense of desolation at the sight, Grif fell to his knees.

"He was right," Grif resounded. The remaining shelter quieted the tempest outside enough for him to be audible. "Who was I kidding? Our house can't withstand The Shades. Nowhere's safe. The Battle Academy was probably our only choice."

Azer didn't know what to say at first.

"Our- our house is still a lot safer! Grif, our house is the only one still standing in the whole neighborhood! It's our only chance!"

Grif looked at Azer, defeat in his eyes, until he suddenly focused on something behind him, horror filling his face. Azer turned around to see what was happening.

Through the gaping hole in the house, the sky had changed again. The clouds no longer flowed and swirled rapidly; instead, they had stabilized into a flat shape at the base of the storm. The winds were slowing down dramatically, the rain slowly thinning to a drizzle. The glowing colors in the clouds had dulled, becoming desaturated, slowly fading to a low white radiance.

Nearly invisible divots and lumps dotted the canopy of clouds, each divot made of wind spinning at incomprehensible speed. The infinite pockets of revolving air at the cloud's base slowly began to descend, each breaking off of the main cloud with a tiny, brief glow of colored light, like a farewell. The shapes of air and vapor, spinning blindingly fast, descended en masse from the planet-coating cloud, falling in a staggered, slow-moving rain.

The endless movement and turbulence in the clouds had all been concentrated and condensed into these spinning shapes, about to reach the ground.

And as they approached, their shape changed further. No longer were they indiscernible blobs. As they fell softly out of the sky, they thinned or expanded, steadily morphing into a familiar form: almost human.

Cylinders became arms, thinning and splitting into an imitation of detached, floating fingers, ambiguous and ethereal. The top of the shape pinched and split, floating just barely above the body, becoming edged, diamond, or pyramidal, or something in-between. The almost-limbs floated apart from each other, connected by some unseen force. When each being was finally formed, it glowed with a remnant of the colored light that had once existed in the now-dormant storm.

But they *were* the storm.

They were The Shades.

When each of the countless Shades made landfall, the water and mist on the ground vaporized and swirled around it. Now that they were inside the remains of the town, Azer could see their staggering size. Each Shade was easily more than ten feet tall, some more than a dozen. They gazed around with hazy eyes.

The Shades began to roam the ruined town, floating inches off the ground, hovering around the land slowly but with purpose. Seemingly meaningless things would prompt them to extend a swirling arm towards an object and run their fingers over it, or turn something over without touching it, or stop abruptly before continuing their bizarre journey. Despite their aimlessness, no Shade came into contact with another, no path ever crossing, no patch of passed earth ever revisited.

Azer and Grif watched the spectacle with dumbfounded awe and terror. The living yet inanimate creatures appeared not to have noticed them yet. They could only wait in their ruined house helplessly and watch.

After a few moments of watching the creatures roam, the two came to another terrifying realization. When a Shade touched something with its ghostly limbs, whatever was touched would be completely erased. A Shade passing by their house came across a rumbling generator. It stopped briefly before continuing along its path. As it passed through the generator, with a sharp and high-pitched noise, the generator was reduced to atoms, ripped apart by the torrential winds that made up the Shade's body. It then turned and began to glide towards Azer and Grif.

Azer heard a shout, followed by scattered sounds of movement. Trudging through the rubble, only a hundred feet from the boys, was the cult leader Kovaki, deeply injured but with a look of wonder on her face. Her arm was severed and was hanging over her shoulder, but she hardly seemed to care. She was fixed on the Shade's presence.

"I knew I was right!" she shouted. "Haise! You've led me to salvation!"

When Kovaki began to move towards the Shade, it abruptly halted in its path.

"Take me, my lord! Take me from this wo-"

When Kovaki moved again, in an abrupt movement, the Shade swung its detached arm through Kovaki, leaving her instantly and utterly erased.

Gathering will and energy, fighting past his terror, Azer uttered to Grif in a whisper.

"We can't move," he said, the Shade growing closer and larger. "It-senses- movement. Only movement. Everything that moves is... gone..."

He let his voice grow quieter as the Shade began to steadily occupy the space in front of Azer and Grif's gaping wall. It approached with purpose. Azer froze, fear paralyzing him as much as it protected him.

The Shade entered the gap. It was close enough for the boys to take in its full appearance. Its ethereal limbs were well-defined, but the edges of its body seemed to fade into the background. Despite the unfathomably fast speed of the air spinning within and around it, the Shade remained quiet, with a low, almost voice-like hum ringing through the air. The acidic stench of ozone filled the room as it entered, only broken by the smell of the cold, clean wind and water that made up its being. Despite being opaque, the familiar colored glow resided inside it, pulsing, ebbing and flowing. Two fathom-deep eyes glowed with the same color, brighter and more pronounced.

As the boys stood inanimate, the Shade reached out an arm towards them.

The atmosphere itself began cutting at Azer's skin, taking the thinnest layer of his body away. His body was being skimmed and disintegrated by the hypersonic spinning air, but Azer remained utterly still in The Shades' presence, not daring to move a single cell.

Its fingers floated closer, and the sharp, encompassing stinging grew almost agonizing. The wind's friction alone was atomizing the surface of his skin. He was afraid he wouldn't be able to keep still any longer.

And then as quickly as it started, the Shade floated away, the slicing air coming to a halt, floating away with a pulse of colored light. A few seconds later, it appeared to fade into nothing, rising into the air and becoming one with the wind.

The rest of The Shades followed suit, each turning its near-infinite rotational energy back into the storm. And, with staggering speed, the storm began to return to strength.

But something was different. No longer did the rain fall from the sky, but, instead, it came from pools of rushing water covering the ground.

The raindrops fell *up*.

A raindrop emerged from a nearby puddle and fell to the sky, then another, then another, increasing in rate and intensity until the reverse rain had fully restarted the storm. Even the winds whipped backwards. Thunder ripped through the town before converging on a spot where lightning struck backwards into the storm. The sickening motions of the clouds played back in an unnatural manner.

The entire storm was playing in reverse.

The intensity had increased a hundredfold, every gust of wind orders of magnitude stronger than before, whipping around, destroying the remaining bits of the town that had previously survived. Before them, Azer and Grif's house was ripped and torn apart, the endless wind threatening to pick them up. Then Grif rose in the air, and in a moment of desperation, Azer dug his fingers into the concrete below, with the other hand clasped to Grif's. His S.R., using up the last of his energy, flowed between Azer's arms as he tried to keep his friend grounded to the earth as the sky tore the town away. He roared with exhaustion and desperation.

"DON'T- LET- GO!" Azer screamed over the deafening scene around them. Grif's tears were being sucked into the wind, he too clinging as hard as he could to Azer's hand, to reality.

They held on for what seemed like an eternity, Azer's strength fading by the second, Grif whipping around in the wind. Azer's body was secured only by his concrete-embedded fingers, the rest of him rising off the ground. Their house was gone, their town was gone. Azer felt as if he couldn't hold on any longer. He cried for help, but his cry was only drowned by the infinite storm. Nobody heard him.

The S.R. in his body, moved by his will, flowed out of his hands. The hot energy moved through his fingertips and into Grif's. With a peculiar sensation, not unlike being struck by lightning again, the S.R. strengthened Grif's resolve. Grif held on tighter, the S.R. strengthening his muscles, and even when Azer couldn't, Grif continued to hold on. Energy spread through Grif's body, if only for a moment, and gave him the strength to live.

Neither would notice it in the mayhem, but the ground in which Azer's hand was dug began to sprout with grass, flowers, and life.

As the winds raged on, the reverse storm began to throw shrapnel back into the air. It stopped at where the houses used to stand, and, steadily, the town began to return to form, rebuilding itself from nothing. The reverse storm was undoing its damage, piece by piece. Azer and Grif's belongings, previously lost to the sky, were now softly floating back into place, their house's walls self-assembling by the aid of the wind.

Before they knew it, the world had reassembled, and the wind began to die. Azer and Grif fell unconscious, falling to the ground on the street outside their home. The houses and buildings in their neighborhood, as if nothing had happened, loomed around them, unlit windows staring down on the boys.

The last thing they saw and felt before exhaustion took them were light-gray clouds rolling away above them, and a soft drizzle falling down on their still bodies.

CHAPTER TEN:
IN CITRO VERITAS

Cloudy. Little to no wind. Ninety degrees fahrenheit. Sunny over the next few weeks, but storms will arrive later.

The only thing Azer's brain processed was a clamoring of voices and a series of harsh beeps. He could tell no sense of passing time, and he wasn't yet conscious enough to feel the rush of pain his body was waiting to give him.

The first thing he consciously noticed was crippling exhaustion, followed by crippling hunger, followed by open floodgates of pain. For a brief moment, processing these things, he regretted being conscious, but it was quickly quashed by an overwhelming appreciation of being alive.

He sat in this feeling for a moment as the memories of what had happened returned in a rush. Some details came back, others didn't, others left him completely awestruck as to how he had survived. Finally, Azer took in his surroundings.

A morass of tubes and wires surrounded him, pumping blood and fluids. His hospital bed was scratchy and plasticky, and he felt another wave of relief at the fact that he would one day sleep in his own bed again.

A tiny table nearby was dotted with gifts, flowers and "Get Well" cards. He recognized the names of his teachers and friends, Dr. D included, silently noting to himself to read them all when he could.

But, for now, he decided he would sleep once more.

His first visitors were Saa and Milo, full of worries and woes in one big stream of run-on sentences and exaggerations. Only briefly did they ask what being in The Shades was actually like, but Azer found himself unprepared to share.

The next person to visit was Mr. Grano. After barely being able to fit it through the hospital door, and barely having it allowed past the nurses and doctors even with his best interests in mind, he delivered, still partially steaming, a massive platter of Azer's favorite food: Grand Soman. It didn't take much encouragement to get Azer to devour the entire thing, slice by slice. He had also brought a basket of fruit and vegetables, of some Azer liked and some he didn't, but appreciated his sentiment nonetheless. Oddly, Mr. Grano was wearing protective plastic gloves when he handed the basket over to Azer.

"What's up with the plastic gloves? You don't have to worry— I'm not sick, Mr. Grano."

Mr. Grano looked at the gloves for a split second, confused, before dismissively waving a hand.

"Allergy," Mr. Grano replied simply.

Azer chose not to press further, instead talking happily to Mr. Grano about business at the diner.

"Take your time to recover, and enjoy your food," Mr. Grano said on his way out.

Azer wasn't sure he wanted to see his next visitors—two members of Team Virga, Mrs. Korca and Dr. D.

"I'm sure you're wondering where the others are," Dr. D started, Mrs. Korca instead opting to sit by his bed worriedly, "or at least one of them."

In a sudden recollection, Azer remembered Delvin's imprisonment, adding another layer to his exhausted mix of complex emotions as he sat in the hospital bed.

"Okta is busy with work right now. And Delvin is... well, you know."

"Is Copycat alive?" Azer asked.

"Yes. He survived. He's stationed in this hospital, too, and it looks like none of you are going to be released anytime soon. He says he survived by getting dragged underground."

Azer felt a small rush of relief at this news. But it quickly faded as he recalled Delvin again.

"And they haven't released Delvin yet?"

Dr. D's face hardened and Mrs. Korca looked seriously at him. Dr. D continued, his tone laced with frustration.

"Even through the storm, even in orbit, they kept Delvin under tight watch. Despite lacking any real or reasonable proof, he's still labeled as a 'suspicious figure' and they're continuing to hold him in prison. They- or, Orbo- wants to get some answers out of him. He wants to keep any information about the relics completely secret, God knows why."

The three were silent once more, until it was broken by the question Azer knew was coming.

"Azer, I don't want to put you on the spot, but can you please tell us what happened during The Shades? You, Grif, and Copycat are the first people to survive it—ever."

Azer finished recalling everything he remembered, bringing the hospital room to a hushed silence broken only by the incessant beeping from the hospital equipment.

"What you described... it sounds like a Val," Dr. D announced.

Azer wasn't following. "What?"

"The Shades. That was no weather event. That was someone's- or something's- Val. A living thing had to have caused that."

The news was hardly processed. *Was this possible?* One person, one thing, with a Val that powerful? To cause and control a storm big enough to encompass an entire planet?

"Thank you, Azer. This, believe it or not, helps our theory."

The last person who visited Azer was both the least expected and the least welcome. With hardly any warning, the door was pushed open and through it entered the town mayor.

Orbo Lindwoter strode slowly up to Azer's bed, a wide smile on his face. Azer was momentarily grateful he had no face to display the sheer distaste he felt.

"Hello there, young man. Your name is Azer?"

"Yes," Azer answered stiffly.

Up close, Azer could notice the similarities Orbo shared with his brother. Like Mr. Grano, Orbo was portly, with a wide, kindly face. Only Orbo's was tainted with age, and the kindness in his eyes and wrinkles seemed to have drained, replaced by the tiredness and subtle wickedness that came with political power.

"You've survived a really rare thing out there. I congratulate you. The people of Nur are dying to know how you did it! Why don't you join us in the Perihelion festival in a couple weeks? You'll get a stage appearance at the centerpiece of the festival; you'll be the star of the show!"

Azer remained silent.

"Of course, you'll be doing it alongside your fellow survivor, Grif, whom I've already invited. I'd ask to hear about your experiences now, but I'm sure that should be saved for the stage! What do you say?"

For a moment, Azer burned with anger. Azer was already having a hard time processing the insanity that had occurred, and Orbo wanted him to divulge such a terrifying experience as a public speaker? Only hours ago he had been visited by Team Virga, and now the sole reason for one of their missing members was sitting in front of him. He wanted to shout about Delvin, and he wanted to yell about the hidden relics. He wanted to point out what a ridiculous and insensitive thing Orbo was asking. But before Azer gave a spiteful "no," he looked at the fruit basket Mr. Grano had given him a few days ago and an idea came to him. An idea that seemed perfect. For now, he would play into Orbo's hands. He would tell the mayor what he wanted to hear.

"Oh, of course! I would love to," Azer said in an upbeat voice.

"I knew that'd be tempting. If it was me, of course I'd accept! And for that matter I'm starting to think you might be a lot like me. Well, just come by the stage during the festival, all you need to do to share your experience with the world. See you then!"

Azer strode up the grassy path to the festival, savoring the waning heat of the setting sun and the sensation of truly walking again. He wore a leg cast, now far less restricting than it used to be, minding it as he walked.

As Azer passed by numerous stations selling food, drinks, and small inflatable toys, he felt a pang of sadness watching other kids his age with their parents, buying them things or talking happily. Today, he would get a little closer to what he sought: the relics. The relics have answers.

He made his way over to Grif, who was hunched over a fruit stand. He stood up a moment later and turned to Azer, pocketing something.

"Bought what you asked," he chimed, joining Azer in step. "Really think we're ready to pull this off?"

"It's our only chance. I can't imagine a way to get what we need otherwise."

Grif sighed apprehensively, training his eyes on the gigantic stage ahead. It was made of neatly polished wood, but showed signs of wear as old as the town itself. A large, desaturated curtain covered the backstage area, suspended by a wooden pole and dotted with modern stage lights.

"What's up? Going headfirst into a plan is usually your strong suit," Azer pointed.

"Eh… it's just…" Grif stared wide-eyed at the stage again, "public speaking has never been my thing."

Backstage it was hard to tell what was happening outside. Azer and Grif sat silent on cheap black chairs, surrounded by other groups, bands, and magicians waiting their turn to present. The two had only recently finished describing their experiences from the stage, divulging as much as they could without seeming totally insane, and now they waited for a fateful figure. The nighttime summer air leaked through gaps in the warehouse-like backstage, along with slivers of light from warmly glowing bulbs. Then, from afar, came Mayor Lindwoter.

"Hello boys," he piped without giving them a chance to speak, "you two were very brave out there. Come with me."

He urged them forward in a fashion not unlike Mr. Grano would, and they obliged. Grif pulled a small, sharp knife out of his pocket, looking at his reflection on it with apprehension, before putting it back.

The mayor led them out of the stage on a short wooden staircase. At its base was an extravagant limousine, polished so thoroughly that every light around it was reflected. Azer and Grif could see their reflections with surprising clarity. A servant opened the door, first letting in the mayor, and then motioning towards Azer and Grif. They turned to each other before following the mayor's lead and stepping inside.

Setting foot in the exquisite vehicle, Azer felt a rush of both resentment and awe. He resented that the mayor could own such a stunning and expensive luxury, but couldn't suppress his feeling of awe at the sight.

Inside of the long vehicle were leather seats lining one entire side of the limo, and a bar and radio on the opposite side where delicate wine glasses hung down from neatly lined racks. LED lights covered almost every surface, many at low power and glowing a dim blue. Azer realized more clearly now that this was how the powerful lived. And the foul man who owned it all was now grinning directly at him and Grif.

"Surprised, huh? I know, it's a lot, but I'm sure—especially after seeing you two today—that you could eventually take my place and earn all this for yourself."

The boys finished taking it all in while the driver closed the door behind them and the car momentarily began its journey.

"So, I'm sure you boys are wondering, 'Why is he letting us ride in his super amazing car?' And to answer that, I want to say that the experience you two have shared makes you truly special. Truly extraordinary. You've awed the audience, my friends. You've revealed a secret to everyone that generations have been dying to know. And for that, I wanted to treat you to something special. But, as the mayor, I can tell that you both left some things out. Why was that?"

He then waited for their response while pushing a button on the far wall. A table rose out from the space between the seats and the bar, and he placed three wine glasses on the table, pouring water into two and wine into one. "Drinks?"

Azer and Grif took the wine glasses and sipped before Grif answered.

"Well, you see, some of the stuff was… well, hard to talk about."

"Yeah," Azer agreed.

"And some of it was… well, frankly, unbelievable."

"But everything you survived was unbelievable!" Orbo boomed before taking a sip of his wine. "How much different could what you left out be?"

"Very," Azer answered, honestly this time. "And it will probably take some effort to convince you that it even happened."

"Of course I'd believe it from the young men who endured it! Please, tell me."

"But, it won't be too comfortable for us to talk about it, either," Grif murmured. Inside of his left pocket, he removed the sharp silver knife, hiding it between two soft cushions. He moved his other hand slowly towards his other pocket, pulling out a citrus fruit and sneaking it between him and his squishy leather seat.

"We'll have to ask a favor of you when we're done," Azer finished.

"Well, I'd be glad to do you boys a favor for getting to hear this! Nobody else in the world knows about it!"

"Alright then. Do you remember how we described hiding in different houses in the neighborhood from the storm?"

"Yes, of course. And in *my* town, I wasn't really surprised that the houses survived a little storm!"

"Well, we lied. None of the houses survived the storm," Azer said, prompting Orbo's facial expression to change and for him to let out a soft, "oh."

Azer carefully observed Grif pulling out the knife before cutting the citrus fruit in two while he had Orbo's attention captured. Azer continued: "The storm continued to intensify way, way more than we thought possible. Probably more than physically possible. A massive tree branch tore the first house where we were hiding in two, nearly killing us. The same thing was happening all over town, and we barely made it to our own house."

Thankfully, Orbo's attention was one-track, for he was still gaping at the absent face on Azer, glancing over where his features should be. Grif managed to push the knife all the way through the fruit, quickly hiding the knife in the gap between the leather seats. He then hid the two fruit halves between his thighs, slowly moving a hand towards an outlet on the base of his seat. He nodded at Azer to continue the story.

"Once we reached our house," Azer went on, "something weird happened to the sky. And, yes, Grif did get struck by lightning. The sky twisted and turned and glowed like we described on the stage, but something even weirder happened to it once we got inside our house. Bits of the storm were spinning and breaking off, eventually forming these... these creatures. It's impossible to describe them, but it was like their limbs were connected to each other by some invisible force, and they looked *almost* human."

Azer put emphasis on his last words as Grif's electric fingers reached the outlet, which briefly sparked before shorting the circuits inside the outlet. All of the lights in the car went dark. Orbo gave a small yelp, and for the brief moment that the car lights were out, Grif snatched the wine bottle from the table. As Orbo called frantically for his driver to help, Grif squeezed as much of the citrus fruit's juices as he could into the bottle, before placing it back on the table and giving the outlet another jolt of electricity. The lights suddenly returned.

"Phew," Orbo huffed, visibly spooked, "that was strange. And right at the scariest part of your story!" he joked. "I'll have to get my assistants to look at the car's wiring. That's never happened before. Sorry, Azer. Please continue."

Orbo downed the rest of his wine and poured himself another glass. If Azer's memory served correct, Mr. Grano and Orbo's species were almost entirely immune to alcohol intoxication. But, the citric acid in fresh citrus, on the other hand, would be potent to them. Orbo took a sip of the citrus-spiked wine, briefly looked at it with confusion, and then shrugged and placed it back on the table. Azer continued his story, now thoroughly relieved. His plan was working.

"These storm creatures must be what gives The Shades its name. It's not the name of the storm; it's the name of the creatures birthed by the storm. These Shades were wandering the ruins of the town, looking for... something. I still don't really know what. They attacked anything that moved, be it a wire or person or anything. Eventually, they came near us."

Now under the citrus' intoxicating influence, Orbo seemed less on-edge. What usually would have prompted a comically big flinch from him just made him open his eyes a little wider.

"The Shades made their way to us, and the spinning of the air in their bodies felt like it was tearing everything apart, including us. It was the hardest thing, to keep still. The terror... It was unbelievable."

"Stranger yet," Grif jumped in, prompting Orbo's relaxed face to turn to his, "is once The Shades were gone, the wind started blowing everything backwards. Like, *in reverse.* All the damage that was done by the storm was being undone. It had to have been some kind of... time reversal. I have no idea what it was. And the wind was way, *way* stronger than before."

The boys paused, and Orbo sat wide-eyed.

"That's everything," Azer finished candidly, Orbo taking another swig of his wine. He looked around thoughtfully for a moment, now swaying tipsy in his seat. Orbo took a breath.

"You know, all of this bizarre stuff you went through... it reminds me of what my brother said."

"Mr. Grano?" Azer queried.

"No, my other brother," Orbo said somberly. "We were three brothers. Of course, we're two now, because my younger brother Tetro—our middle brother—passed away just recently. Well, he was already 'gone' long ago, but it still breaks my heart nonetheless."

Grif urged him on. "Why was he 'gone?'"

"Thirty-three years ago, I became mayor. The town was a lot smaller back then, and much of it was still just overgrowth—y'know, trees and bushes and nothing. Grano was far too young back then to help us, and we were never that close anyway due to how much older Tetro and I were. But Tetro and I were close, only two years apart. He was happy to help me build up the town. One of the first things I did as mayor was clear out more land for the growing town, and boy did we clear stuff out. We cut down so many trees some of the people of the town thought we were going to run out!"

The effects of the citrus were now becoming plain, and Orbo's speech was growing more and more slurred.

"Tetro had always loved archaeology and all that junk, so when we came across some different monuments while deforesting—relics, I think Tetro called 'em—he was very, very intrigued indeed. He'd try and learn everything he could about 'em, but nobody could figure out which language they're in."

Azer's heart was pumping now. "How many were there?" he asked as casually as possible. "How many relics?"

"We'd found three across town, and Tetro bounced between them by the day. He'd still help me out, but his focus was learning the language. He'd tell me his findings all the time. Then, one day, he cracked it. He figured out how to read the 'ancient language,' and one day he stopped coming to help me altogether. I found him glued to one of the monuments after we couldn't find him for lunch or dinner, and his eyes were... blood-shot red. He'd been staring at it for hours."

Orbo took a deeper swig of his wine and then began to tear up a little.

"And... and I don't really remember exactly what he told me; he said it all in a rush. He said these relics were 'ancient documents' from an 'ancient civilization' and he went on and on about a virus, and a 'planet with life.'" He took a pause to hiccup.

"It was so scary to watch my brother, my best friend, become like this. He'd become... crazed, completely crazed, gone—gone insane with whatever he read on those relics. He'd stopped eating, and he wouldn't sleep. He'd just sit at a relic all day and night. He told me that he'd learned the secrets of the planet, and that he was enlightened now. But I knew better. I knew the relics had driven him mad."

He hiccuped again, drunk and teary, and then sighed, looking at the boys.

"I decided, before anyone else found them, I'd hide the relics. Destroying them would have killed Tetro. He was so obsessed with them, so I hid them instead. I hid them in plain sight, burying one, passing off another as a shrine to the town, and building a library on top of the third. I didn't want anyone else finding them... or at least understanding that they *were* ancient monuments... because I didn't want anyone else to go insane. What's on those relics is too horrible to be known. If news came about of poor people in the town... going insane like my brother did... I wouldn't be able to bear it. I'm doing good for the town, and I don't want any ancient piece of rock to take that away."

"One of them is under the library?" Grif asked as if he hadn't known.

"Yes, and the librarian—oh, bless her—Iris helps me guard it. I code-locked it in a trapdoor under a desk, using Tetro's birthday in his honor, and then put it in an area nobody would find. But, that Rawins teacher... Delvin... I think he's working with that forsaken Ortum. If word got out that I was hiding these things from the public, my time being mayor would end. I know, I *swear*... that cursed Ortum is trying to take my position! He's learning about the relics and sending his servants after them to undermine me! They all think I'm paranoid, but I just *know it!*"

He finished with an angry slam of his fist on the table. The glasses and bottles jumped, spilling out. Azer and Grif jumped back, but were too engrossed in what Orbo was saying to stay startled.

"The one mistake I made," Orbo resumed, red-faced, "was letting one of the relics get destroyed. I'd permitted a company to build a parking lot in the place of the shrine relic, and destroy it..." he hiccuped, more tears dripping down his bright pink cheeks, "I thought that, after 33 years, Tetro'd let go of the relics. I even asked the construction company to chase him out—I couldn't bear to do it myself. But he still loomed around them, haunting them, and destroying the shrine relic killed him. He was so shocked, he died of a heart attack."

"The man who died at the shrine..." Grif uttered, thinking of the image of the skinny ghoul they'd encountered, "he was your brother? Tetro?"

"Yes. So, I swore never to destroy another relic again. But I have to... I just have to keep it out of the public eye."

"But," Azer started, "why are you imprisoning Delvin? Even if he was trying to learn about the relics, surely it's not worth imprisoning him for?"

"There's no other way. I don't plan on giving up my position to Ortum, not now or ever. If I have to keep one of his team members imprisoned, then so be it!"

He slammed his fist angrily on the table again, causing one of the glasses to tip and spill water onto the floor. He scrambled to save it, but ended up fumbling and knocking the glass onto the floor as well. He settled for snatching a hand towel from a nearby rack and mopping it onto the ground before using it to wipe his own face. He took another sip of wine.

"I don't think they want to overthrow you," Azer huffed, "Dr. D, Delvin— they're trying to make some important discoveries. That's all we actually want."

Orbo wobbled around in his drunken state for a moment, and then snapped into stillness. His eyes made contact with Grif's, then the spot where Azer's face should be, and then he let out a soft gasp.

"We...?"

Azer immediately cursed himself for his mistake.

"Did... did you say we...? Are... ARE YOU WITH THEM?!" Orbo roared.

Azer and Grif glanced between each other, perfectly understanding what they had to do next.

"Run!" they both exclaimed.

As the two scrambled to open the doors of the limo, Orbo was in a drunken rage, flailing around and shouting: "YOU WON'T HAVE MY POSITION! YOU WON'T TAKE MY TITLE! NO *PRINCIPAL* WILL BE NUR'S MAYOR!"

They threw open the doors and, the car still moving, leapt out. As they rolled and skidded on the grass beside the road, they could still faintly hear the mayor yelling wildly from the receding car. The two panted loudly, watching the headlights shrink, until the limo passed a turn in the road and was out of sight.

CHAPTER ELEVEN:
BEYOND ANCIENT

Mostly cloudy. 11mph winds blowing east. Eighty-four degrees fahrenheit. Heavy rain expected in the afternoon.

"Our time is waning," Okta stated. The remaining members of Team Virga, Azer and Grif included, were walking purposefully together under the blue-gray sky, scarcely graced with fleeting sunshine.

"Indeed it is," Dr. D confirmed.

"Is it really our last chance to get Delvin out of jail? Why can't we break him out?" Grif queried.

"The mayor already knows we're all... well, working against him. Azer, you were right to say that we're not going for his position as mayor. That's not what I want. He only thinks I do because he's paranoid and I'm his only competition."

"Sorry, I didn–"

"There's no need to apologize," Dr. D shot, "just acknowledge what we can do with the information we have. The mayor was already close enough to figure out Team Virga existed, anyway. You two were right to confront him. Now we've gotten everything we need for a pincer attack."

"Pincer attack?" Mrs. Korca echoed. "Surely you don't mean-"

"Yes, I do. While Okta and I attend my trial, the rest of you will go to the relic."

"In the library?" Azer gasped. "Surely not yet?"

"Why not? I can't make any more moves anyway. Even if I'm found not guilty for... well, whatever Orbo's going to try me for—I still can't do anything suspicious. All I can do now is help you all from behind the scenes."

They were approaching the intersection that met the road with Nur's court hall. Then, they would split ways. Whether Dr. D joined Delvin in prison or not, the rest of them would try to find the next relic. Nervousness tore at Azer's insides. Today would end in either a resounding victory or a resounding defeat. He cursed the idea that this might be the last time he saw Dr. D as a free man.

"Are you sure Okta will help you win the case? You said he was an archaeologist, not a lawyer," pointed Azer.

Okta turned his sullen eyes to Azer, and his face grew serious.

"With my Val, I will not lose."

More and more people occupied the seats in the courtroom, filling the building. Five seats stood in the front of the room, facing the podium, but only two people were sitting in them: Dr. D and Okta. Okta Sastrugi would represent Dr. D, and Mayor Orbo Lindwoter, entering the room with a hardened face, would make the case against him. Okta stood and approached the podium with the mayor, and they briefly shook hands. Okta's eyes briefly glinted, but the mayor's remained dull.

The last of the court members took their seats. In a normal trial, Mayor Lindwoter would act as the judge. But since the mayor was the prosecutor in this case, the trial would be judged by a panel of Zystinian government representatives acting to ensure a fair outcome.

Okta sat by Dr. D's side again and the mayor adjusted the mic and took a sharp breath.

"Today we are gathered for the trial of Itell D. Ortum, for reasons of conspiracy and plotting against the government. Defending Ortum will be Okta Sastrugi, and arguing against Dr. Ortum will be me, Mayor Orbo Lindwoter."

"To begin my case, I find that Itell D. Ortum, along with several other teachers and students within his school, the Battle Academy, have been found plotting against the government. Ortum, along with his co-conspirators, including the already apprehended Delvin Rawins, have trespassed in restricted areas and attempted to glean classified information. The purpose of this, of which I almost certainly believe is true, is to bring Ortum to a position of power and to result in taking mayorship from me. The accused is attempting to violate the safety and sanctity of Nur's fledgling government."

Silence fell over the court.

"Mr. Sastrugi, what is your defense?"

Rain began to patter on the windows on the sides of the courtroom. Okta stood from his chair, moved the microphone in front of him, and took a deep breath.

Mrs. Korca slowly pushed open the large library doors with a creak and the cool library air rushed outside over the three. Grif silently followed them inside, briefly reveling in the less humid air, and shut the doors behind them.

"She's probably already waiting for us," Azer pointed. "And, guys, wait."

Grif and Mrs. Korca stopped in their tracks.

"The librarian—Iris—she has some kind of ability. Last time we were here, Delvin and I were completely silent and invisible, and she still somehow found us. Or, at least, she found Delvin. I'm almost certain she's another Valin, but I have no idea what her Val is."

"Should we split up then? Would it make a difference?" Grif asked.

"I'm not sure. I think we should, at least so if she finds us, she only finds one of us. We'll all make our way into the maintenance room since our real goal here is the relic."

"You're the man. I'll take a different path there, provided I don't get lost."

"Then so will I," Mrs. Korca added.

"Great," said Azer. "Let's find this relic."

The three split off into the empty, labyrinthine library, Grif taking the most direct path he knew. He edged his way along the endless shelves, on constant lookout for any sign of the librarian. Every once in a while, he'd stop to scan his surroundings, taking them in before proceeding further. He walked down a blue-carpeted section of bookshelves, the carpet aged and desaturated from years of wear.

Grif was encountering very little resistance, suspiciously little. The mayor had made it clear how much he wanted the relics kept secret, so why wasn't Grif being stopped? Surely the relic wouldn't be left unguarded?

And then, Grif had a terrifying thought. Were Mrs. Korca and Azer the ones being stopped? Grif had easily been the fastest, so what if the others had been attacked? He turned around. What if they needed his help?

A book was lying on the ground in front of him. After a brief moment of shock, he entered a battle stance. *That wasn't there before.* Someone was nearby, and it wasn't Azer or Mrs. Korca. He'd gotten too far ahead of them.

He looked around again, trying to control his breath. His artificial heart was beating quickly. Had she really pulled a fast one on them?

And then, between the books on the shelf on his left, he saw it. An eye, amber yellow, was staring at him.

He swung at the shelf, but the eye and its owner were already gone. Moments later, he heard a voice from all around.

"You already know you shouldn't be here," the voice croaked. It was Iris. Grif thought, the others had to be hearing it, too.

"Turn back now. If you don't... well, this time... the mayor has given me permission to kill. And doesn't that make sense? You'll be completely unable to speak of the relic if you're dead."

Silence followed. Her voice echoed slightly in the gargantuan library, just enough to hear a second imprint of her ghostly croak.

"Oh, how I've waited to hear those orders."

Then, something rushed by Grif's side. For a moment, he felt nothing. But, suddenly, a wave of pain in his abdomen made him gasp, and blood began to pour out of a long gash.

That accursed Ortum sent his goonies into my relics. Of course it's because he wants to dig that up and overthrow me! Everyone in the town will rebel if someone finds out the truth. Not while I'm mayor! Nothing this Sastrugi clown says will make a difference.

Okta heard these thoughts in his own mind, though they were not his own. They were the mayor's. In the brief moment Okta shook hands with the mayor, he had used his Val to temporarily gain access to Orbo's thoughts. Even before the words were spoken, Okta could sense what the mayor was thinking next, and he would use this to counter the mayor's points before he even could say them. It wasn't mind reading in that sense, as he couldn't take access to the mayor's memories. But the thought process was Okta's now, and in a scenario like this, getting in the mayor's head—literally—would be a huge advantage.

Physically, Okta was the weakest of Team Virga. He knew that. His Val's combat potential was dwarfed by everyone else's, even by the kids. Nothing Team Virga did together was a competition, but he knew deep down he was weakest. But in a scenario like this, he was invincible. He'd show the others just how capable he could be.

"I would first like to bring up the possibility of a false accusation," Okta declared. Almost immediately, Orbo's face went white. And Okta's dual mind ability told him that the mayor had just heard exactly what he didn't want to hear.

"Mayor Lindwoter, do you have any proof of the accused having the intention of overthrowing you?"

Oh, this cheeky bastard. Of course I do! I wouldn't be in court if I didn't! It all started with that damned survey a decade ago!

"I would like to firstly disprove the idea that Dr. Ortum wants to take your position as mayor. Ten years ago, a survey of the members of the town said that seventy-six percent of Nur's citizens would prefer Dr. Ortum as mayor over you, yes? I'm sure that could have been a source of paranoia for you, was it not?"

Orbo's face went even whiter.

"But you have failed to consider the fact that briefly afterwards, the same surveyors, seniors at the Battle Academy, interviewed Dr. Ortum and asked him if he hoped to be mayor. And Dr. Ortum publicly declared, 'I have no interest in such a thing. As a principal, I'm already busy enough.'"

Orbo seemed to be choking on his own words. "P- wha- how- how did you-"

"I'm just presenting the evidence as it is, Mayor Lindwoter," Okta answered with perfect, cold diction.

Who is this Sastrugi bloke? Is that really what Ortum said?

Okta listened calmly to Orbo's panicked, frantic thoughts as he prepared his next point. All he needed was Orbo to go in for the attack.

Grif's blood poured onto the carpeted floor of the library, staining the worn, dullish blue shag with a grim red. He fell to his knees, mind racing. Tunnel vision began to settle in, limiting his field of view.

A wound. It's deep. Really deep. I need to stop the bleeding right now.

One hand clutching the gash, he lifted the other and concentrated on it. The warm, familiar crackle of electricity rang out from his fingers. He made a fist with his free hand, save for his index finger and thumb, which were separated from each other and angled like a claw into the air. The electricity he produced arced between his index finger and thumb, hot electricity expanding the air. And as he concentrated the arc into a continuous stream of high voltage, he ripped off the section of shirt that covered his wound.

Prompting a wince of pain, he pinched the skin around the gash to raise it, and then cauterized the wound with the arcing electricity, giving the deep cut a momentary break to heal.

Grif then let out a breath he didn't know he was holding, and the panic subsided, replaced with glaring anger and confusion. The enigmatic librarian came to mind, and he couldn't help but think:

This asshole.

Throwing aside the bloodstained portion of his shirt, he stormed towards the maintenance room, but the blood loss and his ever-worsening lightheadedness made him sway from side to side. The paralyzing fear of death the wound had inflicted was being drowned by rage and determination.

If she wanted to play that game, so be it. Grif had previously intended to leave peacefully, but now he was hellbent. He'd find the relic and step on the librarian's unconscious body the whole way, and he'd depend on Azer and Mrs. Korca to stop him from actually killing her. Now, he was really ready for battle.

First, he'd figure out the librarian's abilities. How did she find him so quickly? Grif wanted to make his trip to the maintenance room quick, but he had been stealthy, too. He had intentionally avoided the sights of every security camera, and he had stayed as quiet as possible. So how was he found?

And he had to figure out how the hell he'd been attacked so quickly. Something incredibly fast and sharp had rushed by him before the wound appeared; did she have some kind of projectile ability? Or, worse—was she invisible?

No, Grif told himself, *she couldn't be.* Azer's description of Delvin's capture didn't involve her being invisible at all—and she had every reason to be invisible then. The really troubling thing was why—and how—he and Delvin had been found, even without leaving any traces of evidence to find them.

With a dubious sense of calm, he continued on deeper into the library. He entered a short hallway, which appeared far more worn and older than the rest of the building. Was he getting closer? If the library was built on top of the relic, perhaps the oldest part would be where the relic was?

Everything in the hallway was covered in dust, hiding the original color of the walls. Grif noticed a raised portion, what looked like it used to be a sign. He wiped a thick layer of dust off the sign, revealing an arrow pointing to the maintenance room.

The dust blew into Grif's eyes, forcing them shut. He cursed to himself as he rubbed the dust out of his eyes, temporarily blinded, before he heard a quiet footstep. He turned to the noise, still semi-blinded, without making a sound. Was it Azer or Mrs. Korca? Had they already caught up?

Red and irritated, Grif opened his eyes to see the librarian. She hadn't seen him, as she was still walking carefully around the shelves as if he wasn't there. Grif sprinted towards Iris, who noticed him with a surprised jolt, only for her to run away and vanish behind a corner.

The mayor was already losing his composure, and his attempt at an authoritative voice was showing its cracks. "But, Mr. Sastrugi, that survey was ten years ago. It's entirely possible Ortum's mind had changed after that point, because only briefly after that was when his goonies—sorry, his *acquaintances*, started to dig around in this town's history for what is plainly politically damaging material."

"Are you referring to Dr. Ortum's practice of science and discovery?"

Orbo was silent again, but his thoughts told Okta everything.

Science? What a joke! That's just a ridiculous excuse for digging up dirt on me!

"Mayor Lindwoter, I believe Dr. Ortum has evidence to show he's been practicing science. Dr. Ortum, can you tell us what you've discovered thus far?"

Dr. D rose, straightened his neat clothes, and then cleared his throat.

"I'll make it brief. I believe there's a danger potentially threatening this town, potentially extending to all of Zysti galaxy. An interplanetary virus we call the Magna virus might threaten the safety of our planet. So, in response, my colleagues and I have been looking for evidence of its existence. Our research might also explain The Shades and why it happens. I believe that the two phenomena may be connected somehow. A major breakthrough in this research are the relics that the mayor has been hiding for many years. The only relic that we've managed to transcribe has given us important archaeological information, helping our cause and mapping the unique history of Manim. However, the mayor has made it clear that he does not want us pursuing this information, despite the potential consequences ignoring it may have."

The mayor stood silent, and Okta heard the mayor's mind race. Dr. D sat down calmly.

These... these must be excuses. He wants my power. Science can't justify that!

"In further defense of the accused," Okta continued before Orbo could retort, "Zystinian law protects the acts of science that Dr. Ortum has described." Okta pulled out a worn, thick pamphlet from a coat pocket, flipped to a page, and then read:

"Section E36 of the Zystinian Laws and Guidelines for Planetary Governance, line 3, states that 'the pursuit of discovery, when acted by a non-governmental party, even while not specifically endorsed by said government, shall not be prohibited by said government, including any governmental leaders, democratic courts, or elected individuals in power.' In that, I believe you, Mayor Lindwoter, are violating this law. We've now established that Dr. Ortum is practicing science, and yet you are trying to halt it with the false, and frankly paranoid, narrative that he wants to take power from you."

Okta was on the dot. The mayor, dazed by the unexpected defense, could hardly form a coherent counterpoint.

"Mayor Lindwoter, I now believe it's your turn to counter," Okta finished.

The mayor's mouth contorted as he tried to articulate a thought, and then his face lit up as he audibly exclaimed, "Aha!" Orbo's attempt at businesslike order was slipping further and further.

"But Mr. Sastrugi, the Zystinian Laws and Guidelines for Planetary Governance don't apply to established planetary countries! They're only made to govern planetary colonies without proper leadership, not government systems already established! Otherwise, every planet in the galaxy would have to obey these rules, and we both know that they don't!"

"But is Manim not considered a colony planet?" Okta replied. "Colonists first set here only 80 years ago. The definition of a country stated at the beginning of Zystinian Laws and Guidelines for Planetary Governance clearly states that it must have existed independently for at least 100 years, and must also-"

"I know what a country is, dammit!" shouted Orbo, slamming his fists on the podium. Uncomfortable silence followed a brief echo in the room. Rain fell on the roof of the courtroom as the mayor glared between Okta and Dr. D. Neither returned the glare.

"Then," Okta began softly, "can we agree that you are, in fact, violating Zystinian law?"

"Ye- wh- *fine,* but-" Orbo stuttered.

"Then," Okta interrupted, "can we both agree that the accused, Itell D. Ortum, is innocent and was falsely accused of attempting to overthrow your position as mayor?"

"I *suppose,* but you can't-"

"*Then,*" Okta interrupted again, danger in his voice, "can we extend this innocence to Delvin Rawins, the man whom you've imprisoned for helping Dr. Ortum in his scientific discovery?"

Orbo looked dangerously close to actually exploding.

"Sure!" he blurted loudly. "Fine! Have it your *damn* way! Trial over! Everyone, out! OUT!"

And as the mayor's seething thoughts began to leave Okta's mind, he followed a free man out of the court and into the storm outside.

Thoughts buzzed through Grif's mind as he witnessed the librarian disappear. Had he briefly cornered her? What he saw in her yellow eyes wasn't a hunting glare, it was surprise. Somehow, in some way, he'd found her before she found him. Had Grif accidentally broken through her ability?

Grif thought, *What was different? Why, that time, could she not find me?* He rewound back to the moment before he caught Iris, and remembered: *I couldn't see.* Was that it? Did him being unable to see produce a gap in Iris' ability?

And then, it clicked. Grif recalled Azer's account of Delvin's capture, Azer's confusion about being spared, and Iris' surprise. It was *sight.* She could possess the eyes of others, so nobody could hide from her view. With her extensive knowledge of the library's layout, just taking in the vision of her target told Iris exactly where they were.

But Azer? He had no eyes. To Iris, Azer was an untraceable enigma. And he could easily be the key to their victory. But first, Grif had to tell the others.

He was careful to keep his eyes closed as he ran back into the library, opening them as infrequently as he could manage. It seemed impossible to find Mrs. Korca and Azer without being able to see properly.

Grif continued to weave around rows of books, now lost. All he needed to do now was to find one of fellow Team Virga members.

He cracked his eyes to find another hallway to sprint down, and then closed them again as he ran. He ran for a while before hearing something land in front of him. He briefly opened his eyes again to see Iris standing only a few feet ahead, and a few rows behind her was—Mrs. Korca!

If Iris had been using her ability when Grif's eyes were open, he'd have accidentally revealed Mrs. Korca's position to Iris. When he opened his eyes again, Grif noticed that the librarian was gone.

Grif realized that Iris could likely only possess the eyes of one person at a time. So, only one of them could be tracked at once. And right now, it was almost certainly Mrs. Korca. He had to reach her before the librarian could.

Grif threw his hands forwards and concentrated electricity between them. He'd short-circuit himself to make a huge explosion and draw Iris's attention. The librarian had to be nearby.

Electricity snapped and crackled between his palms and fingers before exploding brightly and loudly, throwing books all around and knocking the shelf in front of him clean over. In the remains of paper and wood, a surprised Mrs. Korca coughed, looking up at Grif with fear, and then relief.

"Oh, thank goodness it's you," Mrs. Korca managed. "What happened? What's going on?"

"Where's Iris? Did you see her?" Grif demanded, digging his hands through piles of books and lifting up the fallen shelf. But the librarian was already gone.

"Oh my goodness, is that blood?!" Mrs. Korca cried, concerned at Grif's bloodstained clothing.

"Don't worry. I'm okay. We need to find Iris. I've figured out how she can find us, and you're not gonna like the solution to how we're gonna stay hidden."

"C- come to think of it, I did see something. There was something small and dark, I couldn't tell exactly what."

Grif thought back to the sudden slice in his abdomen, and remembered something small and black swooping by him.

"Maybe she can transform?" Grif confirmed.

"That would explain her frequent disappearances and her cutting attacks," Mrs. Korca agreed.

She fumbled with something in her pockets and then pulled out a handful of silver coins, giving one to Grif.

"If she can transform, I might have a way to weed her out of hiding. We know she can only transform into something small, because anything larger than a person we surely would have noticed. Hold onto this, and tell me what her ability is while I activate mine."

Grif held the cool coin in his bloody left hand, and felt his ears pop. The quality of the air immediately changed around him. Surprised for a moment, he took her word for it and began to explain Iris' ability.

"She... she can possess the eyes of another person," he started, looking around warily for a sign of Iris as he talked. Mrs. Korca remained focused on something he couldn't see. "She can switch her vision to the vision of another person nearby, and she can use the surroundings she sees through us to conclude where we are in the library. In other words, we're in her domain. We can only stay hidden if we can't see."

"In her domain, huh?" Mrs. Korca commented, finally looking back at Grif. "I don't think so, not anymore. There's no way she can hide now."

"Huh? What did you do?" Grif noticed a change in the quality of the air. Everything looked dimmer and blurry, the visual effects increasing the further away he looked. It almost looked as if he was underwater.

"Pressure triggers," Mrs. Korca announced. "That's my ability. I can change the density of anything I'd like, and do so through objects I designate as the trigger. I just made all of the air in the library twenty times denser than regular atmospheric pressure."

Grif reached a hand out into the air in front of him, and it felt like his hand had left a bubble. The furthest extremities of his hand were being compressed painfully, and he quickly retracted his hand with a wince.

"Keep yourself close," Mrs. Korca warned. "The pressure too far away from you is dangerously high. The coin I gave you is a trigger. As long as you're touching it, the area around you will be kept under normal atmospheric pressure. Remember the secret doorway to get to the Team Virga lab? That's my doing. My power changes the density of the wall to be so thin you can just walk through it."

"Dangerously high? But, Mrs. Korca, what about Azer? Aren't we hurting him as well? He doesn't have a coin!"

"Azer has thick skin. Literally. I'm sure he's handling the pressure increase far better than we are; if anything, he's probably just confused at the moment. For now, we wait. If Iris has transformed into some small creature, she won't be able to last long in this high pressure. She'll have to transform back, and when she does, we'll find her. Only I can undo the pressure. She has to come to us."

The two waited, standing by the fallen bookshelf and tattered, leather-bound papers. The thick atmosphere inside of the library continued to warp light and sound, the pattering rain on the roof of the library coming to their ears muffled and distant. Then another sound joined the distorted sound of rain.

"This... is... nothing..." the warbled voice of Iris said from all around. "In this form... I am only stronger. Faster."

Then, blindingly fast, something zipped between Grif and Mrs. Korca. And, an instant later, deep gashes were visible on their arms, blood leaking out.

"It's happening again! But she's even faster now! How?!" Grif exclaimed.

"Grif-"

The whoosh happened again by Grif's face, and a deep gash appeared from his cheek up to his left eye. He shouted in pain and grasped his wounded face with his free hand, Mrs. Korca attempting to help him.

"She's faster! How can she be faster?!" Grif repeated, gasping through the pain.

"Grif, if she's faster now, that can only mean one thing," Mrs. Korca said as calmly as she could manage. "The animal Iris can transform into... is a bird. A bird of prey. That means we've just given her more air to glide on! Grif, get up! Hurry!"

Grif put up his arms to shield his face, bracing himself. The librarian's voice rang out again.

"It doesn't seem fair that you don't have to live in this air pressure. Why don't you join me? With this pressure it's painful to remain in my Tessian form, after all."

The black object swooped through the air again, and Grif could faintly make out the outline of a raptor, sleek and muscular. She passed only inches in front of him.

"Tessian," Mrs. Korca remarked. "She's a Tessian! Valins from Tess have multiple abilities!"

"You must have something that keeps the air pressure around you normal, don't you?" Iris droned again. "Why don't you let me have it?"

Iris swooped at Grif again and took something from his hand. He realized too late what had happened.

"A coin..." Iris remarked. "A simple trick."

As the air pressure crushed Grif's body, he could faintly make out the bird holding his silver coin between its beaks before promptly swallowing it.

"No!" Mrs. Korca yelled, processing what had happened. "Grif!"

The twenty atmospheres of pressure compressed his skin, his muscles. His eyes felt like they were being pushed into his skull.

"Mrs. Korca!" Grif managed, hearing his own voice distorted by the thick air. "Undo the pressure regulation on the coin you gave me! We can't get it back from her now! She's protected!"

"Grif... Grif, I can't! I can only make and modify pressure triggers on objects I touch! We can't do anything now! Here... here, I'll undo the air pressure! Hang on!"

"No," Grif gasped, desperate to force the liquid-like gas into his lungs. "I realized something. Don't undo the air pressure in the library. Don't undo it yet... because now... I can do something I couldn't before."

Grif put weight on his crushed legs and began to stand.

"My electricity powers... are only effective... at close range. I can sustain 40 amps of electricity through my hands... enough to power a small house." He stopped to gasp the thick air into his body again. "But at range... I'm useless. I can't make much electricity at all. I can't make arcs of electricity... without a medium. I need a conductor... to use my full power."

He tried to ignore the agonizing pain in his ears as he reached an arm into the air and towards Iris. His eardrums felt as if they were going to burst. Iris, still a bird, approached.

"But with the air being denser... there are more ions in it to conduct my electricity."

Voltage sparked between his fingers before erupting into the thick air in a fountain of blinding electricity. Arcs and tendrils edged their way up through the library, a voltaic threat that licked the ceiling.

But it hadn't hit Iris.

"You missed," she taunted before extending a talon and whizzing by Grif's stomach. Blood spat out of the new wound, and he collapsed to the ground.

"I... wasn't... aiming for... you," Grif wheezed. "I was trying... to signal... *him*."

Mrs. Korca yelped, running to Grif to tend to him, but he was already unconscious. The raptor that was Iris gripped its talons onto a shelf, the razor-sharp claws digging deep into the wood. She perched on it for a moment, taking in the scene. Grif was unconscious. Mrs. Korca was panicked. But who... and where... was *he*? Iris tried to possess the eyes of lifeforms nearby. She could possess Mrs. Korca's glasses-covered eyes, and the eyes of the occasional insect around... but nobody else. Grif was unconscious and his eyes were closed. Who was he signaling?

From behind a shelf Iris saw a horrible sight. A boy, dark gray-skinned and lanky, was emerging.

And he had no face.

Azer took in the sight, not with eyes but with something else inside of him, something alien. He could see Mrs. Korca leaning over Grif, who was bleeding, and a sharp-eyed raptor perched on a nearby bookshelf. He quickly understood what was happening.

"Is she changing the air pressure?" Azer asked.

"No, that was me!" Mrs. Korca cried. "She can transform into... *this* and... and possess the eyes of others. But–"

"You..." Iris seethed at Azer. Her face, still that of a bird, twisted into rage. Her piercing yellow eyes thinned as she glared at him. "How long have you been here?"

"Since you took Delvin," Azer snarled in return. "And I still haven't gotten back at you for that."

"Azer!" Mrs. Korca cried out again. Her voice was distant and warbled through the thick atmosphere inside the library. "Grif's hurt!"

And then, just like that, Iris stepped off of her perch and disappeared. She was already faster than any eye– or otherwise– could see. Attack was imminent.

"Should I undo the air pressure? It will take some time!"

"No, not yet," Azer answered. "Stay with Grif and keep him under regular pressure. We can take advantage of this thick atmosphere. What exactly is your ability? Tell me down to the details."

Mrs. Korca took a deep breath, her glasses-widened eyes glancing around for a sign of Iris. "I can turn objects into triggers that modify the density of materials around them. I can modify the pressure of the air, or I can reduce the pressure of an object to turn it into a gas and pass through it. But I can only affect pressure by setting objects as triggers, and those triggers only work through being touched by something living. I gave Grif a coin earlier, as a trigger normalizing the air pressure in a radius of him. But Iris stole it, and now the high air pressure won't affect her."

"Can your density triggers affect *anything*? Any material?" Azer asked.

"Yes, but I have to establish what is being affected, how the density is changed, and the range in which it comes into effect. I can't do it instantly, either."

Azer thought for a moment, trying to focus on the fleeting signs of Iris swooping around them.

"I've got it," he exclaimed. "Mrs. Korca, I want you to make a pressure trigger that affects only air. Make the trigger's range affect a large area, and make it so the density of the air is decreased as low as you can make it go. After you've done that, give me the trigger, but *don't touch it.* I'm going to use it as a weapon. You said the triggers only happen when touching something organic?"

"Yes, only when touching something living. Dropping a trigger on the ground will do nothing."

"Then this is going to be tricky."

Mrs. Korca pulled a coin out of her pocket and held it between her fingers, concentrating. She then looked up at Azer.

"The moment I let this coin go, the trigger will be active. We won't be able to touch it. Are you sure this is a good idea? The pressure difference this trigger will make could kill us if it touches us. The massive pressure decrease in the air is going to be like an explosion, and even your thick skin won't protect you."

"Which is exactly why I wanted it." Azer leaned down to a fallen bookshelf and gripped a beam on its side. S.R. flowed through his arm, and he ripped the wooden beam clean off and tossed it between his hands. This would be his bat. "I'll hit the coin at Iris and it'll take her out. This is a gamble I'm willing to take. When I say go, toss the coin to me, alright?"

"But Azer! Iris is incredibly fast! Grif and I could hardly see her when she attacked, much less just flying around at full speed! There's no way a little coin can hit her!"

"It's our only chance."

Mrs. Korca looked at him with disbelief, before hardening her expression and nodding. Azer nodded in return.

"I trust you."

"Go!" Azer called out.

As the silver coin flipped through the air, Azer activated his S.R. His senses slowed down, and all movements around him became sluggish. His muscles felt quick and nimble, and his hands gripped the wooden beam tightly. The coin began to fall in front of him, and he trained his focus on the quickly moving image of Iris, a raptor flying through the air twenty feet directly in front of him. His muscles flexed, and he swung.

Azer hit the coin, and it jetted through the air at lightning speed. It whizzed just by Iris, disrupting a feather on her wing, before slamming into the opposite wall with a crack and embedding itself deep inside. Iris immediately used her incredible speed to swoop towards Azer and extend a talon, cutting the right side of Azer's neck. But he hardly flinched. He ignored the warm blood pouring down his neck.

"Again!" he yelled to a mortified Mrs. Korca. "Give me another coin! I've got her movement down!"

"A- already on it! But I only have two left! You have to hit her!"

"I will!"

As Iris flew in circles around Mrs. Korca and Azer, Mrs. Korca set another trigger on the silver coin.

"Go!" Azer shouted.

The coin flipped through the dense air again, light reflecting off its spinning sides. Azer took his aim, S.R. pumping through his veins, and focused on the coin and the raptor. He swung the wooden beam once more.

The beam impacted the coin, damaging the wood, and then launched it through the air. Traveling impossibly fast, it hit the bird of prey directly in the chest.

The pressure trigger activated, causing a cascade of atmospheric mayhem. The expanding bubble of thin air around the coin ejected the thick atmosphere around it in a gigantic shockwave. The shockwave traveled into Iris' small raptor body, jarring her organs and brain. As the coin left contact with her body, the bubble of expanding thin air dissipated, and the thick atmosphere collapsed back with staggering force directly into Iris. The bird coughed a spurt of blood and flew out of sight.

The shockwave rocked and shook the library, bouncing off of the shelves and walls. It sounded like a deafening explosion, but there was no fire or brimstone. Only the staggering force of a shattered atmosphere.

After the shockwave dissipated, only silence filled the library. Every security camera was now shattered, pieces of glass littering the floor. But Azer saw the distinctive shape of a bird still in the air, blood dripping down its beak.

"She's still going!" Azer exclaimed. "Mrs. Korca, one more! Give me the last coin!"

"R- really?! A- alright, I'm doing it! Get her, Azer! Finish this!"

Azer's body felt shaken and his skin tingled painfully. Only one more.

"Go!"

The coin flipped through the air for the last time, and Azer tracked Iris' movement. She was slower this time. S.R. forced his muscles to flex, and he slammed the wooden beam into the coin.

But no coin was shot at Iris. It was as if it had completely disappeared. What had happened? Then Azer saw it.

The silver coin had embedded itself in Azer's wooden beam. It was completely stuck inside a crack in the beam's top. It was over.

Iris noticed the failed attack and swooped towards Azer, who was holding the beam uselessly. Although the coin was stuck inside of the beam's tip, half of it was sticking out. If he could hit her with that, then...

Azer gripped the bottom of the beam with both hands and raised it over his head. He would hit Iris the moment she got within range. It was a contest of speed now.

Iris extended her talons, and Azer used his S.R. to swing the beam down with brutal force. In a fraction of a second, the beam hit Iris, and the coin impacted her head.

The explosion of pressure blew them both back, rocking their bodies and damaging their internal organs. The deafening BOOM echoed through the library, louder than ever, the pressure difference smashing the windows that kept the pouring rain outside.

Azer's brain and body were rattled. He was close enough to the epicenter of the atmospheric explosion to take major damage, and as he tried to push himself up he struggled to form a thought. His head was spinning, but he could barely make out Iris, back to her original form, bleeding from the head and lying on the ground. For a moment, Azer could only process the pattering of rain outside the library, the moist air flowing in, the dense atmosphere of the library no longer contained. The pressure normalized, and all he could feel was the sensation of humid air on his skin.

Mrs. Korca got up first, the farthest from the explosion's epicenter. Blood was leaking out of the side of her mouth, and she held her head with a hand as she rose. Azer found his way to his feet, but collapsed momentarily after.

Azer couldn't process anything, until he heard Mrs. Korca softly saying:

"No... how..."

Azer saw Iris standing up straight and tall. Her mouth was closed and her lips were thin, and her golden-rimmed glasses were cracked.

Blood was still falling from her head. Her piercing yellow eyes looked at Azer with rage.

"I can't go down that easy," Iris said matter-of-factly. "I can't be beat. Your explosion hurt you as much as it did me."

She began to stride towards Azer, tripping over her own feet on the way.

But in her path was Grif, who had risen, too. He glared at Iris and stood firmly in her way, unmoving. They both stood for a moment.

"I will make you know despair," Iris declared. "Faceless boy, I will kill your friend in front of you."

"Did you know that I've been struck by lightning?" Grif asked Iris. She said nothing, only moving her sharp eyes onto his.

"When I survived The Shades, I was struck by lightning. People talk about wanting to know what it would feel like to be struck by lightning, but it's terrible. It hurts. There's nothing fun about it."

"What are you-"

"But I learned something after being struck," Grif interrupted. "I learned how to make my own lightning, and all it takes is a *positive charge*. A conductor. Do you know what Mrs. Korca's coins are made of?"

"You-"

"Silver," Grif answered before Iris could speak. She was growing furious, her face growing red with rage. "It's the most conductive metal there is."

In an instant, Iris lunged at Grif, extending massive talons towards his throat. But, moments quicker, Grif emitted a crack of electricity in front of him. The charge arced from his hand toward a spot pinpointed between Iris' eyes. It traveled through the library air and hit the silver coin Azer had embedded into the wall only minutes earlier. Thousands of amps and millions of volts ripped through the damp library air and straight through Iris' head. The searing, white-hot charge passed between her eyes and blinded her. A final, deafening crack filled the air, and Iris fell limp to the ground.

Grif sighed exhaustedly.

"You should have stayed down. You won't be able to see through anyone's vision again for a while. Especially your own."

Azer pulled open the hatch underneath the desk, and the first thing he and Grif could see was a puff of dust, followed by neverending blackness emitting from below. The two looked at each other wordlessly before Azer positioned himself, dangled his legs through the hole, and jumped down.

The sound of his sneakers hitting stone echoed through what sounded like a chamber. No light was visible except for the small rectangular glow of the trapdoor above.

"It's not too deep," Azer shouted back up. "You should be able to make it."

Mrs. Korca's magnified eyes peeked into the dark relic, occupying the opening of the hatch.

"Grif, be careful," Mrs. Korca warned, turning to him. "I only gave you first aid. Don't push yourself."

"Yeah, this better not open up my wounds," Grif griped. "Azer, I'm gonna kill you if this kills me."

Grif's legs could be seen covering the gap of rectangular light before disappearing again as he fell into the blackness. He landed with a wince and a similar chambery echo.

"Damn, dude! That was a lot deeper than I thought! That hurt!"

"Sorry about that. I guess I'm not that good at judging distance."

They were silent again as the two took in the cold, silent darkness. Neither wanted to walk in either direction for fear that they wouldn't be able to find a wall.

"I'll contact Dr. D," Mrs. Korca said. "You two take your time down there, and let me know if I need to throw you a ladder."

"We will," Azer shouted back up.

"The air smells... weird. Azer, do you smell that? Actually, *can* you smell that?"

The air inside of the chamber was odd, a hint of petrichor along with something almost sour. This smell lingered inside of the chamber, the air feeling wet despite the cold dryness.

"Grif," Azer started, "do you have the energy to make some more electricity?"

"Yeah," he answered, "on it."

Grif moved his index finger and thumb together and sparks arced between them, growing in intensity, sound, and light until the buzzing sound of Grif's electrical fingers illuminated the chamber.

The room was extensive and round, a perfect half-sphere. Symbols and runes lined the walls up to their height, and the top of the chamber was dotted with more than a dozen circles of varying sizes. The top of the sphere was roughly twenty feet up, the rectangular entrance slightly misplaced from the very highest point. The sphere was forty feet in diameter, wall to wall. Azer walked over to what appeared to be the beginning of writing above a deep line in the stone wall.

Azer reached out a finger and touched the stone sigils. It was deeply cold, the kind of cold that instantly chills to the bone. He again felt that unexplainable feeling of familiarity, but it vanished immediately. He rubbed the blackish dust between his fingers.

"Azer, this thing looks... old. Impossibly old. It doesn't even look ancient. It looks like it's straight from another world, a society we can't even comprehend. It looks... *beyond* ancient."

Azer kept this in mind as he read.

"'*This planetarium illustrates the astronomical recordings of the Hivanian society over our time on this planet. On the ceiling of this relic are a number of planets...*' So these things are planets?"

"I guess so," Grif seconded. He stared up at the circular carvings in the stone, scanning them for details.

"I can read some of the labels on the planets... *'Peremil...'* that one says *'Ulbitinum...'* none of these are planets I've heard of. Any of those ring a bell?"

"Nope. Any way that these are just old names for current planets?"

"I don't think so. I read a book on the planets in our area and nothing met these coordinates. There's galactic coordinates on the sides, see?" Azer asked.

"Then what are these?"

"I'll check, the text on the walls mentioned them. It might say something about the planets."

Azer began reading again. *"'... planets which were in the path of the Magna virus. Telescopic observations show that every form of life on the planets were completely extinguished. Extinction is imminent, thus we are taking unexpected measures to evacuate our planet.'"*

Grif stared wide-eyed at Azer, who shared his panic, heart pumping out of his chest.

"Azer," Grif whispered, his mouth dry, "how old is that? Is there a date? How long has... has it been here? The virus? When did this happen?"

Azer mumbled as he paced around the edges of the room, looking between different symbols before he slowly turned towards Grif.

"Sixty thousand years ago."

AUTUMN

CHAPTER TWELVE:
A TRIP TO ARCUS ISLAND

Sunny. 15mph winds blowing east. Seventy-five degrees fahrenheit. Clear weather for the coming days.

Endless research followed the discovery of the Magna virus. Excavations in Nur's soil—and most other places on the planet—yielded a mysterious specimen of virus deep in the earth. It was, through microscopic observation, determined to be the long-sought Magna virus.

But mysteriously, despite existing beneath all of Manim's surface, it had only infected a few people. The virus remained dormant, awaiting its moment. There were no fatalities or even symptoms—it was just sitting there, infecting without hurting.

And more importantly, it wasn't able to be extinguished.

No modern medicine would kill the virus. No organism was able to fight the virus. When infecting a cell, the virus wiped the DNA of the cell clean, replaced it with its own, and then reproduced. It was stubbornly resilient to all forms of attack, leaving the public no choice but to keep a wary eye on it despite inflicting no real harm. Only a day after the virus was discovered and brought to the attention of Zystinian authorities, a planet-wide quarantine was announced, barring any interplanetary travel on Manim to or from inhabited planets.

Fall break had started at the Battle Academy, a long break at the beginning of every long season on Manim. Every student had three months of break before school resumed again, and in Azer and Grif's grade, many were taking advantage of that opportunity. Their classmates and friends had gone away, their parents taking them on vacation elsewhere on Manim, but Azer and Grif were stuck. They had no parents to take them anywhere.

"We have no way of telling how much time we have left!" Dr. D pressured. For over two years, with the help of the Zystinian government, Team Virga had been hard at work developing a cure. The lab was filled with every book and research paper even tangentially related to the Magna virus, from reports of the deadzone planets to accounts of The Shades. Delvin was even reading old Nova Noctis records. Azer and Grif were toiling away too, turning on centrifuges and studying chemicals. Grif's right eye was bruised from looking into the microscope so often, and Azer's fingers ached from managing complicated equipment for so many hours. And at the end of each and every day of stress and work, Azer and Grif would always say the same thing to each other:

"We need a break."

Dr. D looked between them with a pained expression, conflicting emotions swirling behind his white eyes.

"I know, but-" Dr. D started.

Grif interrupted, "We can hardly focus anymore. School was hard enough before the Magna virus, and then we had to fight the librarian and all of that, and then we had to deal with the stress of having to come up with a cure before this planet ends up like the others we saw in the second relic. I've found myself glazing over even my work on the cure now, and I can hardly tell the difference between an amoeba and a bacteriophage. Please, we just… we need a break."

Dr. D looked even more pained for a moment. He looked behind at the rest of Team Virga, hard at work on the virus. Mrs. Korca had taken off her glasses and was rubbing her eyes, Delvin was looking through a series of microscopes and was pinching tweezers, and Okta was typing away on a computer, eyes even more sullen than usual. Dr. D looked back at the two boys, looked down and closed his eyes.

"I… I know. I'm sorry. I've been too caught up in the work, and we don't even seem to be making much progress."

Delvin turned around from his microscope and added, "We're making *no* progress. This thing seems… unkillable. It doesn't have any weaknesses. It's perfect."

"Exactly. Azer, Grif… I apologize. I've apparently been too shocked at the discovery of the Magna virus to use good judgment. I just felt… I just feel like, considering my actions in my past life, I want to make a proper effort this time. I wanted to redeem myself. It just seems… it seems that I've been going too far. Of course you two can have a break."

Azer and Grif turned to each other, elated.

"But," Dr. D shot, "I have a homework assignment for you. And it's not school this time; it's about the Magna virus. All I want you to do is to look for some possible ingredient for the cure. I remember… in my recollections of my past life, there was *something* to the cure that let it work. I have no idea what it was, but… I know it's there. Wherever you go, whatever you do on your break, however long you need… I just want you to look for that. It doesn't have to be major, just keep the cure on your minds. Alright? There are lives at stake here."

On their first day off, Grif had come to Azer, who was sitting on his bed reading a book.

"What's up?" Azer asked.

"I was thinking about what Dr. D said yesterday—about us looking for the secret to the cure. It made me think about, well…"

There was a moment of silence. Grif looked apprehensive.

"Go on," Azer urged.

"The answers to the stuff we've been looking for our whole lives haven't been pretty," Grif said. "I mean, if you think about it, we would have been better off not searching for that Haise girl and never knowing what really happened during The Shades."

Azer's memory flashed to their encounter with the storm, the paralyzing fear of realizing they had been left behind and the endlessly deep eyes of The Shades themselves. The image had been burned into his mind.

"Do we even want to know the secret of the cure?" Grif continued. "Or our pasts? Somehow, we're connected to this, and I'm not sure if I'm going to like it, the way things are going."

"But we still have to explore," Azer said seriously. "What's the point of all this without learning? We can't go on without knowing who we really are. I'd pay any price to find that out. Wouldn't you?"

Grif thought about this, eventually steeling his look.

"Yeah. You're right. Whatever the truth is, we can face it."

Azer couldn't smile, but Grif got the point anyway. "You bet your ass we can."

The doorbell rang, and Azer answered it to see an unexpected face. It was Saa, her split-colored face beaming.

"Hey, is Grif here? I wanted to ask you guys something."

"Uh, yeah. Grif!"

Stomps were audible through the house with growing volume, until Grif could be seen running up to the door by Azer.

"Hey, what's up?" he greeted.

"So, my older brother Erril just got his space license and we were planning on going to a beach trip on an uninhabited planet called Kular, he said I could invite a few people. So I wanted to invite you guys!"

Azer and Grif looked at each other.

"This won't violate Manim's quarantine, right?" Azer asked.

"No, of course not. It would if we were visiting an inhabited planet, but this one's as barren as you can get."

"Then hell yeah!"

"Alright, bring everything you'll need. We plan on staying for a week. We're going to camp out on the beach. It's pretty habitable. We won't have to worry about alien bugs or diseases or anything. This weekend, come by our house at dusk and Erril is gonna take us!"

Azer and Grif arrived at Saa's comfortable-looking house at dusk, the sun setting behind their roof. The door was answered by Erril, a handsome and well-dressed young man who looked a few years older than Azer and Grif. He had a short mustache and sported longer hair than his sister, Saa, with dark bluish-green dreadlocks. He had the overwhelming presence of simply looking cool.

"Hey guys!" he exclaimed. Erril looked like the textbook definition of a chill college student. He ushered Azer and Grif inside.

"I invited some people of my own; they should be in the living room. We're heading out in just a bit. I just have to pack up the rest of my stuff first."

They stepped further inside the medium-sized house and made it to the living room, warmly colored and nicely furnished. On one of the couches facing the TV, Azer saw a wiry-haired girl he didn't recognize, and with her was-

"Copycat?! What the hell are you doing here?" Grif exclaimed.

Copycat whipped towards them, wide-eyed, and the other girl stayed trained on the TV.

"Why are *you* here?! Erril never said anything about *you two* coming!"

"Saa invited us!" Grif responded.

And, right as Grif said this, Saa came into the room, assessing the situation.

"What's going on? You guys know each other?"

"We have... history," Azer stated bluntly.

"History, as in he's tried to kill us more times than we can count on our hands," Grif added.

"Kill you?! *Excuse* me? I have never tried to kill you."

"What about the time when you were chucking rocks at us in the scrapyard? What about the time when you *literally* trapped us during The Shades?"

"I wouldn't have *trapped* you if you two weren't so goddamn slow to leave the school-"

"Don't you DARE put that blame on us! It was a hundred percent you who got us stuck there!"

"Well you two didn't seem to hate it so much since you gave your heroic survival speech about it to the *entire town* and left any mention of me out of it!" Copycat argued.

"You should be glad we left you out of it, because it probably won't be good for your fragile self-image if we mentioned that you were the one who *stuck us there!*"

"Alright, guys, stop!" Saa yelled. "It's been seconds since you got here and you're *already* at each other's throats! Just stop for a moment!"

Grif and Copycat glared dangerously at each other, the girl next to Copycat still idly watching the TV with a glazed look on her face, only occasionally turning around to the source of the commotion. Erril had entered the scene, watching the arguing boys with an apprehensive look. He looked lost for words.

"Just- not everybody here knows each other. Can everyone just introduce themselves? Without fighting? Please?" Saa asked.

An uncomfortable bout of silence followed.

"Alright, I'm Azer."

"I'm Copycat. Erril invited me."

"I'm Erril. I'm gonna be flying all of you tonight, and I invited Copycat."

"I'm Grif. Saa invited Azer and me."

"I'm Saa. Erril is obviously bringing me along. Also I invited Grif and Azer."

Everyone then expectantly looked at the other wiry-haired girl, but she still seemed to be engrossed in the TV.

"Oh…" she gasped softly. "I'm Rena. Copycat invited me."

And then she went back to watching TV.

"Yeah," Copycat added, "I brought her along. She just gets distracted easily. It's alright if she comes, right?"

Everyone else in the living room looked between each other awkwardly.

"I suppose it's fine," Erril concluded.

"Sweet. So when are we heading out?" asked Copycat.

"In just a sec," Erril replied, leaving the living room, "I have to finish the boot-up sequence and stuff. Just hang tight here, alright?"

Some time passed while Azer and Grif caught up with Saa, recalling occurrences and talking about the journey to come.

"So Milo's not coming?" Azer asked.

"Nope," replied Saa. "He's already on vacation with his own family. He said he really wanted to go, though."

"It's been a tick," Grif commented. "Haven't talked to him in a while. Been too busy with finding the cure and all."

"I never asked, how is that going? You and… Team Virga, right? You all are working pretty hard?"

"'Working hard' isn't the right word for it," grumbled Grif. "See this bruise on my eye? That's from staring into a microscope all day, and it's already healed some. It used to be a lot worse than before."

"That sounds awful."

"Worse yet, we're making precisely zero progress," Grif continued. "So far all we've discovered is that the Magna virus is the closest thing there is to the perfect lifeform. Radiation does jack shit, it's immune to disinfectants and alcohol, and worse yet, there's no way to actually make a live vaccine for the thing. Any amount of Magna in the body just multiplies and spreads, and it's not as if we could damage the virus enough to weaken it anyway. All modern medical science has been completely rendered moot."

"And to add insult to injury," Azer added, "it's coming at the cost of Team Virga's sanity. Delvin and Dr. D will sleep in the lab sometimes and skip meals for days at a time. Delvin especially hasn't been well since he came back from prison. He's been... off. I'm not sure how much longer we can hold out."

"Except," Grif added, "Dr. D did tell us to try and look for a 'secret ingredient.' Apparently when he died before, he remembers there being some kind of trick to the cure that let it work and brought him back to life."

"Wait, died?" Saa repeated. "Brought him back to life—what? I don't remember this at all! When did this happen?"

"Oops, probably said too much."

Erril's face popped into the room, his dreadlocks swinging by his head.

"Ship's ready! Everyone on!"

A large spaceship roughly the size of a small house, sleek and edged but not without obvious signs of use and wear, obscured the view of Saa's neighborhood. Its shape resembled an upside-down yacht. Lights in the cockpit and windows glowed, illuminating the front yard and cul-de-sac. The engines on either side of the spaceship's slim shape were wide and deep, like a strange and alien distortion of a jet engine. Awe struck Azer at the sight.

"Look at this beaut, eh?" Erril said, moving his arms in a comical display of showing the ship off.

"Oh, shuddup," Saa groaned. "This is mom's old ship. Don't act like it's yours. And it's super outdated at this point anyway."

"Hey! Don't diss *Stormbreaker!*"

"Diss *what?* What did you just call it?" Saa asked.

"*Stormbreaker*. And she's not *it,* she's a she! Respect your space-ships! All ships are 'she,' everyone knows that!"

"Why the hell is it named *Stormbreaker* anyway?"

"'Cause it's an awesome name."

Azer could hardly take his attention off of the ship. He didn't care about its name or how old it was—he was dying to get inside and experience a taste of space travel for the first time.

"E- Erril? What's space travel like?" Azer asked, trying to get Erril's attention away from his bickering with Saa.

"Hm? Oh, it's dope. You'll just have to see when you get on, I don't wanna spoil it for you."

Erril boarded the *Stormbreaker* on a set of narrow steps to the interior, Saa following not far behind with her own luggage. She stopped and turned to Azer.

"It *is* pretty cool, I won't lie," she added before stepping inside.

Everyone else began to board, including the strange girl, Rena. Azer grabbed his backpack and climbed the steps.

The extendable staircase onto the spaceship was, as Saa had described it, old and creaky. It was made of tough metal that felt hard beneath his shoes, and small rows of rubber dotted each step to provide traction. As he climbed, the light from inside the ship was bright enough to obscure the interior, but once in he could make out the details of the ship.

The main cabin was sleek and beautiful, but aged. The metallic walls were no longer the pure white they had once been, and the brand-new look was long gone, now sporting the occasional stain, scratch, and dent. Still, it was still a sight to behold. It was spacious, with eight seats along the walls. Rather than a constant, flat surface, the walls and ceiling would occasionally dip or jut out smoothly to achieve a more modern and futuristic look. The smooth walls converged sharply to a point towards the front and back of the ship, each a few dozen feet from his position, with doors visible on either end, blocking the view of anywhere but the cabin and the world outside. Erril was by the door towards the front of the ship.

As he followed Erril, Azer ran his hands over the cabin walls and felt the smooth ridges of the metal, in awe at the craftsmanship. It gave him a rush of appreciation for the people who had built it.

Erril pushed open the creaky door and then turned around towards Azer.

"I know you want to explore the ship, but sit down for now. The ride's gonna be a few hours. I promise there'll be plenty of time to tour it soon. First, you're gonna see what it's like to get off this planet."

Azer didn't need much more convincing to sit down.

After a drawn-out pre-flight systems check, Azer sitting as patiently as his excited self could, the *Stormbreaker* was ready for launch. His seat was ever-so-slightly rumbling and he was focused on the window outside. In the window's reflection was Grif, giving him a wide grin and a thumbs-up. Azer returned the gesture enthusiastically.

"Hello, hello, this is your captain speaking," they heard from the ceiling of the cabin. Through the intercoms, Erril was doing his best impression of a generic flight captain, but even an idea like that went over Azer's head. He hadn't been in the sky at all before, much less space.

"Tonight we have clear skies, but we don't really care about that. More importantly our path to the planet Kular is nice and asteroid-free, and we're going to reach max hyperspace, putting our trip at around 3 hours. Buckle up and enjoy the ride."

Just after these words, Azer felt the ship jerk underneath him, and before he knew it, it was rising up into the sky, and the lights of the neighborhood were beginning to shrink.

A faint rumble was audible all around the ship thanks to the ship's roaring engines. The lights of the neighborhood were very quickly shrinking into yellowish specks on a velvety black landscape, and the occasional car could be seen moving slowly beneath.

"Hold on tight, we're accelerating to escape velocity. Don't lose your lunch!"

And without a moment's notice, Azer felt his body increasingly shoved into his seat with frightening force. It was uncomfortable at first, but the cushiony seats lessened the effect. They had been skillfully made to comfort passengers during space travel.

As the *Stormbreaker* accelerated, the whir of the ship's engines grew to a higher pitch. The uncomfortable sensation of being pushed into his seat continued and then, all at once, it stopped. He hadn't even been paying attention outside during the acceleration, and took the opportunity to turn to the window again.

And what Azer saw left a strong imprint on his mind.

All he could make out from the window was a wide curve, a hazy glowing atmosphere separating inky blackness from inky blackness, each void of dark dotted with its own lights. One was Manim, with its own little oasis of light representing the town he'd lived his whole life in. Past the veil of the blurry blue curve was space, dotted with innumerable stars. It was an unfathomable sight, watching the curve that was the roundness of his own planet slowly fall away into the darkness of space.

The next thing Azer realized was that he was completely weightless. His arms, which had only moments ago been gripping the rests on his seat, now floated by his side without any resistance or care. His insides did a funny flip, adjusting to the lack of gravity, but he quickly acclimated and the nausea was drowned out by overwhelming awe. The intercom clicked on again.

"This is the million dollar view, folks. Enjoy it while you can. I'll give you all a moment to look at the planet while I prepare Stormbreaker *for warp drive."*

Azer's mind could hardly comprehend the view. He turned around in his seat, scanning the cabin, double-checking what he knew was real: The cabin and walls around him were real— he had touched them himself only half an hour earlier. Grif was real—he was laughing to himself at his weightlessness, throwing a coin into the air only for it to keep rising and bounce lazily off the ceiling. Saa, Copycat, and Rena were real, too—all of them were reacting to the sights and sensations of outer space.

But it was so hard to believe!

Azer continued taking in the "million dollar view." Though seeing his own planet's atmosphere curve away before him was unbelievable, he took it in, appreciating to his core the sight of Manim in its whole, in its purest form he'd never seen or dreamed of before.

And then, Azer felt his guts settle back into his body and his hands fall back to his side, the ship's artificial gravity turned on. A strange-pitched whirring was audible from the back of the ship as it prepared for warp drive.

"Particle accelerator calibrated. Man, that's fun to say!"

The whirring in the back of the ship grew louder.

"Measuring dion particle wavelength..."

The whirring grew louder still.

"Charging ship to particle wavelength..."

Azer felt a small static shock from all around him. Grif's hair was standing up on end, which amused him.

"Warp drive begins in ten seconds... nine..."

The whirring took on a different pitch, and Azer took his final chance to admire the planet from space.

"Six... five..."

Azer's heart dropped into his stomach as he realized he had no idea what warp drive would feel like. He gripped his arm rests anxiously and tensed all the muscles in his body.

"Two... one. See ya, Manim."

If Azer's mind had not been completely blown from seeing his own planet from space, this would certainly have done it. White streaks whizzed by the window at incomprehensible speed, and with a sickening jolt of shock, Azer realized that the white streaks were entire stars. The window now resembled the static of a malfunctioning television, displaying a haze of innumerable colors that were nebulas, planets, and solar systems, flashing by for nanoseconds at a time.

It looked as if the universe itself was rushing by.

And then as soon as it started, it stopped. For Azer, it felt as if he hadn't moved at all. The stars, which had previously been abstracted to blinding streaks in the window, were now still and unmoving as ever, a new set gazing down upon the ship.

"And we're here. We'll be cruising for another two and a half hours as we get into orbit and slow down onto Arcus Island. Sit tight and we'll be there soon."

Azer didn't know what to exclaim first. They had already arrived? They had been in hyperspace for less than ten seconds! Not to mention the lack of g-forces he felt during the warp, and the unimaginable speed of everything flying by—he was too astounded to form a sentence.

"Pretty weird, right? I haven't even gotten used to it yet," Saa said, unbuckling her seatbelt and rising from her seat. "Hyperspace never fails to be awesome."

Grif was as dumbstruck as Azer. His jaw was dropped, and he seemed to be having a similarly hard time forming words. Saa turned around towards the boys.

"Aren't you going to get up? You don't have to sit in those chairs for the next two and a half hours. The gravity's on."

Orbiting above Kular, Azer could make out with surprising clarity the details on the surface. It was mostly a water planet, great greenish-blue seas dotted only by great white clouds above Kular's surface. Tiny islands hid beneath the clouds. When the *Stormbreaker* orbited to the night side of the planet, Azer was surprised to see no lights whatsoever. But, this made sense in a way—Saa did say it was uninhabited.

And, right on cue, Saa approached him.

"You know, it's *technically* illegal for us to be here. The Zystinian government hasn't really explored this planet yet."

"It's illegal? Why? This isn't a deadzone planet, right?"

"Didn't you pay attention in school? Well, for better or for worse, Zysti doesn't want people visiting uncharted planets without a colonizer's license or Planetary Explorer's license. The colonizer's license you have to get from your planet or country if they want to expand, and the Explorer's license is a title you have to get from the Zystinian government. And no, this isn't a deadzone planet, we're not quite that stupid."

"Why can't we get an explorer's license? Sounds like it'd be better than running the risk of getting arrested."

"Eh, not really. Getting an Explorer's license means you actually have to apply to be part of Zysti's government, which is a whole ordeal, and we're not even old enough yet to do that. Erril could have, but no way he's doing that. Waaaay too dumb to pass the entry exam."

The intercom clicked on, and Erril's voice said:

"I can hear you, you know. No trash-talking the captain."

Saa made a rude gesture towards the intercom in the ceiling and turned back to Azer.

"And besides, everyone does it, anyway. It's harder on Manim because you gotta avoid the deadzone planets, but we're by no means the first ones to do some illegal spacefaring. Zysti can't patrol the galaxy everywhere at once. If they caught everyone who illegally visited another planet, half the galaxy's population would be in jail. Besides, they just don't want you to contract some alien disease or die in an unexpected volcanic eruption. If you're smart about it, there's hardly any risk at all."

"Are we *sure* this planet's safe?" Azer questioned. With the state of his own planet and the virus on it, he felt doubtful.

The intercom clicked on again.

"Don't worry, dude. I personally scanned and visited this planet, and there's nothing here but lush foliage and crystal-clear beaches. No other aliens, no crazy diseases, nothing. This planet even has an almost identical day-night cycle and seasonal pattern we have on Manim. Just relax a bit, you're on vacation."

"See?" Saa assured. "It's fine. He's not taking us anywhere crazy."

Azer shrugged and sat back into his chair, examining the planet again. Maybe he was just worrying too much. It was his vacation week, after all.

The *Stormbreaker* touched down on the coast gracefully despite its enormous size. Almost immediately, Azer felt strangely lighter. Erril entered the main cabin from the cockpit and, observing the bewildered passengers, addressed them:

"I forgot to mention, but gravity is lighter here. This planet is 80% of the mass of Manim. Sorry about that."

"Yeah, you should have mentioned that sooner, and I could have brought nausea medication. This and zero gravity make me a bit queasy..." Saa groaned.

"You guys don't like this?" Grif exclaimed. "This feels awesome!"

"How aren't you nauseous? Everyone gets nauseous when going into different gravity," pointed Azer.

Grif was jumping up and down by his seat, jumping surprisingly high with each leap and falling uncharacteristically slow.

"Guess I just adjust quickly. You guys can stay nauseous. I think feeling this light is pretty nice. It feels more natural."

"Well, anyways, once you guys are feeling well enough for it, I'm gonna put up the staircase and start setting up the tents," Erril finished. "Come on out whenever you're ready."

Azer was feeling well enough, though thoroughly tired, and proceeded to follow Erril through the hatch outside.

He was disappointed to step outside into almost complete darkness. The galaxy shining above them was far brighter than any of the land in front of Azer, and the only visible patches of this new planet were illuminated by the lights of the *Stormbreaker*. All other features above the horizon were reduced to black silhouettes on a starry sky.

"Darker than I thought," Erril remarked. "It'll do. I brought a flashlight, anyway. Azer, would you mind helping me set up the tents?"

"Sure."

Erril hurried back inside the ship, returning with an oversized flashlight which he handed to Azer. Others were beginning to come outside as well, surprised at the inky darkness of Kular at night. Azer, stepping into the sand alongside Erril, hoped he'd get to see the planet properly once it turned day.

"We won't be able to get too much sleep tonight," Erril said, hammering a metal stake into the sand. "It's past midnight on this planet already. But like I said, the day-night cycle here is the same as Manim, so we should adjust quickly enough."

Azer helped Erril finish setting up the tents, and after properly unfolding and raising the supporting poles he realized just how large they were. Each of the two tents reached over a dozen feet into the air at its peak, and there was ample room to sleep and live.

"For sleeping, the guys are getting a tent and the girls are getting a tent," Erril announced to the group, "but there's no restraints or requirements to where you want to be during the day. We got a whole planet to ourselves, guys, we'd better enjoy it while it's ours."

The boys slowly congregated into their tent and the girls into the other. By the time Azer was inside, Erril was already setting up small portable gas stoves and pulling out blankets for the rest.

"Tomorrow," Erril said, now straightening out his own sleeping bag, "I think we'll go for a hike. Explore the new scenery, y'know?"

"Sounds good," Grif said.

Copycat was setting up his sleeping bag now, in a corner of the tent as far removed from Azer and Grif's as possible. Azer's heart sank again at the idea of having to spend his vacation week with his worst enemy.

Azer got into his own sleeping bag and readjusted his pillow.

But, Copycat seemed to be keeping his distance. Maybe Copycat felt the same way, and wanted to stay as far from Azer as Azer did him.

His consciousness began to drift away. *Who knew...?*

CHAPTER THIRTEEN:
SCHISM

A bright sliver of light leaked through a gap in the tent, seemingly cutting the interior of the tent in two. Azer noticed that Erril's sleeping bag was empty.

Azer grabbed one end of the tent's entrance, pulled it open, and stepped out into the light.

Over an endless expanse of still, clear water, the sun was rising and reflecting a long line of lightly twinking sunlight over the sea. The sun was warmer than usual on Azer's skin.

The ocean was shockingly infinite. But it was infinite in a different manner from the endless black of space Azer had first seen a night prior. Space was infinite in its nothingness, but the ocean, Azer discovered, was infinite in its vastness. The watery horizon went on and on until it couldn't be seen anymore, and then continued this expanse sideways on every field of view that touched the water, splitting the sky in two. Birds dotted the sky, occasionally opting to cross the border of sky and sea before returning with a fish in their beak.

Azer quickly discarded his sandals he had put on inside of the tent, leaving them in the orangish sand, and slowly walked up to the shore.

As he approached, he noticed the ocean's sound, too. It was a soft sound, a whoosh from every corner of the ocean of waves that rose and fell, lapping at where the water met the land.

When Azer found himself at the edge of the water, he took another moment to admire it. A small, cold ripple of water rushed up the beach, covering Azer's ankles, before receding again into the sea. Azer quietly laughed to himself before walking a bit deeper into the water and striding down the coast.

Azer noticed a sound accompanying the quiet singing of the waves. It was music, not the natural kind. The music's source was Erril, humming to himself while he grilled something on a portable gas stove. Azer approached him.

Erril had stationed himself away from the tents, a beach umbrella over his head and a fish on the grill. An old radio was by his side, playing music that Erril was singing along to poorly, skipping words and mumbling parts he didn't know. Upon noticing Azer, Erril turned down the volume on the radio.

"Azer! You're up early."

"Aren't you, too?"

"Well, I figured I'd try and catch the prime time for fishing. I packed plenty of food, but I figured we could have fish for breakfast, y'know? Living off the land. Oh! You wanna know something awesome?"

"Yeah?"

"So, I brought my radio for the trip, but I realized that there's probably not gonna be any signal here on a planet like Kular. No radio stations, y'know? But I did a bit of tweaking on this baby-" he patted the radio by his side- "and it turns out there's a station broadcasting a bunch of music all over this part of the galaxy! Isn't that cool! Someone really thought this stuff through. I wouldn't wanna know how expensive it must be to upkeep a radio tower strong enough to broadcast music across whole light-years. Guess they've been doing it a while, too. The music is dated as hell. Great, though."

"Wow, that– that is cool. What kind of fish is that?"

"Oh, this?" Erril chuckled. "No idea! But I guess we'll be finding out the hard way if it's good to eat or not. I wouldn't think so. Our noses would tell us if something's harmful, and this smells pretty good. That's why we have noses, after all. Oh, wait, that's right. Sorry."

"It's alright."

There was a painfully long silence, the radio still quietly playing music over the sounds of sizzling fish.

"You, uh," Erril started, breaking the silence, "ever fished before?"

"Nope. Never."

"Oh, yeah, that's– sorry. Well, do you want to learn?"

"Totally."

Erril promptly grabbed his fishing pole with one hand, the radio with another, and strode towards the ocean, motioning Azer to follow.

They stopped a few feet from the water and Erril turned up the volume on the radio. He held up the fishing pole with both hands as if it was a sword and looked over to Azer seriously.

"Fishing's awesome. It's fairly easy, too. You take bait–" he pulled a small, rubbery bait from his pocket– "hook it onto the hook at the end of the fishing pole–" Erril hooked it on– "and you're ready to cast. Make sense so far?"

"Mhm."

"When you're casting, you want to hold onto this button, and whip the fishing pole so the hook goes out far. Usually, the further, the better. Like this."

Erril made a show of holding down a button near the pole's handle and then whipped the fishing pole towards the ocean, the machine on the pole buzzing as the line flew further and further. Finally, the bait fell into the ocean, the buzzing stopped, and a small ripple emerged from the spot where the bait landed.

"And now we wait. Now, all we need to do is wait until a fish bites. Thankfully for us, this planet is barren of intelligent life, so the fish are gonna be way too stupid not to bite. We should get a bite aaaany second-"

Just then, the spherical bob on top of the water sank, prompting Erril to let out an "ah!" of satisfaction. He began rapidly spinning a handle on the pole's side, and the bob slowly came closer, leaving a tiny wake behind it.

"Now," Erril explained, still spinning the handle, "a fish has bit, and we're trying to reel it in. Depending on how much of a fight it puts up, you're going to want to reel it in *hard*, just spin this thing and it retracts the line. And- eventually-"

With one huge tug of the fishing pole, Erril had pulled the fish to shore and it flung up into the air. It gleamed in the sunlight for a moment, gorgeous green scales shining like a disco ball, before landing on the sand in front of Erril and flopping around.

"Haha! Look at this beaut! It's huge!" Erril laughed.

"That thing's the size of your leg!" Azer exclaimed. He'd never seen a live fish caught before, only dead and frozen in a supermarket.

"Now, why don't you give it a try?" Erril offered, holding down the fish with a knee and handing Azer the fishing pole.

"Really? I probably won't be too good at it."

"Of course you will! They're practically asking to be caught! C'mon, give it a try."

Azer obliged, holding the fishing rod in his hands. After a moment of hesitation, he checked the bait and held down the button, rearing back the pole.

"Swing it away from me. I'm not the one you're trying to hook. Also, swing it *hard*. The further, the better."

"Hard?" Azer repeated.

"Hard. I mean it. As hard as you can."

"Are you sure?"

"Well, how hard *can* you swing it?"

"Hard."

"Oh, I'm going to regret this, aren't I?" Erril said.

Azer reared his arms back, mimicking the motions Erril had made before he swung the rod, and, activating S.R., he swung the rod forward full force and let the hook fly.

The hook soared through the air at astonishing speed, the reel aggressively buzzing at a high pitch. The reel began to smoke from the speed of the line, Erril looking at the smoking pole with horror. Finally, the hook hit the water, and a large splash was visible from afar— then another, then another, and another. The hook was skipping across the ocean, splashing seawater into the air as it flew further and further away. Finally, the hook came to an abrupt stop, the line having run out and the fishing pole jerking forward in Azer's hands.

"Uh... Sorry," Azer apologized.

Erril, mortified, could only stare between where the hook had disappeared and the still-smoking fishing rod.

"No, that one's on me, but... Azer... that was hundreds of feet of line! Did you actually extend all of it?"

"Does that not usually happen?"

"No! That never happens! Well... I suppose you just have to reel in a fish now. If the line's still intact, at least."

They quietly stood on the beach for a moment, Azer patiently waiting, the radio by their feet still idly playing music. Azer didn't mind how long it took—he felt as if he could take in the ocean and its vastness forever.

"Hey, uh..." started Erril. "Sorry about the nose thing. I wasn't paying attention."

"No, it's really alright. I'm used to it."

Azer then realized his poor choice of words.

"Well, not the insults, I mean, I'm just used to, well, not having a face. Though I've been through my fair share of teasing. Sorry about the fishing rod, though. Hope I didn't break it."

"I'm sure it's fine. That thing's pretty sturdy. It gave me a shock, though, I won't lie. Say, how did you cast the line that far? No normal person could do something like that, I mean—you made the hook *skip* across the water. Do you have—"

"Yep. A Val. It's called S.R., don't ask why I called it that. It's a long story. Basically it gives me super strength, and I can kind of 'concentrate' the energy into different parts of my body. I can transfer it to other people, too. Only downside is that it uses a massive amount of energy, and I usually have to eat a huge amount of food to make up for the burnt calories."

"So you'll probably have to eat a lot now, right? Good thing you picked fishing."

Azer chuckled. "I hadn't thought of that."

There was another moment of silence.

"Honestly, I'm glad I have my S.R. And, in a way, I'm glad I don't have a face, too."

"Really?"

"Well, yeah. Really, it just makes me who I am. I mean, don't get me wrong, I'm still dying to know *why* I don't have a face, and who my parents were, and where I came from, but there's no point in me being upset over not having a face. It's different, but it's... well, kinda cool in a way. Does that make sense?"

"I suppose so."

"The only thing I really wish I could change would be for me to have parents. Or at least meet them. It's stuff like this—y'know, fishing and whatnot—that I sometimes feel like I've missed out on. It might be part of why I want to know my past so badly."

Only a moment later, Azer felt a great tug on the line, and immediately began reeling in the line with full force.

"Yeah, go! You've got a lot of line to reel back in!"

Azer reeled and reeled, far longer than Erril had, until finally he dragged a large fish onto shore, flopping and writhing in the sand.

"Well done! These fish are huge! Here, let's take it back to the tents. It's probably about time to wake up the others, anyway."

Dragging along their catches, they reached the tents thoroughly sandy. Upon reaching the tents, they found everyone else up and ready.

"Where were you guys?" asked Saa. "We've already started preparing for the hike. We had to have breakfast without you."

"Oh. We were getting breakfast. Thought we could have fish," Erril answered.

"Those look goooooood…" Grif drooled, gazing intently at the large fish Azer and Erril were holding by their sides.

"We'll eat them on the road," Erril said. "Or, I guess, trail. Or, wait, there aren't either of those here. We'll eat them later. Let's go."

Erril led the group into the mass of trees bordering the beach, hiking along a path he knew shockingly well.

"I explored this place a few times while scouting this planet," Erril explained. "I've hiked through this forest already."

"You didn't get lost?" Copycat asked.

"This planet has a magnetic field and I had a compass. Not only that, but I'd mark the trees I pass like this—"

Erril took out a shiny knife from his pocket and cut a vertical line in a nearby tree, tiny fragments of bark flying in every direction.

"I'd do a line like this in the trees I pass and find the marks on my way back. I'm just following the marks I already made. Speaking of, we're about to get to where I left off."

"Should we turn back?" Copycat asked.

"Already? No way. I'm fairly certain there's a perfect spot for fishing or swimming up ahead, look at how the ground gets rockier and wetter up there."

"Erril, you should have said if we were going fishing, I didn't bring my pole," Saa said testily.

"I was hoping to keep it as a surprise. You don't keep your fishing pole on you?"

"No! Why would I?!"

"I didn't bring a swimsuit, I thought we were just going out for a hike," Grif added.

"Neither did I," Copycat agreed.

Erril looked at the unprepared offenders, visibly disheartened.

"Should we turn back?" Saa suggested. "We can always do it again later. Or we could just do the hike now and then come back and fish later."

"We've come out quite a ways, though," Azer pointed. "And I'd like to practice fishing again if I can."

"Me too," added Rena. "I've never fished before."

"Should we, uh, just meet you all back here?" Grif suggested. "That way we don't have to call off the trip. You guys can keep hiking and we'll catch up."

There was a moment of silence, Erril still looking disappointed.

"I suppose that works," he conceded with a sigh. "We won't be going far, anyway. You all should be able to catch up as long as I'm making the marks in the trees for our trail. Just, be sure to follow it on your way here and back, alright? I don't want you getting lost."

"We won't. You said it yourself: it's pretty easy to stay on track as long as you're paying attention," Grif said. "As long as all of us can do that," he added, giving an extra long look at Copycat, who gave a rude hand gesture in return. Saa elbowed Grif's side.

"We're off," Saa told her brother, disappearing into the woods behind them. Azer, Erril, and Rena watched for a moment before proceeding towards the water hole.

Twigs snapped beneath Grif's feet as they trekked back towards their campsite, thinking angry thoughts about Copycat. *Why did Copycat have to come with them, anyway?* Grif thought this could be a nice vacation from his stressful research and worrying about the virus, but Copycat just had to sour it for them.

Hoping to get out of earshot of Copycat, Grif ever so slightly quickened his pace through the trees, Saa maintaining the pace with him.

"Why'd you have to elbow me like that?" he asked Saa, who immediately rolled her heterochromic eyes. "Copycat's a total ass, you know that. We've told you how many times he tried to kill us."

"Yes, Grif, and I trust what you and Azer are saying. But *please*, can we just enjoy this vacation without you bickering with him for once? In all honesty, he probably doesn't want you here, either."

"Wha-"

"Not to mention," Saa interrupted before Grif could retort, "Copycat is Erril's friend. I have no idea what's up with that Rena girl or why she's here, but Copycat is my brother's friend. I have to keep my brother in mind, too, whether his friends are nice or not."

This didn't satisfy Grif. He would let it slide for his friend Saa, but Grif made sure he would convince Saa that Copycat was trouble. Surely she could see that?

Then, all of a sudden, Grif stopped. His artificial heart sank.

"Hey, Saa."

"What's up? Why'd you stop?"

Grif stared at the tree in front of him for so long that Copycat caught up. He looked at Grif with confusion.

"Grif, what the hell are you doing?" Copycat said.

"Am I crazy?" Grif replied.

Both Saa and Copycat remained silent.

"Are you?" Copycat asked. "Because you're giving us the impression that you ar-"

"This cut is sideways," Grif observed. He reached out a hand towards the cut in the tree and ran his finger over the scarred bark. It was a horizontal mark in the tree, obviously cut with a knife or sharp object.

"And?" Copycat asked impatiently.

Grif glared back at Copycat before continuing. "It's wrong. All of the other cuts Erril made were vertical. Remember?"

The three looked around them at the cuts in the trees they'd been following. All of them were horizontal.

"They're *all* sideways, dude," said Copycat. "If you're going to stop in the middle of our walk, at least have it be for some important reason. I'm going back towards the camp. I actually want to keep hiking instead of stalling and gawking at marks in trees."

As Copycat stormed off, Grif looked hopefully at Saa. Neither of her colored eyes showed full belief.

"Erril could have just switched to making vertical marks in the middle of his trek. He came here on multiple trips. It's possible he didn't follow the same pattern."

Grif sighed sullenly.

"Though, I do agree, I recall some of the marks being vertical on the way here as well," Saa continued.

Grif's expression turned thankful.

"What's with that face? What, you thought I actually thought you were crazy? I'm your friend, remember? Cmon, we'll ask Erril about it after we meet them at the water hole. Let's just keep following the trail."

But as they continued to follow the trail of marks in the trees, Grif's sense that something was wrong only heightened. He felt as if the cut trees felt unfamiliar, but he assured himself that all of the trees in the forest were; he had only been on this planet a day. Saa was probably right, Erril wouldn't necessarily be consistent with how he made the marks.

But then something unexplainable prompted all of them to stop. Copycat walked towards Grif and Saa, hearing the same sounds they did.

"Is that…" Copycat started.

"Voices?" Grif finished Copycat's sentence. "It has to be."

"What the hell is that? We're too far from the others by now," Saa pointed. "Who else is here?"

They listened to the unmistakable clamor of voices coming from the woods ahead, and Grif approached the horizontal gash in the tree in front of him, running his fingers over the cut. It was far deeper than he had realized from afar, and there were obvious signs of age in the cut– the tree had grown since the cut was made, and it was far rounder and deeper than anything Erril could have made with a knife. Erosion had smoothed the cut into a uniform gash.

And then, seemingly from nowhere, fingers emerged from within the tree, then hands, then arms, and then a face. The hands grabbed Grif's head and shoulders, and then, before he could scream, he was pulled inside.

Azer was preparing fishing bait, squatting down on a rock, while Erril helped Rena fish. The water hole was a large pond, jagged, rocky edges bordering the sides, two fishing bobs near the water's center, rippling the water ever so slightly. It was oddly quiet by the water's edge, save for the quiet boom of Erril's radio.

"So, where'd you meet Copycat?" Erril asked her.

"We had chemistry class together last year. We're also in the same neighborhood, which I didn't know until then."

Erril looked expectantly at Rena again, hoping for elaboration, but she seemed trained on the fishing bob. To a chatterbox like Erril, Rena was excruciatingly untalkative. After another moment of uncomfortable quiet, Erril attempted to break the ice again.

"Copycat and I have been on the school's track team forever. I became the captain last year, so I got to know him better then. Has good determination, that kid. Knows what he wants. You go to the Battle Academy, right?"

"I do," Rena answered, still not looking away from the bob.

"Wait till you get to the college level of the school. It's a blast. Should you decide to go to college at the Battle Academy, at least, there's still plenty of good colleges off-planet."

Suddenly, the bob sunk into the pond and, without a second's delay, Rena began furiously reeling in the line. It got closer and closer, the image of the writhing fish clearer and clearer under the surface of the water, until she finally pulled it all the way up to the end of the fishing pole.

"Well done! That one's a weird color, though. It might be poisonous. We'll have to see later."

"Can I kill it?" Rena asked.

"Uh... go ahead, I suppose."

Rena immediately picked up a long, thin rock, placed the flopping fish on the ground, and, in a swift motion, stabbed it in the head. It went limp immediately. Erril looked at the dead fish with a mixture of shock and amazement.

"W- wow, I thought I would have to tell you where to stab it, but nevermind, You've already figured that out. You sure you haven't gone fishing before?"

"Positive."

Erril turned back towards Azer.

"Azer, you wanna give it another try? Have you finished preparing the bait yet?"

"The others are taking a while," Azer pointed. "Did they get lost?"

"They couldn't have. All they had to do was follow the lines in the trees."

"It's still worrisome, though. They've been gone for a long time."

"If they got lost, I'd know. Saa's Val could tell me where she is."

Azer stood up. "Her Val?"

"She can make light," Erril explained. "Infrared light. And a lot of it, too. She used to think her Val was just lighting things on fire from afar, but that turned out to just be concentrated beams of infrared light that she couldn't see. Overtime, though, she learned to see it."

"Really?" Azer recalled Saa's early sparring matches with Grif, and the strange heat she could create at will.

"Yeah, it's pretty cool. I never had Vals growing up in the Battle Academy, so I'm pretty jealous, but I'm happy for her."

"I never knew. We haven't had classes together in a while."

"Yep. And should there be an emergency, she can just emit infrared light into the air, and I should be able to pick it up with this." Erril held up an IR camera from his heavy backpack and turned it on. "So if they were *really* lost, we would know about it."

"Maybe we should go back anyway to check," suggested Azer. "Worst case scenario, we find them on the way up to us."

"I suppose we could. A break couldn't hurt."

Grif opened his eyes to see complete, overwhelming darkness. His skin felt cold with a mysterious tingling feeling all over. Pushing himself up, he could feel dirt and dust beneath his hands, and warm liquid on his head. Blood.

But before he could panic or process the pain in his head, an opening of orangish light appeared behind him. Through the opening Grif could make out a sickeningly familiar figure shouting at him to stand up. Now lit, he could see he was being held in some kind of dirt cell, a massive boulder having previously blocked its entrance. In the cell with him were the unconscious bodies of Copycat and Saa. The figure stormed into the cell, grabbed him by the collar and dragged Grif outside.

And when Grif got a look at the person dragging him out, he thought he was looking into a mirror. The boy was Grif's age and shared the same tinted color of Grif's skin, even the shape of his eyes.

The boy threw Grif to the dirt-lain earth in front of a large bonfire, illuminating the surrounding camp. *A camp?* It was nighttime. Where was he? Was it night already? Who were the unnervingly familiar people surrounding him?

"Get up!" the boy shouted at Grif. "Don't make me drag you again! Answer the chief's question!"

The chief? Was Grif in some kind of tribal camp?

At that moment, Grif saw a figure from behind the dancing fire, tall and menacing, with a massively scarred face. He had to be the chief, and the woman to his side his partner, only slightly shorter with equally scarred features. Upon closer inspection, the chief was missing an eye.

"I said," the chief boomed, "why did you come here? We're shocked to see you again. Why do you tread on our lands?"

Grif didn't know what to process and how to process it. His mind was overflowing with shock at a hidden civilization on this barren planet, the jarring familiarity of everyone around him in the back of his mind. And, *"Again"?* Had Grif really been here before?

In a moment of shock, Grif realized: *He could understand what they were saying.* He tried to form a reply, and felt his mouth and lips speaking a strange language.

"W- who are you people? My friends and I had only come here to visit. We didn't know there was anyone else here!"

"You don't remember?" the chief said in the same foreign yet familiar tongue, his voice softer now. "It's no surprise. You were young. We are the society of the Schisms, and this is our home. I'm surprised you've survived, Grif. My son."

CHAPTER FOURTEEN:
PRINCE

The sun hovered over the ocean and the sky slowly darkened, turning the beautiful colors of the sky redder and redder. The sun would set soon.

Erril let out a terrible yell from inside the girls' tent, a guttural yell of fear and desperation.

"Where is she?!" he repeated, bursting out of the tent and panting heavily.

"There's no other footprints in the sand but ours," Azer announced. "And there's nothing in the boys' tent either. It's like they're just... gone."

Erril yelled with anguish, falling to his knees in the sand. Even Rena's usually tranquil expression was grim.

"Although," Azer continued, pointing a finger towards the tall woods, "we've narrowed down that they have to be in the forest somewhere."

"But we've searched the forest all day!" Erril retaliated. "We checked every inch of our path!"

"But that's exactly it. They might not be near the path at all. If we want to find someone who's lost, we have to get lost ourselves."

Grif pondered long-ago spoken words from Dr. D as he sat in his dirt cell again.

"Where did you come from? Well, I found these old news articles from a while ago about two young children who were found soaking wet in sea-water. If I could guess, those two children were you."

This made him think. What was the significance of him being found covered in seawater? And if the Schism chief was telling the truth, then how had he gotten to Manim in the first place?

Grif had been unceremoniously tossed back into the cell after attempting to ask further questions about the Schisms. He could hardly feel the scrapes and bruises they had inflicted on him over the cacophony of shocked thoughts buzzing through his injured head.

He had no idea where he was from or who his parents were. He wasn't sure what he expected. But this—the people who'd imprisoned him—seemed to be about as bad as it got. Grif had always envisioned his biological parents in a tragic but noble light—maybe there was some heroic reason he had been sent away, why his heart had been removed and replaced. A primitive tribe of barbarians wasn't anywhere in that picture.

He thought back to his conversation with Azer several days ago. Maybe he was better off not knowing the truth.

Grif felt a stirring beside him, and then a weak "ugh..."

"Where are we?" groaned Saa's voice from behind him.

"I'm not sure," Grif replied, trying to keep his voice measured. His throat was impossibly dry, and he tasted blood. "We've been captured. We weren't alone here on Arcus Island."

"But... how? I thought-"

"I'm just as stupefied as you are. And to make matters worse, the chief of their tribe said I'm his son. Knew my name and everything." He let the silence hang. He could almost hear Saa's shocked expression. "I don't know what's supposed to happen to us next."

"For real?" Saa's disbelieving voice said. "Damn…"

They were silent. Grif didn't know what to say.

"Well, we have to get out, don't we?" Saa said, accompanied by the sound of shuffling dirt. "I mean, unless you want to stay. Here, stand up. I need to show you something."

Following Saa's lead, Grif stood up in the choking darkness of their cell.

"I'm gonna have a hard time seeing what you want to show me if it's dark as shi-"

All of a sudden, Saa grabbed Grif's shoulder, and the cell lit up with bizarre light. His eyes briefly burned before the pain reduced to a low ache, leaving him able to focus on the unimaginable things in front of him.

Grif couldn't recognize a single color in the room. The dirt walls were faintly lit with a reddish light. Grif thought every color he was seeing was red. But it also wasn't red. It was as if he was seeing indescribable variations of the color red, none of them truly crimson, everything unfamiliar and alien to his eyes. All of the colors were somehow… *below* red. Infrared.

"How did you-" Grif sputtered.

"My Val is the control of infrared light, remember? Or has it really been that long? I just gave you the ability to see in the infrared wavelength. As long as I'm touching you, you can only see infrared light. Here, turn around."

Grif whipped around to see Saa's face, but it was a distortion of it that he didn't recognise. He could only see her heat, a strange temperature map of his friend. And, behind her, still collapsed, Grif could see the heat of Copycat's body.

"Can you… usually see in the infrared?" Grif asked, still bewildered. He wasn't sure if he could ever adjust to the incomprehensible colors.

"I can see both infrared and visible light, or just either of them if I want. But, isn't this better? A lot better than just pure darkness, right?"

Grif gave his cell and surroundings a proper look-over, and was shocked to see how much detail he could make out inside the cell. He could even distinguish small pebbles within the dirt walls of his enclosure.

"Y- yeah. Not gonna lie, it's off-putting, but yeah."

"Great. Make your way to the boulder at the front. We might be able to see the body heat of everyone outside. And don't drift off, I have to be touching you for you to see infrared light."

Grif walked over to the massive boulder that blocked their cell, Saa's hand still on his shoulder. There was a hotter shade of color peeking out from around the edges of the large stone, most likely residual heat from the bonfire outside.

"Looks like moving the boulder back and forth over the entrance of the cell cracked the dirt a little bit. Look, the dirt's dislodged where the boulder meets it," Saa pointed.

Still fascinated by the fact that his fingerprints left temporary heat marks on the boulder's face, he refocused on escaping. Saa looked up to a light-emitting break in the earthen wall of the entrance.

"Yep, there's people out there. A huge fire, too. Here, you try."

Saa moved out of the way to make way for Grif, who pressed his face up against the crack and tried to look outside. He could make out the figures of people, glowing in different spots, the sides of their bodies that faced the bonfire colored significantly warmer. Then, without warning, another glowing humanoid shape crossed his vision and approached the boulder.

"Wait, I think people are coming. Get back!"

Saa and Grif stepped back, and Saa's hand left his shoulder, plunging the area back into total darkness. Then, with a shuddering slide, the boulder was pushed out of the entrance, and three figures, one being the familiar boy Grif had seen earlier, filled the light.

"Get up again, all of you!" the familiar boy shouted in his guttural language. "Get up! Now! You're coming with me!"

"He's telling us to come with him," Grif said to a very confused Saa. Copycat was beginning to stir now, and another boy with similar stature appeared from behind the first and grabbed Copycat by the collar, pulling him to standing.

"Hey- what the hell are you-" Copycat shouted.

"Copycat, just go with them. Don't resist," Saa warned.

Three spear-armed guards pushed, shoved, and pulled the prisoners out of their cell and into the fire-lit camp.

Grif found himself thrown to the ground again in front of the chief, his war-torn face staring down at him with a single eye.

"Grif," the chief growled. While Copycat and Saa didn't know the Schisms' language, they recognized Grif's name, prompting them to go wide-eyed. "Your fate is already decided. But you two—" the chief trained his eye on Saa and Copycat— "you two are foreigners. If you have powers... then show me."

Saa and Copycat looked at Grif expectantly, the flickering fire illuminating their panicked expressions.

"He... he wants you to show him your Vals," Grif said.

Reluctantly, Copycat created a clone of himself that quickly dissipated, and Saa briefly heated up a leaf on the ground until it burst into flame. The chief looked at the two scrutinizingly.

"As I thought. I should have assumed one accursed boy would only bring more accursed children. But your timing is impeccable. Our deities demand sacrifice, and you three will be perfect for the ritual. Take them away," he ordered.

"Wait, wait!" Grif shouted as the guards began to drag the three towards a tunnel at the end of the camp. "Why are they cursed? I thought you would leave them alone if they showed you!"

"I have no words for a child possessed by the devil. I spared you once, and though you are my son, you will not be spared again."

Then the chief's face disappeared behind the fire, and the camp fell away behind the receding mouth of the tunnel.

Azer, Erril, and Rena stood bewildered in front of a horizontal cut in a tree. Erril ran his fingers over the gash, shock overcoming his panicked thoughts.

"We weren't alone..." he uttered.

"Didn't you only make vertical cuts in the trees?" Rena pointed.

"I did. These definitely aren't mine. The cut's too wide to have been from my knife. Here, look-" Erril pulled out his knife and rested it within the horizontal cut. There was ample space between it and the borders of the scar in the tree. "They had to have followed these instead of my cuts. But, look at this- the horizontal cut is pointing towards another."

Erril put his knife back into his pocket and traced his finger along the cut's path. He moved his finger off the tree, following its path forward until it hit another tree, right where a new cut started, pointing in a new direction.

"Someone's using these to get back from somewhere. It's marking a path," Azer pointed.

"Then we just have to follow it," insisted Erril.

"But, wait, listen," Azer interjected. "If we follow it back, we're sure to find whoever made the trail in the first place. And at the bare minimum, we can assume that they have a knife. And if they happened to take Grif, Saa, and Copycat, then-"

"Then we'll just have to fight them."

"Are we even ready for a fight? Erril, I thought you didn't have a Val?"

"I do," Rena quietly interjected. The two turned to her, surprised.

"You do? What is it?" Azer asked.

"It's not important. I can hold my own if I need to."

"Vals or not," Erril said testily, "we need to follow this trail. No matter what, we have to get back to the others. I can hold my own, too, thank you very much."

Azer thought for a moment, pondering Erril's determination. Erill wasn't afraid to encounter anything to get his sister back, despite the innumerable risks. *Maybe he could get behind that, too.*

"You're right. We'll be able to take whatever's waiting for us. Let's go."

After hours of being forced through earthen and rocky tunnels, lit only by the flickering flame of a torch, Grif, Copycat, and Saa were thrown unceremoniously into yet another cell, barred with old and rusted iron. From the glimpses Grif could manage, it was one of many along a long, hastily-dug wall of cells, with remnants of other poor souls inside. Grif could have sworn he saw bones in some of them.

With iron shutters slammed behind them, the faces of the torch-lit guards stared down at the three. The tallest one, holding the torch, said:

"You'll be sacrificed at dawn. Any attempt to escape will be met with torture. Save your blood for the ritual."

The three guards then turned back around in perfect unison, backs to the cell, distanced just out of reach. They gripped their spears tightly. After a moment of silence between the three prisoners, Saa spoke.

"Did you see the conditions of the other people in the cells?"

"Unfortunately," Grif replied. Copycat was silent, maintaining a glare on Grif, who ignored it.

"They were *skin and bones,*" Saa hissed. "They looked like walking corpses. I saw some of them missing fingers and limbs."

"Well, we won't have to worry about being in here that long since the guards just said we're being sacrificed at dawn."

"At dawn?! It's already night!"

"They also made it pretty clear that we're gonna be tortured if we try and escape."

"Holy shit," Saa said, pacing the cell with her hands on her head. "Holy shit."

Grif couldn't process anything anymore, as if his body had shut down all outside stimulus. His parents and people—the things he'd dedicated his whole life to finding—were trying to kill him.

Now it was Copycat's turn to speak. "Grif, what did they say earlier?"

Grif snapped out of his trance. "Who? When? You mean when they asked you to show them our Vals?"

"Yeah. What was the chief saying?"

"He said we had to show him our Vals, and when we did, he told us that our Vals were 'evil' and said we were going to be sacrificed."

"Why didn't he ask you to show your Val?"

"He already knew it. Apparently I'm the chief's son."

"Figures."

Grif looked at him incredulously as Copycat stood up, visibly angry.

"What did you say?" demanded Grif.

"Figures you're his son. You've been plotting with them, haven't you? You already know their language, after all. What do they call them-selves, huh?"

"The Schisms. But, Copycat, what–"

"Enough!" he shouted. "Just shut up! You brought us here, didn't you? You led us to the Schisms' camp! You're oh so special enough to deserve being spared while Saa and I get tortured and sacrificed to a tribe of primitives! Isn't that right? You said it yourself, the Schism chief said 'your fate is already decided.' He just wants to spare his darling son!"

Now Saa was looking at Copycat incredulously. "Copycat, what are you saying? Grif was captured, too. He doesn't know why he's here any more than we do!"

"You shut up, too! How can you defend him? He's the only one here who knows their language! He told us to show them our Vals! And he's the chief's damn *son!* He has every reason to be helping the Schisms!"

Grif's fists clenched and his knuckles went white. Another word, and he'd slam his fists into Copycat's hateful face.

"He and Azer just want to be special! Of course he'd want to be the Schism's damn prince!"

"Copycat, STOP IT!" Saa yelled. "Grif didn't even want to come here! It was my fault we even followed the Schism's false trail in the first place! Remember? When we were following the trees back, he didn't even want to come this way! Grif was the first to be captured when we did encounter them! And besides, he would have no reason to betray us! He's our *friend!* Can't we trust in that?!"

Copycat was breathing deeply, his face still red with anger, Grif's even more so. Copycat was still glaring into his eyes as if daring him to attack. Grif held back. Barely.

"We have no reason to be arguing and every reason to be escaping! We really *will* be sacrificed and killed if you keep this up!" said Saa.

"Alright," Copycat conceded. "Fine. We'll focus on escaping. And Grif, if you overstep your bounds, I'll-"

"I can promise you that I want answers more than you," Grif interrupted. "I wanna know what the hell is going on."

Copycat glared for a few seconds more.

"Saa, what's your plan? Do you even have one?" Copycat asked.

"I do. I know how we can get out, get rescued, and get answers, all at the same time."

"Seriously?" Grif urged.

"A lot of it is gonna depend on my Val, especially getting out and getting found by the others. And Copycat, your Val is how we're gonna get answers. Though we might have to get violent to do so."

"And how are we going to do all that?" Copycat demanded.

"Well, we need to get out. And to do that, we're gonna have to fight."

The cool night air of autumn chilled Azer's skin as he stepped and trekked through the forest just behind Rena and Erril. They had to have followed hundreds of marks by now, walking beside a small creek that weaved along their path.

"Haven't you noticed," Rena said quietly, looking at the ground intently as she walked, "that we haven't come across any footprints? None of the leaves we're stepping on are crushed."

Azer focused on the satisfying crunch of dried, fallen leaves under his shoes. "Yeah, you're right. I wonder why?"

"We've also passed a lot of diverging paths," Erril added. "Whoever or whatever made these paths must have made each one for a different purpose, to a different location. I've just been taking us on the main path that the others connect to."

"Maybe nobody's been on this trail for a while," suggested Azer. "The cuts in the trees, like you said, *are* pretty old."

"No, Rena had the right idea. There should at least be some footprints in the leaves. There's no way that Saa and the others would have gotten this lost without something happening to them. Whoever made these marks had to have kidnapped them, and they had to have left some kind of trace."

They continued walking silently, taking in the dark forest lit only by the stars overhead. The trail of marks seemed to continue forever, and more enigmatically, not a single crushed leaf was to be found along it. Then, from afar, they heard the sound of rushing water.

"It sounds like a stream," Rena pointed.

"It does. And the trail looks like it's taking us right to it," said Erril. "We should refill our water bottles."

Slowly, the sound grew louder, until the source of the splashing came into view. It was a small waterfall inside of a clearing, rocks and stones lining the stream. The still parts of the water reflected Zysti galaxy above, bright and clear, fathoms of stars clustered in the sky. The waterfall stretched two dozen feet into the air, its top out of view from the clearing below. Autumn-colored leaves pooled and grouped in the water, getting stuck behind sticks and rocks as they marched along the stream's surface.

"It's really pretty," Azer pointed.

"No kidding," agreed Erril. "But we can't stay. Let's refill our water and get back on the path."

Azer unscrewed the lid of his bottle and dipped it into the clear water, watching the reflected stars rippling over the surface. The bottom of the stream was rocky, Azer noticed, and the clarity of the water was astonishing. As the water topped off, Azer admired the waterfall up ahead and the white mist it made as it fell.

And underneath the waterfall, barely visible, Azer noticed a shimmer. For the briefest of moments, it reflected Erril's flashlight, dangling off his wrist from a looped string.

"Wait, guys."

Everyone went still and looked towards Azer.

"There's something under there." Azer pointed at the waterfall. He got up, replaced the cap, and walked closer to the waterfall along the water's edge. "I saw it reflecting."

"You sure it wasn't just the water?" questioned Erril.

"Certain."

As close to the waterfall as he could get now, Azer began removing his socks, shoes, and coat.

"Whoa, Azer, what are you doing?"

"I'm gonna get a look at it. I'm sure I saw something in there."

Then, Azer leaped into the water.

The cold was paralyzing. Below the water was a freezing abyss that made Azer's mind reel. Underneath the foamy white blanket of bubbles from the falling water, Azer could faintly make out a shiny object, rectangular in shape. But as he swam closer, he realized it didn't stop there. The rectangular, metallic object was a thin flap, one of many attached to a large wheel much taller than him. The wheel-like machine lay flat on the bed of the stream, mostly covered in silt.

Azer, freezing down to his bones, threw himself onto the rocks, shivering violently.

"I saw... a wheel," he managed.

"What? In the water?" Erril asked.

"Yes. Under... the falls. It looked... like a water... turbine."

Erril grabbed a towel from his oversized backpack and draped it over Azer, still shivering.

"A turbine? For real?"

"I don't know... why it's there... but... I saw a wire... connecting to it. Going up the waterfall. Just under the surface of the water... most likely."

"Are you saying..."

"We need to follow it," Azer stated, more determined now. "I think that's going to take us... where we need to go."

"Are you sure? If we stray off the trail, we might not ever make it back."

"I'm pretty sure about this."

Erril looked at the top of the waterfall and then sighed apprehensively. "If you insist. At least climbing this thing might warm you up."

After Azer retrieved his coat, the three began to climb up the rocks that surrounded the waterfall, the cold surface freezing Azer's fingers further. By the time they reached the top, Azer noticed that he did in fact feel warmer.

"Hey, Azer. You were right," Azer heard Erril call.

Erril was already hunched over the stream, his arm shoulder-deep into the moving water. He had uncovered a wire under the silt and mud, looking as if it continued upstream.

"Let's see where this thing goes."

They followed the stream's path a ways, staying close to the water's edge, until Erril broke the silence.

"You know, there could very well be wildlife here. The path might have been protecting us."

Azer took in his surroundings in the dark forest. For a moment, the shadows all seemed to be staring down at him. Then, all at once, he realized how isolated they were now that they were outside of the marked path of the cut trees.

"You're right. We should be on guard," Azer replied.

As they walked, Erril frowned, looking at the stream apprehensively. Azer, too, shifted his attention to the stream to see plump, camouflaged fish swimming around, only their movement noticeable against the grayish waterbed. Some of the larger fish had sharp, menacing spines on them. Some were almost as long as his whole body.

"Why would these fish need spikes?" Erril pondered, leaning down towards the water. "They're pretty big."

Erril turned to the other two. "You guys know what this means, right? There might b-"

In a swift moment, a massive, scaled creature erupted from the stream beside them, soaring through the air. It had rows of jagged teeth and shrunken eyes, its jaws agape and ready to clench down on Erril.

Massive pounding sounds rocked the earth, and then a bigger creature suddenly grabbed the first within its maw midair. With a sickening crunch, it gulped down viscera, scales, and bone, until it had swallowed the scaled creature whole.

The predator was colossal in size, with six clawed legs standing on the wet rocks by the stream. Its mouth was bloody, its teeth dull and lining an elongated jaw. The creature was battle-scarred, its fur-covered body sporting numerous gashes and cuts, and as it turned its tiny eyes towards the three shocked travelers, it took the new prey into its gaze.

Azer, Erril, and Rena backed up slowly. The creature had already killed in the blink of an eye. There was no way they could outrun it. Azer, maybe, with the full use of his S.R., but Erril and Rena? Not a chance. Azer's mind was racing, processing what to do, how to escape, while faced with the slowly approaching, hostile predator in front of them.

Suddenly, the creature made an agonized noise, and the bloodthirst in its eyes died out instantly, replaced by an expression of immense pain. Brief puffs of smoke came from its eyes, nose, and mouth as it gasped for breath, and it swayed left and right trying to maintain its footing. It continued growling and whining, reddish-orange glows now visible from inside its open jaw, until it let out the loudest roar yet.

"RUN!" Rena yelled.

The creature exploded in a massive blast of fire, meat and guts flying in every direction. A mix of burning brimstone and chunks of flesh whizzed by the three, and by the time the carnage was over, the only evidence of the creature left were stains of blood on their clothes and a red mist hanging in the air where the creature used to stand. Nearby, Rena stood resolute, hands pointed towards where the creature used to be, a sick look on her bloody face. She wiped her face with the back of her hand.

Erril, panting heavily, looked at Rena with disbelief.

"What the SHIT?!"

"I told you I could hold my own if I needed to," Rena said stoically, still wiping blood off her face. She pulled a piece of flesh out of her wiry hair and threw it to the ground.

"What did you do?" Azer asked. Erril was too shocked to say anything.

"My Val is to control sodium. The element."

"That doesn't help!"

"I just concentrated the sodium in its body into its stomach. Sodium reacts with water, there was plenty of water in its stomach, so the sodium reacted and exploded. Almost every living thing has sodium and water in it."

Azer turned towards the bloody mist cloud and the falling chunks of the creature splashing into the water. *Hold your own? That's going a bit further than that.*

"On the count of three, kick down the melted bars, alright?"

Grif was positioned in front of the iron bars of their cell, Saa standing beside him. Saa had already melted through the top of a few of the bars, concentrating infrared light onto them until they became red-hot and decayed. The three guards in front of the cell were oblivious. Saa finished melting the final bars and they were ready to be kicked down.

"One... two... three!"

Grif kicked the weakened bars with all of his might, and the red-hot molten metal that was holding them in place snapped and fell away.

In unison, the guards lunged at them with their spears, but the escapees swiftly dodged or leaped over the metal tips. Grif unleashed an electric kick onto one of the guards, Copycat kneed another in the face, and Saa squarely punched the last in the temple. All three of the guards reeled at the impact but steadied themselves again only a moment later, returning more vicious and more powerful. As Grif dodged blow for blow, now too focused to notice what was happening with Saa and Copycat, he realized the sheer bloodthirst of the guards. Their moves were brutal, aiming to gouge fingers and eyes with their spears and to break bones with their muscular and war-torn arms. It was nothing like the punches and kicks Grif and his friends were taught to use in the Battle Academy.

At last, Grif's opponent faltered in his stance, and Grif swept his leg, knocking the guard to the ground with a thud. The guard still conscious, Grif decided he would try to end the fight with a swift punch to the face. He reared back his fist, swung, and-

The guard, in a blinding fast movement, grabbed Grif's wrist before the punch could land, stopping it in midair. But there was something wrong—where the guard's hand met his wrist, Grif could feel a bizarre tingling sensation. And then he realized, in a sickening moment, that the guard's hand was *sinking into his arm*. The guard was looking up at Grif with a cruel stare.

Grif raised a leg and slammed it into the guard's face, knocking him out instantly. The guard's hand released, and blood poured out of where the hand once held. Grif looked at the wound in horror, seeing the skin and muscle where the guard's hand had been was removed, wiped away. All that remained was a hand-shaped wound with blood pouring out of it.

Grif promptly tore a piece of cloth off of his shirt and wrapped it around his wound. He turned to Saa and Copycat, still fighting.

"The guards have some kind of weird ability! Don't let them touch you!"

Saa, without hesitation, stepped away from the guard she was fighting and opted to blind him with infrared light before finishing him with a blow to the head.

"It's a little late for that!" Copycat shouted. The guard had already grabbed Copycat's arm and was pulling it closer to his face, a steel glare fixed on Copycat's eyes. Copycat was desperately trying to release his arm from the guard's grip, but the guard was too strong. When Copycat's struggling hand touched the guard's face, the tips of his fingers began to disappear.

"WHAT THE HELL IS HE DOING?!" Copycat yelled.

Now all of Copycat's fingers had disappeared, absorbed into the guard's face, still glaring coldly at him. Then his hand disappeared, then his wrist, before one of Copycat's clones drop kicked the guard, forcing the guard back. Copycat's arm was now missing its hand, and blood was pouring out of the wound. The guard lunged at Copycat again, and—

With a loud yell, Saa slammed the guard in the head with one of the torn metal bars. The guard fell to the ground with a thud, unconscious. Grif ran over to Copycat.

Copycat was breathing heavily, holding his right arm with the missing hand in horror. Grif began tearing off another piece of cloth.

"It doesn't hurt... it didn't hurt... but what the hell did he do? I'm missing a hand and it doesn't even hurt?!" Copy said between heavy breaths.

"Take this," Grif offered. He held out the cloth. "I don't know how we're going to get your hand back, but this should help stop the bleeding-"

"It's fine," Copycat said, a clone of himself he had made earlier walking over to him. "I'm lucky I copied myself so much during the fight. I ended up with a few clones left over."

"What do you mean?" Saa said, now approaching Copycat as well.

"Here, Saa, give me the iron bar," Copycat's clone said. Saa obliged, handing over the bar with the sharp tip.

The clone turned the bar over to its sharp side, put his hand on the ground, and pointed towards a spot on his wrist.

"Here?" the clone asked Copycat.

"Yeah," the original answered. "There."

"Don't look if you know what's good for you," both Copycats said in unison. The clone lifted the bar into the air, aimed it over the spot on his wrist, and, realizing what was about to happen, Grif looked away.

There was a sickening *thunk* sound, and then the sound of Copycat picking something up off the ground. When Grif turned back around, the clone was gone, only dust left, and Copycat was holding a brand new hand tight onto where his bloody wrist was.

"Did you just-" Saa exclaimed, horrified.

"Yeah. Not fun," Copycat answered. "Grif, could I have that cloth now?"

Grif handed over the cloth, thoroughly nauseated now. To Grif's own surprise, he was looking at Copycat with a mix of horror and sympathy.

"If I lose a limb and I have a clone available, I can just take the limb from the clone. We're all exactly identical, down to the cell, the only difference is I'm the original. I can't be replaced."

"What if you don't have any clones?" Saa asked.

"Then I'm screwed. Any clone I make copies my current physical state, so if I copy myself with a missing arm, the clone's gonna have a missing arm, too. I got lucky this time."

Grif had a brief moment of respect for Copycat.

"If you're not in too much pain, we can keep going," Saa said.

"I'm fine," Copycat answered. "It didn't hurt much anyway... it just felt really, really weird."

"I'm alright too," Grif answered. "I just lost some blood."

"Then we'll proceed with the next bit of the plan," Saa said. "And for that, you guys are gonna have to get closer."

Copycat and Grif slowly edged their way closer to each other. Then Saa walked behind them and put her hands on each of their shoulders.

And then everything went dark.

CHAPTER FIFTEEN:
SACRIFICES

In an instant, the darkness in Grif's eyes flashed into the bizarre mass of impossible colors that was infrared light. He was now seeing in temperature. Copycat, unfamiliar with the sensation, let out a yelp of surprise as his eyes adjusted to the new wavelength of light.

Taking in the environment, Grif could see the extent of the tunnel system they were in. It seemed to stretch on forever, twisting and curving, and there were strange, glowing lines along the walls he couldn't understand. His mind was still reeling at the idea of perceiving infrared light, and he still couldn't get ahold of *what* the impossible colors he was seeing were.

"What did you do?!" Copycat exclaimed, looking around frantically. "What's going on?! Why is that so bright?!" He pointed at a bright light on the ground behind them.

Hands still on Grif and Copycat's shoulders, Saa turned around, and Grif got a look at the light Copycat was referring to. Copycat was right; the light was blinding. It was like looking at the sun in the sky—he couldn't make out its shape or anything else near it from the brightness.

"You're seeing infrared light," started Saa, "and that thing on the ground is the torch the guard was holding earlier. It got knocked to the ground when we escaped."

Saa began stomping on the torch, snuffing it out until the glowing somewhat dissipated.

"Whoa, whoa, what are you doing?!" Grif exclaimed. "Don't we need that to see?!"

"Do we?" Saa said. From what Grif could gather through heat, Saa was looking at him with an eyebrow raised. "We can see infrared light now. Would you rather use a torch and let all the guards know exactly where we are at all times?"

"No, of course not."

"What we're going to do is sneak through these tunnels, find a guard, and Copycat, you're going to copy him. We're going to interrogate the guard's copy until he gives us answers, and then be on our way. That way the guard never goes missing and there won't be any trace of where we were. Actually..."

Saa released an arm from Copycat and pointed it towards some rocks on the tunnel wall. All of a sudden, a bright beam of light emitted from her hand and hit the rocks, making them glow brighter and brighter.

"Is that..."

"Infrared light? Yes. I'm heating up some rocks on the wall."

She replaced her hand on Copycat's shoulder and led them forward through the tunnel. Both his and Copycat's eyes were trained on the hot rocks.

"I kind of lied about not leaving a trace. You see, Erril has an infrared camera on him in case of emergencies. If I get separated from him, I can beam IR light from somewhere and he can pick it up and find me. If they make it into these tunnels, Erril should be able to find the hot rocks and follow our trail. As long as I don't make them hot enough to glow visible light, we should be good."

"Damn," Grif said. "You're a genius."

Saa just smiled.

They proceeded through the cold earthen tunnels, watching the faint heat signatures of the other prisoners receding. Saa occasionally would let go of Grif or Copycat to heat up more rocks before proceeding, leaving a trail Erril could find. The frigid tunnels made everything appear dark, but they could still make out an astonishing amount of detail in the rocky walls. The one thing that bugged Grif was the faintly glowing lines that stretched up and down the tunnels, sometimes crossing over to the other wall of the tunnel along the ground or roof.

"What are those?" Grif asked curiously. "Those lines?"

"I'm not sure. Let's check it out." Saa suggested.

"Yeah."

They walked over to the wall and Saa examined the lines. She removed her hand from Grif and ran a finger along it, plunging Grif back into darkness.

"It's a plant root," She pointed. "It isn't giving off much more heat than the rest of the tunnel."

"Why are there roots down here?" Grif asked. Saa replaced her hand and Grif's strange infrared vision returned.

"Your guess is as good as mine. I can't think of why the Schisms would need roots along their tunnels. Did they mention anything about it?"

"Not a thing."

"Huh. Let's just keep going, then. Nothing we can do."

They trekked for a while longer, taking the path that moved them higher when encountering splits. Grif was getting intensely cold now, unsettled by the fact that he could see his own skin getting dimmer and dimmer.

"Wait," Copycat said. "Stop. There's a guard." His now clammy fingers pointed towards a warm humanoid figure trekking along a break in the tunnel. The guard's body heat radiated out, heating up the places his bare feet stepped.

"Go for it," Saa whispered. "I'll stay close to give you vision."

They creeped up behind the guard, staying as quiet as possible, until Copycat reached out an arm and grabbed the guard's shoulder. Copycat then gripped the shoulder and pulled back, and another identical heat signature to the guard's was created out of the back of the first, Copycat violently dragging it closer. The first guard hadn't noticed a thing.

Grif saw the mouth of the copied guard open for a brief moment and cupped his hand over it.

They waited until the real guard walked out of sight, and then Copycat whipped his hands towards the guard's and restrained his arms tightly. The guard struggled for a moment, but stopped when Grif started to make cracks of electricity. Saa let go of Copycat and Grif and they could see only visible light once more.

Grif tapped his index finger and thumb together with a series of electric cracks until a constant stream of electricity was shooting between them. Holding his thumb and index finger an inch apart, he had his own electric torch. Grif's electric torch illuminated the guard's young face. Grif removed his hand from the guard's mouth.

"It's the devil child," the guard said as soon as he could speak.

"Don't call me that," Grif hissed in the Schism language. He moved his sparking fingers closer to the guard's face, which writhed in horror.

Copycat reminded him, "Remember, he doesn't know he's a clone. Threaten his life as much as you want."

"Tell me who I really am. Why am I here? Why did the chief send me away?" Grif demanded.

"I- I don't know. I don't know why ch- chief Kirottu sent you away. I don't know what happened to you either," the guard stuttered.

Grif moved the electricity closer, increasing in intensity.

"No! Really! I was too young! I don't remember any of it! We were always told that chief Kirottu's son had died!"

Grif looked again at the guard's young face. *He's probably telling the truth.* Grif turned back to Saa and Copycat and relayed the information.

"He doesn't know what happened to me."

"Really?" Saa exclaimed. "Then, ask him why we're being sacrificed. Ask him why it was bad for us to have Vals."

"Why are we being sacrificed?" Grif demanded. "What's wrong with our Vals?"

"You... you have the devil's powers. You and your friends. You're being sacrificed to appease our gods and... and to remove the devil from this world."

"Why are they devil's powers? Your people have Vals, too. You probably have one as well."

"We... why would we? The devil's powers are different. We... there's a legend that says we had to imitate the devil to make him stop ravaging our lands, giving us our own version of the devil's powers. But, by making a sacrifice to our gods, we can purge our sins. Our ancestors had to make devil's powers of our own... during a time of great calamity. The devil was attacking us. We barely survived only because of our imitation of the devil's powers. But in doing so, we were cursed. We can only become blessed again through sacrifice."

Grif could only stare blankly after hearing this. The guard's clone was still breathing heavily, terrified. But the way he looked at Grif's electric hands, it wasn't because he feared for his life—the guard probably didn't even know what electricity was. He was more afraid of Grif's "devil's powers."

"That's all we need," Grif told Saa and Copycat. "We're done with him."

Copycat obliged and the clone dissipated into darkly colored dust.

"What happened?" Saa asked. "What did he say?"

"The Schisms have some kind of legend that boils down to 'Vals are the devil.' It has to do with why the Schisms have their own Vals and why they're so corrupt. They don't even understand that they have their own Vals."

"Why?"

"Hell if I know. Everything he told me was part of some superstitious legend."

Grif stopped his electric torch, Saa grabbed their shoulders, and they continued into the tunnels.

Unbeknownst to them, a Schism leader was stationed behind the three, hiding in wait, slowly advancing on them. She was determined to recapture them in time for the sacrificial ritual. And behind her, reinforcements were arriving, materializing from within the roots in the walls, joining her in step.

Saa briefly noticed a slight change in brightness from behind her. She turned around to see the multitude of heat signatures, bright in color, with more appearing seemingly from within the roots, their bodies rapidly warping and morphing into a normal size.

The Schisms grabbed the three before any of them could scream, pulling them promptly into the organic highway of the roots in the walls.

The wire Azer was following had long since abandoned the stream, now leading the group into a downward sloping tunnel inside a mountain in the middle of the island. From the entrance, none of them could see the rocky peak.

Inside the tunnel, the darkness was crushing. Visibility was reduced to the small circle of light from Erril's flashlight and no more. It was cold and dry, unlike the moist air outside, and it seemed to get darker and colder with every step they took into the descending cavern. Azer relished the warmth of his coat.

As they walked, they noticed another wire traveling along the floor. They all stopped, Erril's flashlight following the wire's path until it met up with another running adjacently along the wall. As they proceeded further, more and more wires along the walls of the tunnel connected and traveled deeper into the cave in unison. Azer's curiosity and confusion grew and grew. Enigmatically, the wires and tunnel all had an inexplicable sense of intense age to them. The wires were slightly buried in the dirt-lain walls, and the tunnel wasn't round and earthy like a cave. Instead, it was squarish, a shape that became more and more defined as they descended deeper and deeper.

After what felt like hours of walking, the wires on the walls now innumerable, coating one side or another, the tunnel suddenly changed in nature.

With Erril's flashlight focused on the ground, the three saw a metal stairway just barely poking its way through the earth. And below that another, and another, and another. Each descending stair was covered in less and less dirt. As they went down the staircase, the true identity of the tunnel was revealed.

They had been walking down an ancient, metallic, sturdily-built structure with rivets in the walls and fluorescent lights that had long since been snuffed out. And this staircase was taking them to the end of a corridor, a massive room that became more expansive as they got closer to its maw.

Within a colossal room of finely crafted metal was a gargantuan spaceship, immeasurably tall and hundreds of feet long. Its shape was indescribable by nature, made of some kind of deeply forieign material. Its composition could only be dreamed of. Capsules surrounded the ship's underside, most missing but some remaining, each large enough to comfortably fit a person. A faint, blush glow illuminated the craft from above, a massive window of clear material surrounding the top of the chamber from edge to edge, letting the three see the heavens with striking clarity. Structures in the room stretched up and down the walls, each as tall as an entire building. The walls had countless lines running down them, coming from numerous entrances into the main chamber. Azer couldn't place what the lines were yet—until he realized, they were wires like the ones they had followed here. Countless wires from countless places, all funneling power into this one craft.

The ship's magnitude; the unfathomable technology within every square inch of it; the staggering complexity of the whole spacefaring vehicle; all of it surrounded by the husk of an advanced society–

Azer had seen it all before.

He fell to his knees and collapsed to the cold floor. His skull felt like it was going to split in two, thoughts and visions whirling through his mind, none of them his own. Every time he tried to process the colossal ship in front of him, he perceived it through different eyes. The sense of familiarity with this ship that Azer had felt throughout his life grew stronger and stronger.

Until Erril's gloved hands tapped Azer vigorously on his shoulder.

At once, the pain and the déjà vu came to a halt, and awareness of his surroundings came back to him.

"Hey, Azer," Erril said, concerned. "You alright?"

"I- I'm okay. Thanks, Erril. I'm alright now. We can keep going."

"If you're ready. But... man. I just... I can't really describe this thing. That something like this has just... been here. All along. And nobody's known."

Azer's familiarity spiked again before dissipating. *Maybe not nobody...*

"I've never seen anything like this before," Rena added. "It's like... you know how if we were to show someone from the past our current technology, they wouldn't be able to understand it? That's how I feel now."

"And it looks as if some kind of civilization had been using it," Erril finished.

They all stood and took in the sight for a moment before Erril turned back and began climbing up the stairs again.

"I think I saw another tunnel branching off of ours on the way here," Erril said. "Let's follow that one back and see if we can get any closer to Saa."

With that, Azer turned his back on the ship and began climbing the stairs after Erril. He tried to ignore the beckoning feeling he felt towards it as he left the room.

It was a terrorizing realization for Grif to wake up to scorching air burning his skin and a bubbling pool of lava beneath his feet. Realizing the situation, he began to hyperventilate, only further singeing his lungs, his chest pressing against the ropes that bound him to the metal behind him.

The metal—what *was* he bound to? Grif looked up and down the structure he was tied to by scratchy, bloodstained rope—only to see a towering steel cylinder stretching up as far as he could see and down into the pool of lava beneath. Countless pipes and wires stretched into the walls of the chamber and down the massive steel cylinder. Grif recognized the structure as an ancient geothermal power plant. To his left and right were Copycat and Saa, both awake, also tied to the structure with blood dripping down their heads.

"O devil-possessed child of mine," Chief Kirottu boomed into the sweltering cavern. "Today you will meet your end for the greater good of this society and to appease our great God Ydin. He will bear the blood of our sacrifices for the benefit of the world."

Grif squirmed within the ropes around him, but they didn't budge. His arms were tied tightly to his body. The way Kirottu spread his arms out towards the massive geothermal vent—*did he think the structure was a god?*

As Kirottu continued, Grif frantically surveyed the scene for a plan of escape. The entire Schism tribe appeared to be standing behind the scarred figure of Kirottu, the majority armed with spears. Grif assumed that most, if not all of them, possessed the Val that let them travel through the roots in the tunnels and absorb into organic matter, like Copycat's hand. It was as if they could pull other organic matter "inside" as well, which would explain how the three of them had gotten dragged here in the first place.

"With these spears," Kirottu continued, with Schisms beside him picking up three colossal spears with razor-sharp tips. Stains of blackened blood colored the iron shafts. "We will impale the sacrifices all the way through their cursed bodies, snapping the rope behind them that keeps them tied to Ydin's holy shell. Then, they will fall into his burning cauldron below, and the smoke they leave behind will cleanse our people."

Grif became acutely aware of the knotted rope behind his back, keeping him from falling into the lava beneath. He shivered at the idea of meeting such a gruesome fate. Seeing the executioners with their massive spears move closer to the rocky ledge, eyes fixed on where they would stab him, Saa, and Copycat, Grif made a last-ditch attempt to stall.

"W- wait!" he cried in the Schisms' language. "Chief Kirottu, you never explained what happened to me, your son! Why was I sent away? Why am I being sacrificed now?"

Chief Kirottu's face hardened, his remaining eye reduced to a scrutinizing glare. His partner beside him, who Grif presumed to be his mother, flinched at the question but stayed resolute.

"You *were* my beloved son, up until the devil took you from me. Since you do not remember, I shall detail to you the chance I gave you when you were young, before you foolishly returned here. A year after you were birthed, during a terrible storm, a bright light from the sky, the sun itself, decided to strike you down. This was but a terrible calamity at first, until it happened again. And when it happened a total of seven times, over seven different storms, I knew that God was striking you down because you had the devil's curse. God tried so hard to kill you, but yet you survived each time, until the seventh, when the heart within you stopped. Desperate, I tried to save my son. I instructed the members of our tribe to replace your faulty heart with a sacred stone, passed down through generations. My father told me that the stone had come from another world. And after the operation was complete, the light above struck you one final time, and you breathed again. Your heart had been replaced by the stone, but we made a terrible realization."

"The power of the sun that had struck you down during those fateful storms still resided within you, and at your fingertips you were able to create sparks of light that I knew only a God and the devil himself were capable of creating. I should have killed you then and there, but the compassion within me couldn't bear to do it. So we took you to another of our gods, Kaari, within a massive, sacred site within our mountain, and prayed for her boon. The prayer was answered and we received a better fate for you. With Kaari's holy blessing, we took you away from the land of the Schisms and into the heavens. We had hoped that by doing so, God would remove the devil from your body. But, alas, you have come back here, the devil only stronger within you. Now you must die, and be retaken by Ydin's jaw and sent into the gates of the underworld where you belong."

The cavernous walls rung out with the last word Kirottu spat, not a soul making a sound. The lava below bubbled, as if beckoning Grif to his fate.

"Make no mistake, Grif," Kirottu growled again. "You are cursed. The world will be better without your presence tainting it. And I realize now the mistake I made in saving you from God's will, who tried to strike you down when you were young."

Infinitely more than the heat below scorching Grif's bare and torn feet, Grif burned with rage, visceral and blinding. His own father wished him dead. The father and mother he'd been seeking for as long as he could remember wanted to burn him alive, seeing his powers and who he was as a curse. Grif wanted to make Kirottu see who he really was. Show his parents the real him.

Kirottu gestured to the spear-wielding Schisms to begin the ritual, and they approached the sacrifices, ready to strike.

Rage filled Grif's entire being, every molecule in his body, until the molecules themselves began to split apart, dividing into their essential components, protons, neutrons, electrons. All of Grif's body and soul slowly reduced to electrons, a conscious flow he could control. And in this refreshing new form, he slipped out of the bindings of the ropes around him, weaving between their atoms and moving around the polymers.

Grif had become electricity itself.

And he had never felt more alive.

In an instant, he arced to the iron tip of the spear that had intended to impale him, letting himself flow through the metal, down the handle, and into the hands of his to-be executioner. He electrocuted the guard from his hands to his arms to his head, who collapsed with steam emitting from his mouth. Grif then shot through the air at 1/7th the speed of light to the next guard, then the next, before promptly returning to a corporeal form in front of his father.

"Go to hell," Grif spat.

Grif reared back an arm, clenching his fist, and punched Kirottu in his battle-scarred face with all he had, breaking his nose beneath Grif's fingers. Using the confusion to his benefit, Grif rushed over to Saa and Copycat to untie them. At a glance, Grif couldn't tell who was more shocked—his fellow sacrifices or the Schisms.

Every single one of the Schisms—man, woman and child—was dead set on killing the fleeing sacrifices. With the ability to freely move through organic matter or take organic matter into themselves, each had a formidable power that made it impossible for Grif and his friends to defend themselves.

Grif became electricity again, zapping between the bodies of the attacking Schisms one by one, clearing a path for Saa and Copycat to escape. He became corporeal again, standing in front of his two comrades.

"We gotta escape! Focus on getting out of here!" he yelled over the chaos. They nodded, making a beeline for the path, but–

The corpse of a Schism guard, a bloody hole in his chest, flew through the air and onto the ground in front of Saa and Copycat. Kirottu emerged from it, his arm soaked in the guard's blood, lunging at one of

Copycat's clones. When Kirottu touched it, the clone withered away into nothing, becoming a shriveled husk.

"A clone," Kirottu growled.

Their path out was now blocked from all ends, Kirottu blocking their way and the rest of the enraged Schisms behind them. What Kirottu did to the clone was different, Grif noticed. It wasn't the absorption of organic matter—it was something far more sinister. The original Copycat looked at the defeated clone with horror.

Grif gazed at the corpse Kirottu had hidden in, his bloodsoaked arm the telltale murder weapon.

"Why did you kill him?" Grif asked the chief.

"Corpses struggle less. Better for transportation."

The fallen Schisms were being used as transportation too, the living jumping from corpse to corpse with no regard for their fallen brethren. It made Grif sick to the stomach.

"What will you do, Grif? Will you abandon your comrades to escape? Or will you stand with your friends and be tortured to death?"

Grif looked between Kirottu and the approaching Schisms, still traveling from corpse to corpse to get closer. Time was running out...

"I barely found it in time!" Erril gasped, sprinting down the tunnel. "Saa, I'm coming! I found the heated rocks!"

"Erril!" Rena shouted as they ran. "If there's an enemy, will you give me permission?"

"Permission to do what?!"

Rena looked seriously at Erril, a grim hint of malice in her eyes. Erril's jaw dropped. *Would he?*

In a quick movement, Grif shoved Copycat and Saa past Kirottu, into the tunnel, but before Kirottu could reach out to touch them, Grif grabbed Kirottu's arms, holding them tightly. Saa and Copycat fell past him, out of harm's way.

"So be it," hissed Kirottu.

Grif felt the most peculiar sensation in his hands. It felt like his hands and wrists were dying before his eyes. Kirottu was the harbinger of decay, and Grif was his target.

The spread of decay reached further and further up his body, reaching his chest, then his neck. Then the decay crept up Grif's face at a terrifying rate, numbing his lips—it was becoming hard to breathe from his now rotten lungs. But just before the decay reached his eyes and killed his brain, he saw a haunting sight. Kirottu had finally let go, gripping his own stomach with agony. He coughed and gasped, and every time his mouth opened Grif could see a reddish glow within him. Kirottu began to shake, training his one bloodshot eye on Grif.

"CURSE YOU!" Kirottu screamed, lunging at Grif's face.

Then, he exploded. Kirottu disappeared, and in his place there was a colossal explosion of fire and the dustlike remains of his body. The shockwave echoed through the cavern, reverberating over and over. The only evidence left of Kirottu was the occasional fleck of blood on nearly every surface of the cavern.

Grif breathed heavily through his dying lungs, terror and shock clouding his mind. Was Kirottu... gone? Grif turned around, most of his face decayed, drops of Kirottu's blood on his body.

And he saw his friends.

There was Rena, her arms extended towards where Kirottu had just been, her eyes shining with malice. There was Erril, a look of mortified disgust on his face, and Azer without one.

They were finally here.

Grif turned back towards Copycat and Saa, also covered in blood, and motioned them back towards their rescuers. They wordlessly obliged, but Grif found his body unable to move.

The Schisms toppled or killed their fellow people to try to reach the escapees, using their corpses as means of transportation. Their hands would claw and snatch at the fleeing teenagers, screaming and cursing at them, enraged at their lost chief. Just before Grif could be pulled into the wave of wrathful Schisms, Azer grabbed his hand.

Azer's arm began to smoke with his S.R. Grif felt the energy of life flow into his afflicted limbs, liveliness filling his chest and healing his dead internals. And as quickly as Kirottu had almost killed him, Azer had undone all of Kirottu's work, and then some. Grif felt like he could run faster than anyone else, hyper-aware and filled to the brim with adrenaline. They raced past the Schisms and through the ascending tunnel, following the moving illumination of Erril's flashlight up the labyrinth.

"You're better," Azer pointed as they ran, surprised.

"I am," Grif said. "How did you do that?"

"Don't worry about that right now. We need to get out of here!"

Now deeper into the tunnels, the Schisms were utilizing the roots that ran along the cave walls to get ahead of the escapees. The six of them barely threw the approaching Schisms away, some Schisms able to grab on to someone before being shook off. Grif ran towards a wall as another Schism was emerging from the root, and he touched the root with his index finger. Electricity jolted through the root, shocking the Schisms within.

"I'm destroying their means of travel," Grif told the others. Erril, Azer, and Rena were confused, but Saa and Copycat gave him an approving nod.

Now that the Schisms couldn't use the burnt roots, they had no choice but to chase the escapees on foot. The tunnel weaved higher and higher, the Schisms growing closer and closer, before the light of dawn was finally visible from afar.

"We're almost there!" Erril yelled to the others. Running on nothing but pure adrenaline, they could only nod in response.

Finally, they emerged. They had entered the Schism camp again. Grif realized there was a network of tunnels throughout the camp.

Hardly processing his surroundings, the group blindly sprinted into the dimly lit forest. They weren't even looking at the markings. All they had time to process was the light of the sun—towards the ocean.

Now, the Schisms were shrinking into the trees and materializing from the trunk's other side, before leaping back into another tree. They never touched the ground. They just hopped from tree to tree, racing after the escapees with astonishing speed.

"That's why the leaves were untouched!" Erril yelped at the sight, gasping as he ran. "They don't even touch the ground!"

Just then, a Schism leapt from a tree next to Erril and scratched his face with overgrown nails. Erril winced with surprise and faltered in his step. The Schisms had caught up now and were striking at the escapees without mercy. Saa had part of her shoulder cut by a knife-wielding Schism, Azer's head was hit with a club, and even Grif couldn't avoid the grasping hands of the attackers.

Then, finally, they ran into the light of morning, out of the trees and towards the glistening sea, running as fast as their bodies could take them on the cool sand. The Schisms could utilize their powers no longer. The beach was a sanctuary.

The *Stormbreaker* came into sight. They ran further and further from the snarls and screams of the malicious Schism tribe, until finally, Erril pressed open the hatch.

They clambered inside frantically. Not an instant after the last person's foot entered the ship, Erril slammed the door behind them. Erril ran to the cockpit, and soon the *Stormbreaker* ascended with furious pounding on the hull, until, finally, the ship was out of reach. Out of the window, as the *Stormbreaker* flew higher, the remaining Schisms were furiously gathered underneath them as if they would come back.

Finally, all was quiet. Copycat coughed somewhere across the ship.

As the ship accelerated and rose into the atmosphere, and Arcus Island shrunk to become a speck in a bluish-green sea, Azer noticed something haunting underneath the water's surface.

Between the planet's continents and islands were the sunken remains of a colossal bridge, hardly visible under the water's surface. But the craftsmanship was there, the engineering and genius of a long-lost society, sunken under the ocean and gone from sight.

Forever.

And Azer's head ached with familiarity once more.

Dr. D could hardly believe the recounted experiences of the disheveled boys and girls, having returned from their misadventures far sooner than anticipated.

"All of this... really happened?" he uttered.

"Yes. It's... impossible to believe, really," Azer said. "Grif's own father was the leader of the Schisms."

"And you think the guard you interrogated was telling the truth? About the legend?" Dr. D asked.

"I'm certain," Grif affirmed.

Dr. D looked nowhere in particular for a moment, the gears turning in his head. His face looked simultaneously hopeful and haunted.

"What this leads me to believe..." he started, "is that we might be dealing with a Val."

"What?" asked Grif.

"The Magna virus. It's a Val. It's a Val-based virus. That's why it can't be cured, the virus itself is a Val, no modern medicine can beat a Val."

"Then what can?"

"Another Val. The cure has to be Val-based as well. Grif, you said that in the legend, the Schisms were 'attacked by the devil' and 'had to create their own devil's powers to survive?' And we already know the Schisms think Vals are the devil, right?"

The answer was dawning upon Grif now, too. His face twisted with shock.

"Then they must have tried making their own Val-based cure to fight the Val-based virus. And I think I know just the way to do the same."

After months of tireless engineering, Dr. D held in his hand a small vial of darkly colored liquid. The entirety of Team Virga had gathered, each of them standing or sitting, eyes trained on the vial. Mrs. Korca was jittery, Okta's stoic expression had been replaced by a determined glare, Delvin looked disheveled as ever, and Azer and Grif sat down in front of the vial with cautious hope within them.

The number of infections had risen since their return from Arcus island. The first deaths had already occured. The virus took over a month to kill each of its victims, and dozens had died in the time it took to develop a cure. But, finally, there was hope.

There had been no recorded instances in Zysti galaxy's history of a manmade Val up until now. An ancient group of Schisms had done so—but their cure was imperfect. Bodies not suited to handle Vals were damaged and corrupted by the Val-based cure. Dr. D's cure aimed to avoid that problem.

Like its ancient counterpart, the new cure used a synthetic Val to destroy the virus. But there was a clever exception to the rule of the body giving something up in order to contain a Val. A small amount of corvyte, the revolutionary material that made up the majority of Nur's exports, was injected into the body alongside the Val-based cure. The corvyte mimics an organ within the body, acting as a buffer against the negative effects of the injected Val. Instead of a vital organ or bodily function ceasing to work, the corvyte organ acts as a sacrifice. The body gives up the corvyte organ to hold the Val instead of damaging anything essential.

Dr. D held the vial to the light above them within the room. The liquid was translucent, a grayish color with a hint of blue, and appeared to glow and move within itself. He prepared the vial within a syringe and held the needle up to the light.

"You all know why you're here," Dr. D said. "The cure is done. But before that, I have an important revelation for you all."

Dr. D's ghostly eyes trained on Azer.

"Azer."

Azer stood from his seat. "Yeah?"

"I analyzed this thing last night, to double check its composition. To make sure it's safe for consumption and all. And I found that, minus the corvyte, this Val-based cure... it has an identical composition, down to the very molecule...

...to your S.R."

CHAPTER SIXTEEN:
THE CALM

Mostly cloudy. 13mph winds blowing south. Forty-eight degrees fahrenheit. With wind chill, forty-two. Unusual weather patterns incoming. Forecasts may be unreliable.

"**B**efore," Delvin started, breaking the shock in the room and speaking loudly to attract the attention of the others, "you all do anything with that... cure. I want to tell you something important. Or, ask, rather."

All eyes were on Delvin, who was standing tall in the center of the room. Tension filled the air.

"The fact that we've created this cure leads me to believe that we have been observing different things through the microscope over the past few months."

Dr. D was growing angry. "Delvin, what are you on about? You've hardly even been helping us develop the cure."

"Yes, and I have a reason for that. This virus... we can't kill it."

"Delvin, you are out of line. What are you-"

"But we can," Grif interrupted. "The Schisms—my species—they ended up how they were because of the cure they tried to make. It's all in the legend they told me. The Schisms got infected by the Magna virus a long time ago, and when they tried to make a cure for it, it corrupted their bodies and gave them mutated Vals. It made their brains permanently underdeveloped. But we fixed that, didn't we? Wasn't the corvyte supposed to fix that?"

The group looked at Grif with apprehension, then relented. Delvin spoke again.

"No, that's not what I mean. The cure you've developed will work, yes. What I mean is… we *shouldn't* kill it. In the time that I spent studying the virus, not only did I come to the conclusion that it was incurable, I realized that I felt, how do I put this… *blessed.*"

He paused.

"I found a certain holiness… maybe an unholiness within the virus that I found beautiful. Godly. And with my research I found several unsolved documents from long ago. I uncovered every record of a barren planet that may have once supported life—every planet in the Manim deadzone—and found that every single one contained organic matter that had its DNA wiped—the exact deadly properties of the Magna virus we've been studying. What we're dealing with isn't something that medicine can cure; no, it's far beyond that. Far beyond the scale of us and our small lives on this planet. The Magna virus has killed *trillions.* Dozens and dozens, maybe hundreds of different intelligent species in our corner of the galaxy have been wiped out by this single virus. But we aren't actually dealing with a virus, we're dealing with perfection. The perfect lifeform. We're dealing with the barrier to life itself, the single filter that stops life from evolving. Do you all *really* think you can beat that? There are five of you in the room with me—do you all think five lifeforms can compete against something that has killed trillions? Can you really fight *perfection?*"

Delvin paused again. Nobody said a word.

"Science is discovery. It is experience. And so, I want to ask you all to join me in the discovery of perfection. We've seen a glimpse, yes, but there is so much left in store for us. I found inspiration long ago in Nova Noctis, the group dedicated to the pursuit of The Shades. Their methods were flawed, but the idea of searching for the ultimate answer to our world is one I can relate to. The Magna virus is the answer to all of the questions we've asked together. Wouldn't you like to experience it in its full glory? If we stop the Magna now, we'll miss out on what it feels like to experience the ultimate lifeform. Frankly, I'm excited for it. So I want to ask you, my lab partners, my colleagues, my friends and fellows in science to join me as we experience perfection before we die. Wouldn't you like to get a glimpse of God?"

Azer's heart was pumping madly. Was it terror he was feeling? Everyone in the room was looking at Delvin with horror and disbelief. But what sickened Azer most was the look of hope and joy on Delvin's face.

"Of... of course not," Mrs. Korca croaked, her voice breaking. "Delvin, people are going to *die!* How can you just stand there like that, like it's a good thing!"

Delvin's look of excitement quickly fell off his face into an expression of genuine disappointment.

"I'd hoped..." he murmured. "Do you all... really?"

"Delvin," Dr. D said, more shocked than enraged. "No. We don't. You're completely mad. Get out of here now. NOW."

The moment Dr. D's free hand pointed towards the door, Delvin snatched the syringe from Dr. D's other hand. Without a word or change in expression, in a flash of movement, Delvin injected the cure into Dr. D's chest.

Dr. D groaned and fell to the floor. His tall figure no longer obscuring Delvin's face, the others could see a look of sadness on his visage.

"I didn't want to do this," Delvin said quietly.

Amid screams, Delvin approached the rest of the group. Azer had to get to Dr. D, fast. Something in the cure was killing him.

"Ortum was the easiest to take out, and my only real challenge," Delvin explained as he strode closer to the rest of Team Virga. "His body is a glitch between life and death, so injecting him again with the cure that originally revived him has reversed his fate."

Azer activated his S.R. and tried to jump past Delvin to get to Dr. D. In a swift movement, Delvin grabbed Azer's arm.

"He can't be saved," Delvin explained. "Who knows what will happen to his body now? Besides, *you* aren't my next target."

Delvin threw Azer against the wall with frightening force, then continued walking. Quickly, Azer realized Delvin's intentions.

Mrs. Korca, too, was frantically trying to reach Dr. D. Upon seeing Delvin approaching her, she screamed again. She was cornered.

Azer tried to lift himself up, but he was too dazed from the impact. Grif tried to tackle Delvin, but Delvin easily threw Grif aside.

And in a quick moment of disbelief, Mrs. Korca grasped at her own throat, choking, and then collapsed to the ground, dead.

Delvin watched her body fall to the floor.

"This is what you chose!" Delvin thundered. "Your death was a waste! A meaningless death at my hands! You could have chosen to experience the ultimate lifeform, but your sentimentality got in the way! You are nothing but a fool!"

Grif was breathing heavily, looking at Mrs. Korca's motionless body.

"No," Grif breathed.

"WHAT DID YOU DO?!" Grif roared at Delvin. He looked back at Grif, unfazed.

"She was next on my list. There's a method, you see, to getting rid of you all. I know your Vals. I'm not a haphazard berzerker. Dr. D was the only truly strong fighter among us, so I took him out first with the cure. Korca could have used her density triggers to thin the air, rendering my wind Vals useless. But, after removing the air in her lungs, I only have Okta, Grif, and Azer to remove from my path."

"You're a madman, Delvin," Okta growled. "You're unhinged."

"And you can imagine how insane I think you all are to deny a glimpse of the ultimate lifeform before death."

On one end of the lab stood Delvin, the bodies of Dr. D and Mrs. Korca at his feet. Grif breathed heavily, tears in his eyes at the sight of them. Azer was too shocked to believe it. On the other end of the room were Azer, Grif, and Okta, horrified at the sight.

"Our first move," Okta said to the boys, lowering his voice, "is to escape the lab. We're at Delvin's mercy in this enclosed space."

"HE KILLED MRS. KORCA!" Grif yelled. "HE KILLED HER! AND DR. D IS DYING TOO!"

"I know," Okta growled, voice still lowered. "But it doesn't change our first move. We'll all be dead within the next minute if we don't leave *now*."

And, right on cue, Delvin began to walk towards the three. Air whirred through the holes in his hands, a sound that resembled a scream.

"But... we can't leave them!" Azer said with a shaking voice.

"Our priority is to escape. We can't save them by dying here."

Azer took one last look at Dr. D and Korca and then steeled himself. He turned towards the entrance and sprinted up the stairs, followed quickly by Okta and Grif.

Delvin chased the three up and out of the lab. Azer, Okta, and Grif ran up the staircase and pushed open the door, emerging into the outside world.

The sun above shone on Nur with altered light. The ground had an orangish tint as if it were lit by a great fire. Its color held a corrupted quality.

Azer, Grif, and Okta burst out of the Battle Academy, panting. Only seconds behind came Delvin, not bothering to touch the door, having it float open from a gust of wind instead. They ran into the Battle Academy courtyard, trying to distance themselves from the haunting whir of Delvin's wind.

Okta turned back towards Delvin.

"Delvin's a powerhouse," said Okta. "He's mastered his wind Vals to an incredible degree. And he's no longer bound by the moral restraints he'd obeyed before."

"How does that help us?" Grif retorted. "I think we could infer that much. He killed Mrs. Korca instantly."

"I'm saying that there's no chance of beating him through brute force. Delvin knows every attack you have, and he can and will counter each one."

"I thought we were trying to get away!" Grif exclaimed.

"And then what?" Okta snapped. "He gives up? Delvin's unhinged. His insanity won't stop at killing us. He truly believes experiencing the Magna virus is like experiencing God. Nur isn't safe from him."

"You said it yourself, he's nearly invincible," Grif replied.

"*Nobody's* invincible. We can win if, and *only* if we have a plan."

"Then what's your plan?"

"Two things: One, we need to get out in the open. Two, I need to touch him. Even a brief graze will do."

"Why in the open?" Azer asked.

"It gives him fewer weapons to work with. What kills isn't the wind, it's what the wind throws around. We need to get to the outskirts of town, ideally the plains."

It was just then that a car slammed down only inches in front of the three, sending shrapnel in every direction and partially embedding itself in the ground. Azer looked behind to see Delvin in hot pursuit, running by parked cars.

"Get out of the parking lot!" Okta yelled. "NOW!"

The three scattered in every direction. Air whirred behind them as the holes in Delvin's hands circulated immense amounts of the atmosphere. The wind, moving fast enough to create trails of water vapor, flowed through and around his hands, circling behind him into an exponentially growing tornado. The tornado swerved through the parking lot, launching cars into the air with stunning accuracy. They fell only inches away from the three, grazing them with ripped and torn metal shards and glass. Okta and Azer found themselves running side-by-side just as a car soared in Azer's direction. He activated S.R., his senses sharpened, and dodged the car as it slammed into the pavement with a horrific crunch, showering them in fuel and scrap.

The three gathered again at the parking lot's edge. The area around them was slowly growing hillier and grassier. They had reached the Octane fields on the outskirts of Nur.

They stopped at the plains and turned back to see Delvin still approaching. He wasn't touching the ground, rather floating just above it on a layer of wind.

"You've chosen a foolish way to disarm me, Okta," Delvin said. "Just because there's nothing around doesn't mean I'm powerless. Never have you had to truly *fight* me before."

"That's objective one," Okta muttered to Azer and Grif. "Ignore what he's saying. This is an ideal position. Now, your next priority is *me.* I need to touch him, and I need to survive."

"Why you?" Grif challenged.

"I am his next target. He realizes what I can do and therefore wants to kill me next. He's calculated. Ortum was the strongest—he took him out first. Korca was the best counter to wind—she could reduce air pressure. She was taken out next. I have dual minds, I'm a master strategist. My Val may be our only chance to get into that head of his and figure out what his next moves are before they're made."

"Fine. Let's do this."

Delvin carefully dropped himself to the ground and aligned his arms in a strange manner, as if he were holding an invisible spear. The whirring sound climaxed for a moment, becoming a high-pitched whistle, and Azer noticed water vapor circling around and around through the holes in his hands, spreading out in a line. The line of spinning air grew more and more visible, the speed increasing further and further, until it looked like

Delvin was holding a ghostly white spear through the holes in his hands. He brandished it at the three.

"It was without a doubt from the beginning that the rest of Team Virga would try to stop me should they not decide to join me," Delvin said. "Enough of the heroics. Your empathy is getting in the way of human discovery."

Delvin swung the spear. The cylinder of spinning air extended from his hands and cut downwards, barely missing Okta. The ground that the spear touched was instantly cut and wiped away, erased by the cyclone.

Azer dashed towards Delvin, his S.R. activated, his senses sharp and his surroundings moving slow. His body went on overdrive, watching the wind spear in the air as he charged.

Azer noticed something about the rotating spear: the wind had picked up bits of the ground that it had cut away. Pieces of rock and dirt, while miniscule, swirled around the cylinder of air Delvin wielded. Seeing it now, it seemed obvious: the spear didn't erase what it touched, it eroded its surroundings at a nearly instant rate. The material that was ground away stayed spinning inside of the spear. This gave Azer an idea.

He dodged under the spear's cutting wind and distanced himself from Delvin, making his way over to Okta. But before he could speak, Okta said:

"Tell me exactly how your ability works. S.R, was it?"

"It's a supercharge of the body. Your senses go on overdrive, your muscles go on overdrive, and from what I saw from saving Grif on Kular, even regeneration goes on overdrive. It's pure life at the cost of massive amounts of energy, and I can temporarily give some of it to other people as well."

"Perfect. I need you to inject me with as much of your S.R. as possible."

"What?!"

"Do it. The longer you wait, the worse our odds will get," said Okta.

"I just told you, it drains your energy like nothing else. It could kill you."

"Do it."

Azer stood in front of Okta in the heat of battle, thinking quickly.

"Fine. You probably have a plan, but indulge mine as well. His wind spear is just rapidly rotating air, it doesn't just erase things. You know how Delvin was throwing cars at us? We're covered in fuel now. If you can get that fuel inside of Delvin's spear, and if Grif lights it up, it'll make a huge explosion. The spear is constantly circulating air; it'll be oxidizing the fire big time."

Okta peered at Azer for a moment before dodging the incoming wind spear. Azer grabbed Okta's arm and let the S.R. flow through his body. It moved through his chest to his arm to his hand and fingers, moving into Okta's body, until Okta's own skin began to steam, and he nodded at Azer.

Okta dashed away towards Delvin, sprinting faster than any organic body should allow. His shoes pounded on the grass of the fields beneath him, the fields he felt like he was flying over. Delvin turned his focus to Okta and was surprised to see the speed he was moving at. Immediately, Delvin wielded his spear and swung it downwards just as Okta extended an arm towards his face—

A slashing sound rang through the turbulent air. For a moment, nobody moved, all of the combatants on the field watching the scene. Delvin was holding his wind spear below Okta, and Okta's hand was only millimeters in front of Delvin's face.

"Touched you," said Okta.

But just then, Okta's arm began to fall, sliding off his body and landing in the grass with a thud. Blood poured out of a stump on Okta's shoulder, and he grasped it while letting out a groan of agony.

"You..." Okta growled between labored breaths. "You made one... fatal... mistake. Smell that?"

Delvin looked down at Okta's severed arm to see that another liquid was dripping from it other than blood. Liquid fuel. It soaked the sleeve and dripped between the blades of grass below. And in Delvin's spear of wind, alongside vaporized crimson blood, the fuel swirled in a potent vapor.

"NOW!" Okta shouted.

Grif shot a bolt of electricity towards Delvin's wind spear, igniting it instantaneously. Arcs of spinning flame ignited the fuel vapor, exponentially increasing in speed, the rotating explosion making its way down the entire spear. The flames were fanned by the rapidly moving air. In the blink of an eye, the colossal explosion traveled down to the holes in Delvin's hands, surrounding him and Okta in a ball of fire.

The heat of the explosion reached as far away as Azer and Grif, and the air around them was sucked into and then pushed away from the blast. When the smoke and dust subsided, the two were lying on the ground apart from each other, charred and bleeding.

"OKTA!" Azer and Grif yelled in unison.

They sprinted over to Okta, frantically trying to help him up and distance him from Delvin, who was stirring. Okta remained limp, groaning as Azer and Grif dragged him away.

Delvin pushed himself up to a kneel and looked at his bloody hands, shaking.

"DAMN YOU!" he yelled. His face was enraged. "DAMN YOUR TRICKS!"

In Azer and Grif's arms, Okta began to stir now, too. He attempted to move his legs to standing.

"He's... not... done..." Okta groaned. "He's... coming."

Delvin, after several attempts, pushed himself up to a standing position and turned towards the three.

"I must admit that some compliments are in order," Delvin said briskly. "You found an opportunity and acted upon it. And for that, I must thank you. I cannot grow until I am challenged, and I am being challenged indeed. But your attempts are still useless. You cannot beat me."

Delvin took a sickeningly familiar stance and air began to hiss through the holes in his hands. The hissing rose in pitch until it became almost inaudible, and Delvin's figure slowly faded away into invisibility.

"NO!" Azer yelled. "Get him! Quick!"

Grif sprinted forward towards Delvin to try and catch him. But by the time Grif arrived at his old position and fired a small bolt of lightning, he was gone. All signs of Delvin had vanished into thin air.

Then, a familiar voice boomed around them from all directions.

"Have you ever wondered what truly makes us intelligent?" Delvin asked from nowhere in particular.

Azer and Grif were back-to-back, looking around frantically for the source of Delvin's voice. Okta, hardly conscious, propped himself up by putting his remaining arm around Grif's shoulder, back-to-back as well.

"I can hear his thoughts," Okta managed. "I managed to touch him before my arm was severed, I can hear his next moves."

"Yeah, but that's not gonna help us much if we don't know *where* he's thinking them!" Grif retorted.

"Grif, you need to-"

Just then, a slash of cutting wind impacted Grif's torso. He began to bleed profusely, wincing and desperately searching for Delvin's presence.

"It's been found that a number of species on a vast number of planets show intelligence," Delvin said again, his voice from all around. "Some creatures have the mental capacity to play games or solve puzzles, even build and communicate with each other. So it makes you wonder, why is it *us* who are considered the intelligent ones?"

"Azer," Okta muttered, "Azer, HE'S COMING-"

Azer barely managed to throw his guard up before a glimpse of Delvin appeared before him and sent a blast of slicing air at his throat. It hit Azer's forearms, leaving deep cuts behind.

"The answer is curiosity," Delvin went on. "All other creatures but us have failed to *ask*. No beings other than us Zystinians have ever truly wondered about the world around us, not to the extent that we do. Apes don't conduct science, but we do. Our intelligence is built off the back of questions and answers and the pursuit of both. We aren't intelligent because we are, we're intelligent because we have the capacity to *ask*."

"Science is the greatest pursuit of humankind. Science is what brought us out of the primitive age, and it is what brings us into the world we live in today. Science is to ask, and to ask is to be human. So for you all to deny me of my ability to ask, to deny me a chance to experience the most perfect creature to ever roam the universe is the greatest crime there is. You are denying me my curiosity. You are denying me my humanity. You are denying me the ability to ask before I'm taken into oblivion. Don't you see that?"

"You're a madman! A madman and nothing else!" Okta yelled into the air.

"You will not deny me my curiosity," Delvin's voice growled.

Then, the air went silent. All that was left was a light wind.

"Something's coming…" Okta warned. "I can feel it. He's preparing something. Something big. Get ready."

"We are," Grif replied.

"He's… he's thinking about attacking… all of us. All three of us. The next attack isn't just one particular target. He-"

Everything around them then went eerily quiet. It wasn't just quiet—there was *no* sound. Okta's mouth was moving, but no sound was coming out. Then, in a sick moment of realization, they covered their mouths. *The air was gone.*

Immediately, Azer felt his skin begin to swell. The sweat on his body was evaporating, and the blood within him was beginning to boil. Their wounds were bleeding profusely, the blood immediately vaporizing as soon as it left their bodies, disappearing into the vacuum around them. Azer felt claustrophobic, trapped in a bubble without air.

Azer ran as fast as he could in no direction in particular, but his shoes made no sound on the grassy earth. He tried as hard as he could to not focus on the timer counting down the seconds in his mind, the 15 seconds of consciousness he had remaining before his body shut down. *This is how Mrs. Korca died,* he thought grimly.

In a panic, Azer stopped. There was no time left. Something had to be done now. The hypoxia was setting in, his vessels and veins increasingly blocked by the gas bubbles of his boiling blood. He allocated the last of his thoughts to *finding Delvin.*

Okta and Grif were already unconscious on the ground. Their wounds were worse than his—they didn't stand a chance. *If the air is gone,* Azer thought, *then Delvin must be somewhere nearby to take it away.*

But Delvin was invisible. There was no way of finding him. *Unless...*

Air refracts light. Anywhere in the atmosphere, refraction is unnoticeable due to the fact that the air pressure is mostly uniform. But like a spoon in a cup of water is refracted due to the difference between water and air, the difference between a vacuum and an atmosphere should be noticeable as well.

As his vision darkened, Azer frantically searched his surroundings for a shadow. Any difference in the light, any sign of refraction. Delvin was nearby, and he had to be in an air bubble of his own to stay invisible and continue breathing. And then he saw it. The shadows of the sun on the grass, in a small patch only a few feet across, were different—a bubble of pressurized air.

With the last of his energy, Azer sprinted towards the barely-distinguishable refraction, fist reared back. With all of his might, all of the rage and anger he felt, he slammed his fist into the bubble with frightening force.

Delvin's face was crushed with the trauma of the impact, jettisoned from his protective bubble at high speed. With a loud whoosh and a small boom, the atmosphere returned.

Azer heard Delvin groaning and yelling in frustration, grabbing his bloody face. A tooth had fallen onto the grass beside him.

"You made one mistake," Azer told Delvin, fists clenched. "You messed with Team Virga."

Azer rushed forward, S.R. burning through his veins, charging directly at him. Delvin summoned his wind spear, streaks of water vapor taking form. They ran towards each other, accelerating and accelerating, until—

They impacted. Azer threw a fist into Delvin's head once again, shattering skin and bone, the wind spear cutting at Azer's flesh, until Delvin went flying backwards at a stunning speed. But Azer wasn't done yet—he followed Delvin as he rapidly flew through the air, sprinting beneath him. When Delvin began to fall, Azer lifted a leg and mercilessly kicked Delvin back into the air again. By the time Delvin landed once more, they were at Nur's town scrapyard, Delvin leaving a dirt trail behind him on the ground.

Azer stood over him, watching the man's chest rise and fall with labored wheezes, but he could feel nothing but contempt at the sight. Azer didn't have an ounce of pity for him. Azer groaned as blood dripped from his chest, a wound inflicted by the wind lance during their clash. *Was it critical?*

"Stop," Delvin wheezed, trying and failing to push himself to standing. "Stop this. Don't... kill me."

"I wasn't going to," Azer said quietly. "As horrible as you are, I don't want to take your life."

"I need..." Delvin breathed, "I need to see it. I can't die without seeing it."

Azer felt another pang of fury. This close to death, and the man still wanted to die at the hands of the virus?

"I'm not letting that happen. We're curing this damn thing. My S.R. is the cure, just like Dr. D said. Even though the one we've made is gone, I swear we're stopping this."

Delvin then looked at Azer scrutinizingly. He breathed on the ground, staring at Azer, a look of disappointment on his face.

"What a... waste," Delvin said. "At the library... our search for discovery together... I could have sworn I saw myself in you. Like my own face could have gone where yours should be. But I see now... what an oversight that was. You never felt the passion for discovery like I did."

Then, in a flash of movement, a massive gust of wind pushed Delvin to standing. The air moved past Azer faster and faster, getting stronger and stronger as Delvin reached out his hands towards Azer.

"I *will* make my escape! I will complete my goal!"

The wind grew stronger and stronger yet, pushing harder and harder on Azer's body. *How does he still have energy left?* Azer tried to push forward against the gust, bracing his feet into the dirt, but even the dirt was getting blown away. A terrible clanking noise filled the air as the immense piles of scrap began to fall, carried away by the monstrous gale.

And beneath the largest pile of scrap a gargantuan relic was revealed, glimmering and resolute in the sunlight. Azer took in the sight, astounded, until the wind was finally too much, and he was blown far past the scrapyard's borders, never to see Delvin again.

Azer stepped through scattered scrap and trash, littered between the trees, until he finally stood on ancient stone again.

The final relic, now revealed, was well-preserved for its age. Unlike the shrine relic that they had come by long ago, this relic was full in size. It featured a large series of towering walls, the tallest stretching almost twenty feet into the air, every inch covered in strange symbols. It had been hidden in plain sight all along, underneath the heaps of scrap Mayor Lindwoter had placed atop it.

But just as Azer began to read the text on the final relic, his head was knocked back with the force of the memories that hit him. His mind spun and whirled, he fell unconscious...

And then he Remembered.

CHAPTER SEVENTEEN:
FILTER BREAKER

SEVENTEEN YEARS AGO

"**H**ave you ever heard of the 'Great Filter'?" Enik asked.

Revel accessed her memories. She searched back and back, stopping what she was doing and putting down the beaker to search. Her eyes went vacant for a moment as she sifted through the countless memories of her ancestors, before she returned to her task.

"Nope. That's a new idea, isn't it?" she answered.

"Yeah. The astrophysics division coined the term recently as a way to explain the lack of alien life out there."

"Go on, now I'm curious."

"So you know how, statistically, there should be lots of alien life out there? With how many stars and planets there are in our galaxy alone, we should be seeing spaceships flying all over the place by now."

"Why should we assume other life out there is more advanced than us?"

"It's just statistics. Us Hivanians have had a hard time expanding off-planet because of this stupid virus. Statisticians estimate we would already be an interplanetary society if we weren't constantly fighting the Magna virus."

"That would be nice."

"You're telling me. Anyway, the Great Filter is a means to explain why we're not seeing other life out there. All of the planets nearby are completely dead and barren. Basically, the Great Filter is a barrier that life has to pass while emerging. And the astrophysics division pretty much unanimously agrees that the Magna virus is the Great Filter that's been killing all life on other nearby planets."

Revel gazed once more at the crimson, pulsing mass of Magna specimen on the petri dish in front of them. Her expression hardened.

"I wouldn't be surprised," she murmured.

"The filter can either be in front of us or behind us. And in this situation, I think we can safely say the filter is in front of us. It has been for a while. We won't be able to expand outwards again until we can conquer this thing," Enik finished.

"And now that the infection's finally started here, we'll be hitting the filter soon."

"Exactly," Enik added. "But we can only pray that we make it through."

Revel stood in front of dozens of rows of seats, all filled with watchful, waiting eyes. The lecture hall lights shone on her, prompting her eyes to squint for a moment before adjusting. She took a deep breath.

"It has been 62,506 years since our species left our home, our old planet behind, fleeing the imminent Magna virus. And ever since we left our old planet, we've been searching for a cure without success. I, Revel Ytiva, head scientist of the Hivanian Disease Research Division, am unfortunately not presenting a cure to you all today. Not yet. I'm here to outline the Hivanian Disease Research Division's recent discoveries on the Magna virus and its properties. In today's crisis the division needs more brilliant minds than ever, which is why I'm talking to you all, the next generation of scientists. One among you may even be the one to cure the Magna."

The projector clicked on and displayed a diagram of the virus behind her.

"The Magna virus is a variety of virus we had not seen before. It spreads through contact and through the air, but most importantly, the Magna spreads terrestrially. It does not discriminate between species— the Magna can and will infect anything living, flora, fauna, or other. Once patient zero touches the surface of a rocky planet, the Magna virus, over the course of a few hours, deconstructs patient zero into more of itself, seeping into the ground where they once stood. It spreads through the crust of the planet over the course of dozens or even hundreds of years, lying dormant there for what we know could be hundreds of thousands of years."

"Once another living thing touches the infected planet, the virus infects it, as well. It will continue to infect any and all life on the planet, lying perfectly dormant, seeming perfectly harmless until one specific condition is met. Once an infected individual travels to a new planet, the Magna activates."

"Almost at once, as if receiving a simultaneous signal, all infected life on the original planet becomes sick. The first symptoms for humanoid entities are coughing and chest pain, followed by the symptoms intensifying greatly in the first week of sickness. In the following week the individual suffers migraines, the mind becomes clouded, and the individual has a hard time thinking. After two weeks, small blobs of Magna will form in the bloodstream and on the skin. In the third week, the patient's DNA will slowly be erased and replaced by strains of Magna virus, exponentially accelerating the infection. After one month, the patient is dead."

Revel took in the grim stares of the students. She only wished the facts she was presenting to them weren't true.

"It is believed that the pandemic on our planet has been triggered by our first interplanetary mission, by attempting our first colony on Planet U. The first Hivanian on another stellar body inadvertently triggered this

illness, and now, it is our duty as a species to stop it. We must expand outwards. We must conquer the Magna virus before it conquers us, else our
legacy will be lost forever."

It was a ghastly sight.

Inside of massive white rooms, Revel could see countless sick and
dead, taken by the Magna virus.

The Hivanians possessed the ability to access the memories of any
of their deceased ancestors—and right now, new memories popped into
her head faster than ever.

Revel stepped back into the massive lab from the sick rooms, trying
to ignore her nausea. A rookie lab worker approached her.

"Dr. Revel, the mortality rate is still 100%. Those who fall ill never
last more than a month. Are we making any progress towards the cure?"

Revel sighed defeatedly. "Nothing. Nothing we try can kill the virus.
I've put together the best thinkers on the whole goddamn planet, the best
medical technology our society has, but nothing's working. It's killing every
form of life on the planet at a staggering rate."

The rookie looked down at the ground, murmured, and walked off.

Everyone in the lab was grim. *There must be something different,*
Revel thought. *Some kind of weakness that sets the virus apart.*

She strode through the colossal laboratory, making her way towards
the center room of the lab. She passed by hundreds and hundreds of
doctors, officials, and world leaders until she finally reached the center
room where the first sample of the Magna virus was held. It was a piece
of earthy stone in a thick glass case, a cut made in the center of the rock,
and a gash on its side.

Revel Remembered that her ancestors had lived on the planet
where this rock came from. After discovering the Magna's existence, they
were forced to evacuate with the help of the Schisms. What irony, to think

that the Schisms had been the whole reason for the Magna virus to spread around the galaxy anyway.

The Schisms—what had truly happened to them? Revel dove into her ancestors' memories once again, from thousands and thousands of years ago. She Remembered how, following the Hivanians' evacuation, the Schism and Hivanian species became close, exchanging gifts and information. The Hivanians gave them their abundant knowledge of the world, thanks to their species' collective memories, along with an ancient stone from their old home. In exchange, the wealthy Schisms gave them faster-than-light communication devices to ensure planetary contact, and a dozen escape pods from their spaceship.

And the Schisms themselves had thrived in the years following the migration; their technology and society had skyrocketed, all thanks to their own faster-than-light spaceship—the *Kaari*, it had been named. The interplanetary resources granted by the *Kaari* let the Schisms advance further and faster than any other species.

But maybe they had flown too close to the sun.

Shortly after evacuating the Hivanians, the Schisms went radio silent—attacked by the Magna. Originally, it was thought that the Magna virus had caused their extinction, but it was discovered several decades later that the Schisms had survived. Only, they weren't the same; the cure that they crafted for themselves had succeeded in killing the virus, but a combination of population bottlenecking and the cure itself had corrupted the Schisms' bodies, reverting them to a band of primitives on a single island. It was a tragic end to the Hivanians' companion species.

But if the Schisms had survived the Magna, then there had to be a cure somewhere out there. And if the Schisms could do it long ago, the Hivanians could certainly do it now.

The center laboratory was cold and empty, full of the remains of failed experiments and fruitless tests. In the middle was the first sample of the Magna in a glass case, the virus embedded in stone. Revel and her colleagues had spent hundreds, maybe thousands of tireless hours in this lab. Now that the technology within it was outdated—the Magna crisis had spurred fast improvement in lab technology—it was now but an artifact of past failures and a symbol of where it all began.

Built of stones like the sample she was looking at were relics her ancestors had made eons ago, three relics describing the Hivanians' society and warning of the virus that resided there. And Revel Remembered, her ancestors long ago had done research into the truth of Manim before they were forced to leave. There was a special trait to Manim's land that they had yet to discover...

Revel pressed a button on a dashboard nearby and the glass casing surrounding the sample sunk. When they took the sample of the Magna virus long ago, it was from this rock. But, then, they had only been focused on the virus within, not the stone itself.

She scraped off a sample with a drill and then put it in a chemical analyzer. She waited a moment in silence as the loading bar filled, and then gazed at the results.

Within the silicon, oxygen, and aluminum there was a hidden element. Ingrained within the molecules of the rock was something new.

4.679% VAL

Val? That's what the Hivanians called their memory-accessing ability. It was the mystery element that they found embedded within their DNA and within the virus that ravaged them. And the sample she picked didn't have any of the virus in it—was it possible that the earth itself had power?

Revel stormed out of the testing room, hands bloody and panting frantically. A single thought was ringing through her mind.

Horrible... so horrible....

The first patient to be injected with a Val-based cure had died terribly. It was as if their body itself rejected the cure, rejected the Val she had tried to put inside them. It had *corrupted* the body. She didn't want to recall the experience. She wished it never happened.

Enik walked out of the same room, eyes wide and filled with terror. He stopped by Revel.

"It's okay," he reassured. "Everything's alright. The patient's dead, but, please, Revel, don't let their death be in vain. Please don't give up."

"I don't want anyone else to lose their lives if this cure is faulty," Revel stated simply, still gathering herself.

"But it's not," Enik said. "Didn't you see? The cure worked. The spot where the patient was injected became free of the virus for a moment."

Revel stopped her panicking. "Really?"

"Yes, it did. We just have to figure out how to adapt it to the Hivanian body."

Dozens and dozens of failed trials taught Revel something: every time a patient was injected with the Val-based cure, they lost something. Some lost their minds, or their sight, or their senses, but none of them survived. Their bodies, only adapted to handle a single Val— their collective memory—simply couldn't handle the new Val being added. And worse yet, she noticed the symptoms of the Magna virus developing within herself now, too. Not one living thing on their planet was still healthy anymore. The clock was ticking, and time was running out.

What if instead of adapting the cure to the Hivanian body, Revel thought, *the Hivanian body should be adapted to the cure?*

The remaining doctors and scientists began their ceaseless work on the genetic modification of developing babies. Pregnant mothers volunteered their lives and their children for hope of a functioning cure. Something had to be "lost" in order for the Val to reside in the body, and losing too much would only kill the subject. Revel thought, *what can someone lose*

while still surviving? The options were running out, and anything physical the subject lost turned out to prove deadly.

Revel wheezed on her desk chair, her mind spinning. The infection was taking hold—she wouldn't have a week left. Something had to happen. There had to be *something* one could lose at birth that wasn't an arm or a leg or a mind.

She looked once again at the countless lab reports of Magna patients, all of which showed the exact same pattern of slow demise. The symptoms at first were like a regular, worsening sickness, but once the Magna virus began to delete the victim's DNA, all was lost. Symptoms akin to radiation poisoning began to show themselves, leading to a painful death. Revel tried not to think about the fact that her own DNA, her own identity was being deleted at that very moment.

Then, at once, it hit her. Why hadn't she thought of it sooner? It was right in front of her the whole time—*identity*. The virus itself was practically giving the answer to her.

What if identity was lost?

Everything was in order. The injection would insure the child would be birthed perfectly healthy, only without a face. All functions a face performed—sight, smell, hearing, taste—would be replaced by an artificial organ within the brain. Where the mouth should be, the surface would be able to melt away for consumption and partial digestion of food.

The only thing lost was the given identity of the child.

In front of her was a pregnant woman, the last Revel could find. She was desperate.

"My husband's life has already been taken," the woman cried when Revel found her. "Please give some hope for my child."

In the laboratory room were the woman, Revel, and Enik. Enik prepared the cure inside of a syringe while Revel lay exhausted in her chair. She could hardly stand up anymore.

"Revel," Enik called once the cure was ready. "Do you remember what I told you about the Great Filter?"

Revel turned her pale face to Enik, who too was showing signs of the illness.

"Yes?" she managed.

"I've been thinking about what's gonna happen if this cure works. When this child is born, he'll be the only Hivanian to conquer the Great Filter. The Magna virus... he'll be able to destroy it. If this works... we Hivanians will have broken the Great Filter. Life will be able to pass through."

"You're... right..." Revel breathed.

"I'm gonna give it a name. The child, the cure, I'm not sure yet. *Serterin Rebau*. In our language, that means 'filter breaker.' And, for short, we'll call it..."

Enik paused as he injected the cure into the woman.

"S.R."

Only two hours after the child was born, it was placed in one of the escape pods the Schisms had gifted the Hivanians sixty thousand years ago. Despite its age, the escape pod's incomprehensibly advanced craftsmanship ensured perfect functionality for eons. In the pod, the child would develop, obtaining all necessary nutrients in a coma-like state.

The entities that had created the pods weren't Hivanian—they weren't Schisms, either. They were something greater, something different. It supported the child's humanoid form regardless.

The last Hivanians alive, only moments away from death, placed the child in the escape pod and sent it into the heavens. Far from now, it would land on the planet where everything started.

Long, long ago, thousands of years before Revel's or Azer's time, the last Hivanian to be evacuated off of Manim, a little girl, boarded the *Kaari*, a sophisticated spaceship able to travel lightyears in a blink. It looked like nothing she'd ever seen or ever would see, foreign beyond foreign, a level of advancement in its technology that exceeded comprehension. Now, it was being used to evacuate the Hivanian species off of a planet that would be called Manim tens of thousands of years later. She felt sick as she walked inside, but it wasn't enough to warrant telling her parents.

Walking deeper, she passed by the waiting eyes of a number of Schisms, conversing in their unfamiliar language. She marveled at the Schisms and their different features. Finding her parents and sitting down, she looked out a window at her former home.

The ship appeared to be rising slowly, but she felt no motion. Below were the rolling hills and tall mountains she'd lived near her whole life. But they were not lit by the usual warm glow of the sun—instead, great shadows darkened the entire landscape. She looked up.

Wall-like clouds were consuming the ever-shrinking window of clear sky above, dark and foreboding. Flashes of light tried to escape the tempest, glowing briefly from deep within the storm, the horizon-to-horizon front giving a vertigo-inducing sense of scale.

On cue, the mood within the great ship shifted. The Schisms began running to different stations, manipulating devices the girl didn't understand and shouting to each other. The windows in the ship became the main source of attention to its passengers, many of her fellow Hivanian refugees letting out gasps of surprise and awe.

Sensing the tension around her, the little girl turned to her mother.

"What's going on?"

The girl's mother had a hard time keeping the fear out of her face when she turned from the window to her.

"It's okay, baby. It just looks like a storm's coming."

"Will we be okay?"

Her mother turned to one of the passing Schisms and shouted something in their language. The Schism shouted back, accompanied with expressive hand motions. The little girl looked to her mother for an answer.

"They said we should be fine," her mother answered, rubbing the girl's cheek. "We'll get out of here in time."

But still, her mother continued to look out the window with apprehension.

Hardly a few minutes passed before the clouds, once distant and harmless, began to consume the spaceship *Kaari*. The girl's view of the sky was completely obscured, becoming an opaque sea of water vapor and darkness. The ship began to shake in its ascent. She kept her view through the window steady.

For a while, nothing except distant yellow-white flashes penetrated the darkness. But, as they rose, she noticed more and more colors present within the storm, first dim, then bright. Then, abruptly, the flashes stopped.

For a moment, the girl could see nothing but her own reflection in the window. She noticed the features of her own face, the shape and color of her eyes. Then, it looked as if her eyes were beginning to glow.

A face, not her own, was staring back at her from beyond the window, only crudely resembling a face at all and with large, glowing eyes that looked somehow impossibly deep.

The *Kaari* shuddered with a huge *boom*, and with a collective scream, the passengers were tossed to the side. The Schisms piloting the vessel yelled to each other, and a strange sound filled the ship. The girl's mother held her tightly. She looked to the window again, and the apparition was gone.

"What's happening? I'm scared!" the girl shouted to her mother.

"It's fine, it's fine," her mother reassured. "They're saying a piece of the ship was torn off, but it sounds like it was just a communications device. They're calling it an emergency transponder. They said we'll be out of this storm in a second. Hold on, okay?"

With the image of the face outside burned in her memory, she nodded apprehensively.

After several more minutes of turbulence and fear, the *Kaari* emerged from the storm. It fell into a slow and sluggish orbit above their planet. This sight, too, was too advanced for her to understand—space travel was far outside of her species' daily activities of hunting and gathering. She had never seen an ocean before, much less a planet.

The ship drifted away from their old home, and then, with a flash, it blasted away.

Azer woke with a jolt on the cold stone of the third and final relic. Grif was looking at him with joy seeing that he was awake.

"I... *Remember*," Azer muttered, pushing himself up.

"What?" Grif's face grew concerned.

"I Remember everything. Everything about my species, my people, the cure, *everything* that happened. The virus... the Magna virus..." Azer paused. "My S.R. *is* the cure. All of the Hivanians sacrificed themselves to let me live."

Azer was overcome with a wave of profound sadness for his parents, his people, the ones who had died at the hands of this virus. So many people. But with it was a sense of improbable hope: *he* was the only one who had the cure.

For the first time Azer no longer questioned his identity. He realized then, he was a Hivanian. He was hope. He was Azer. He was the Filter Breaker.

"We were afraid you had died," Grif lamented, Okta trudging along behind. "We just got back from the fields, and when we saw you, we weren't sure what had happened."

The sun illuminated the relic in its dignity, shining and beautiful in the light. The three shared a moment of awe at the sight.

"This was the last one, huh?" Grif commented. "It's stunning. The whole thing was just-"

"Hidden in plain sight. I know."

"Delvin's gone," Okta said, "but his injuries aren't letting him go far. He can't take refuge in Nur anymore. Stranded and with all his strength gone, he'll eventually succumb to the virus."

Azer felt a sick feeling of fear and disgust well up within him. "That means that... he completed his goal. He'll get what he wanted."

"He will," Okta said. "And now we have to face the aftermath of his actions. Azer, your S. R... it is an incredible thing. Can it really cure the Magna virus?"

"It can."

"Would it be possible to distribute it to everyone?"

"No. The S.R. is a chemical cure, yes, but it's also my Val. It's a chemical my body can produce and utilize at the cost of my energy. Producing enough of it for the entire town– or the entire planet–would kill me. Long before I can make enough."

"Then what else can we do?"

Azer looked again at the final relic, reading its contents. A meaningless act, he knew, since he could now Remember his ancestors who built it.

"We have one last chance at defeating the virus," Azer said, "but this one's a stretch and relies on a huge 'maybe.'"

"In what?"

"My ancestors—the Hivanians—who used to live on this planet a long time ago wrote their society's discoveries and findings on these relics before they left." Then, seeing confusion in Okta and Grif, elaborated: "The Hivanians were evacuated from Manim after the virus got here. They were helped by, well… the Schisms. It's a lot, I know. But before my ancestors left, they discovered a few things about this planet."

Azer strode over to a spot on the relic's wall and ran his finger over the symbols as he read them out loud.

"'Recent excavations have found veins of red and blue at varying depths in the earth.' One of those 'veins' in the earth was the Magna virus, lying dormant, but what was the blue? It can't just be roots. They're described as *veins*. All throughout this relic there's mention of the blue veins and what they could mean, along with strange lights coming from the north, towards the mountains. That's where I want to go."

"All the way to the mountains?" Grif repeated.

"There has to be something there. Through all of my ancestors' memories, it was the one enigma they couldn't solve, the one place nobody reached. And yet all of the signs point towards the mountains."

"Your time will be limited," Okta warned. "Now that the Magna is killing, we have only weeks left until it infects everyone, maybe less."

"This won't take weeks. We could do it in a few days."

Okta looked between the two, his expression unrecognizable. He held his cloth-covered arm stump with his remaining hand.

"Then take my old car. Out to the mountains. All that's left now is to wish you two good luck. Please, for the sake of all of us, find a way to stop this."

Air rushed by the car's hull as it sped over the grassy hills around Nur and towards the faraway mountains. Grif was silent as he drove, Azer too as he sat in the passenger seat.

Azer rolled down his window and let the passing air whip over the patch of skin where his face should be.

And, from far in the North, with the air passing the car came a cold wind.

WINTER

CHAPTER EIGHTEEN:
THE STORM

*Cloudy. 9mph winds blowing southeast. Thirty-seven degrees fahrenheit.
Rain expected.*

Belongings bounced around in the back of the trunk as the car rode
along the expansive hills of Nur's northern plains, the Octane fields.
Gradually, the rolling landscape had been flattening, fading from hills to
plains that stretched from horizon to horizon. Almost three hours had
passed since the encounter with Delvin, and the wounds he left on them
still stung. The people he'd taken from them still beckoned.

The sun had long since fallen behind the growing clouds, covering
the vast plains with a grayish tint. Though night had yet to fall, it still felt
like the sun's comforting glow had left them for good. Far ahead was the
forest at the mountain range's base, a thick dark sea of pine-like needles
that slowly grew closer and closer by the minute. Above them, unseen, a
wall of darker clouds was floating towards them.

Grif's eyes moved from the steering wheel to the fuel gauge
on the dashboard. The thin plastic line was wobbling just above the
"empty" symbol.

"We're almost out of fuel," he pointed. Without hesitation, he let go of the gas pedal and let the car slowly coast to a stop.

The moment the wheels came to a halt, Azer opened the door.

"I'll get the can," he offered.

They each hopped out of the car and went around each side to the trunk. Grif pressed a button and it opened with a beep, Azer grabbing onto one of the four spare fuel cans sandwiched between the rest of their hastily-prepared items. The car they were using was an extremely old model—it still ran on liquid fuel. They had no choice—electric cars would be useless in the wilderness without a place to recharge.

Azer made his way to the fuel cap and pressed it open. He began to fill the tank, the fuel's strong odor filling the cool air.

A drop of rain landed on Azer's hand.

"Damn," Azer cursed. "Seriously?"

Another drop hit Azer's shoulder, and then the top of Grif's head.

"That's not good," pointed Grif.

"Here, that's enough," Azer said hastily, throwing the empty can in the back and closing the car's fuel lid. "We've gotta outrun the storm."

"I don't think that's happening," Grif said, looking up. "It's coming our way."

As more and more drops splattered on the roof of the car, the two got in and shut the doors, hearing the *pitter-patter* of rain on metal. As soon as he was set, Grif hit the gas.

There was a lot of ground left to cover before they would reach even a single tree in the forest ahead, and the sheets of rain visible from far ahead only worsened their prospects of staying dry. As the thumping grew more and more frequent and falling water began to obscure the windows, panic set in. They were trapped.

Grif maintained speed through the increasing downpour, careful not to let the car slip over the unpaved grass plains. The wind began to pick up, whipping along the windshield of the car, shaking the car ever so slightly.

Then, a flash. Far away, a bolt of lighting struck the top of a tree. A couple of seconds later, the sound of thunder rocked the car and wobbled the windows. The rain intensified more and more until it clouded out the expansive forest ahead. Up above, the gray clouds were beginning to swirl, ever so slightly, stirring and rolling like a turbulent sea.

And the rising torrent—the drum-like rhythm of thunder—the swirling sky—it seemed all too familiar.

"There's no way…" Azer said, dumbfounded.

"There's nothing else like this," Grif shot, desperately trying to maintain control of the car.

"The Shades! This is just like The Shades! How?!"

"I know!" Grif agreed.

The sheets of rain were battering the windshield now, like a chorus of drum beats on the glass. It was sensory overload; they couldn't see or hear anything over the mayhem. The car began to lose control, sliding over the grass on a layer of floodwater. The vehicle continued to shift, the steering wheel rendered useless.

Unable to turn and obscured by the rain, the car slammed into a tree and came to a violent stop, tearing apart the windshield and releasing the airbags. After the shock subsided, they pushed open the mangled front doors and fell onto the soaked grass.

Blood mixed with rainwater dripped down Azer's head as he tried to right himself and pull to standing, but the shock of the crash made it hard to form a thought, much less walk. Grif, a few dozen feet ahead, managed to get on his feet, trudging his way through the storm and helping Azer up.

They walked to the trunk of their smoking car, grabbing everything recoverable that they could, and moved onward into the ceaseless storm, towards the mountains beyond.

Without a word, they trekked together through the tempest, freezing rain beating on their bodies, the lightning-lit landscape rolling and endless. The water washed away their blood, carrying it into the raging wind.

Tall trees loomed above the two. Hours after the storm began, it had barely died down, instead growing colder and colder as they got closer to the mountain and under the needle-filled sanctuary of the forest.

Upon reaching a drier spot at the base of an evergreen, Grif threw down his items to the damp earth and punched the tree with rage.

"DAMMIT!" he shouted. "God DAMMIT!"

"It'll be weeks before we can get back at this rate," Azer stated grimly. "*If* we can get back now."

Grif only let out a roar of fury and punched the tree again. All the events of the day, all of the rage, grief, and terror were too much to handle.

"Grif, stop. You're making your knuckles bleed. There's nothing we can do now."

Grif turned back towards Azer, tears and raindrops dripping down his cheeks. He was breathing heavily, a desperate look in his eyes as he gazed helplessly at Azer. Neither of them could say a word.

"Why did it have to be like this?!" Grif shouted. "Why us?! Why our town, why all this?!"

"It's a curse," Azer said simply, darkness still in his voice. "This virus is a curse that's been chasing us for thousands, and thousands, and thousands of years. Both of our species suffered and died at the hands of the Magna virus. It's a curse we have to break. Both you and I."

Grif tried to form words, his mouth moving helplessly as he tried to respond.

"Can we even make it?" Grif cried quietly. "Can we still save everyone?"

"All we can do for tonight is rest. Too much has happened today for us to continue like this," Azer responded.

Grif nodded and then turned to his scattered belongings. Silently, as the last light of day began to fade, they prepared a shelter for themselves under the protective needles of the tree, huddling under blankets and drifting off to sleep.

Grif was woken by a small, sharp coldness on his nose. He opened his eyes slowly.

A white snowflake had landed on the side of his nose, gradually melting on his skin into a drop of frigid water. Aching and sore from the previous day, he moved to sitting, taking in the surprisingly bright landscape in front of him.

Bright white snow coated the landscape between the trees. Previously wet, grassy earth was now buried under a thick coating of snow, turning everywhere but circular patches of brown earth under the trees a stark, beautiful white.

Grif put a hand on Azer's thick blanket and shook him without taking his eyes off the blanketed forest. Azer woke with a groan and, upon seeing the snow, also got up with a start.

"What in the world?"

"It snowed!" Grif exclaimed. "Real snow! Man, we haven't seen this stuff in *years!*"

Both of them were silent for a while, simply taking in the magical sight of dusty white flakes falling from the heavens. All was utterly silent, not even wind was blowing around the peaceful snowfall. The shades of nature had been muted, reduced to simple whites and browns, and the color of the snowy ground and cloudy sky were nearly identical, giving the impression that they had fused together in a bizarre marriage of nature. Azer reached a finger out of the tree's protective circle and the two watched as a six-sided snowflake landed on it before returning to its liquid form.

"I hardly remember the snow," Azer commented. "It's been a really, really long time, I don't think I was really old enough to appreciate it then."

"I don't know about you, but all I remember was that it was really fun."

"Well, let's enjoy it *after* we save the world."

"Oh, that's right. We should get going."

The two geared up, picking their thickest clothing for the snowy weather, and then Grif stepped a boot into the snow outside of the tree they'd been sleeping under.

"But, damn," Grif said, his shoe sinking into the powdery blanket. "This stuff's gonna be impossible to walk in."

Azer followed suit, stepping ankle-deep into the snow.

Over the course of the trek, trudging through endlessly falling snow, the two noticed that the forest at the mountain range's base was far larger than it had previously appeared, and the snow blocking their path only lengthened their travels, minutes turning into hours and hours turning into days. The monochromatic landscape was disorienting and seemed to stretch in every direction, just white and brown everywhere the eye would land.

The second thing they noticed, even more alarming, was that the snow failed to cease. Since the storm began, now approaching a full week ago, there had been no end to the precipitation in any direction. Sunlight was nowhere to be found anywhere on any horizon, even on top of the scant boulders they climbed. Everywhere, endlessly, was the storm, be it the snow that continued to fall over the mountain they were approaching or the distant rain over Nur.

Azer and Grif were hours into their seventh day, relishing in the fleeting warmth of their winter clothes. They built a small fire under a tree at the end of each day, the nighttime slowly but steadily growing longer and longer with every rotation of the planet. Neither knew exactly what time it was, but the fading grayish light from the clouds above told them nightfall was near.

They'd packed enough food and water for three weeks of travel, but the crash had rendered some of their food inedible and punctured their water bottles. They tried to eat berries between rations, a feat that proved effective earlier on into the journey, but Azer swore some of the berries were starting to glow an infected red. Azer's fingers went numb after especially long stretches of hiking, prompting the two to make a quick fire with their remaining car fuel before proceeding.

Azer had been trying to ignore the bright red bubbles he'd seen flowing out of tree sap over the last few days while passing thousands of evergreens. He tried his hardest to ignore the fact that the Magna virus was already spreading, infecting one lifeform or another, flora or fauna.

Through the eerie silence of snowfall they walked, step after step, foot ahead of foot. The monotony of it all had dulled the senses, and neither of the two noticed at first the rustling sound from up ahead.

Crack.

Then, unmistakably, they heard the sound of a breaking branch. Azer and Grif stopped dead, listening.

Somewhere ahead, obscured by the snow and trees, something was trudging its way toward their direction. A dark shape slowly came into view, pieces at a time poking out from behind the sheets of stark white.

It was apparent that the creature wasn't human. It looked as if it was native to the mountain, with four lanky legs and a thick fur coat. It was obviously predatory, baring its bloodstained teeth at them with malice.

"Don't move," Grif whispered.

"Yeah."

"I don't know if it's noticed us yet. I've heard of these things before, they're called mountain gurats. I have no idea why it's all the way down here in the forest."

"Maybe we're close to the mountain?" Azer guessed.

"Shh. It's coming closer. Back up a bit."

The gurat wandered closer, and then stumbled, its face sinking into the snow. Nearby, they could hear its labored breaths and see a large, bright red mass of pulsating Magna on one side of its head. The sight of it repulsed Azer.

All of a sudden, it made a noise and turned its head towards the two. Its eyes were glazed over and it wavered in its place as it observed them.

With a growl, it lunged at them, the two barely dodging out of the way. The creature was taking wild snaps at them as it chased, desperate to sink its teeth into new prey. Azer waited for the gurat to lunge at him once more, and then once it leapt into the air, he landed a well-placed kick onto its side, throwing it away and into the snow.

Belly-up for a moment, Azer noticed a particularly large blob of Magna in the place where its stomach should be. It already looked dead. But it was as if the gurat didn't feel the blow, because it got back without a moment's wait. One of its legs that Azer had dislocated from his kick snapped back into place as if with the aid of an invisible hand. The creature continued its wild attempts to bite and scratch.

"Kill it already!" Grif yelled.

"It's possessed by the virus somehow!"

"Then kill the virus!"

Azer's long-lost memories of the S.R.'s healing effects then returned in an instant, and he focused himself. Now, when it lunged, Azer dodged to the side and removed one of his gloves. He aimed a punch at the side of its head, letting his S.R. flow, until it landed with a crack.

Immediately, as the S.R. flowed into the infected gurat, the lump of Magna on the side of its head burned and sizzled away, turning into dire red-black smoke. The gurat flew backwards from the impact, making a groaning noise as the virus burned and bubbled away. The gurat pushed itself to standing and managed one final bite, flying at Azer with its mouth agape.

"One more time!" Azer shouted.

Azer grabbed its head in the air and the Magna burned away again. Finally, the glowing red mass disappeared, and the gurat fell limp to the ground. Azer and Grif approached it, cautiously. It didn't move. Grif reached a glove down to its neck.

"We were too late," Grif said quietly. "It's already dead."

"W- what? That can't be! I made sure to-"

"You didn't kill it," Grif said reassuringly. "The Magna had already inflicted too much damage. It had to have been keeping the poor thing alive, probably just to spread the virus further."

Azer was quiet for a moment, observing the gurat with pity. "Can that... can that even happen? The virus, keeping it alive? I've never even seen it do that before in my memories."

"I wouldn't rule it out. The beast was being controlled by the virus somehow, without a doubt. And it's pretty clear the Magna has been able to do things no virus should be able to do."

They stood there for a few more moments, Azer taking a silent moment of grief for the creature. To die in such a way seemed unthinkable.

The light of their seventh day was quickly fading now, the two trying to fit in as much walking as possible before nightfall. But as they trekked, the trees were beginning to grow more sparse, the elevation slowly increasing. It was without a doubt—they were approaching the mountains.

Grif led the two up a small, snowy cliff, steep enough to warrant caution but not enough for the snow to make their climb impossible. The trees around them were getting lower and lower to the ground as they climbed, until, finally, they could see above the canopy.

Before them was a gargantuan mountain, stretching well above the clouds with every inch covered in trees, ice, and snow. They stood just at its foot, elevated enough to make the faraway plains seem low, but they were hardly close to the peak. Pieces of the towering monoliths of rock poked out from behind the blanket of snow, breaking the monotonous two-tone world they had been traversing for the past week.

Grif started, "We're here."

"Took long enough."

Grif fell backwards onto the snow with a thud.

"Whoa, you okay?"

"I'm fine..." Grif wheezed. "Just... very... tired. And hungry. We've had a week of walking. Let's set up camp. I'm not ready to climb a mountain today."

Small orange flecks of ember floated silently through the air over the fire, dancing in the cold winter air before landing on a nearby patch of ground of snow and turning to black. The flames illuminated Azer where his face belonged, a sanctuary of warmth that the two shared at the end of each exhausting day.

Several more days had passed since they had first reached the mountains. Slowly, they had been approaching the rocky peak, and gradually the air was becoming thinner and thinner. Neither had said a word since the fire was lit, both opting for silence, a rest for their tired selves. Hunger and exhaustion were setting in.

"You know," Grif started, "we probably aren't going to be able to get help."

"I was assuming not. We're too far out here to be found, anyway. Who's gonna look for us in the mountains? Hardly anyone from Nur has gone this far out here before."

"No, not that. Well, yes, that too, we probably aren't going to get any help reaching the summit or getting back. But what I mean is the whole planet. If this whole endless storm is really like... like a 'mini Shades' or something, it's probably going to be blocking all signals in or out of the planet. I don't even think the Zystinian government is coming for us."

"Not to mention ships can't get in."

"Yeah, you're right. Or out. The clouds are probably too thick everywhere to fly anything."

Another moment of silence. Grif watched some snowflakes fall outside of their makeshift shelter under a large tree. Grif put his backpack on the ground beside him, then placed his head on top of it as a makeshift pillow as he pulled his sleeping bag closer. Azer unzipped his own backpack and pulled out a sheet of paper, silently scribbling on it to the light of the campfire.

"Whacha got there?" queried Grif.

"Makin' a map."

"Handy. Been working on it long?"

"Whenever I get the chance. I started a couple days in, you know, so we wouldn't get lost, but after a while I kinda started enjoying it."

"Enjoying it? Really?"

"I'm sure it sounds weird, but it's just kinda fun to be able to map out our surroundings, getting to explore everything and write it out. I used to map out my neighborhood in Nur when I was younger. I made dozens of little maps of that place; I knew every nook and cranny. And I figured, since now we're deep in the mountains and Manim is just a colony planet—we're probably exploring somewhere nobody's ever been before."

"I guess if you think about it that way, yeah, it is kinda cool."

"Even though our trip to Arcus Island was short, getting to tread new land was amazing. When Rena, Erril, and I were trying to find you guys, we saw some incredible things. Mapping all that out takes all of that mystery and makes it ours."

Azer turned his head to the cloud-covered sky for a moment, focused on nothing in particular. Without turning back to the fire, he said:

"You know, I want to try and map the stars someday. Allllll the way out there. Getting to travel through space on the *Stormbreaker* was amazing. If we can get through all this, that's what I want to do."

"Not a bad idea," Grif agreed.

"And Saa. I'd like to spend some time with Saa if we all survive this."

"That's not a bad idea either." Grif adjusted himself to a more comfortable position. "All I wanna do after this mess is sit down in front of a hot plate of Grand Soman and eat my heart out."

"You're telling me," Azer seconded, turning back to his map. "I've never wanted a bite of Grand Soman more."

"After we save the world though."

"Right. After that."

They remained silent, their surroundings in utter silence, save for the scratching of pen on paper and the crackling of the fading fire.

Grif placed his torn, snow-dusted gloves on another rock and pulled himself further upwards. Visibility was but a few feet ahead or behind for the large, wet cloud the two were climbing within. The air was dangerously thin at this altitude, forcing Grif to take frequent breaks of heavy, unproductive breathing at every flat part of rock. Azer was only just behind, faithfully climbing the peak through the stark white cloud.

Then, Grif placed his hand on a flatter surface. He pulled himself up and out of the cloud and onto the mountain's summit, a peak of bare rock that looked out over everything. Azer pulled himself up just behind, and the two got a view of the mountain range in the dead of night.

The black sky was dotted with hundreds of thousands of stars, no longer obscured by the ceaseless clouds that coated Manim's atmosphere. Millions of worlds looked down on them alongside the inky, colored streak that was Zysti galaxy, painted from horizon to horizon across the void.

Wordlessly, the two viewed the heavens above, before training themselves back down onto the swimming clouds just beneath them.

A peak ahead was another mountain, the tallest one yet, blueish glowing light emitting from its summit, the clouds that surrounded them pouring out of its raised top like a ceaseless waterfall.

CHAPTER NINETEEN:
SHATTERED

WEATHER STATION INOPERABLE UNTIL FURTHER NOTICE

The rocks that Azer and Grif were climbing now were strange, warped, jagged in shape. In the immediate area around the tallest peak there was no snow—just a clear, circular patch of earth around the mountain. Circling around the summit were freshly-formed clouds, flowing out from the mountain's pointed top. Underneath the rock and dirt were sturdy roots of pulsating blue, closely resembling veins or arteries. Each vein trailed up and up to the top, flowing into a hidden cave just below the peak.

As they rose higher and higher, the air's quality grew strange, warm but cold, wet but dry. The mouth of the cave came into view, blue veins lining the walls and converging onto an unseen point. Boots ascending moist earth, they climbed into the blue-lit cave.

The cave was flawlessly round inside, marbled stone lining every inch of the interior. Suspended in the middle of the cave was a spherical blue object, its diameter just surpassing their height. The blue orb was gel-like in texture, warping and oscillating slowly in place, a multitude of thick blue veins from every part of the wall connecting to the glowing blue orb. It was undoubtedly alive.

The light within the orb grew slightly whiter and brighter upon Azer and Grif's entrance. They were peering into the cave with bewilderment. The orb pulsated slowly before the liquid-like light converged on its side, facing the visitors.

"They arrive."

A voice filled the spherical cavern, echoing slightly. The voice was genderless, like everyone they knew was talking all at once in a unified sound.

Grif looked at Azer with a mix of horror and shock.

"There are no words I can give for you to properly understand, but I am what you seek. I am what you call Manim, the planet you reside on."

"You... you're a planet?" Grif stuttered. His mind could hardly process what they were seeing and hearing.

"I am the planet you reside on," the voice restated. "I am the dirt you tread and the stones you climb. Time passes for me differently than it does for you, but I live and understand everything that happens on and around me. I can hear and replicate the language you speak."

Azer could hardly think. Manim, alive? Questions swirled in his head. He opted to ask the one that he sought in the first place.

"The virus," Azer started. "The Magna. What is it? How can we stop it? The old Hivanians... did you see them here, long ago?"

"I did. Thousands of years ago. What you call the Magna virus is not a virus, but a superweapon that was placed here, not by accident. Around the time of your old kind, a faraway race sought to kill me and any future life that may emerge here, burying the Magna's core in my surface, beneath the crust. Slowly, it spread in my dirt and stone, eventually emerging onto the surface as a thin layer. What you call The Shades is simply my self-defense mechanism against the Magna every time it emerges. Like you, I am a Valin. I cannot explain my Vals to you in terms that you will understand, but I control the weather."

There was a moment of dumbfounded silence between Azer and Grif, before Azer spoke again.

"Then... this constant storm... is it The Shades too? Only smaller?"

"It is. Like your bodies develop fevers to fight infections, mine produces a storm. Only, this storm won't cease until I am safe from the Magna. All of my defenses, even my corvyte, are rendered useless against this virus."

"Wait. Corvyte? *Your* corvyte?" Grif said, shock reverberating through his voice. The light within the blue orb shifted a few degrees until it faced him.

"Your kind are harvesting my organs. What you call corvyte is an organ I use to repair any damaged parts of me, like the heart you two stand before. It adapts to organic matter, healing my and your wounds. But corvyte only heals wounds, not infections like the Magna. My only immune system is what you call The Shades."

"But then... how can we stop the Magna? The last Shades didn't work."

"The Shades works because as soon as the Magna emerges every ten years, I erase every suitable vessel on the surface and cleanse the land, forcing the Magna back down for another decade. The last Shades failed because a suitable vessel for the Magna survived. There were three living things that survived the last Shades: you two and the one you call Copycat. His survival against all odds let the Magna reside within him and spread the virus through me. And now, the virus will kill me too. There is only one way to kill it: destroy it at the source."

"The source?"

"The source of the infection. Patient zero. The Magna has sentience—it behaves like a hive mind, much like your old kind did. That's what allows it to function across an interplanetary scale. But it knows now you're aware of it, so the Magna's core has left its hiding place underground. Now, it's concentrated within Copycat, just like my sentience is concentrated within this cave. It is keeping him alive. Manipulating him. Controlling him. He can no longer think for himself, and the infection has spread such that there is very little time left. Azer, your power is great, but you do not have enough strength to cure every person—or me. But if you destroy the Magna's core—the source of its interconnectedness—all of this will be over."

Gusts of falling snow whipped against Azer's coat as he set foot in Nur once again. But it wasn't the town he knew. Only a desolate white landscape was to be found, the blizzard obscuring the streets, not a soul in sight. Every door and car was coated with ice and snow, piled against houses and buildings, obscuring life, obscuring light.

As he and Grif walked deeper into Nur, they saw a light glowing in the distance. A sinister crimson red, beginning as a faint glow behind a myriad of snow but slowly growing brighter, redder as they approached. The source of the light could not be seen.

And then, sound. Faint sounds of crying came from the light, hidden beneath the endless whoosh of wind. Behind the obscured glow emerged two shapes, the silhouettes of two men: Copycat and Okta. They were facing each other with Copycat's back to Azer and Grif, who remained unnoticed.

"I've already told you. The fate of the galaxy comes first." The voice was deep—Okta's.

"How can you do this?" Copycat said between sobs. "I'm your own son. How can you let me... *die* like this?"

"I cannot in good consciousness let all of humanity die to save one person. I must find a way to distribute the cure first. We cannot use it all just on you," Okta said, danger in his voice.

Copycat continued crying for a moment before his voice began to change. Okta took a step back into the blizzard, obscuring him, and Copycat took several steps forward towards his father. The snow hid them from sight.

"Ecat, stop this!" Okta's voice cried out.

There was a loud, wet thud, an inhuman roar, a grunt from Okta, and the red light emanating from Copycat flashed for a moment. Azer and Grif went still for a moment, unsure whether to proceed, before the sounds of Copycat crying were audible again. They stepped forward.

Copycat was on his knees, large masses of brightly glowing Magna on his ravaged body. They shook and shivered with each sob.

"Dad…" Copycat cried, "why did you leave me? Please…"

Azer and Grif stopped where they were, unsure whether to approach.

"Copycat?" Azer said, just loud enough to be heard.

Copycat sprung upwards and turned to face Azer. His face was partially covered in Magna, one of his eyes turned a bright glowing scarlet. Tears were running down his face.

"What happened?" Azer inquired.

"It's going to kill me," Copycat whimpered. "Dad wouldn't give me the cure. He always leaves me. He always does this. I don't want to die."

"Your dad- Okta? There's another cure?" Grif exclaimed.

"Copycat, don't move. I can cure you. Just don't do anything," Azer said, taking a step closer.

Suddenly, Copycat's face twisted with pain, and his head reared back. The globs of Magna on his body glowed brightly, and beneath his torn shirt, in his chest, a sinister crimson glow flashed.

Copycat screamed, "How can you cure me? Dad has the new cure. How can I trust you? You- you just want to kill me, don't you?"

"No, of course n-"

"I WON'T LET YOU KILL ME!" Copycat screamed, an alien voice speaking beneath his own. "I'LL KILL YOU BEFORE YOU CAN KILL ME."

Copycat stood steady on his feet, glaring menacingly at Azer and Grif. His face was crazed, deranged, devoid of sanity.

"It has too much control over him," Grif pointed, attaining a battle stance. "We have to kill it with force."

"I know," Azer replied.

Copycat began to move towards them, his wheezy breathing making steam in the freezing air, snow quietly crunching beneath his feet. Step after step, without breaking eye contact, Copycat walked closer. He extended a gloveless arm. Beneath his skin, in the veins leading to his fingertips, luminous Magna moved and flowed, transforming his cold-nipped arm into an limb of pure red infection. Then, in a sudden movement, it shot out towards Azer.

The Magna hand flew by Azer's head. Azer prepared to counter, but the extended, goo-like arm suddenly whipped sideways into Azer's chest without warning. As Azer flew back from the impact, Grif ran in for the attack, becoming a bolt of lightning that zipped towards Copycat's chest. The arm and hand of Magna swiftly returned to Copycat's side and threw itself at Grif before detaching itself, becoming a flying glob of goo. With nowhere else to conduct, Grif impacted the severed arm, conducting through it, before it fell to the ground. Grif returned to a tangible form and tried to orient himself in a defensive stance, but too late: the now one-armed Copycat had already appeared in front of him. After rearing back his remaining fist, Copycat punched Grif in the face.

Grif flew backwards, blood from his broken nose and teeth staining the stark white snow. Dazed, he could see Copycat standing over him again, who was watching his own missing arm regrow before his corrupted eyes, globs of pure Magna recreating the arm down to every vein. Copycat looked at his arm of virus with wonder, flexing his scarlet fingers, intoxicated with the power of the Magna.

He had become a meld of virus and man, an amalgamation of an intelligent, adaptive bioweapon powerful enough to kill trillions and a boy too weak to understand that his humanity was dissolving before his very eyes.

Azer righted himself and charged again, watchful of Copycat's weaponlike arm the Magna had granted. When it extended in Azer's direction, snaking out for an attack, Azer grabbed it midair and pumped as much of his S.R. as he could into it. The glowing red goop died and disintegrated before his eyes, losing its glow, the death spreading down the arm. But then something unexpected happened. As the S.R. flowed down the arm of Magna, killing it, the arm began to regenerate back faster than the cure could do its work. Copycat's smile was wider than should be possible, watching the sight as Azer's S.R. was outpaced by the Magna's vitality. The arm grew massively, throwing Azer backwards once again with an impact like a car crash, tossing him around the snow and hitting everything in his path. Azer crashed through a metal gate, feeling a rib break from the force, before finally coming to a stop on snow-covered ground.

Grif was not far behind, flying from the force of the arm's impact, leaving a trail in the snow beside Azer, flecks of blood mixed in. Still reeling from the pain and force of the impact, and the shock of the Magna's regenerative strength, Azer pushed himself up and found himself looking at a snow-covered obelisk. Beneath the dusty snow it detailed the death of someone in his town, killed by the Magna's infection. Rage and grief pumped through his mind. Behind the obelisk was another, and another, rows and rows of deaths at the hands of the Magna. They had landed in Nur's cemetery.

"They had to expand it to make room for the new bodies," Copycat's corrupted voice explained from afar, the glow glowing brighter, closer. "My influence has already spread to everything on Manim, and the fatalities are piling up. Would you like for me to bury you here, too?"

Azer fought the urge to cry at the sight of Nur's freshly-built gravestones. He had to continue. He had to fight.

Copycat strode up to the broken gates of the cemetery, his Magna arm effortlessly bending the metal out of his way as he walked.

"You are trying to finish the fight for your species. But I am this close to snuffing your embers out," Copycat said. The voice hardly sounded human anymore. Copycat's tone and inflection were sacrificed for raw malice. The virus was speaking now, using Copycat's body as a vessel.

Copycat raised his Magna arm and it began to morph midair. It lost its hand-like shape and the fingers molded into a pointed tip, the gel-like virus hardening into a luminescent blade. It fell toward Azer's damaged body, then—

The Magna blade suddenly retracted towards Copycat as Saa sprinted out from the blizzard and threw a punch at Copycat's infected head. The blade blocked her blow, cracking slightly, before he recoiled and Saa turned to the two.

"Go! C'mon, now!" Saa shouted.

Azer and Grif didn't hesitate to take the opportunity, following Saa while running on injured legs and labored breaths. Behind, Copycat let out an inhuman roar of frustration as he followed behind, tearing apart walls, fences, and houses. Azer and Grif found themselves running down snow-covered streets and alleys, the sound of the Magna's destruction slowly getting further and further behind them as they ran. Finally, Saa stopped behind a brick-walled building, panting, and sat down in the snow, urging Azer and Grif to join her.

They plopped down beside Saa, trying to control their ragged breathing, hoping that Copycat was far enough behind for them to be safe.

"What... what are you doing here?!" Grif exclaimed.

"I should ask you the same," Saa replied. "Said you'd be gone for five days, and you took almost a month. We all thought you'd kicked it."

"Our car broke down in the-"

"The storm, I know," Saa interrupted. "We wouldn't have expected you to get through that smoothly anyways. Here in Nur, we could hardly function, the mountains would have seemed impossible."

"What's happened here?"

"Exactly what it looks like. The Magna's been ravaging the town, and the ceaseless snow isn't helping. Every day it looks like the sky is crying."

Grif looked at Azer knowingly.

"Well, it probably is," Azer commented.

Saa's faced twisted into confusion. "Wha-"

Her words were cut short by a violent bout of coughing. Azer and Grif looked worriedly at her, but after she finished, teary-eyed, she said, "Here, get inside the building. I'll fill you in once we're safer."

Azer got up and walked over to the backdoor of the building, kept shut by a chain lock. Azer pumped S.R. through his arm and broke the lock with a swift chop before opening the door and letting the other two inside.

Saa fell into another bout of violent coughing, coming to her knees on the floor of a utility room. Grif rushed over to help her to her feet, but Azer was more focused on the flecks of glowing red that she was coughing up.

"Everyone is dying now," she said after wiping her mouth. "Just after you left, Nur was put under lockdown and people stopped being able to leave their homes. It was futile by that point, though, since the Magna had already infected most of us."

"Saa, are you okay?" Azer asked. "You don't have to-"

"Copycat was patient zero, he was the first one to get hospitalized," Saa interrupted. "We'd thought it was amazing how long he'd lasted but it looks like he's just been a vessel for the Magna. I never would have thought it, but the virus started... controlling him. Just yesterday Copycat and his dad disappeared."

"Okta? Well, we know where he is now," Grif commented.

"Okta had been working on a new cure from what was left of Team Virga's plans. A couple of us, me, Erril, Rena, and Milo, included, helped him develop it. We thought Okta was going to give Copycat the first dose, but he withheld it saying that it should be saved until we can distribute it to everyone. Then, the snow ended up blocking travel, and everyone started getting sick and this shitshow got to where we are now."

Saa leaned herself up against a wall and slowly let herself fall down to a seated position. She coughed again, trying to hide it under her hand.

"Damn it. I think I overdid it back there," she cursed.

Azer noticed a faint red glow coming from under Saa's sleeve. Looking closer, he saw a glob of red Magna, connected to a larger mass that seemed to run up her arm.

"Saa! You-" Azer pointed at the Magna.

She looked at her wrist and then pulled her sleeve over the offending red glow.

"I'm fine. You two are probably in worse shape than I am; you got hit pretty hard by Copycat."

"You're not fine! You're going to die if we don't do something! I can produce the cure!" Azer reached out a hand.

"You can? Great. Save it for Copycat. He seems to have it the worst."

"No! The core of the Magna is in Copycat, it's controlling everything! The virus is *alive*."

"If the Magna's core is in Copycat, that's all the more reason to save the cure for him. If killing the core kills the virus for good, then that's what we should be doing. You're probably going to need a hell of a lot of cure to kill the Magna at the core."

"But-"

"Enough. Save the heroics and actually *be a hero*. It's do or die here. Just ignore me and kill the Magna."

From afar, there was another faint inhuman roar. The three went quiet.

"I couldn't produce enough S.R. to kill the Magna the last time I tried," Azer hissed. "It's a losing battle. It regenerated faster than I could kill it."

"Then you just have to try again. There might not be any other way to end this."

"I've already used up a good portion of my S.R. At this rate, I'm going to run out before I can cure him."

"Then we need more. And thankfully, we can get it. Okta's second cure is still in the Team Virga lab, just sitting there. The only issue is, if Copycat really is being possessed by the Magna, then he's going to try and destroy the cure soon. We have to get to it before Copycat does and then pump all the cure we can into the Magna's core."

"Which is located in Copycat's heart," Grif added grimly. "He's never gonna give us an opening."

Saa looked at him seriously.

"We'll do what we can."

There was another faraway roar and a faint *boom*, prompting the three to come to standing.

"If the other cure is in the Team Virga lab, then we don't have any time to waste," Grif said. "We need to get to the Battle Academy."

"I can help us get there without Copycat seeing us," Saa added. "His heat signature should help us figure out where he is, especially in the cold snow."

"Good. Get us there."

Saa walked through a door in the utility room and emerged into a kitchen, untouched pots and pans hanging over sinks of stale water. Another door later and they found themselves behind the counter of *Anak-Lespin*, looking out on large, clean windows and dozens of empty seats. Snow was collecting on the base of the windows, reflecting the only light inside of the dim, now-abandoned restaurant.

Saa walked up to a window and, after fussing with triggers on the window's side, popped it off and set it carefully down onto the floor, letting snow fly inside.

"What the hell are you doing?!" Grif exclaimed.

"Infrared light can't travel through glass. Copycat's too far right now to be seen with visible light, but his and the Magna's heat should be easily visible from behind the cold snow."

Saa looked back and forth through the open window and then pointed into the snow.

"There, he's out there," Saa said.

"Where?"

"You can't see him with visible light. Get behind the window, I'll show you two."

Azer and Grif hunched behind the window and Saa put a hand on each of their shoulders. Azer, not used to the sensation, made a small wince of pain, but Grif was more familiar and could quickly make out Copycat's faint heat signature behind the falling snow.

In infrared light, the snow appeared almost black in comparison to the brighter colors within the restaurant. Behind innumerable snowflakes was a faint, body-shaped glow, misshapen by the warmer-glowing virus corrupting him.

"He's looking for us," Saa noted. "He'll be in here soon."

They watched Copycat's figure move through the snow again for a moment, getting closer and closer.

"Once he gets close enough, follow me and *quietly* open the door," Saa said. "We're gonna sneak as far as we can, because we sure as hell won't be able to outrun him for long."

Copycat disappeared from the window's view, wrapping around the other end of the restaurant. The three ran back to the front entrance before they pushed the door open and sprinted out into the blizzard.

They ran for a moment longer, at first unaware of the red glow they were running towards. Then, with a sick realization, they stopped, throwing themselves behind another wall as fast as their damaged bodies could manage.

"Did he... copy himself?!" Saa exclaimed.

"Must have," Grif panted. "There's no way he could have gotten here that fast, in front of us much less."

"We need to focus on leaving, and fast," Azer interjected. "The longer we wait here the more of himself he can make."

"Let me give you two infrared vision again," Saa said. "We can see him from further away."

Their visions went from stark white to dark and reddish, impossible colors dimly shining at them from every direction. Brighter shades were glowing from several places behind the dark snow around them, indications of Copycat's clones.

"He's made a lot," Saa noted. "Quick, around this way."

They moved around the other side of the building, avoiding the faraway warm glows, running along the backside of a number of stores before yet another figure came into view from up ahead. They turned into another alley, coming back to the front of a strip mall, devoid of its former life. The snowy ground made running near impossible, slowing their pace and trapping their feet with every step. Azer could hear Saa wheezing as she ran beside him, producing small puffs of steam with each raspy breath. It took but a single curb, hidden underneath the coat of snow, to trip her and put their flight to a halt.

Immediately, Saa descended into a paroxysm of coughing. Flecks of Magna and blood fell into the snow, and she gripped her stomach with agony. Azer and Grif stopped in their tracks, looking at her with horror. A moment later a number of bright red glows lit up behind the snow around them like an activated machine. They were completely surrounded.

The numerous Copycats came into view, each one massively infected. Saa was hardly well enough to stand, much less run, but Azer wouldn't even consider leaving her behind. Each passing second resulted in another Copycat coming into view, blocking what was previously an escape route. Every horizon was filled with crimson light but the ground and the sky.

That's it.

Beside where the three stood was a brick-walled building, dozens of feet tall. Azer could scale it with a single S.R.-fueled jump, but the others wouldn't stand a chance without help.

So he would help them.

Azer grabbed Grif and Saa and pulled them close, circulating S.R. throughout his bloodstream. Massive amounts of the chemical flowed into his blood, warming and scorching the veins with distilled power. He let it rush to his fingertips and into the bodies of his friends, who winced at the amount of power being transferred to them. The globs of dire red on Saa burned and dissolved away into blackish smoke, sizzling as if put over a flame. In the stead of the infection was the raw force of life, restoring their fatigued bodies.

"JUMP!" Azer bellowed.

Azer concentrated the S.R. into his legs and bent them, descending into a ready stance. The Copycats quickened their pace and prepared to attack. Azer jumped into the air, aiming for the roof of the building beside them, and felt a rush of air and snow fly by him as he rose higher and higher.

The red glows shrunk beneath him as he flew, finally losing his vertical velocity and landing gracefully on the snow-coated roof. Saa and Grif were just behind, rising up through the snow before falling back down. Saa fell roughly onto the roof and Grif nearly missed, fingers barely catching the rim of the building's edge. The snow threatened to slip him off, but Azer grabbed Grif's wrist before he fell, pulling him up to standing.

Without a word, the three began sprinting across the roof towards the Battle Academy, its silhouette now looming in the distance. Below, dozens of Copycats were following in hot pursuit. They leapt from roof to roof, soaring over alleyways.

Above, a bolt of purple lightning cut through the air, followed by a long period of the silence brought upon by a blizzard, the snowflakes soundlessly falling to the white ground. Then the tranquil soundscape was abruptly shattered by the deafening clap of booming thunder. It echoed across the town, muffled by the snow around them, creating an alien roar from the sky. It was enough to distract the attention of the fleeing Azer, Saa, and Grif, looking up to the heavens briefly while the thundersnow took their town into its jagged, electric claws.

And just ahead of them at that very moment, Copycat had scaled a building to cut the three off. By the time the three returned their senses to the chase at hand, it was too late. Copycat had reared back his Magna arm and was ready to slam it into Azer's head.

The glowing fist grew and stretched as it soared through the air, hitting Azer with staggering force and knocking him clean off the building. After a long fall, Azer skidded in the snow at the foot of the Battle Academy, reeling with pain at the impact. There was a brief scuffle at the roof of the building before Saa and Grif joined him, falling to the ground, bruised and bloody. Azer pushed himself to standing and engaged with the Copycat that had ambushed them, landing and trading blows, before another Copycat promptly hit him from behind, knocking him to the ground again. Most of the clones had vanished now, leaving only three.

"Go for the cure!" Azer yelled.

Saa and Grif obliged, making a run for the Team Virga lab. One of the Copycats blocked their path, flexing his Magna fingers menacingly. He raised his virus arm for a strike, then-

The clouds directly above them then abruptly swirled into a spiral shape, accompanied by a bright, multicolored gleam. The clouds swam and swirled in place for a moment, just like in The Shades, before a purple bolt of lightning emerged from the center of the spiral, edging downwards and superheating the falling snow. It struck the tip of the Copycat's raised arm, electricity surging through his infected body and into the ground.

A deafening explosion followed, shaking the three to the core, reverberating off of every surface in the town. And it occurred to Azer, they had another ally:

"Manim," he uttered. They weren't fighting alone.

The shock of the sudden lightning had momentarily stopped all movement between the fighters. Then, their senses returning, Saa and Grif sped past the steaming clone, running off towards the lab.

"And while they're gone," Azer wheezed, turning to the other two Copycats, "I'll take care of you."

The clones disappeared, the original Copycat's face twisted with rage at the sight of Azer. Copycat breathed angrily, sending puffs of steam out of his mouth with each rasp. They lunged at each other.

Azer landed an S.R.-fueled blow to Copycat's face, burning away Magna globs on his head. Simultaneously, Copycat landed a superpowered strike to Azer's chest, breaking another rib. Azer put up his guard, anticipating the next strike just before Copycat sent his Magna arm out, molding and morphing into a ring that crushed Azer further. Azer pumped more S.R. through his arms, melting away the Magna that bound him. More and more of the virus died, the cure spreading up and up the arm until, horrified, Copycat severed it. The arm fell into the snow as the last of the Magna died off.

But just as the Magna's core within Copycat's heart radiated brighter, prompting the arm's regeneration, Azer tackled Copycat to the ground and landed blow after blow to his face. He would end this right now, before the Magna could regenerate. Azer saw Copycat's heart, glowing under his shirt with the concentrated virus within it, and he placed a hand on it, preparing to inject as much S.R. as possible. It began to flow through Azer's arm, then-

Copycat's normal arm reached over to Azer's and swiftly broke it, causing Azer to yell in pain. The Magna heart flashed with light again and Copycat's other arm remade itself out of virus in an instant, grabbing Azer's neck and choking him.

"You've shown me I might need a few more," Copycat said, pushing himself to standing.

The Magna heart gleamed and long tendrils of Magna emerged from it, replicating four or five arms from nothing. The arms sunk into the ground and lifted Copycat, who was still choking Azer, into the air.

"People are already dead. More are dying. Every second that passes, something on this planet perishes. So why bother trying? Even if you were to kill me now, the losses would still be insurmountable. You've seen the graves."

"Because..." Azer choked, scrambling to remove the Magna fingers from his throat, "that's... who... I... am... If I can kill you... now... people can still... be saved..."

"And that makes a difference?!" Copycat taunted. "I am a living weapon. I've slaughtered trillions of beings. I've stopped entire civilizations from forming. You expect the lives on this planet to even have any meaning anymore? I'm the filter that destroys life itself!"

"And I'm... the filter breaker."

Copycat threw Azer to the ground with rage just as Grif appeared behind him with the second cure in hand. Copycat whipped around and threw a Magna tentacle, but Grif narrowly dodged, evading each attack as he made his way back around to Azer, Saa just behind. The two helped the injured Azer up to standing.

"The other vigilantes," Copycat spat. "A band of fools, cursed to fight a losing battle."

"You know, you talk a lot like Delvin did, and we beat the hell out of him," Grif retorted.

"*I* killed him," Copycat said, raising his voice and glowing dangerously as he lunged at Grif. "I gave him the wish he desired. You have achieved nothing but becoming a scourge on your people whom I have reduced to a tribe of primitives. I see everything inside this boy's mind." Copycat tapped his own head with a finger of Magna. "And I know that all of you are nothing but people who play the hero, scrambling to make a difference in a world that they have no power to change."

Copycat sent Magna tentacles at the three, who dodged around them and prepared to attack again. Copycat retaliated, and the battle renewed.

"You may think that I am manipulating Copycat, but I do not need to make him attack. The hatred is real, an influence I do not need to provide. Every time he sees you he's reminded of just how insignificant he really is, tortured, knowing he will be forever obsolete in comparison to the 'special' Azer and Grif. He sees that they are without parents and family and becomes intoxicated with jealousy, wishing for any alternative to his neglective and abusive father who would prioritize anyone in the world over his own son. He wants to be a hero and tries so hard. But all he does is make EVERYTHING worse."

Even in the midst of battle, this was a startling revelation. Saa, after avoiding Copycat's fist, looked at Azer.

"We need to reach Copycat! We need to put S.R. in his head, not his heart!"

"Are you insane?! I hardly have any left! I'm hitting my limit!"

"I know! But there's no way in hell we're going to be able to reach the heart at this rate, the Magna is protecting it too well! The Magna is literally in his head, manipulating what he thinks! If we can just reach Copycat, the *real* Copycat, we might be able to end this!"

Azer stopped attacking Copycat for a moment to step back and look at him. The Magna had ravaged Copycat's body, mutating it into the perfect fighting machine. His glowing red eyes looked insane, his humanity hardly looked apparent anymore as he lunged at Grif and sent viral tentacles at his foes. Looking at his nemesis, Azer realized that not once had he considered actually talking to him. He had questioned Copycat's resentful actions for as long as he could remember, but never truly asked *why*.

Azer dashed towards Copycat, weaving carefully between his attacks, feet pounding on the snow. He sent S.R. through his veins as the Magna tendrils sprung towards him, stepping on each one and rising higher and higher into the air until he was level with Copycat. Azer pretended to aim for the heart, prompting Copycat to guard his chest, but at the last second he whipped his hand up and grabbed Copycat's head.

S.R. pumped from Azer's fingers into Copycat's skull, the Magna on his head burning away violently, globs of the virus popping and vaporizing as the cure destroyed it. Copycat's glowing crimson eyes went blank for a moment before the red slowly dissipated, revealing Copycat's original eye color. They both fell backwards into the snow, Azer exhausted and Copycat gripping his head in agony.

"Azer..." Copycat snarled, "what the *hell* did you do?!" He raised his Magna arm and began striding towards Azer, who was motionless in the snow.

"Copycat, stop!" Saa yelled, getting in his way. "The Magna is controlling you! You're not yourself!"

"Just shut up, Saa! You and Azer and Grif are getting in my way! I'm about to finish Azer off. He's finally weak!"

"Getting in the way of *what*?!"

Copycat stopped for a moment. His expression went blank, confused.

"The Magna is controlling your body, and up until just a second ago it controlled your mind," Saa repeated. "It wants nothing but death and destruction! Just, please, help us!"

Copycat looked at his hands. One of them was his own, covered in their blood and nipped by the cold, and the other was a deep ruby color, pulsating, alive, but belonging to something sinister.

"What's happening to me?" Copycat asked quietly.

"You need to help us kill it!" Saa replied.

"But- but Azer and Grif wouldn't help me," Copycat said, spiraling. "They hate me. Dad hates me. Everyone- everyone just hates me." A tear ran down his cheek. "I'm all alone."

Tears sparkled in Saa's heterochromic eyes. "No, you're not. We really do want to save you."

"It doesn't seem right," Copycat said again. "They always get what I want. They always get to make the difference I want to make. They always get to play the hero."

Grif then slowly limped towards Copycat, the cure in hand. It was grayish, translucent, contained within a large syringe. When Grif held it out, small snowflakes landed on it.

"Then finish this," Grif said. "Finish the job. I don't think anyone should do it but you. *Be* the hero."

Copycat looked silently at it for a moment.

"Will I ever be able to make up for what I've done to you?"

"This is probably the best you've got. You don't need to apologize to Azer or me. Just put us aside for a moment and save the world."

Another moment of silence, then Copycat reached out and took the cure. He held it in his own hand for a brief second before he jammed it into his heart.

A gargantuan flash of light emitted from the Magna's core, followed by a high pitched screaming sound from every direction. The Magna all over his body, all over the town, all over the world, the entire galaxy, flashed with bright light for a brief second before it slowly, steadily, faded away. The Magna core lost its glowing red color and dimmed to black until it vanished entirely, leaving only Copycat's wounded body.

And after the last bit of Magna had disappeared from his body, Copycat collapsed.

"Copycat, are you okay?" Grif said, trying to support him. Copycat coughed, and a huge spurt of blood came up. Azer stood up and walked over to Copycat.

Upon seeing Copycat's body, Azer realized how ravaged it had truly been—the true effects of him being used as a vessel.

"No, no, no, no! Hey, hang in there, Copycat, alright? We're gonna get help," Azer panicked, trying to hold him steady.

"It's... fine. I should have died a long time ago. I was the first... to be infected... after all. But the Magna is gone now... for good."

"No, don't talk like that. We're gonna fix you up, okay?"

Copycat looked at Azer for a moment, staring at Azer's bare skin where his face should be like he was making direct eye contact—like he was truly seeing Azer properly for the first time.

"Can you... stay with me?" Copycat asked. "You know... while I-"

"Yeah," Azer interjected. "We're here for you."

Copycat managed a small grin.

"Thanks, guys."

And there, in that moment, an infinite lifetime of burdened souls felt as if they left Azer's back, generations of ancestors finally meeting their wish and floating off into the firmament.

There, in that moment...

The Great Filter was shattered.

CHAPTER TWENTY:
THE SUN

Cloudy. 3mph winds blowing east. Forty degrees fahrenheit.

Over time the winter storm waned, weakening until it turned into light snowfall, then to a mere coat of white clouds covering the sky. The citizens of Nur slowly left their homes, no longer plagued by the glowing red virus. A few more graves filled the town cemetery to the grief of many, but even the abundant funerals waned and ceased with time. After the last of the fallen were buried, the cemetery remained untouched for a long time, going from a tragic site that the town visited regularly to a beautiful series of treasured monuments. The largest headstone at the front of the graveyard, ordained with dozens and dozens of flowers and gifts, read as such:

Ecat "Copycat" Sastrugi

3277-3294 ZST

The only thing surpassing the tragedy in the town was the shock of the true nature of the planet they lived on, a new lifeform of unfathomable proportions. A higher being. Though the discoveries this would set in motion would not be realized until much later.

One day, after helping with reconstruction, Azer met his friends at Grano's diner. Azer took a window seat and tried to look outside, but a thin layer of snow from the latest snowstorm obscured his view. He made a glove-covered fist and bumped the window, knocking some snow off. Reflecting in the glass were his friends' faces, looking at him expectantly.

Azer turned to face them. They were all still wearing their winter clothes—Grif, a thin-looking dark green jacket, Milo, a thick vest over a long-sleeved shirt with snow encrusting the top of the sleeves, Saa, a large winter coat with fuzz around the hood, and Azer with his own brown winter jacket a size too large. He liked the way he could tuck his hands into the sleeves when it got cold. Azer took off his gloves.

"I'll state the obvious. We've been through a lot, haven't we?" Azer said.

The words resonated through the other three, though none of them flinched. Milo's scar from Kovaki's attack twitched almost subliminally.

"It's a miracle we're all still here," Milo commented.

It was still overcast outside. It had been for many months now. The sky was still the same bright, desaturated gray as the ground.

"How do we even begin to process what's happened?" Azer said. "I mean everything. It's like our whole lives have been chaotic from start to finish. The fact that it's just… *over* now… is so hard to believe. Grif and I have been intertwined with everything from the beginning, and we dragged you all into it, and, amazingly, still came out of it as friends."

Milo frowned, but there was no unhappiness in his face.

"Dragged us into it? Buddy, we were a part of it the moment our parents decided to live on this planet. You and Grif dragged us out of it. This group—all of us–" Milo gestured around the table. "There's nobody else I'd want to be friends with."

"Thanks, Milo."

The waiter passed menus to the four of them. Grano's Diner, like many other restaurants in Nur, had seasonal menus, changing substantially by the season. The menus they had just been handed featured an entire corner dedicated to different types of hot drinks. The four of them ordered, then turned to each other once more.

"Hey, Azer, Grif," Saa started, "You know what's bugged me ever since you guys told us about what Manim said? About the Magna virus?"

"What?" said Grif.

"Who put it here?" Saa asked. "The Magna virus isn't even a virus. It's a weapon. And you guys said the planet said someone 'put it here' long ago. Who the hell was that?"

"The Schisms?" Grif suggested.

"No, it can't be," Saa said, waving a hand. "The Schisms almost died from the virus, right?"

"Maybe they lost control of their own weapon?" Grif said.

"But then why go through the trouble of rescuing the Hivanians? Wouldn't they put it there to kill the Hivanians?"

Azer sent his memory back thousands of years ago, Remembering what happened the day the Schisms took the Hivanians off of an ancient Manim.

"It couldn't have been the Schisms," Azer added. "They were benevolent. I can see it."

"Who else could it have been?" Grif said. "The Schisms were the first ones ever to master space travel. They did it while every other species in Zysti was hunting and gathering."

"The first ones we *know*," Saa corrected. "What about their ship? The *Kaari*, was it? Who the hell built *that?*"

"Part of me wants to know," Milo commented, his face grim, "but part of me thinks we shouldn't ask any more questions. Some things might be better off staying unknown."

Azer felt a small, brief pang. Part of him disagreed. Something in him still hungered to know. The four of them went silent for a moment.

"Do you guys think," Saa said, "we'll ever fully recover? This town?"

"I don't think we'll ever fully recover," Milo said. "Not fully. I still think about Torbe a lot. I still miss him."

"I'm still coming to terms with the fact that I'll never attend one of Mrs. Korca's science classes again," Grif said. "Or do a Team Virga mission."

Then, Azer had a sudden idea. He jerked up, and the others looked at him.

"Why do we have to let Team Virga die just because the members are gone? There's still the four of us. No matter what happens to us, no matter how long it takes to recover, we'll do it together. How does that sound?"

Everyone looked between each other, but there was no dissent. Grif bumped Azer's shoulder.

"Now there's a good idea," Grif said with an ear-to-ear grin.

Everyone's food came, each dish served with a steaming mug of warm drink. They each picked up their drinks.

"A toast," Saa started, "to the new Team Virga. To the town. To our friendship."

They all clinked mugs.

Eventually, the gloomy snow and winter weather gradually took on a different context. Azer and Grif would return to their home after days of work and, for the first time in their lives, they would simply *live*. A type of calm and peace came to their lives that they had never known, a chance to sit in the window and watch the snow fall with a hot drink in hand without a single other care in the world.

And they could still find it in them to make a jolly snowman,

And the light and beautiful snowflakes would still fall,

And sleds would still be carried up and ridden down hills.

Children would still play, and the adults, too,

Friends would still hug,

Lovers would still love,

Smiles would still cross everyone's faces,

And all the wounds of the world would heal.

And one day, somehow, in some way,

The inhabitants of Nur all knew it was time to go outside,

In pajamas and robes and slippers and shoes,

Alone or together, out in the snow,

And they all looked up

And, finally, between the stark clouds coating the sky...

The sun came out.